CASANOVA
ACEDIA

MATT FRACTION
FÁBIO MOON
MICHAEL CHABON
GABRIEL BÁ

colors by Cris Peter
letters by Dustin Harbin
edits by Lauren Sankovitch

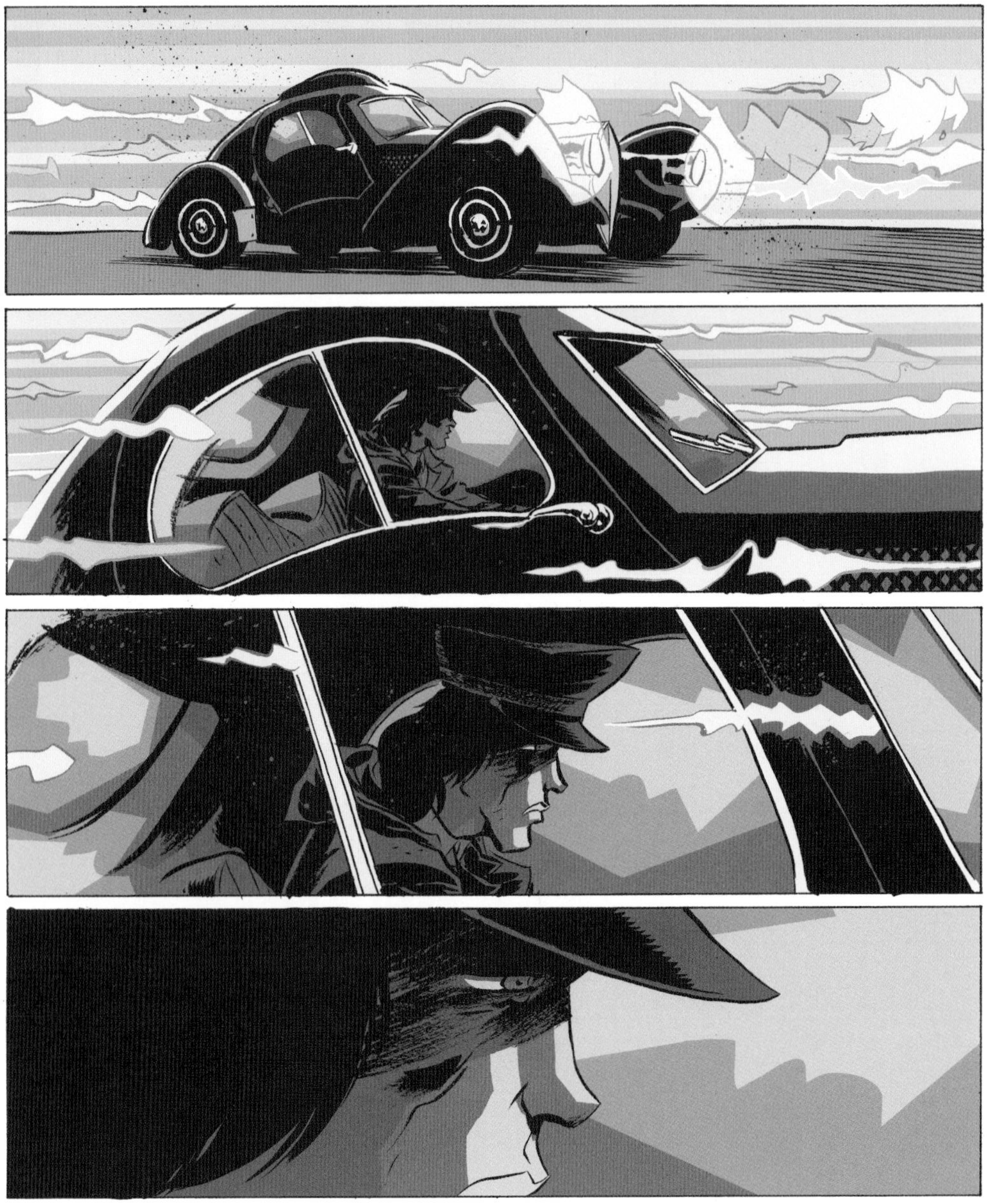

For my father. Goodnight, Dad.
—Matt Fraction

For Hugo Pratt and Guido Crepax.
—Fábio Moon

To Matthew Fritchman.
—Michael Chabon

To Héctor Germán Oesterheld and Francisco Solano López.
—Gabriel Bá

"Time forks perpetually into countless futures. In one of them I am your enemy."

The Creation,
"Frankenstein" by Mary Shelley

"I hope that I was of some little service, here and there, over the years."

The Old Man,
"The Final Solution" by Michael Chabon

"Let's drink to character."

Gregory Arkadin,
"Mr. Arkadin" by Orson Welles

CHAPTER ONE
NINE DAYS NOW

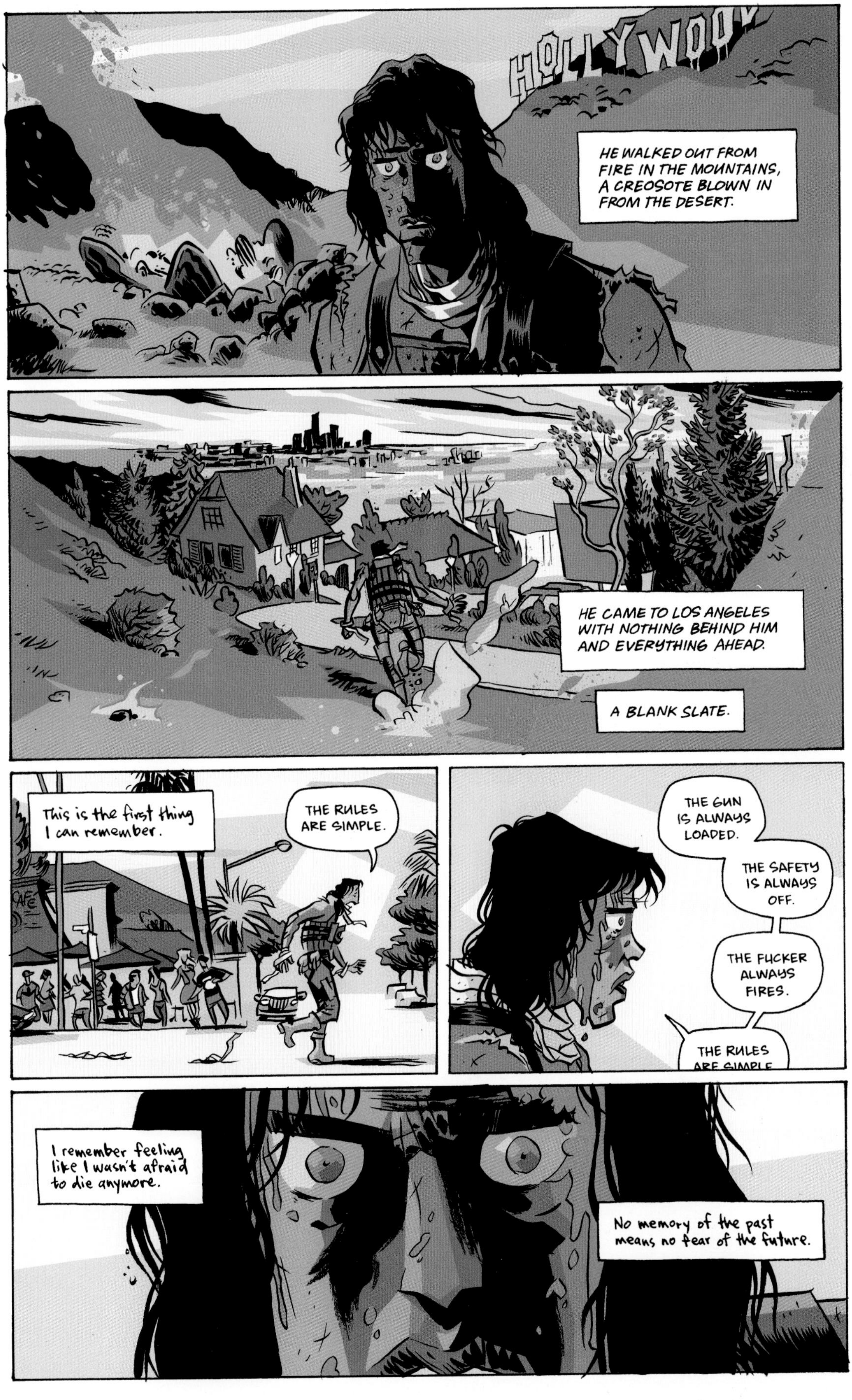
HOLLYWOO
HE WALKED OUT FROM FIRE IN THE MOUNTAINS, A CREOSOTE BLOWN IN FROM THE DESERT.
HE CAME TO LOS ANGELES WITH NOTHING BEHIND HIM AND EVERYTHING AHEAD.
A BLANK SLATE.
This is the first thing I can remember.
THE RULES ARE SIMPLE.
CAFE
THE GUN IS ALWAYS LOADED.
THE SAFETY IS ALWAYS OFF.
THE FUCKER ALWAYS FIRES.
THE RULES
I remember feeling like I wasn't afraid to die anymore.
No memory of the past means no fear of the future.

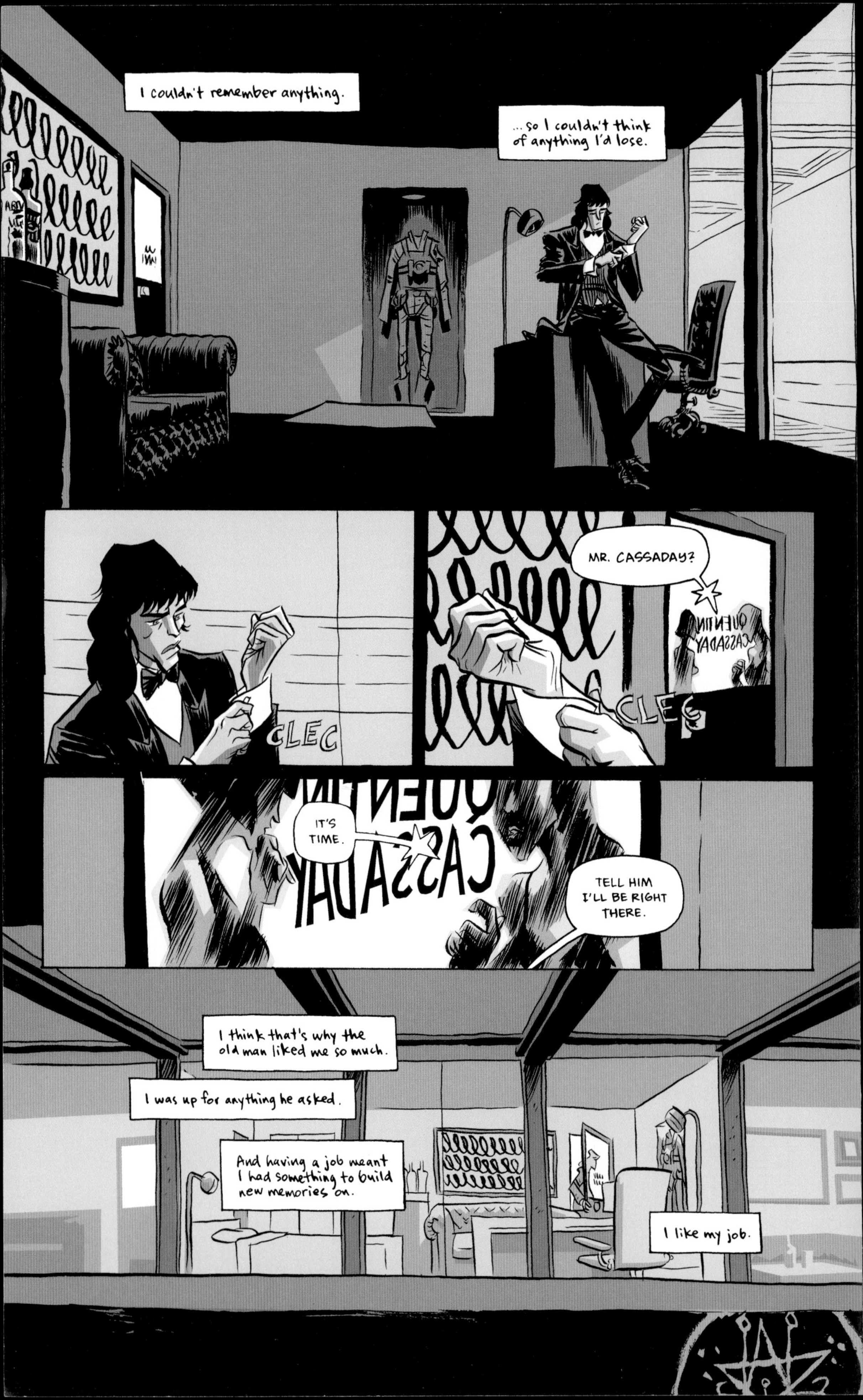
I couldn't remember anything.
...so I couldn't think of anything I'd lose.
CLEC
MR. CASSADAY?
QUENTIN CASSADAY
CLEC
IT'S TIME.
QUENTIN CASSADAY
TELL HIM I'LL BE RIGHT THERE.
I think that's why the old man liked me so much.
I was up for anything he asked.
And having a job meant I had something to build new memories on.
I like my job.

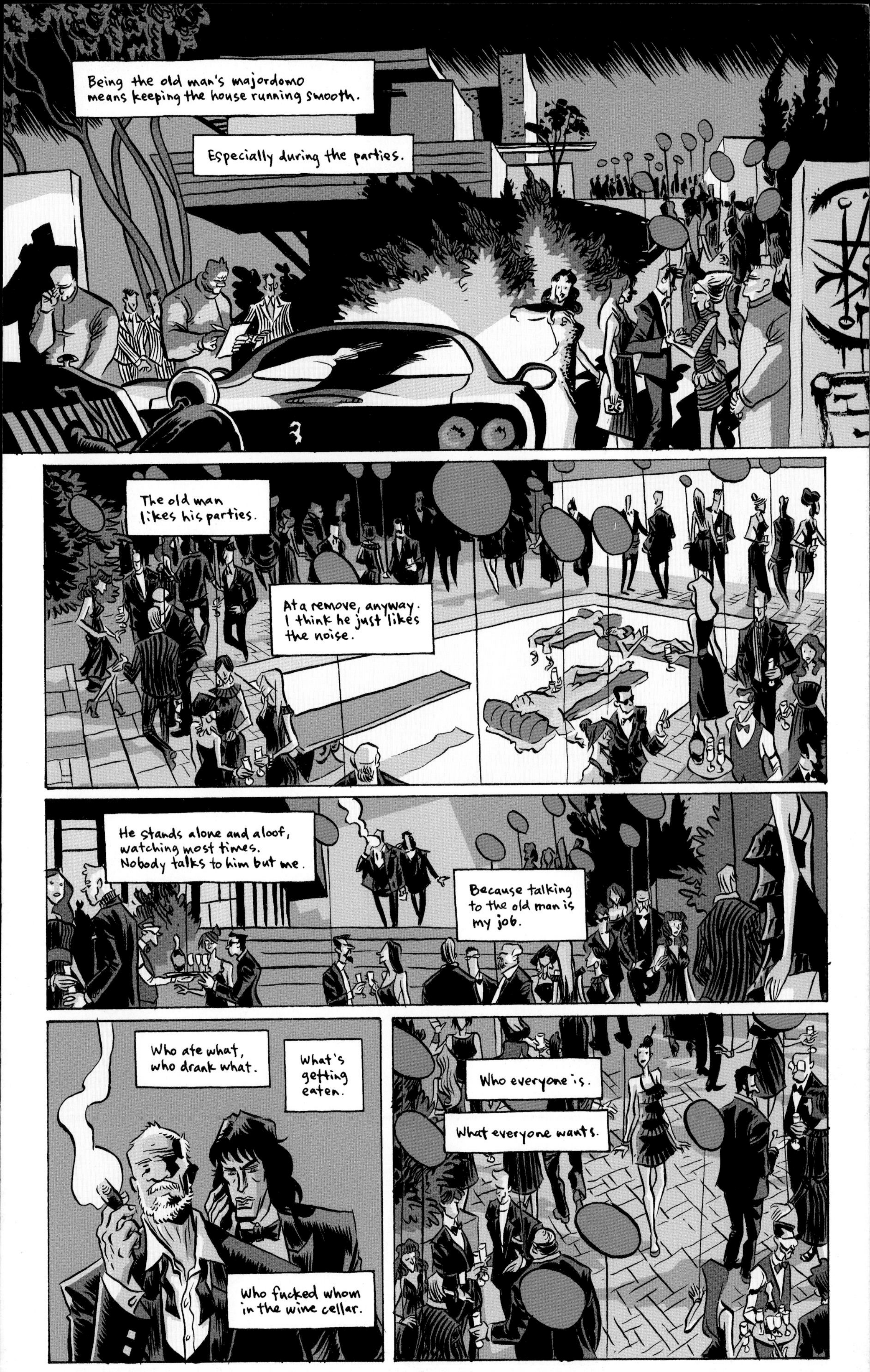
Being the old man's majordomo means keeping the house running smooth.
Especially during the parties.
The old man likes his parties.
At a remove, anyway. I think he just likes the noise.
He stands alone and aloof, watching most times. Nobody talks to him but me.
Because talking to the old man is my job.
Who ate what, who drank what.
What's getting eaten.
Who fucked whom in the wine cellar.
Who everyone is.
What everyone wants.

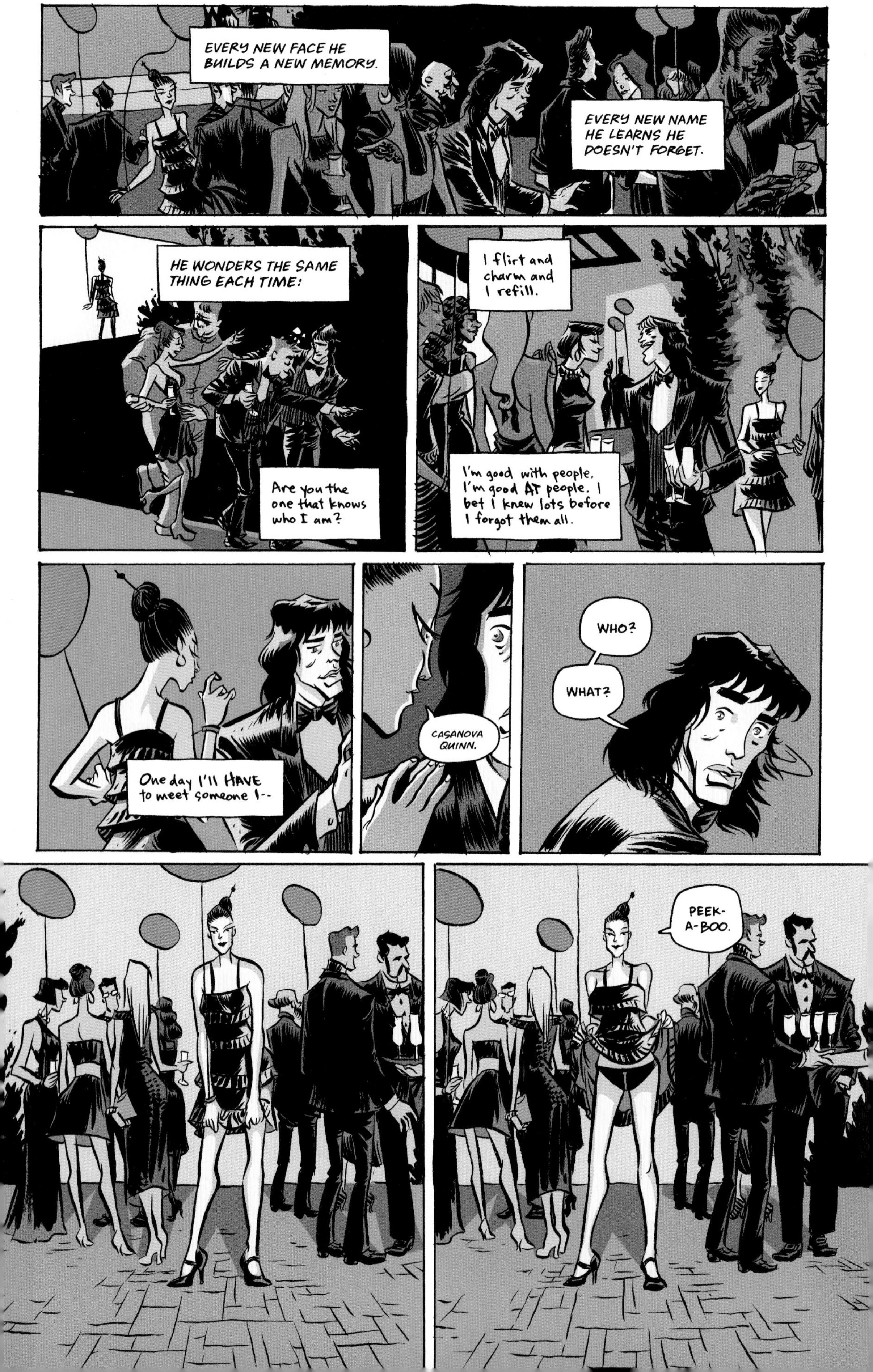
EVERY NEW FACE HE BUILDS A NEW MEMORY.
EVERY NEW NAME HE LEARNS HE DOESN'T FORGET.
HE WONDERS THE SAME THING EACH TIME:
Are you the one that knows who I am?
I flirt and charm and I refill.
I'm good with people. I'm good AT people. I bet I knew lots before I forgot them all.
One day I'll HAVE to meet someone I--
CASANOVA QUINN.
WHO?
WHAT?
PEEK-A-BOO.

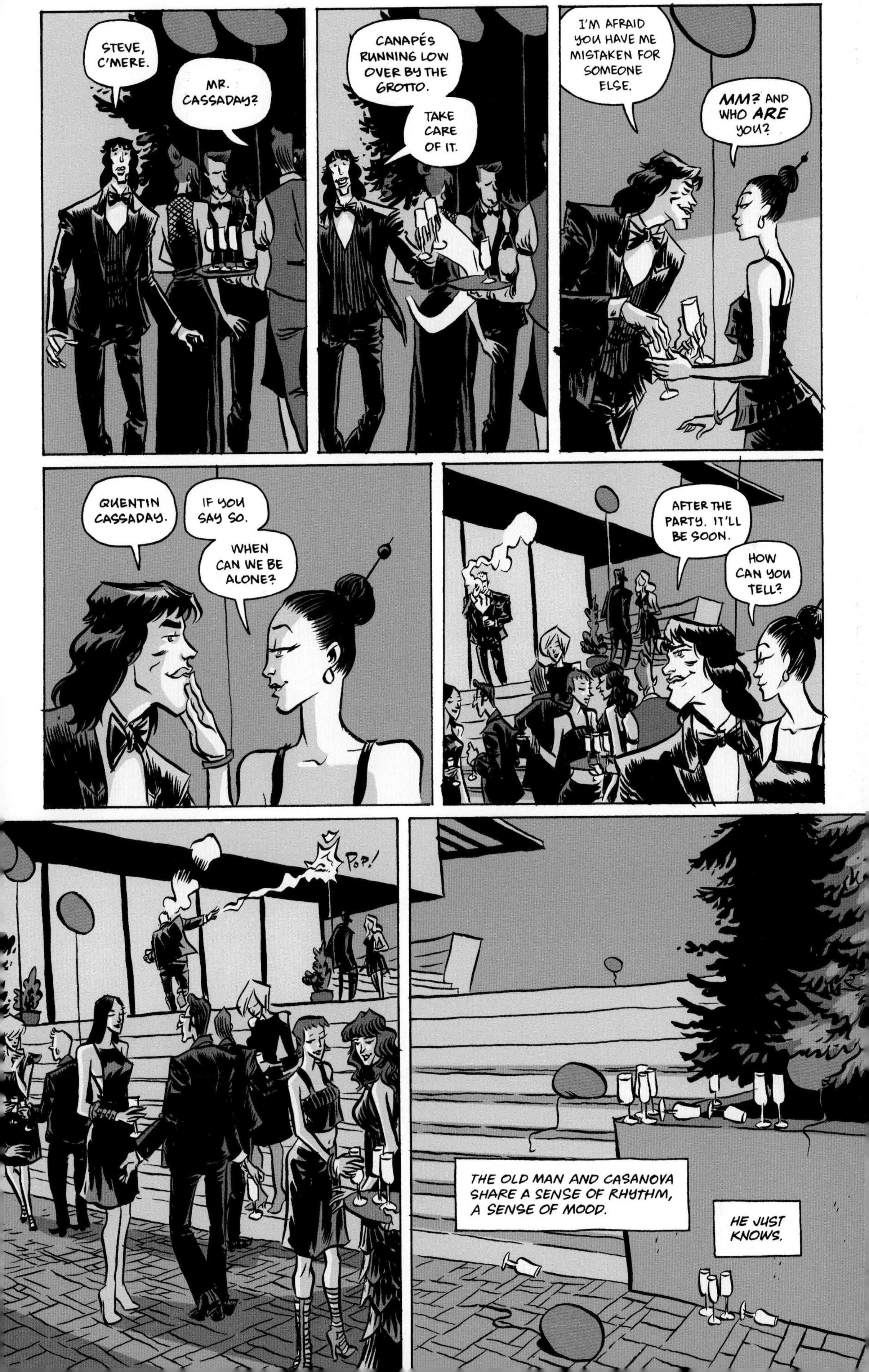
STEVE, C'MERE.
MR. CASSADAY?
CANAPÉS RUNNING LOW OVER BY THE GROTTO.
TAKE CARE OF IT.
I'M AFRAID YOU HAVE ME MISTAKEN FOR SOMEONE ELSE.
MM? AND WHO ARE YOU?
QUENTIN CASSADAY.
IF YOU SAY SO.
WHEN CAN WE BE ALONE?
AFTER THE PARTY. IT'LL BE SOON.
HOW CAN YOU TELL?
POP!
THE OLD MAN AND CASANOVA SHARE A SENSE OF RHYTHM, A SENSE OF MOOD.
HE JUST KNOWS.

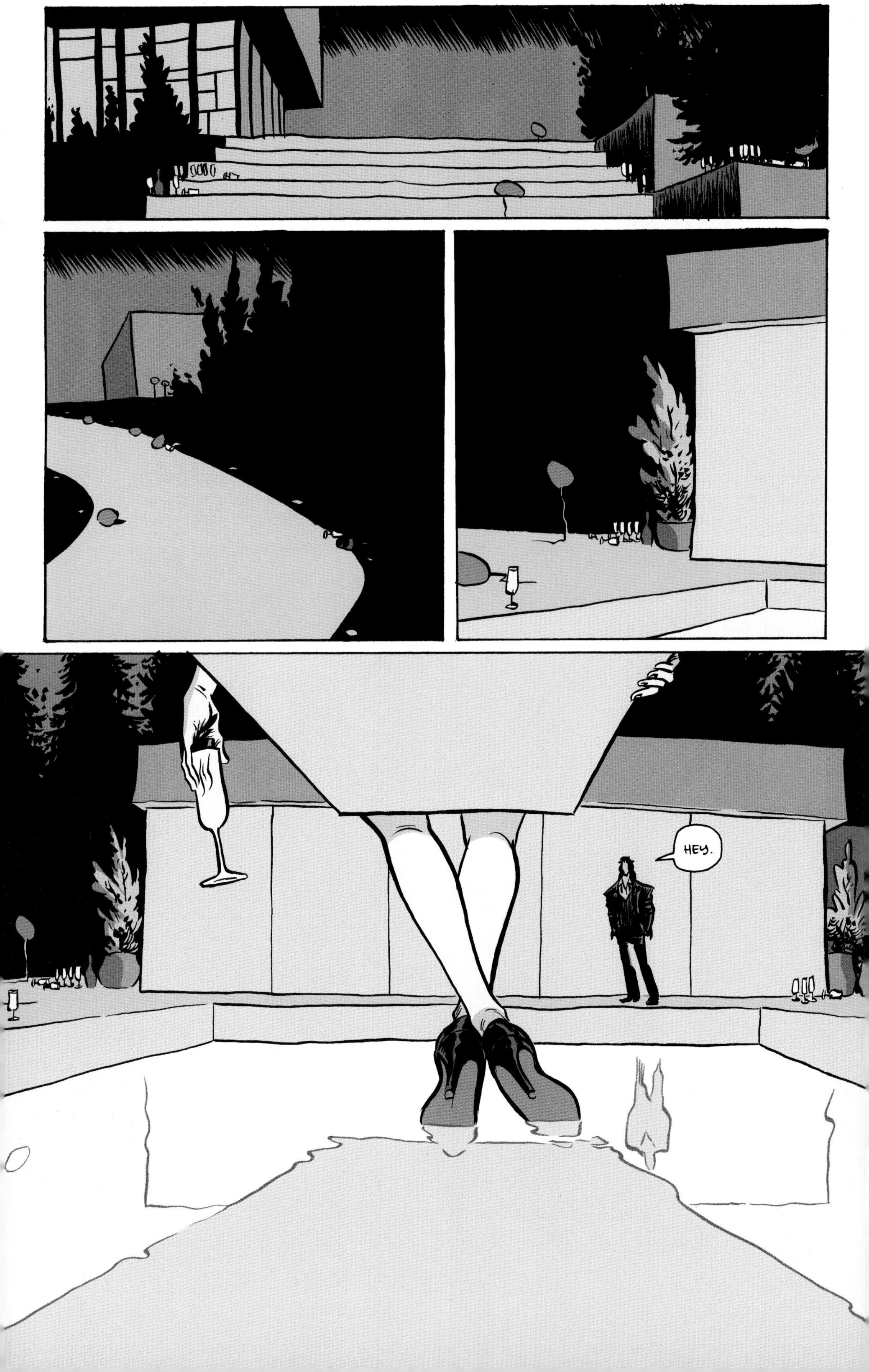
HEY.

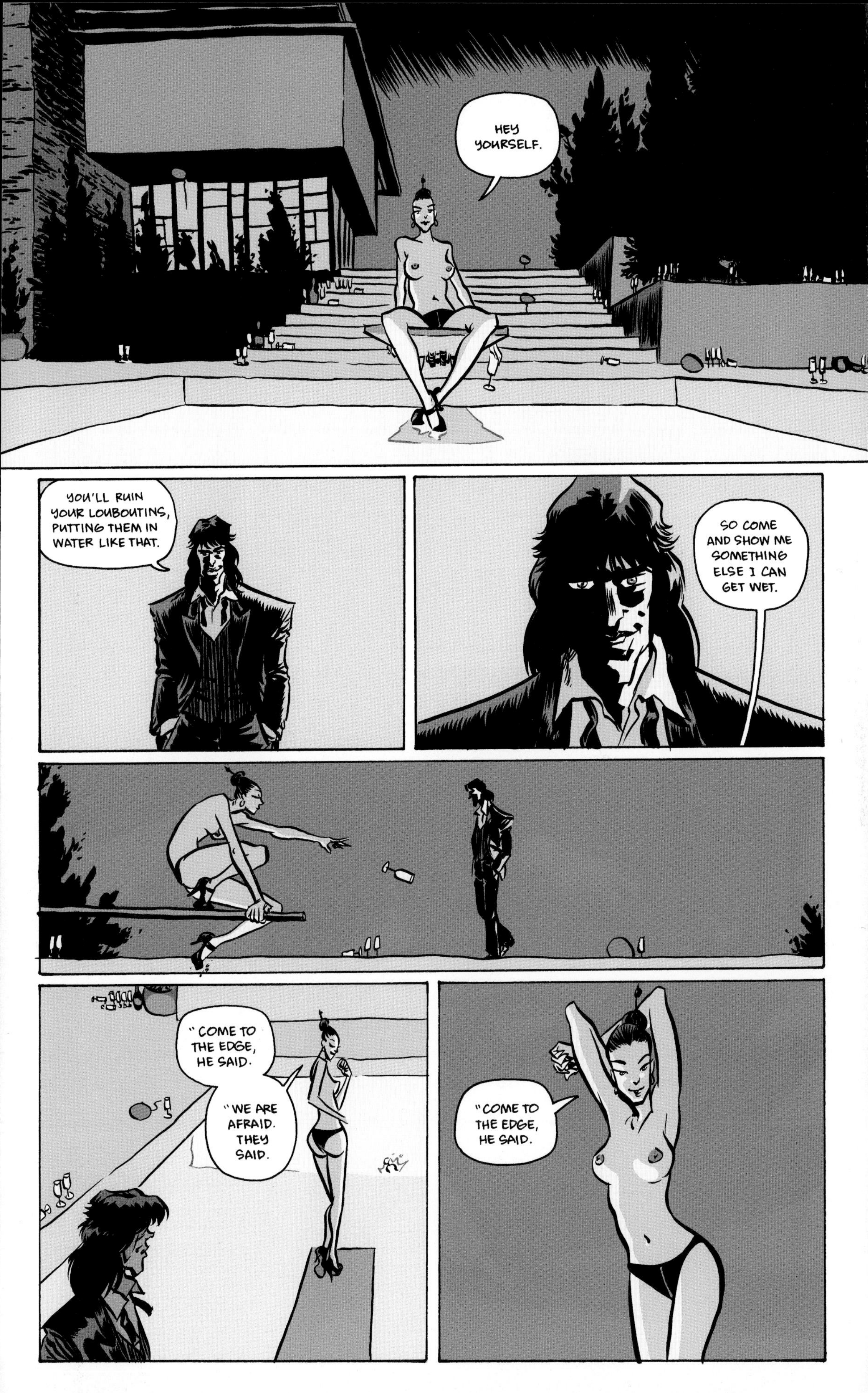
HEY YOURSELF.
YOU'LL RUIN YOUR LOUBOUTINS, PUTTING THEM IN WATER LIKE THAT.
SO COME AND SHOW ME SOMETHING ELSE I CAN GET WET.
"COME TO THE EDGE, HE SAID.
"WE ARE AFRAID. THEY SAID.
"COME TO THE EDGE, HE SAID.

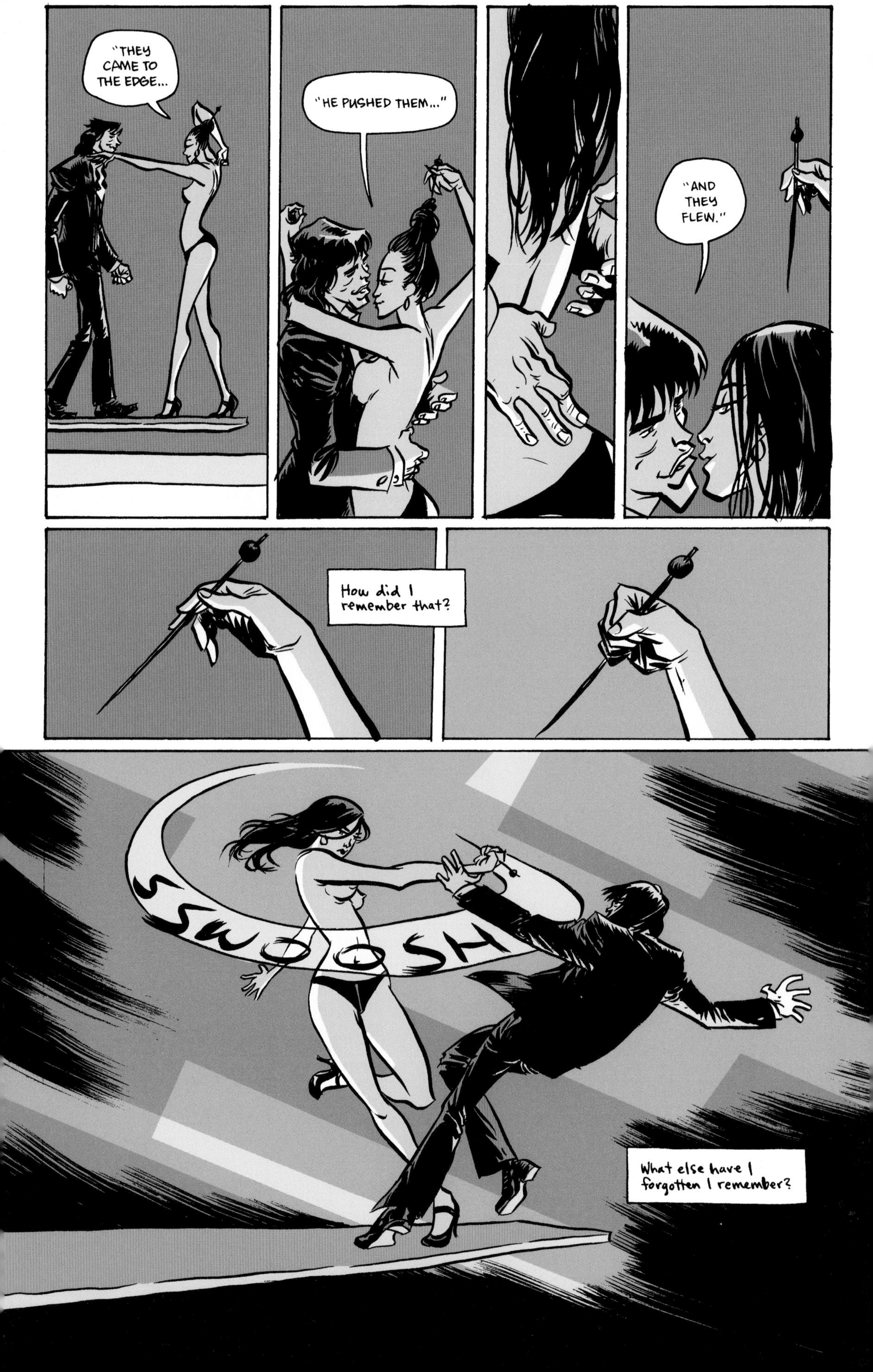
"THEY CAME TO THE EDGE...
"HE PUSHED THEM..."
"AND THEY FLEW."
How did I remember that?
SWOOOSH
What else have I forgotten I remember?

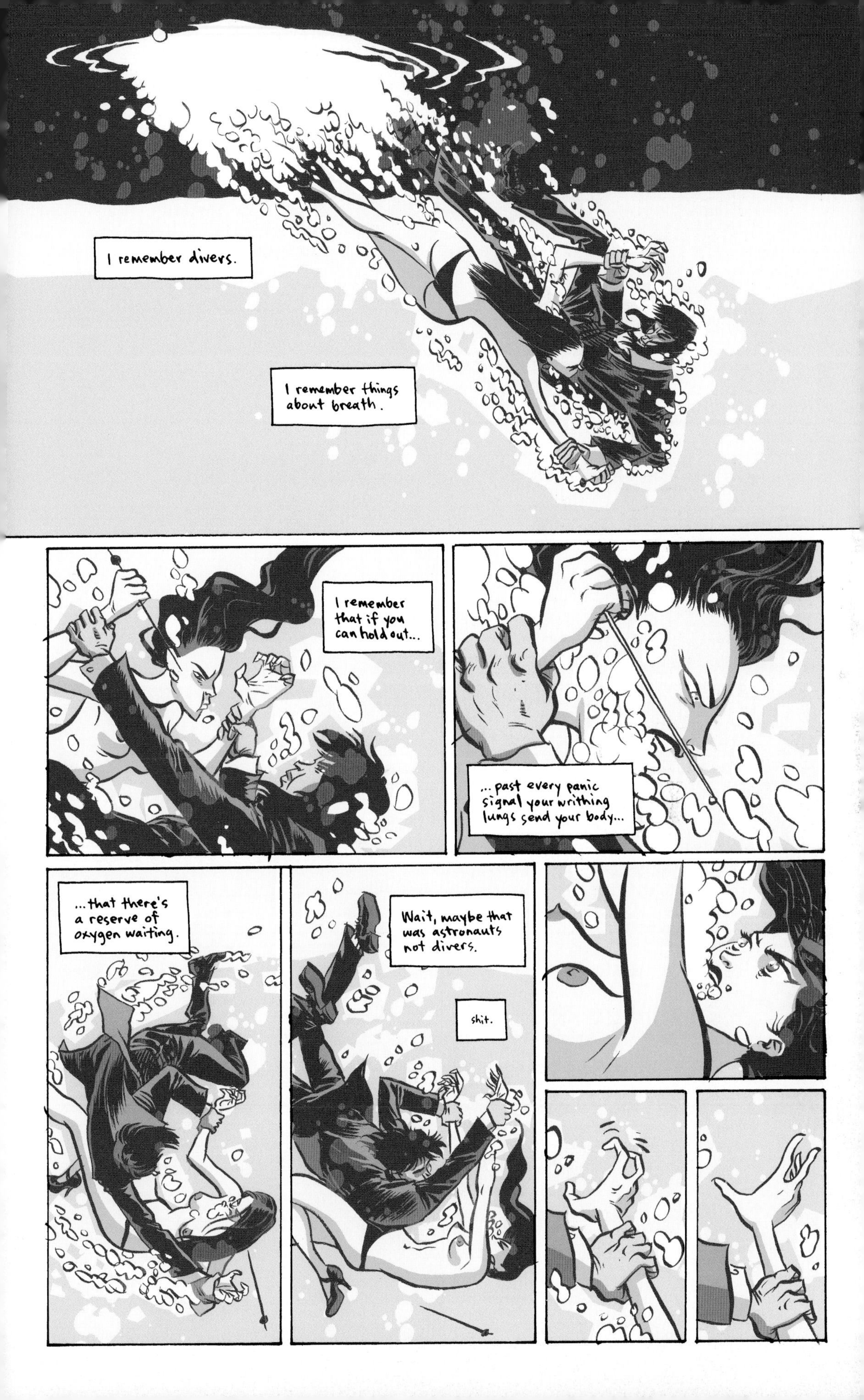
I remember divers.
I remember things about breath.
I remember that if you can hold out...
...past every panic signal your writhing lungs send your body...
...that there's a reserve of oxygen waiting.
Wait, maybe that was astronauts not divers.
shit.

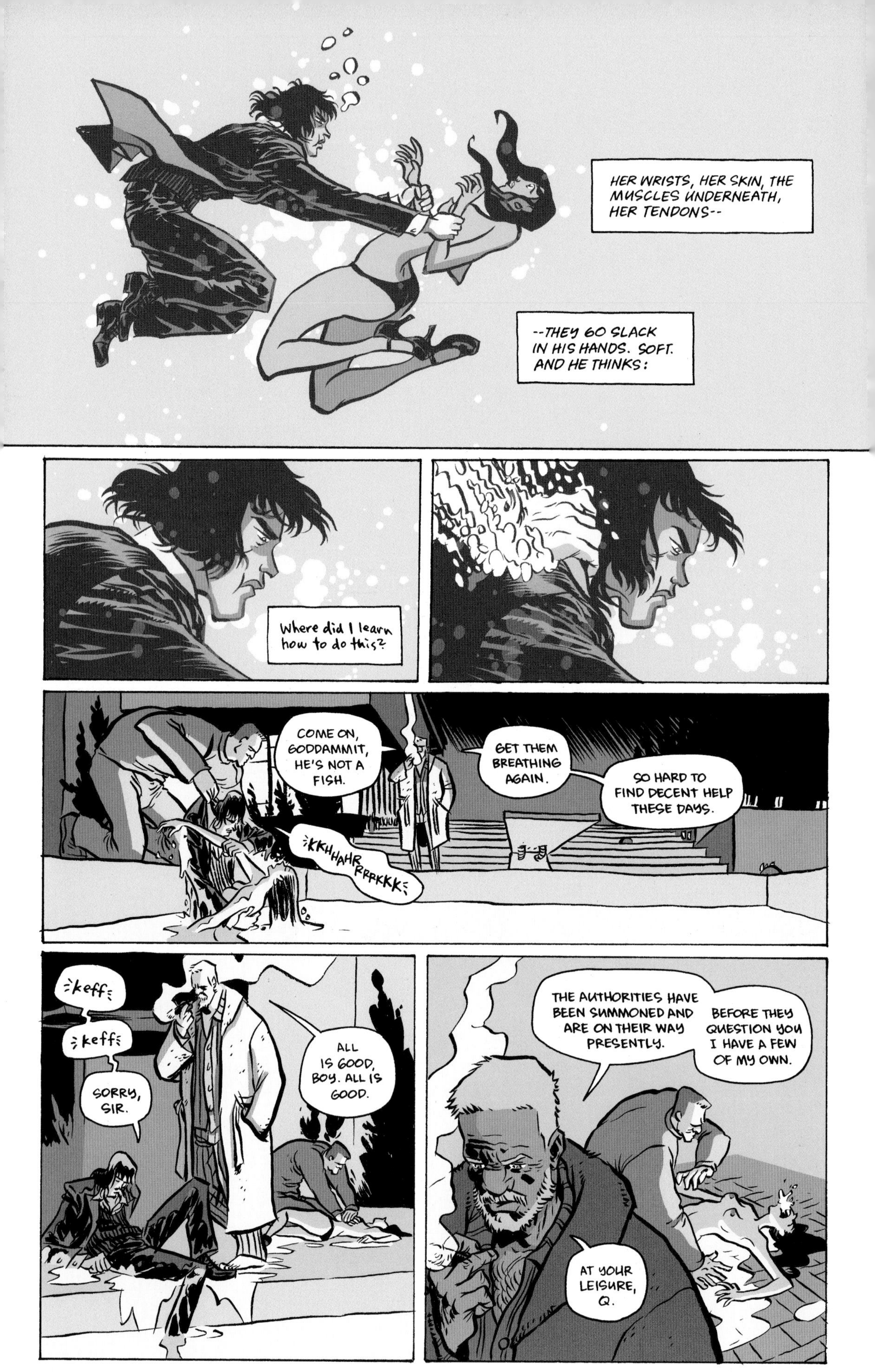
HER WRISTS, HER SKIN, THE MUSCLES UNDERNEATH, HER TENDONS--
--THEY GO SLACK IN HIS HANDS. SOFT. AND HE THINKS:
Where did I learn how to do this?
COME ON, GODDAMMIT, HE'S NOT A FISH.
GET THEM BREATHING AGAIN.
SO HARD TO FIND DECENT HELP THESE DAYS.
KKHHAHRRRRKKK
keff
keff
SORRY, SIR.
ALL IS GOOD, BOY. ALL IS GOOD.
THE AUTHORITIES HAVE BEEN SUMMONED AND ARE ON THEIR WAY PRESENTLY.
BEFORE THEY QUESTION YOU I HAVE A FEW OF MY OWN.
AT YOUR LEISURE, Q.

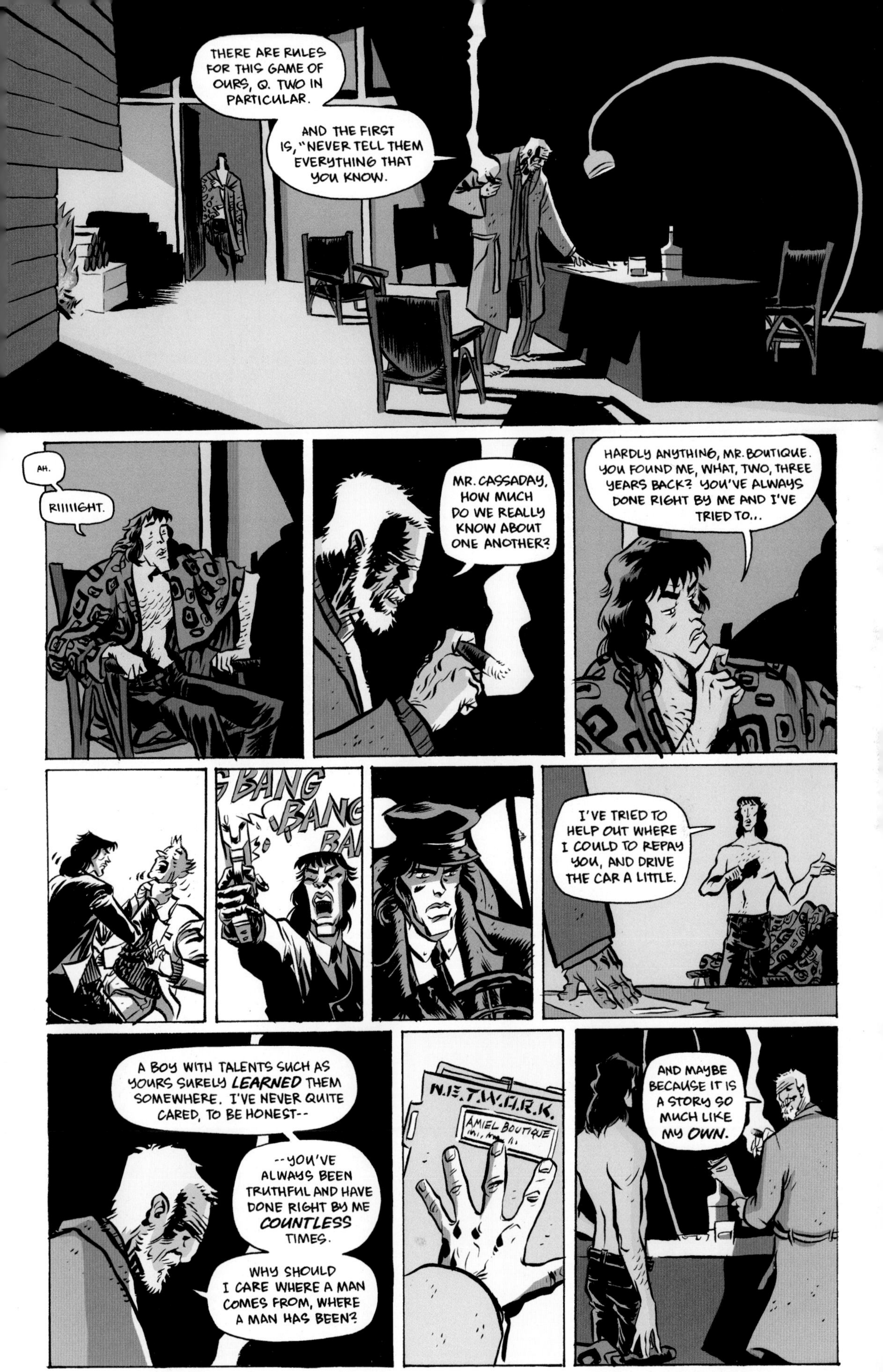
THERE ARE RULES FOR THIS GAME OF OURS, Q. TWO IN PARTICULAR.
AND THE FIRST IS, "NEVER TELL THEM EVERYTHING THAT YOU KNOW.
AH.
RIIIIIGHT.
MR. CASSADAY, HOW MUCH DO WE REALLY KNOW ABOUT ONE ANOTHER?
HARDLY ANYTHING, MR. BOUTIQUE. YOU FOUND ME, WHAT, TWO, THREE YEARS BACK? YOU'VE ALWAYS DONE RIGHT BY ME AND I'VE TRIED TO...
BANG
BANG
BA
I'VE TRIED TO HELP OUT WHERE I COULD TO REPAY YOU, AND DRIVE THE CAR A LITTLE.
A BOY WITH TALENTS SUCH AS YOURS SURELY *LEARNED* THEM SOMEWHERE. I'VE NEVER QUITE CARED, TO BE HONEST--
--YOU'VE ALWAYS BEEN TRUTHFUL AND HAVE DONE RIGHT BY ME *COUNTLESS* TIMES.
WHY SHOULD I CARE WHERE A MAN COMES FROM, WHERE A MAN HAS BEEN?
N.E.T.W.O.R.K.
AMIEL BOUTIQUE
AND MAYBE BECAUSE IT IS A STORY SO MUCH LIKE MY *OWN*.

PAH.

MY MEMORY OF MY OWN LIFE BEGINS WELL INTO MY *THIRTIES*. I HAD WEALTH AND MEN FEARED ME.

BUT I HAD NO IDEA WHERE ANY OF IT HAD COME FROM.

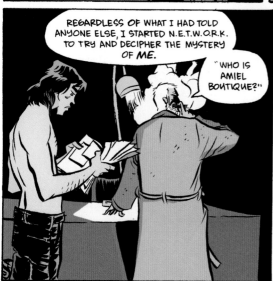

REGARDLESS OF WHAT I HAD TOLD ANYONE ELSE, I STARTED N.E.T.W.O.R.K. TO TRY AND DECIPHER THE MYSTERY OF *ME*.

"WHO IS AMIEL BOUTIQUE?"

WELL, HERE WE ARE, EH?

TWO MEN WITHOUT PASTS.

I HAD NO IDEA.

NO ONE DOES.

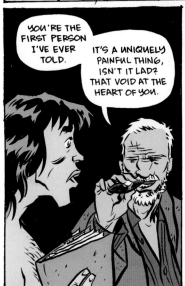

YOU'RE THE FIRST PERSON I'VE EVER TOLD.

IT'S A UNIQUELY PAINFUL THING, ISN'T IT LAD? THAT VOID AT THE HEART OF YOU.

WHERE DID I PUT THAT GODDAMN--

--HERE, SIR--

--HANG ON--

AH.

SEE? EMPATHY. SYMPATHY.

YOU'RE NOT SOME, SOME, WHAT. SOME DARK PSYCHOPATH, SOME AMNESIAC MURDERER, REGARDLESS OF YOUR TALENTS--

WELL, YOU'RE NOT THE TYPE TO GET SICK AT SEA, ARE YOU?

NO, SIR.

WHERE'S THAT FROM? THAT LINE.

I DON'T REMEMBER.

HEH.

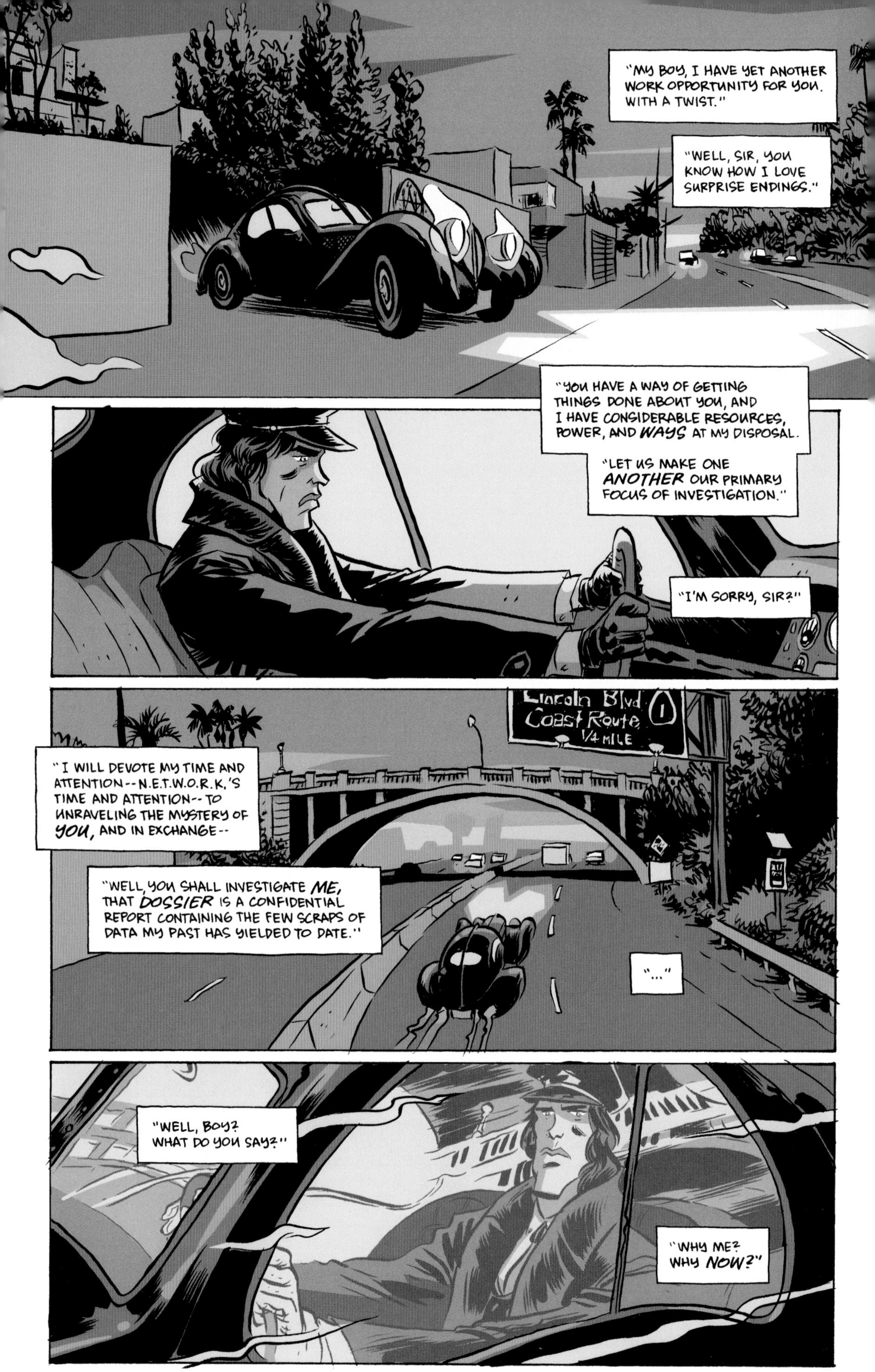

"MY BOY, I HAVE YET ANOTHER WORK OPPORTUNITY FOR YOU. WITH A TWIST."
"WELL, SIR, YOU KNOW HOW I LOVE SURPRISE ENDINGS."
"YOU HAVE A WAY OF GETTING THINGS DONE ABOUT YOU, AND I HAVE CONSIDERABLE RESOURCES, POWER, AND *WAYS* AT MY DISPOSAL.
"LET US MAKE ONE *ANOTHER* OUR PRIMARY FOCUS OF INVESTIGATION."
"I'M SORRY, SIR?"
Lincoln Blvd
Coast Route
1
1/4 MILE
"I WILL DEVOTE MY TIME AND ATTENTION--N.E.T.W.O.R.K.'S TIME AND ATTENTION--TO UNRAVELING THE MYSTERY OF *YOU,* AND IN EXCHANGE--
"WELL, YOU SHALL INVESTIGATE *ME,* THAT *DOSSIER* IS A CONFIDENTIAL REPORT CONTAINING THE FEW SCRAPS OF DATA MY PAST HAS YIELDED TO DATE."
"..."
"WELL, BOY? WHAT DO YOU SAY?"
"WHY ME? WHY *NOW*?"

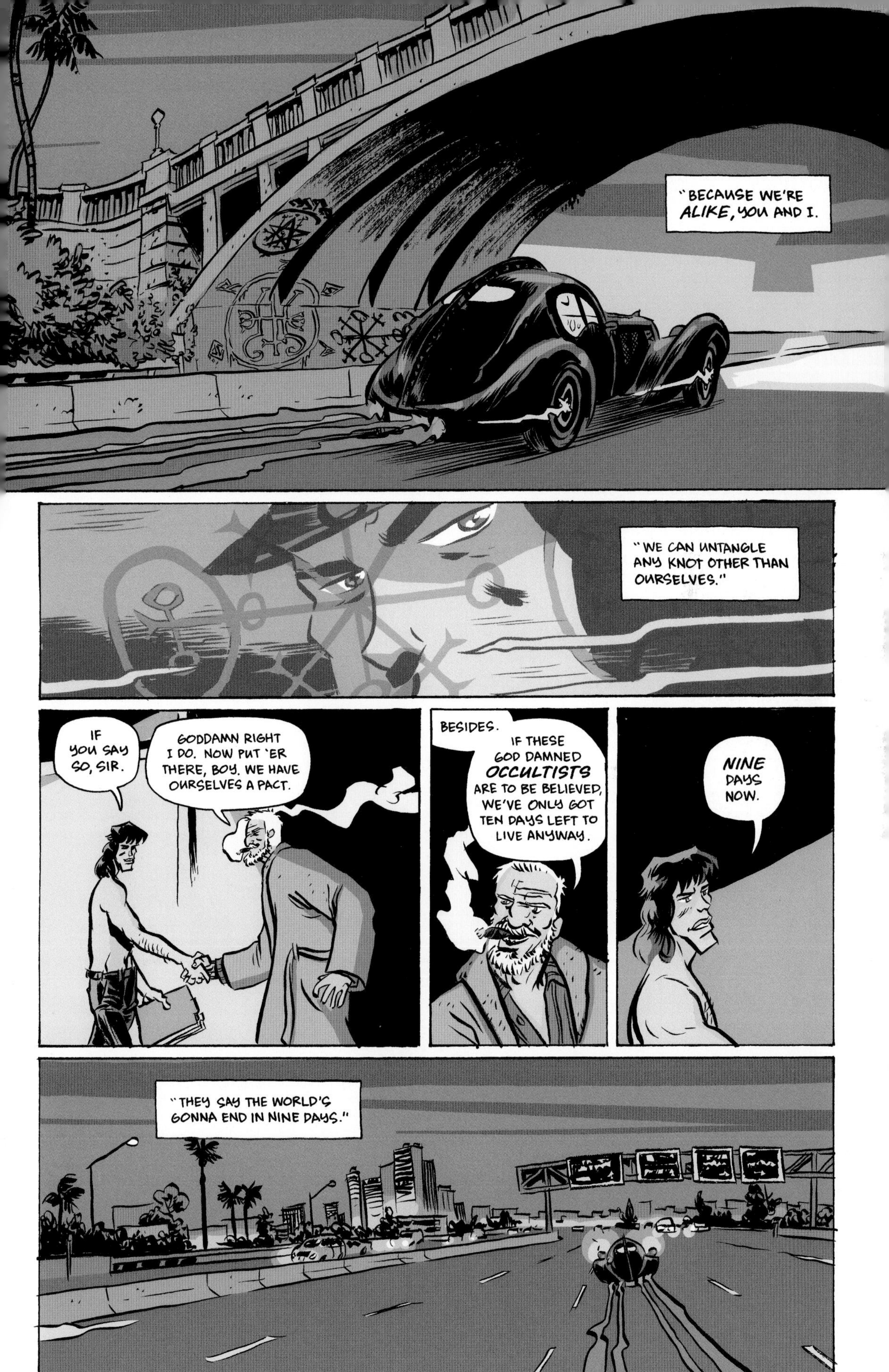
"BECAUSE WE'RE ALIKE, YOU AND I.
"WE CAN UNTANGLE ANY KNOT OTHER THAN OURSELVES."
IF YOU SAY SO, SIR.
GODDAMN RIGHT I DO. NOW PUT 'ER THERE, BOY. WE HAVE OURSELVES A PACT.
BESIDES.
IF THESE GOD DAMNED OCCULTISTS ARE TO BE BELIEVED, WE'VE ONLY GOT TEN DAYS LEFT TO LIVE ANYWAY.
NINE DAYS NOW.
"THEY SAY THE WORLD'S GONNA END IN NINE DAYS."

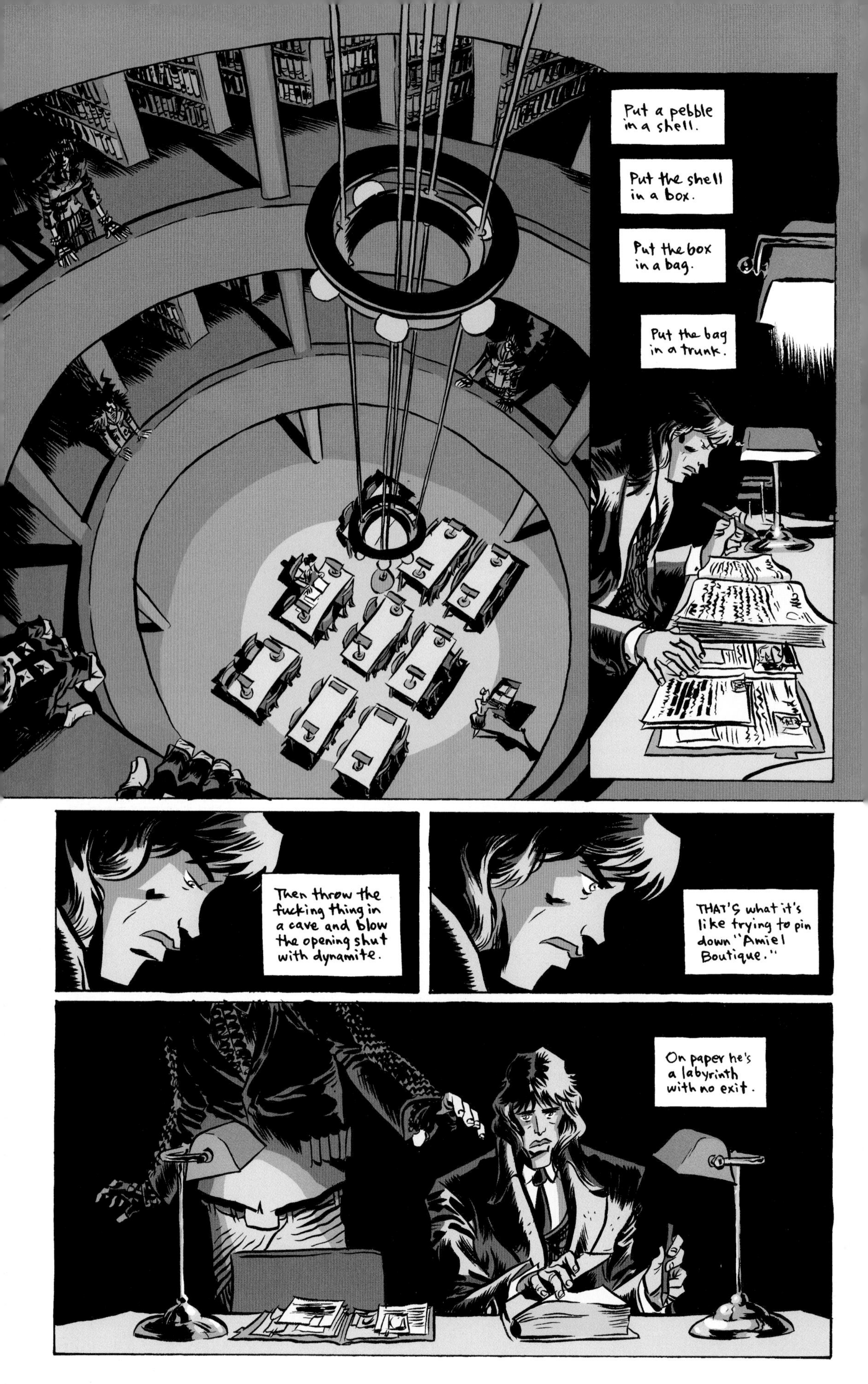
Put a pebble in a shell.
Put the shell in a box.
Put the box in a bag.
Put the bag in a trunk.
Then throw the fucking thing in a cave and blow the opening shut with dynamite.
THAT'S what it's like trying to pin down "Amiel Boutique."
On paper he's a labyrinth with no exit.

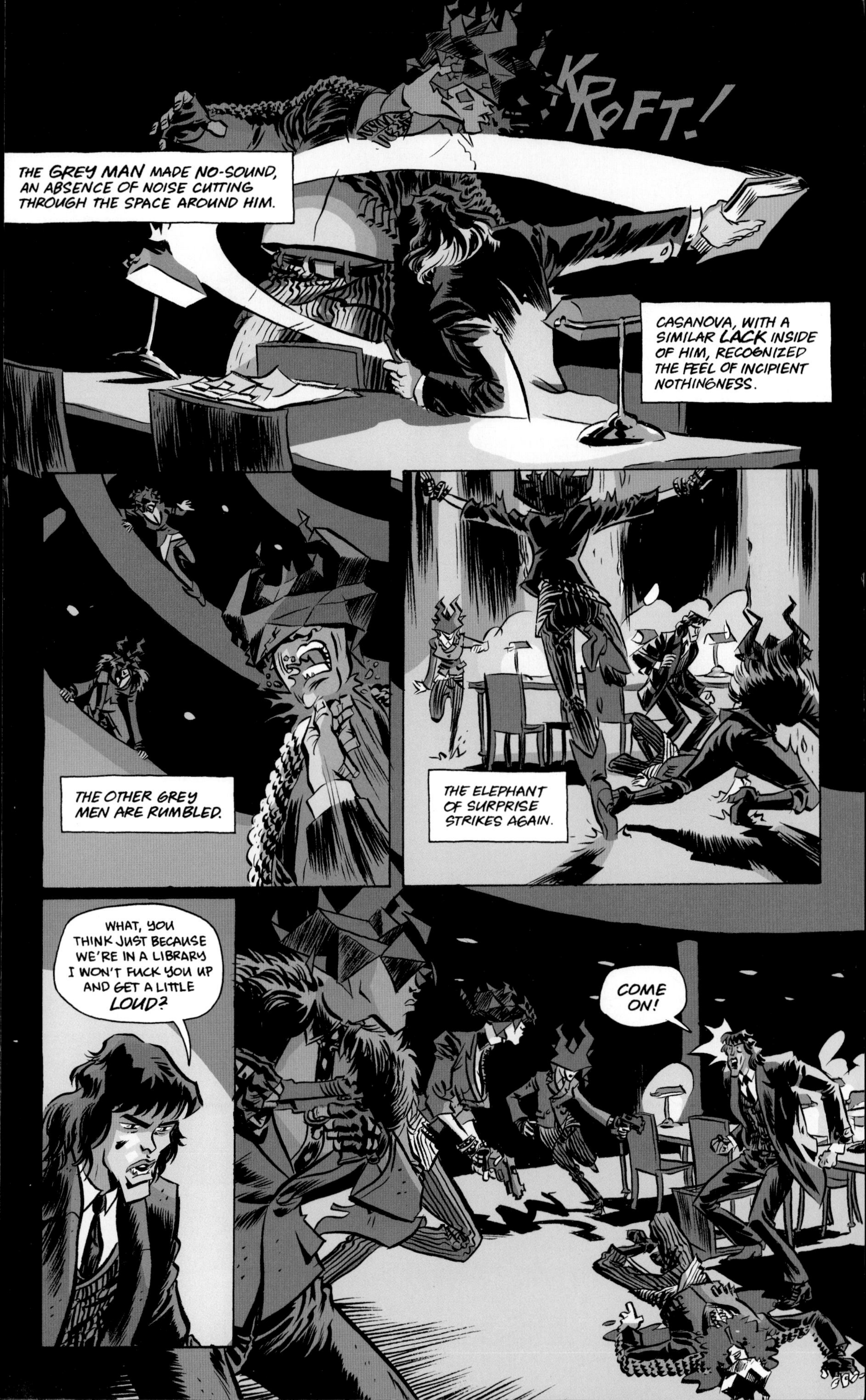
KROFT!
THE GREY MAN MADE NO-SOUND, AN ABSENCE OF NOISE CUTTING THROUGH THE SPACE AROUND HIM.
CASANOVA, WITH A SIMILAR LACK INSIDE OF HIM, RECOGNIZED THE FEEL OF INCIPIENT NOTHINGNESS.
THE OTHER GREY MEN ARE RUMBLED.
THE ELEPHANT OF SURPRISE STRIKES AGAIN.
WHAT, YOU THINK JUST BECAUSE WE'RE IN A LIBRARY I WON'T FUCK YOU UP AND GET A LITTLE LOUD?
COME ON!

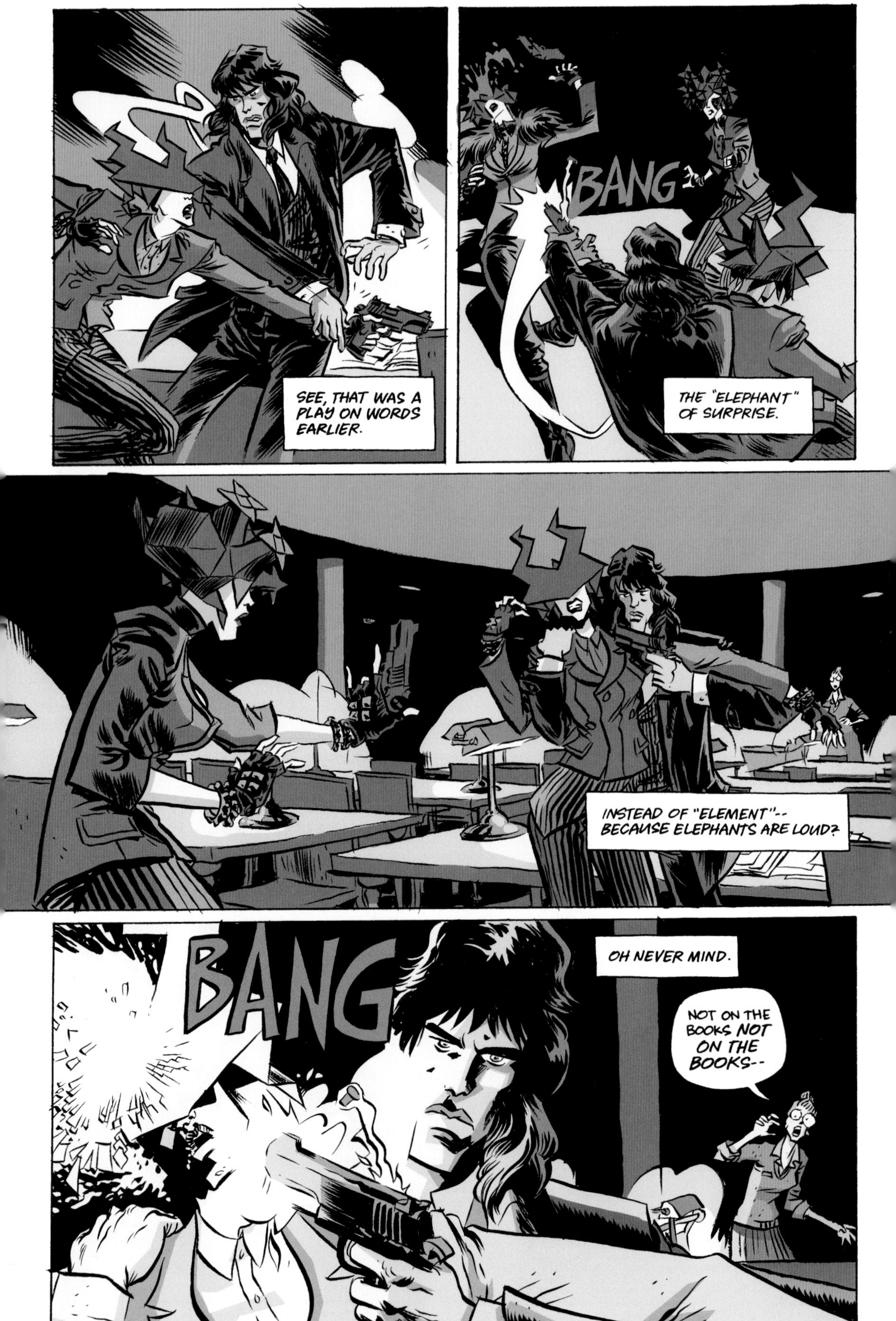
SEE, THAT WAS A PLAY ON WORDS EARLIER.
BANG
THE "ELEPHANT" OF SURPRISE.
INSTEAD OF "ELEMENT"-- BECAUSE ELEPHANTS ARE LOUD?
BANG
OH NEVER MIND.
NOT ON THE BOOKS NOT ON THE BOOKS--

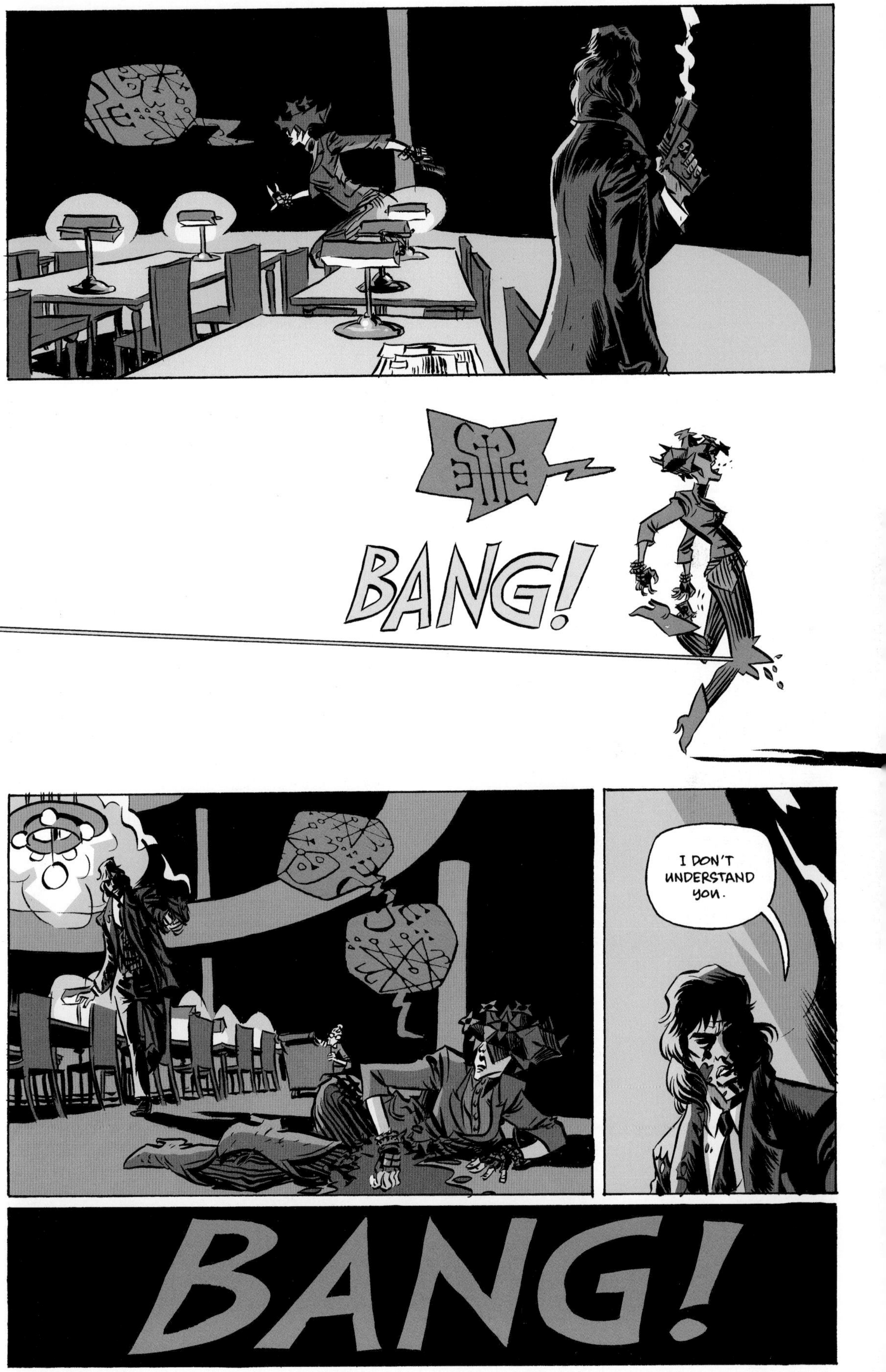
BANG!
I DON'T UNDERSTAND YOU.
BANG!

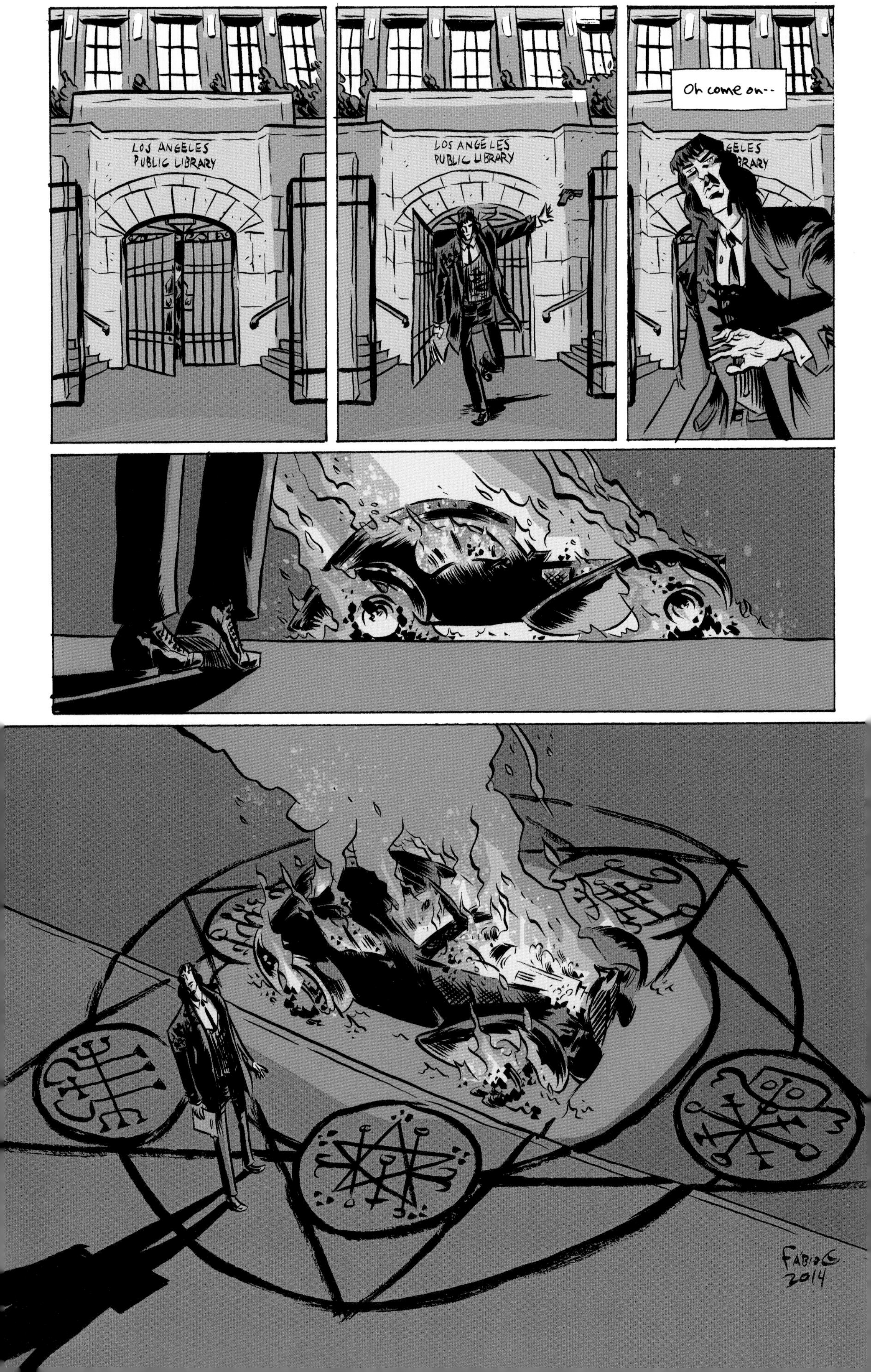
LOS ANGELES
PUBLIC LIBRARY
Oh come on--
FÁBIO
2014

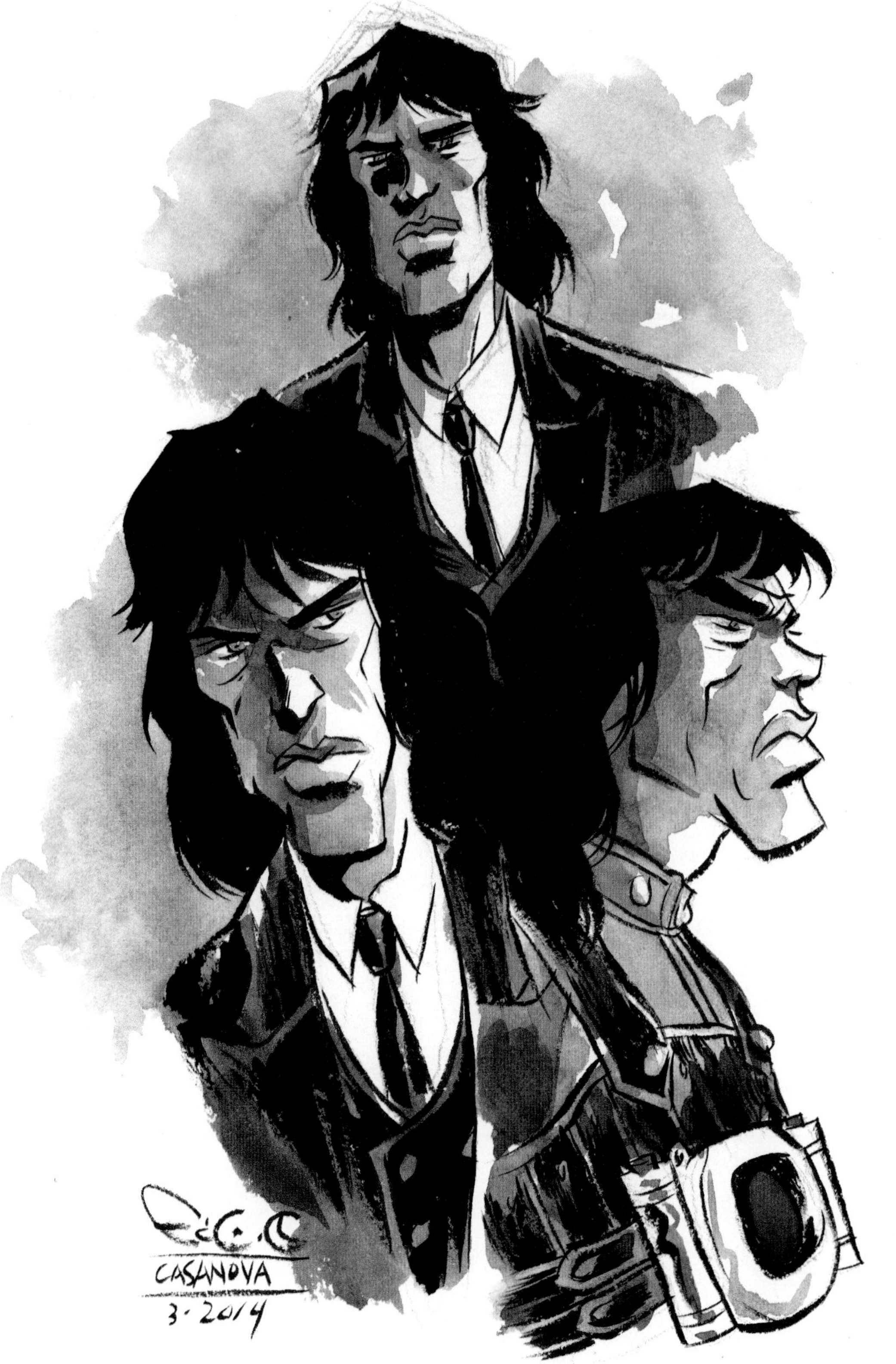
CASANOVA
3-2014

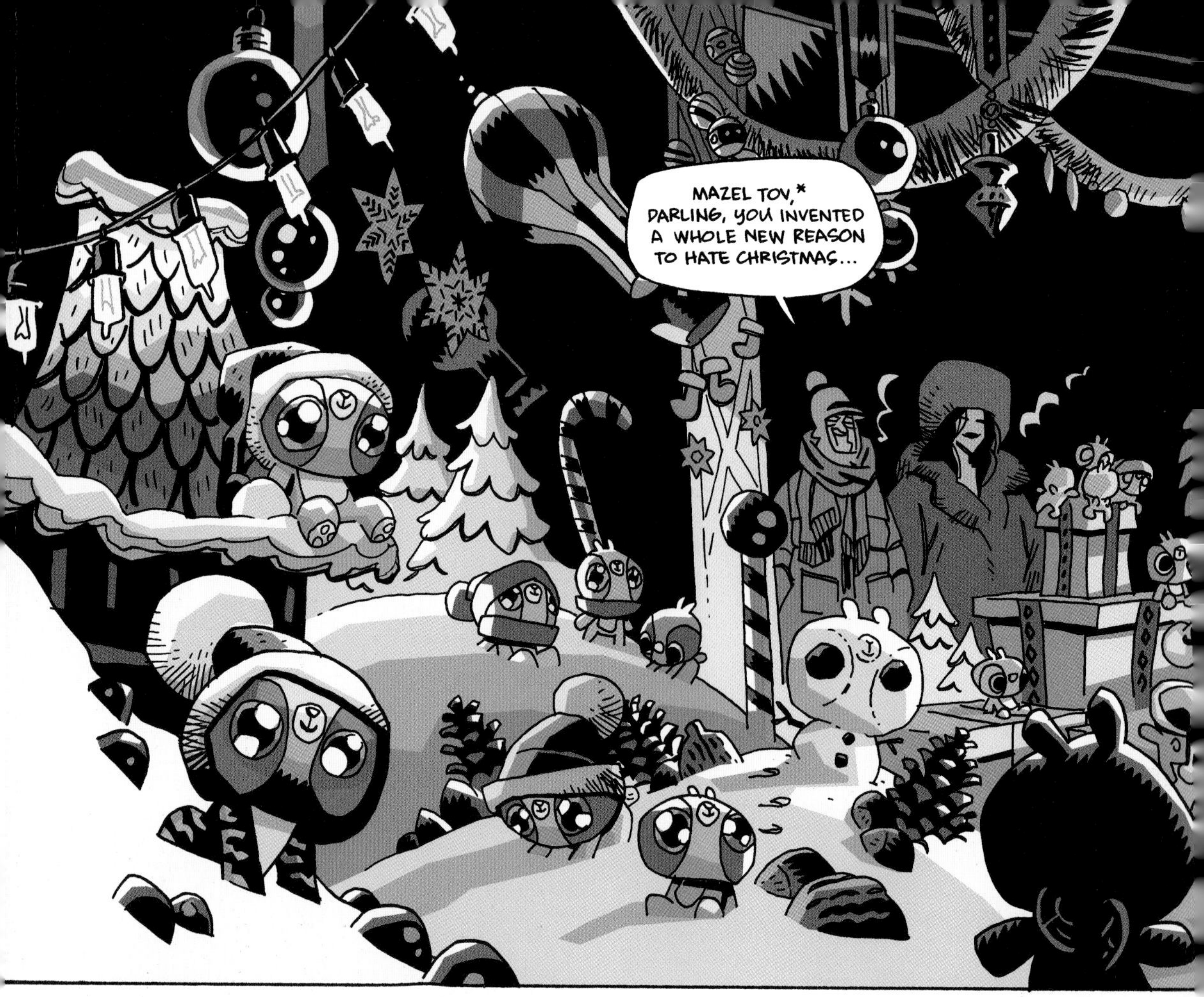
MAZEL TOV,* DARLING, YOU INVENTED A WHOLE NEW REASON TO HATE CHRISTMAS...

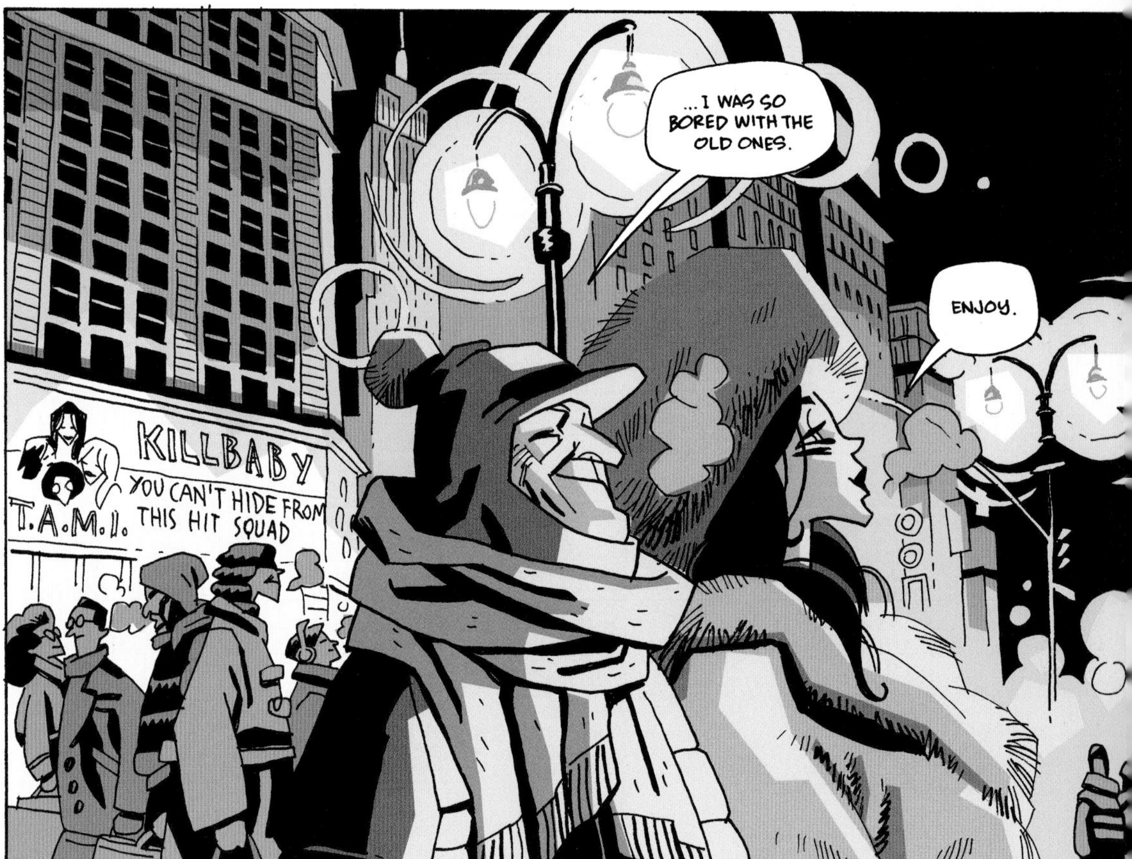
...I WAS SO BORED WITH THE OLD ONES.
ENJOY.
KILLBABY
YOU CAN'T HIDE FROM THIS HIT SQUAD
T.A.M.I.

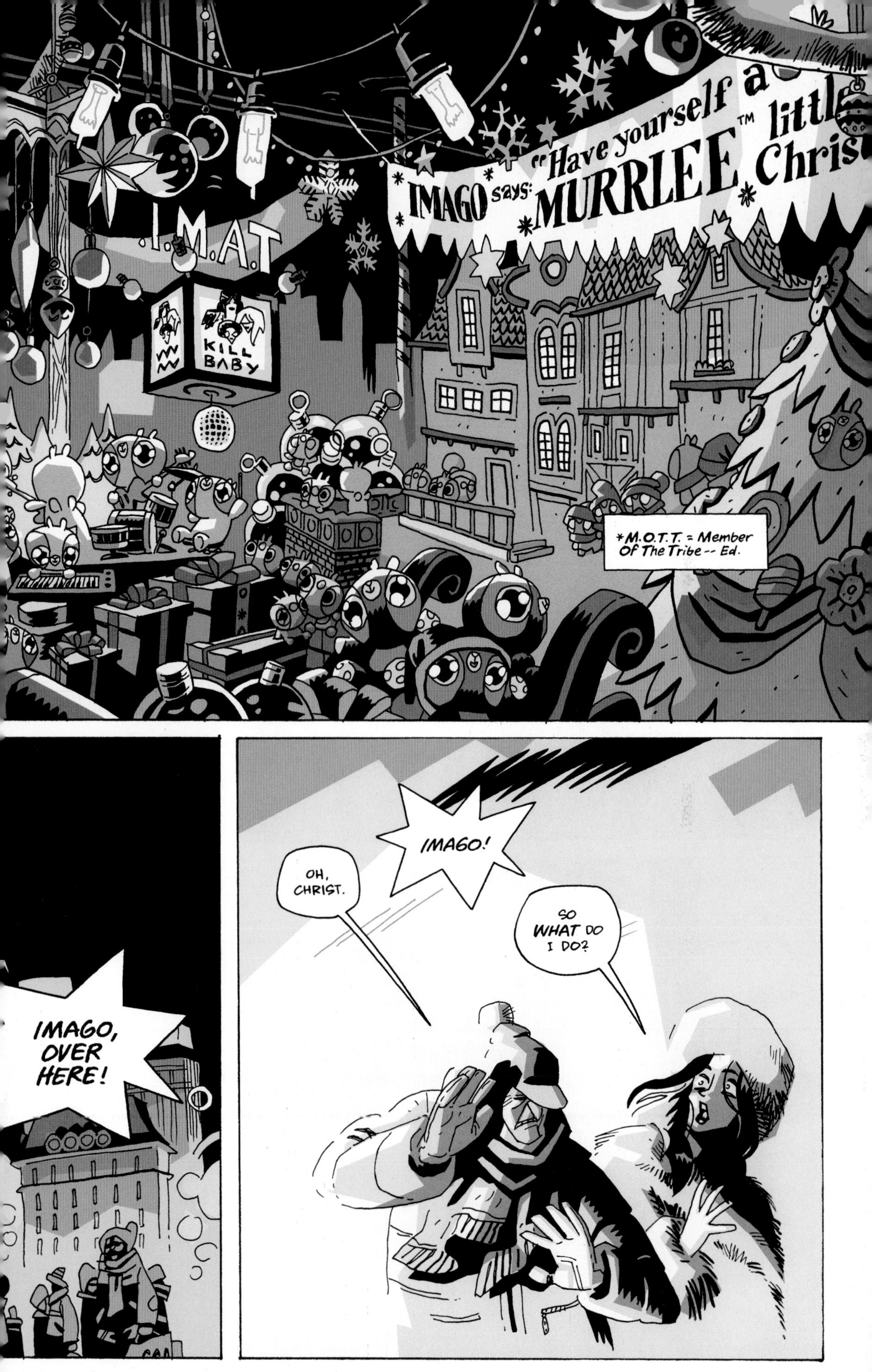
I.M.A.T
IMAGO says: "Have yourself a MURRLEE™ little Chris
KILL BABY
*M.O.T.T. = Member Of The Tribe -- Ed.
IMAGO, OVER HERE!
IMAGO!
OH, CHRIST.
SO WHAT DO I DO?

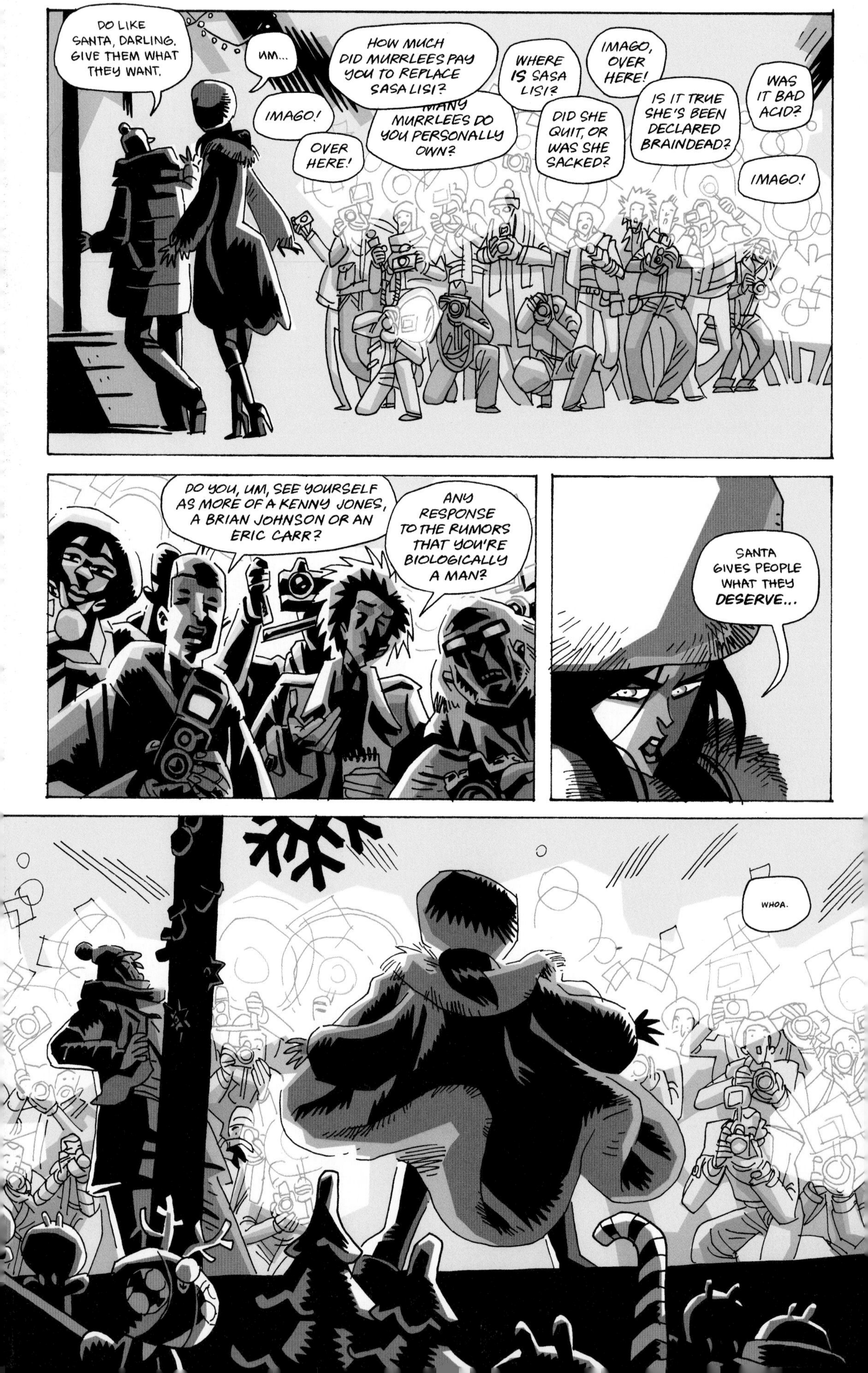
DO LIKE SANTA, DARLING. GIVE THEM WHAT THEY WANT.
UM...
IMAGO!
OVER HERE!
HOW MUCH DID MURRLEES PAY YOU TO REPLACE SASA LISI?
MANY MURRLEES DO YOU PERSONALLY OWN?
WHERE IS SASA LISI?
DID SHE QUIT, OR WAS SHE SACKED?
IMAGO, OVER HERE!
IS IT TRUE SHE'S BEEN DECLARED BRAINDEAD?
WAS IT BAD ACID?
IMAGO!
DO YOU, UM, SEE YOURSELF AS MORE OF A KENNY JONES, A BRIAN JOHNSON OR AN ERIC CARR?
ANY RESPONSE TO THE RUMORS THAT YOU'RE BIOLOGICALLY A MAN?
SANTA GIVES PEOPLE WHAT THEY DESERVE...
WHOA.

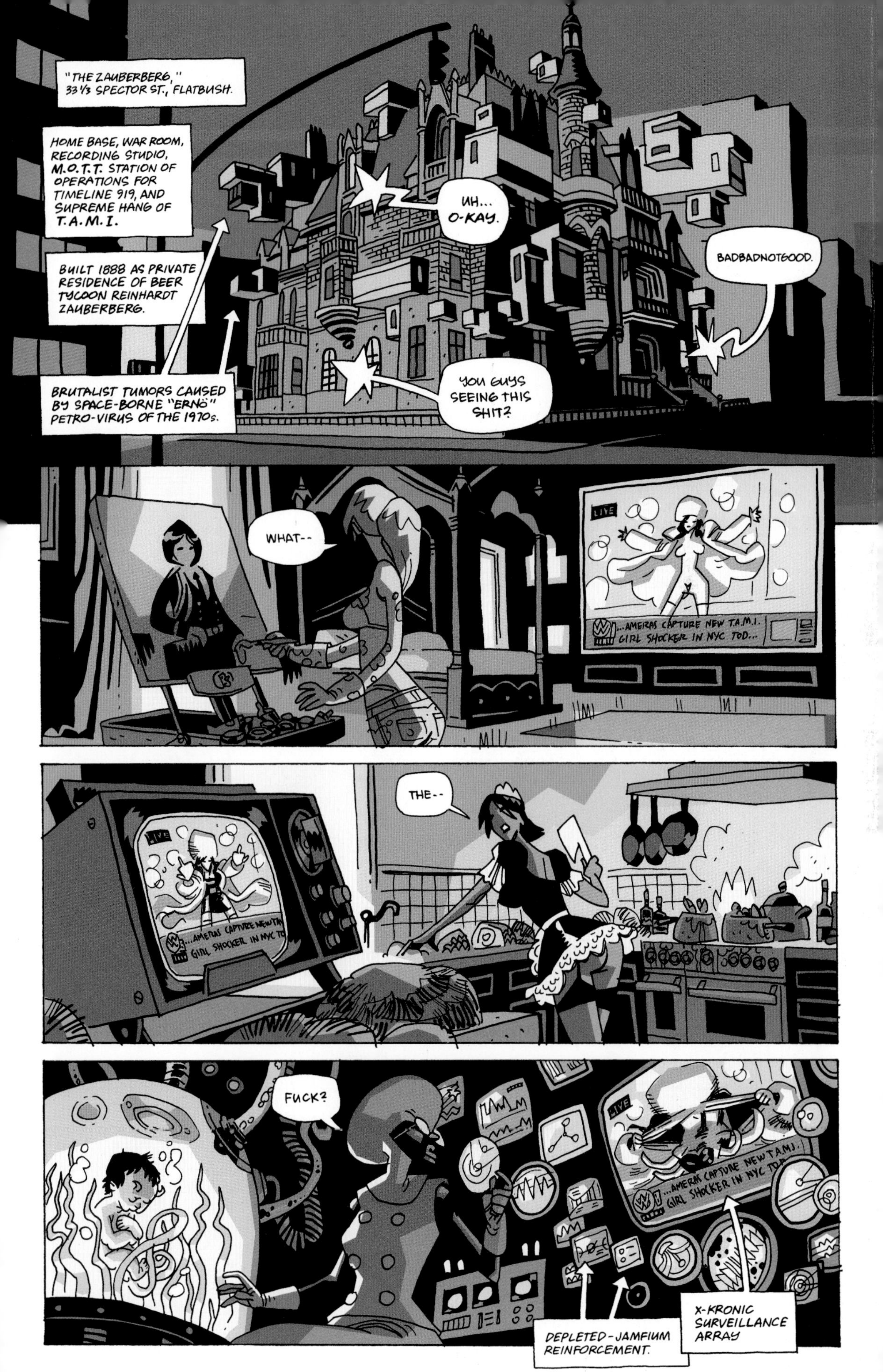
"THE ZAUBERBERG,"
33 1/3 SPECTOR ST., FLATBUSH.
HOME BASE, WAR ROOM, RECORDING STUDIO, M.O.T.T. STATION OF OPERATIONS FOR TIMELINE 919, AND SUPREME HANG OF T.A.M.I.
BUILT 1888 AS PRIVATE RESIDENCE OF BEER TYCOON REINHARDT ZAUBERBERG.
BRUTALIST TUMORS CAUSED BY SPACE-BORNE "ERNÖ" PETRO-VIRUS OF THE 1970s.
UH... O-KAY.
BADBADNOTGOOD.
YOU GUYS SEEING THIS SHIT?
WHAT--
LIVE
...AMERAS CAPTURE NEW T.A.M.I. GIRL SHOCKER IN NYC TOD...
THE--
LIVE
...AMERAS CAPTURE NEW TA
GIRL SHOCKER IN NYC TO
FUCK?
LIVE
...AMERAS CAPTURE NEW T.A.M.I. GIRL SHOCKER IN NYC TO
DEPLETED-JAMFIUM REINFORCEMENT.
X-KRONIC SURVEILLANCE ARRAY

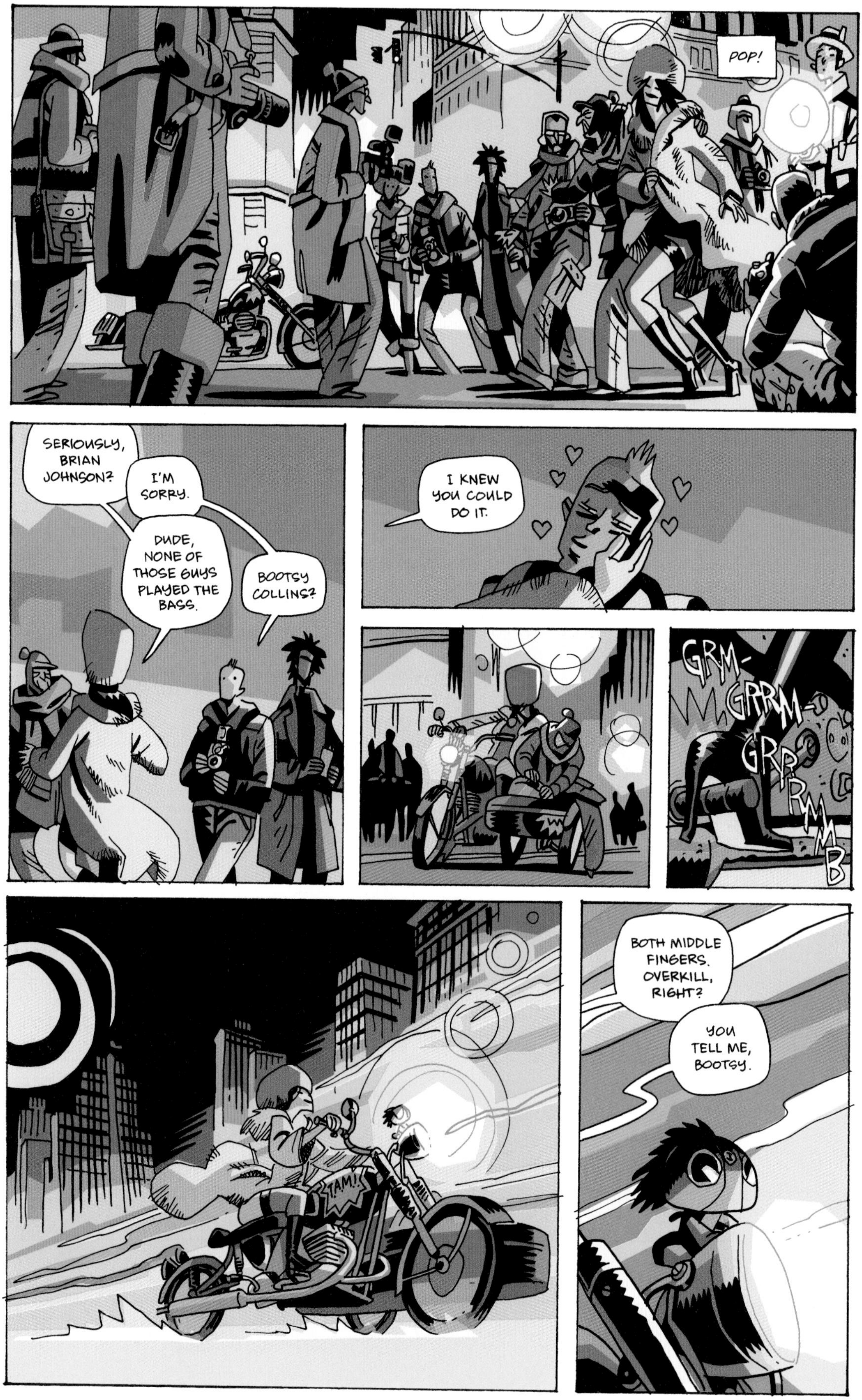
POP!
SERIOUSLY, BRIAN JOHNSON?
I'M SORRY.
DUDE, NONE OF THOSE GUYS PLAYED THE BASS.
BOOTSY COLLINS?
I KNEW YOU COULD DO IT.
GRM-GRRM-GRRRMMB
TAM!
BOTH MIDDLE FINGERS. OVERKILL, RIGHT?
YOU TELL ME, BOOTSY.

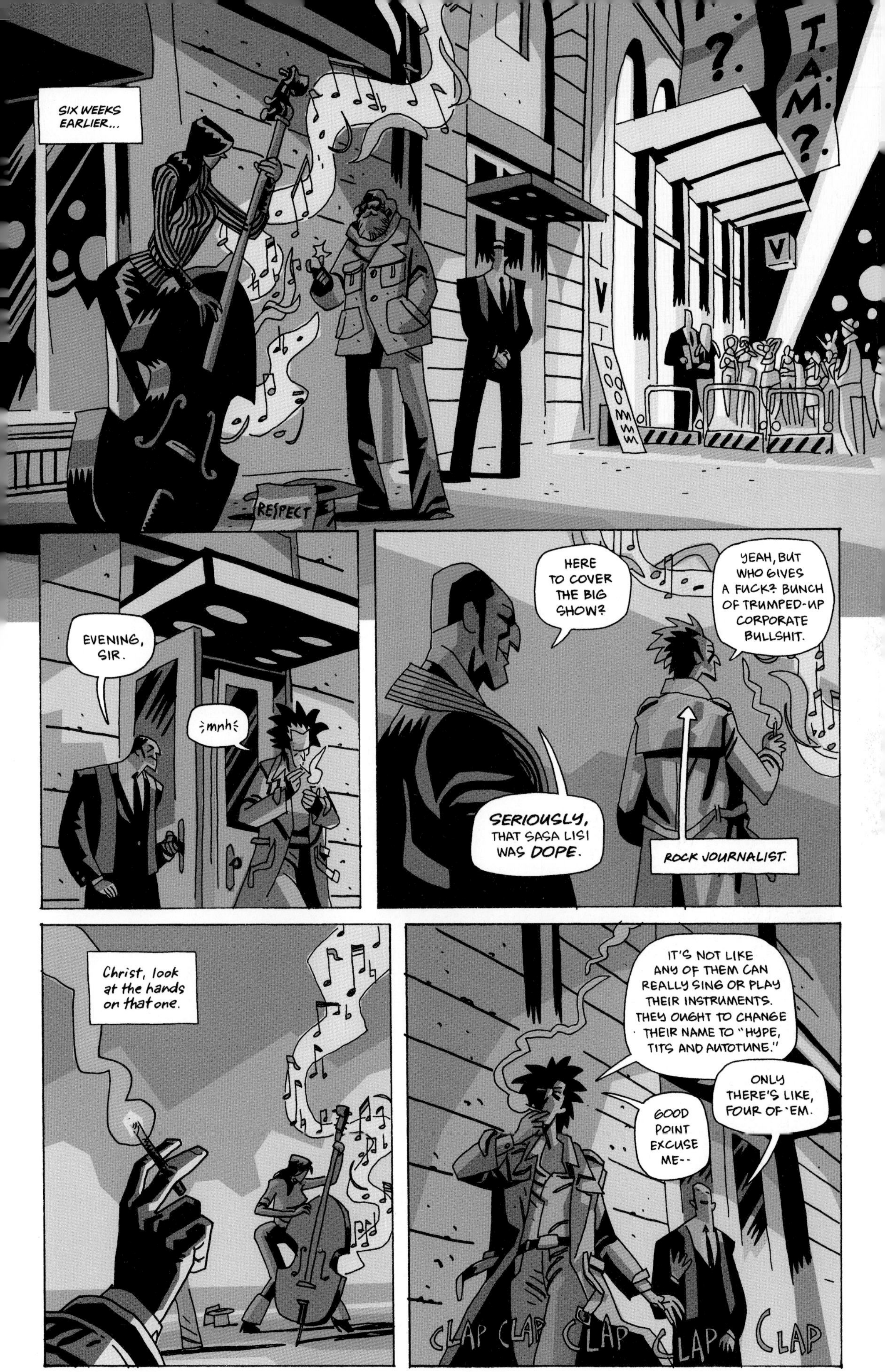
SIX WEEKS EARLIER...
T.A.M.?
RESPECT
EVENING, SIR.
mnh
HERE TO COVER THE BIG SHOW?
YEAH, BUT WHO GIVES A FUCK? BUNCH OF TRUMPED-UP CORPORATE BULLSHIT.
SERIOUSLY, THAT SASA LISI WAS DOPE.
ROCK JOURNALIST.
Christ, look at the hands on that one.
IT'S NOT LIKE ANY OF THEM CAN REALLY SING OR PLAY THEIR INSTRUMENTS. THEY OUGHT TO CHANGE THEIR NAME TO "HYPE, TITS AND AUTOTUNE."
ONLY THERE'S LIKE, FOUR OF 'EM.
GOOD POINT EXCUSE ME--
CLAP CLAP CLAP CLAP CLAP

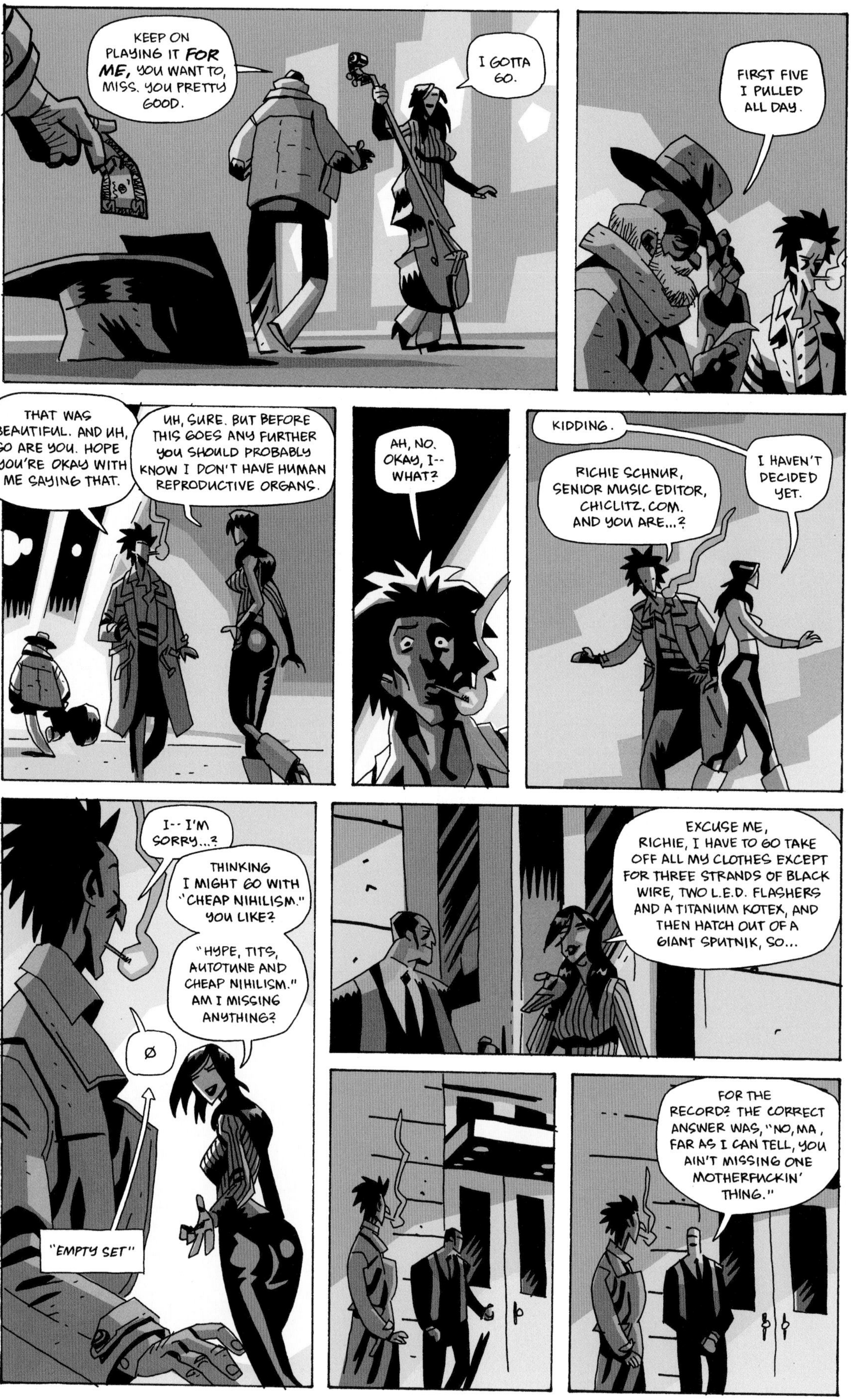

KEEP ON PLAYING IT FOR ME, YOU WANT TO, MISS. YOU PRETTY GOOD.
I GOTTA GO.
FIRST FIVE I PULLED ALL DAY.
THAT WAS BEAUTIFUL. AND UH, SO ARE YOU. HOPE YOU'RE OKAY WITH ME SAYING THAT.
UH, SURE. BUT BEFORE THIS GOES ANY FURTHER YOU SHOULD PROBABLY KNOW I DON'T HAVE HUMAN REPRODUCTIVE ORGANS.
AH, NO. OKAY, I-- WHAT?
KIDDING.
RICHIE SCHNUR, SENIOR MUSIC EDITOR, CHICLITZ.COM. AND YOU ARE...?
I HAVEN'T DECIDED YET.
I-- I'M SORRY...?
THINKING I MIGHT GO WITH "CHEAP NIHILISM." YOU LIKE?
"HYPE, TITS, AUTOTUNE AND CHEAP NIHILISM." AM I MISSING ANYTHING?
Ø
"EMPTY SET"
EXCUSE ME, RICHIE, I HAVE TO GO TAKE OFF ALL MY CLOTHES EXCEPT FOR THREE STRANDS OF BLACK WIRE, TWO L.E.D. FLASHERS AND A TITANIUM KOTEX, AND THEN HATCH OUT OF A GIANT SPUTNIK, SO...
FOR THE RECORD? THE CORRECT ANSWER WAS, "NO, MA, FAR AS I CAN TELL, YOU AIN'T MISSING ONE MOTHERFUCKIN' THING."

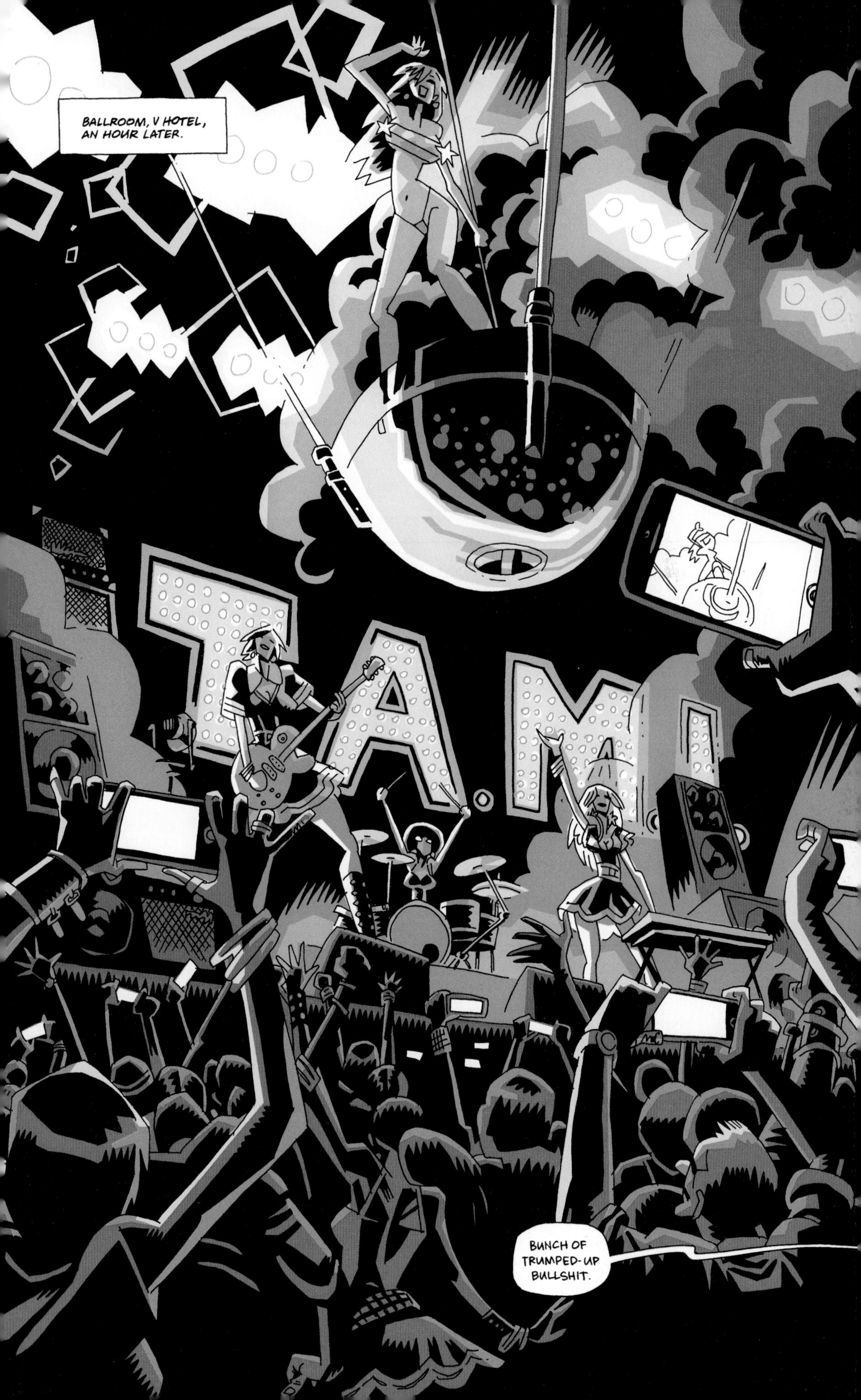
BALLROOM, V HOTEL, AN HOUR LATER.
T.A.M.
BUNCH OF TRUMPED-UP BULLSHIT.

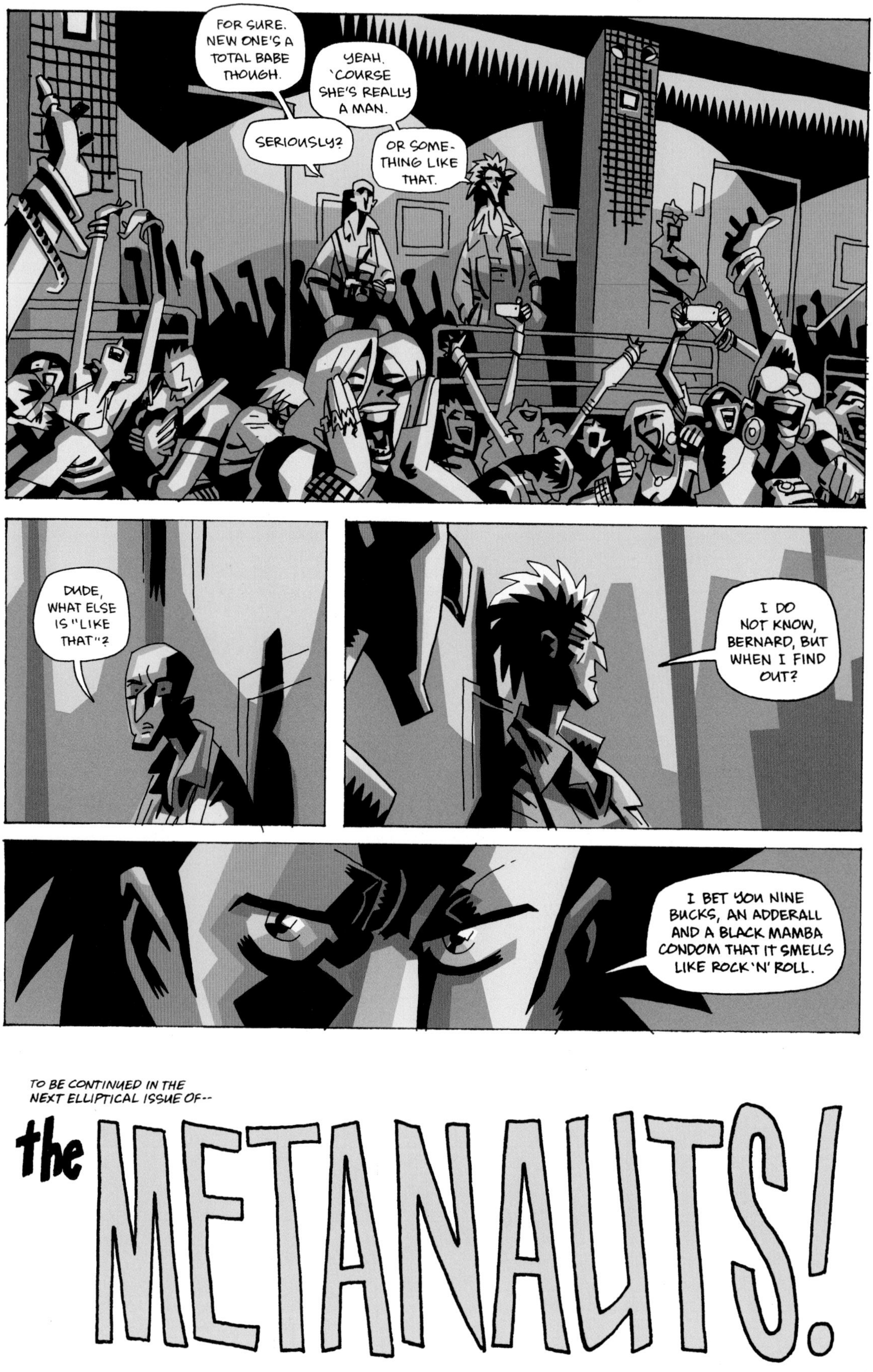
FOR SURE. NEW ONE'S A TOTAL BABE THOUGH.
SERIOUSLY?
YEAH. `COURSE SHE'S REALLY A MAN.
OR SOME-THING LIKE THAT.
DUDE, WHAT ELSE IS "LIKE THAT"?
I DO NOT KNOW, BERNARD, BUT WHEN I FIND OUT?
I BET YOU NINE BUCKS, AN ADDERALL AND A BLACK MAMBA CONDOM THAT IT SMELLS LIKE ROCK 'N' ROLL.

TO BE CONTINUED IN THE NEXT ELLIPTICAL ISSUE OF--

the METANAUTS!

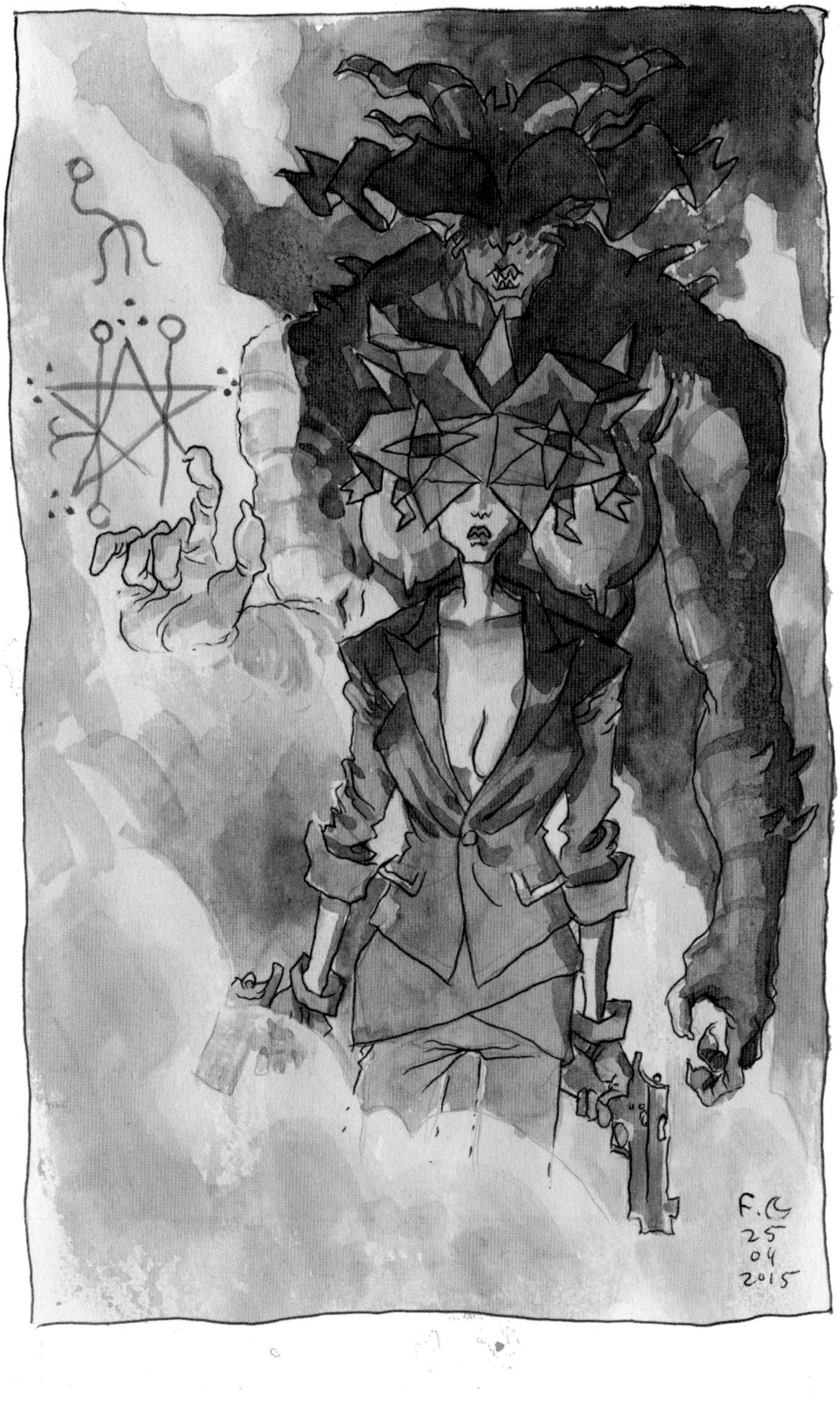
25
04
2015

CHAPTER TWO
O KILLERS I HAVE KNOWN AND LOVED

COULD EVERYONE JUST PLEASE--

--GENTLEMEN PLEASE--

--COULD YOU ALL JUST *PLEASE* MOVE BACK FOR ME--

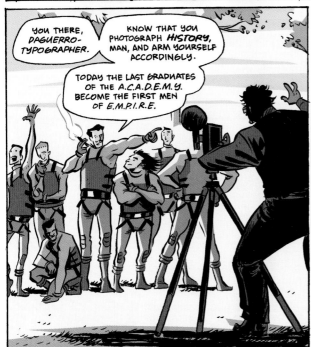

YOU THERE, DAGUERRO-TYPOGRAPHER.

KNOW THAT YOU PHOTOGRAPH *HISTORY*, MAN, AND ARM YOURSELF ACCORDINGLY.

TODAY THE LAST GRADUATES OF THE *A.C.A.D.E.M.Y.* BECOME THE FIRST MEN OF *E.M.P.I.R.E.*

"NOW WE ARE ALL SONS OF BITCHES."

I THINK THAT'S THE LINE HERE, RIGHT?

GOD, JUST SHUT THE HELL UP AND LET'S GET THIS RIDICULOUS EXERCISE OVER W--

--DAMMIT *AKIM* KNOCK IT OFF!

HAH.

EVERYONE *PLEASE*, CAN YOU JUST HOLD STILL, STARE AT THE CAMERA, AND PRETEND WE LIKE EACH OTHER LONG ENOUGH TO LET THE MAN DO HIS JOB--

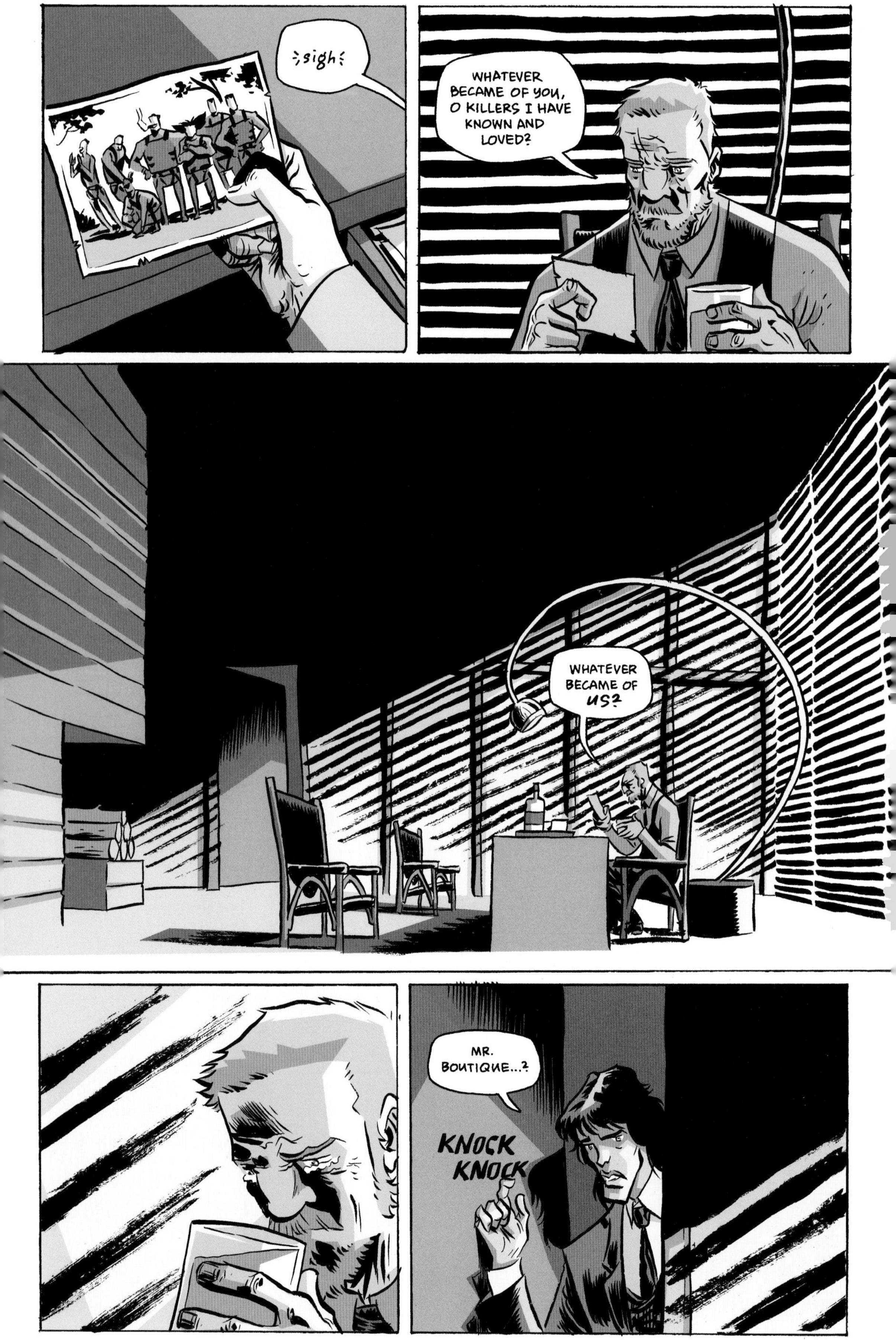
sigh
WHATEVER BECAME OF YOU, O KILLERS I HAVE KNOWN AND LOVED?
WHATEVER BECAME OF US?
MR. BOUTIQUE...?
KNOCK KNOCK

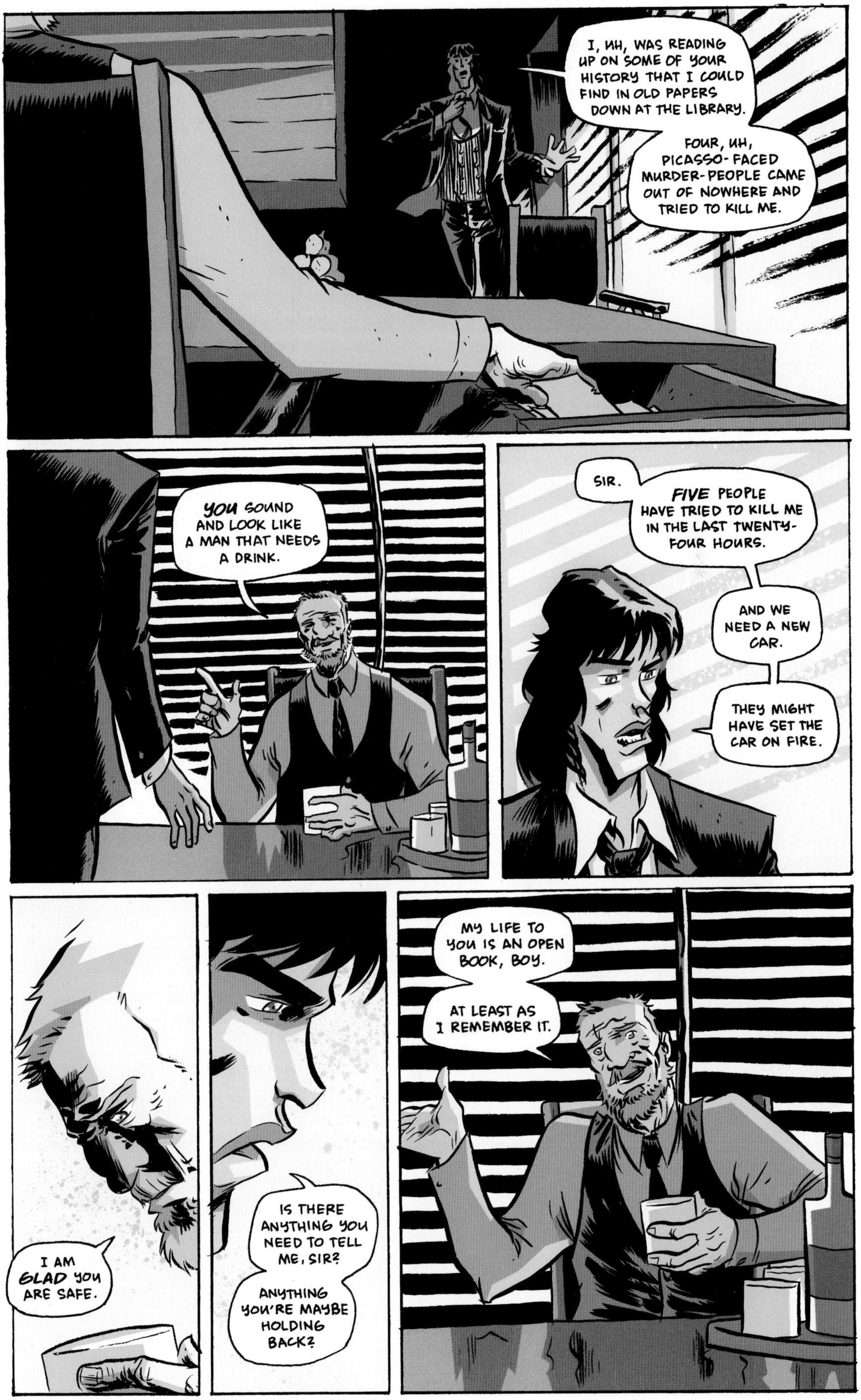
I, UH, WAS READING UP ON SOME OF YOUR HISTORY THAT I COULD FIND IN OLD PAPERS DOWN AT THE LIBRARY.
FOUR, UH, PICASSO-FACED MURDER-PEOPLE CAME OUT OF NOWHERE AND TRIED TO KILL ME.
YOU SOUND AND LOOK LIKE A MAN THAT NEEDS A DRINK.
SIR.
FIVE PEOPLE HAVE TRIED TO KILL ME IN THE LAST TWENTY-FOUR HOURS.
AND WE NEED A NEW CAR.
THEY MIGHT HAVE SET THE CAR ON FIRE.
I AM GLAD YOU ARE SAFE.
IS THERE ANYTHING YOU NEED TO TELL ME, SIR?
ANYTHING YOU'RE MAYBE HOLDING BACK?
MY LIFE TO YOU IS AN OPEN BOOK, BOY.
AT LEAST AS I REMEMBER IT.

I'M JUST NOT A FAN OF COINCIDENCE IS ALL.

AND I'LL *TAKE* THAT DRINK NOW.

GOOD MAN.

HERE.

TO "COINCIDENCE."

AND HAVING ENOUGH OF IT AROUND TO *CHOKE*.

THERE WAS *WEIRD CULT SHIT*, SIR. THAT END-OF-THE-WORLD STUFF.

ALL AROUND THE CAR AND...

...AND IN THE WAY THEY SPOKE.

WHAT'S THAT, NOW?

IT WASN'T A LANGUAGE, IT...

...IT WAS LIKE HEARING IT FROM THE CORNER OF YOUR EAR.

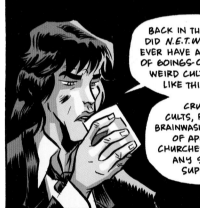

BACK IN THE DAY, DID *N.E.T.W.O.R.K.* EVER HAVE ANY KIND OF GOINGS-ON WITH WEIRD CULT SHIT LIKE THIS?

CRUSH ANY CULTS, RESCUE ANY BRAINWASHED DEVOTEES OF APOCALYPSE CHURCHES, SHUT DOWN ANY SORCEROR SUPREMES?

"SORCERORS SUPREME," AND *NO*.

I DON'T KNOW MUCH ABOUT *MAGIC*, I'M AFRAID.

WELL, SHIT, BOSS.

...THEN I GUESS I'M GONNA GO FIND US A MAGICIAN.

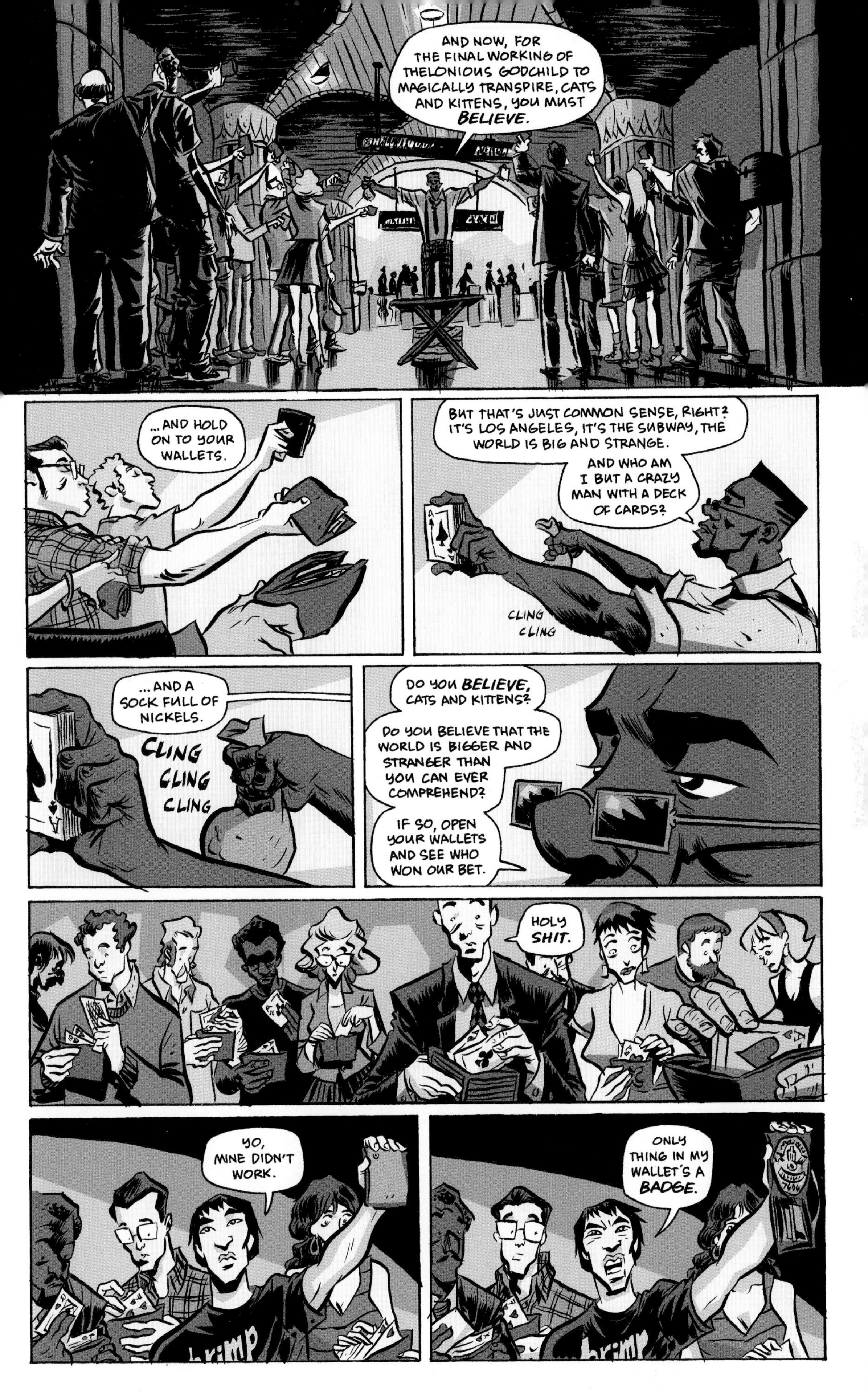
AND NOW, FOR THE FINAL WORKING OF THELONIOUS GODCHILD TO MAGICALLY TRANSPIRE, CATS AND KITTENS, YOU MUST BELIEVE.
...AND HOLD ON TO YOUR WALLETS.
BUT THAT'S JUST COMMON SENSE, RIGHT? IT'S LOS ANGELES, IT'S THE SUBWAY, THE WORLD IS BIG AND STRANGE.
AND WHO AM I BUT A CRAZY MAN WITH A DECK OF CARDS?
CLING
CLING
...AND A SOCK FULL OF NICKELS.
CLING
CLING
CLING
DO YOU BELIEVE, CATS AND KITTENS?
DO YOU BELIEVE THAT THE WORLD IS BIGGER AND STRANGER THAN YOU CAN EVER COMPREHEND?
IF SO, OPEN YOUR WALLETS AND SEE WHO WON OUR BET.
HOLY SHIT.
YO, MINE DIDN'T WORK.
ONLY THING IN MY WALLET'S A BADGE.

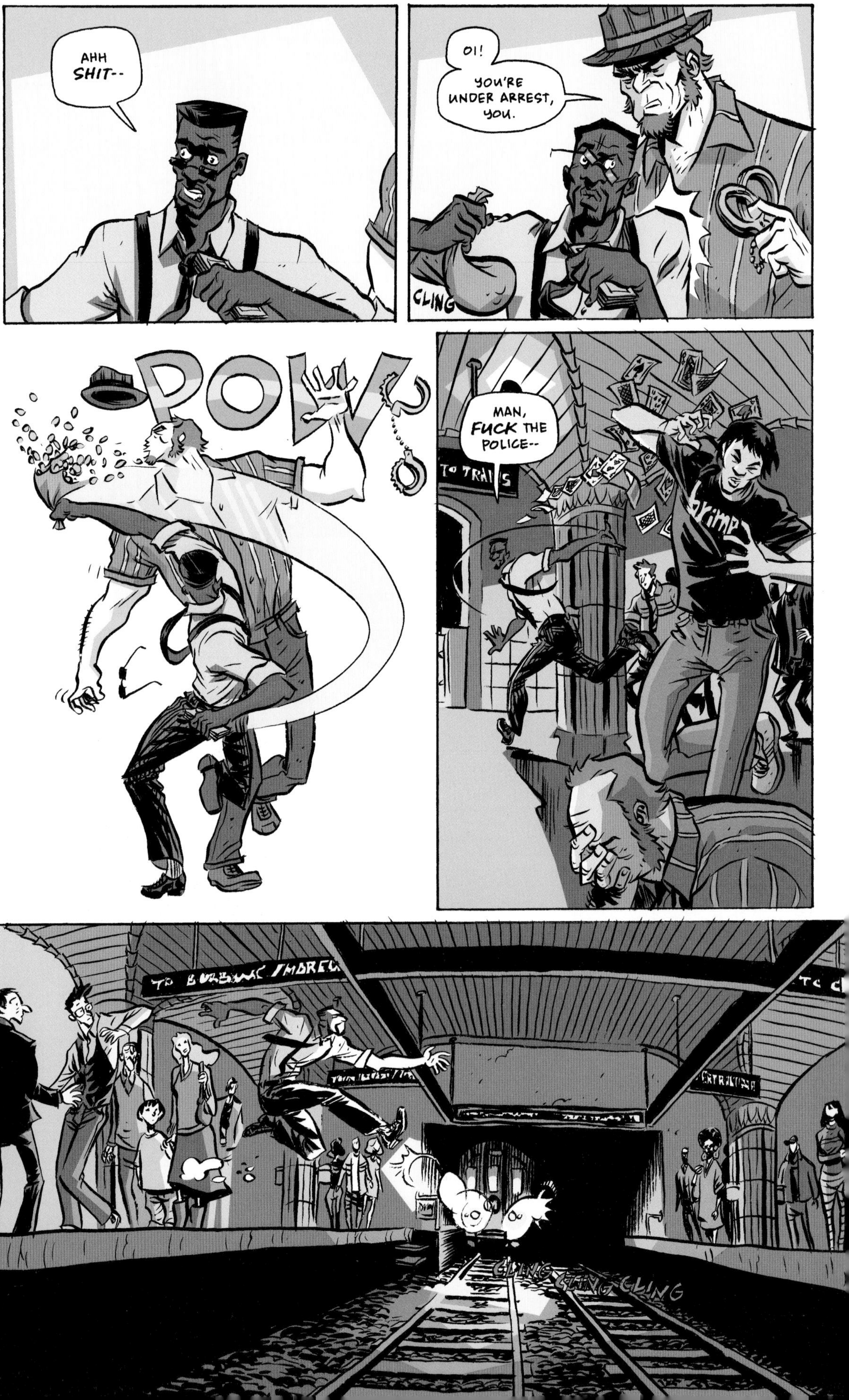
AHH SHIT--
OI!
YOU'RE UNDER ARREST, YOU.
CLING
POW
MAN, FUCK THE POLICE--
CLING CLING CLING

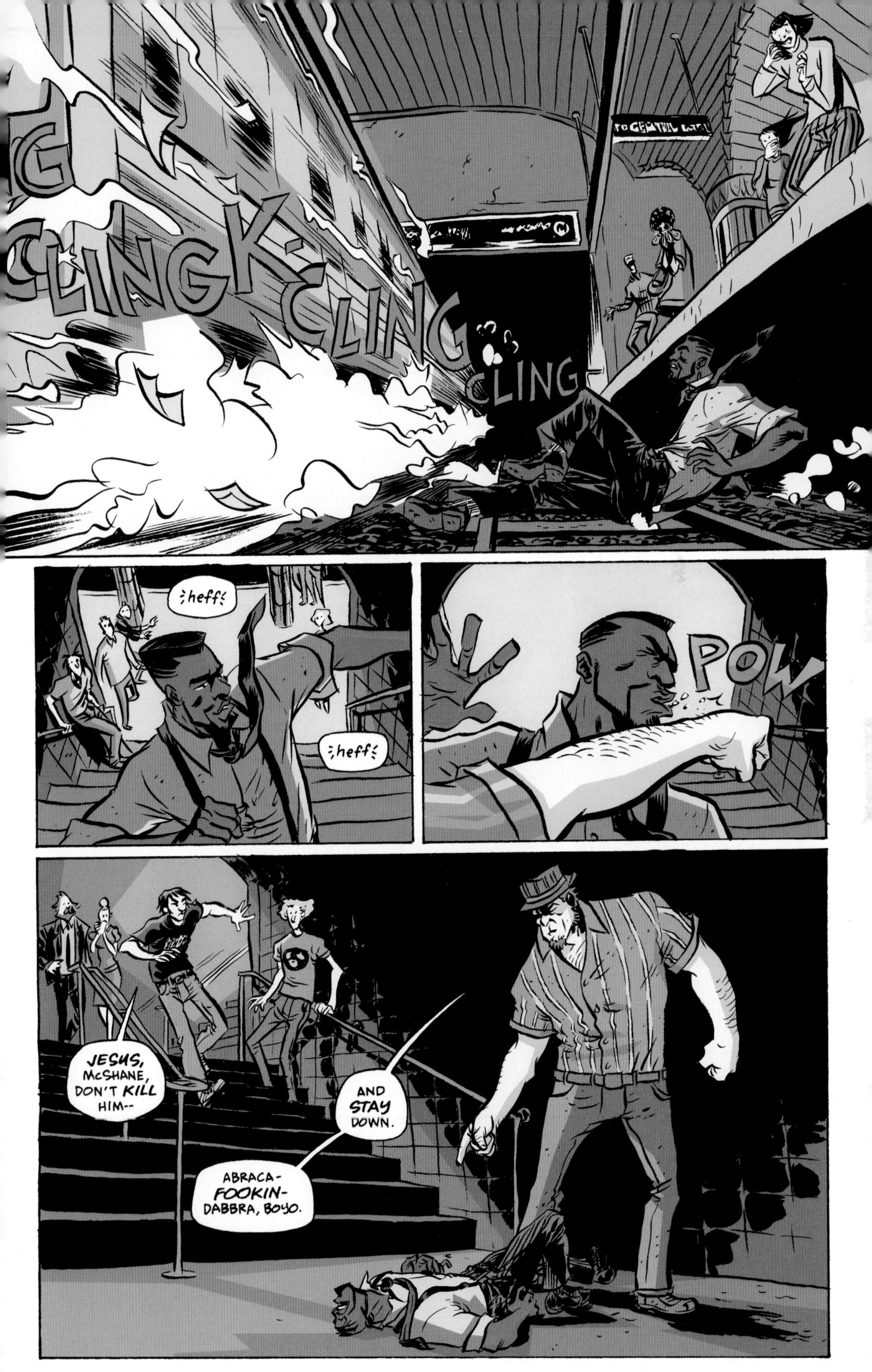
CLING-CLINGK-CLING-CLING-
heff
heff
POW
JESUS, McSHANE, DON'T KILL HIM--
AND STAY DOWN.
ABRACA-FOOKIN-DABBRA, BOYO.

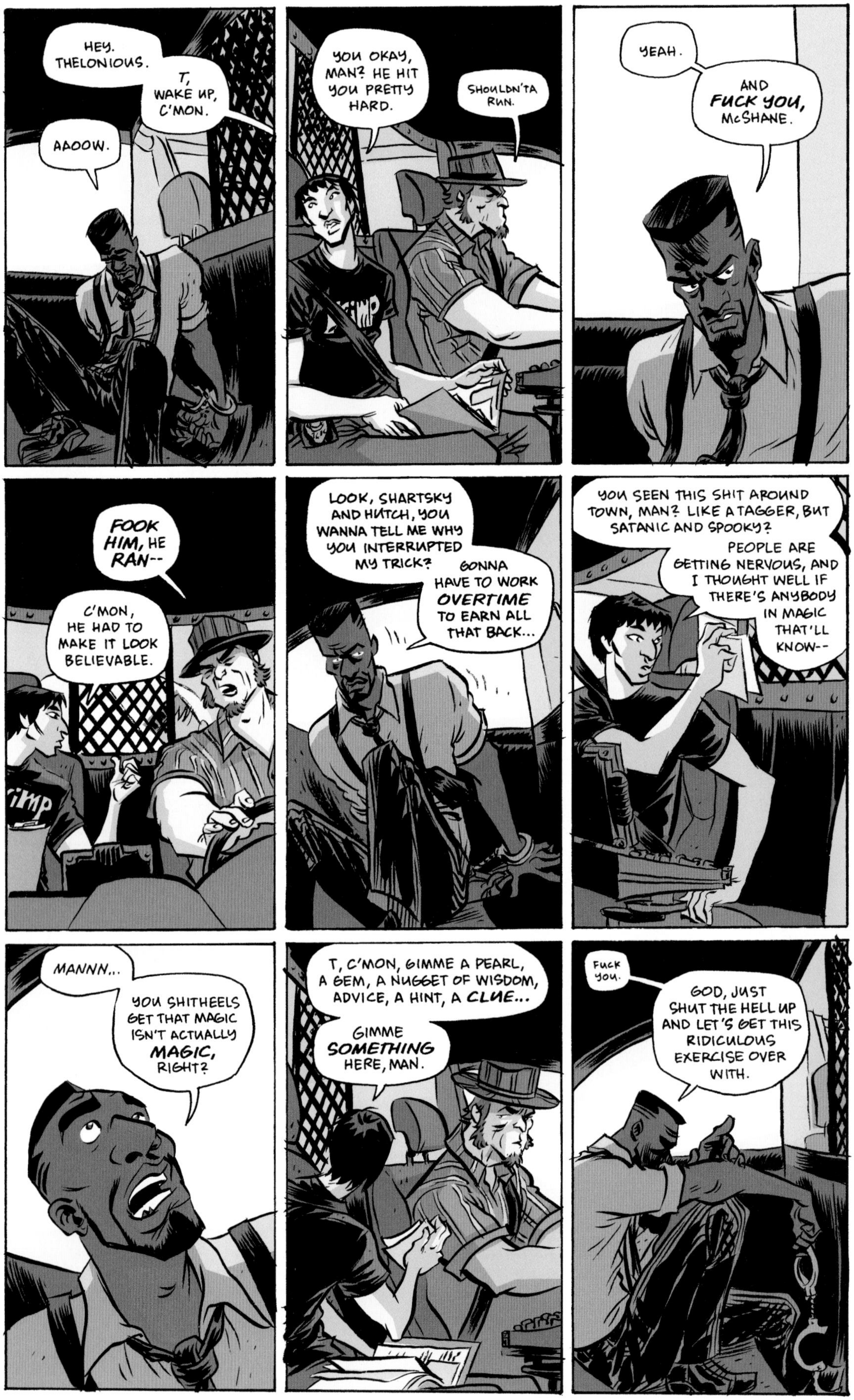
HEY. THELONIOUS.
T, WAKE UP, C'MON.
AAOOW.
YOU OKAY, MAN? HE HIT YOU PRETTY HARD.
SHOULDN'TA RUN.
YEAH.
AND FUCK YOU, McSHANE.
FOOK HIM, HE RAN--
C'MON, HE HAD TO MAKE IT LOOK BELIEVABLE.
LOOK, SHARTSKY AND HUTCH, YOU WANNA TELL ME WHY YOU INTERRUPTED MY TRICK?
GONNA HAVE TO WORK OVERTIME TO EARN ALL THAT BACK...
YOU SEEN THIS SHIT AROUND TOWN, MAN? LIKE A TAGGER, BUT SATANIC AND SPOOKY?
PEOPLE ARE GETTING NERVOUS, AND I THOUGHT WELL IF THERE'S ANYBODY IN MAGIC THAT'LL KNOW--
MANNN...
YOU SHITHEELS GET THAT MAGIC ISN'T ACTUALLY MAGIC, RIGHT?
T, C'MON, GIMME A PEARL, A GEM, A NUGGET OF WISDOM, ADVICE, A HINT, A CLUE...
GIMME SOMETHING HERE, MAN.
Fuck you.
GOD, JUST SHUT THE HELL UP AND LET'S GET THIS RIDICULOUS EXERCISE OVER WITH.

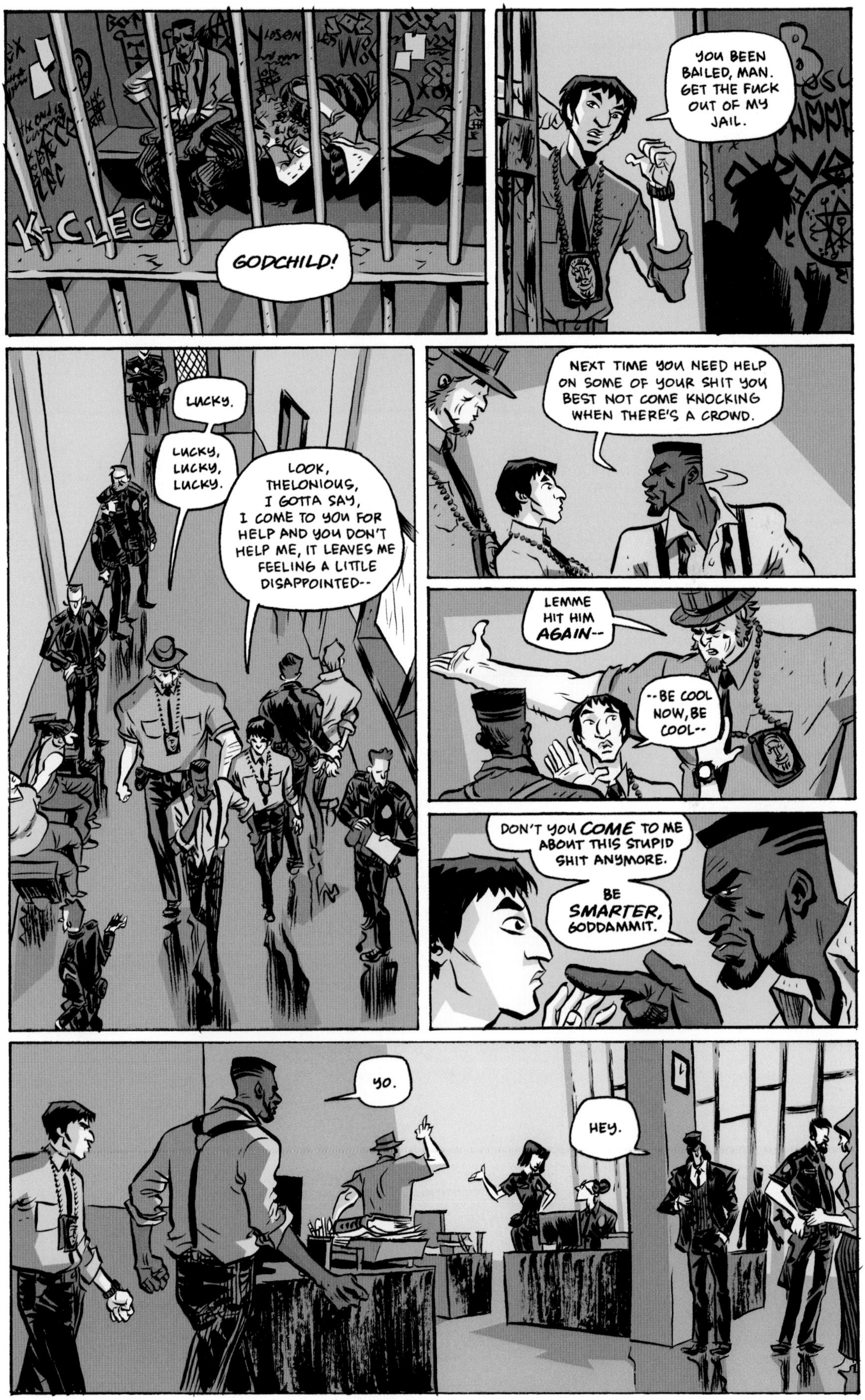
K-CLEC
GODCHILD!
YOU BEEN BAILED, MAN. GET THE FUCK OUT OF MY JAIL.
LUCKY.
LUCKY, LUCKY, LUCKY.
LOOK, THELONIOUS, I GOTTA SAY, I COME TO YOU FOR HELP AND YOU DON'T HELP ME, IT LEAVES ME FEELING A LITTLE DISAPPOINTED--
NEXT TIME YOU NEED HELP ON SOME OF YOUR SHIT YOU BEST NOT COME KNOCKING WHEN THERE'S A CROWD.
LEMME HIT HIM AGAIN--
--BE COOL NOW, BE COOL--
DON'T YOU COME TO ME ABOUT THIS STUPID SHIT ANYMORE.
BE SMARTER, GODDAMMIT.
YO.
HEY.

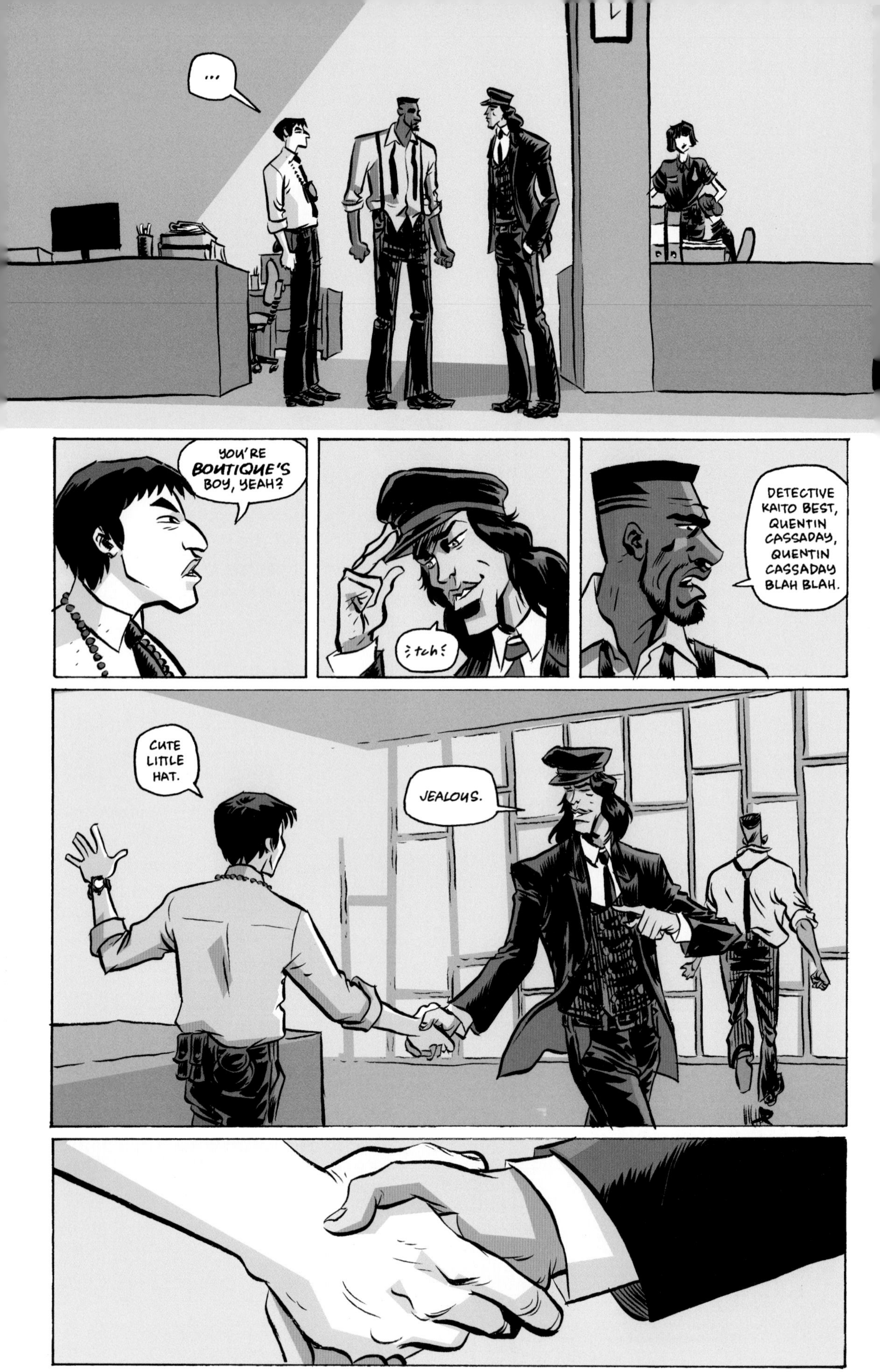
...
YOU'RE BOUTIQUE'S BOY, YEAH?
tch
DETECTIVE KAITO BEST, QUENTIN CASSADAY, QUENTIN CASSADAY BLAH BLAH.
CUTE LITTLE HAT.
JEALOUS.

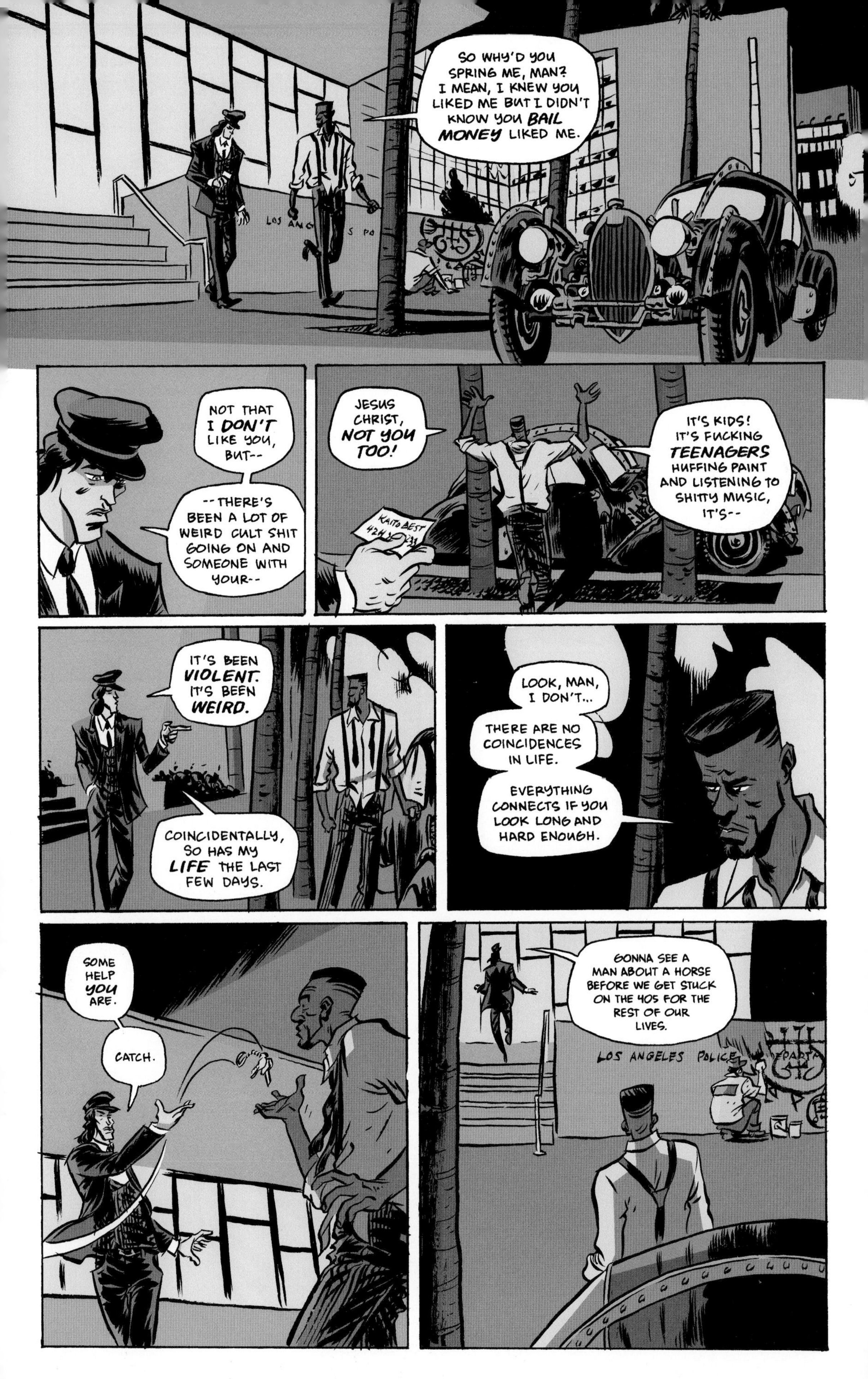
SO WHY'D YOU SPRING ME, MAN? I MEAN, I KNEW YOU LIKED ME BUT I DIDN'T KNOW YOU BAIL MONEY LIKED ME.
NOT THAT I DON'T LIKE YOU, BUT--
--THERE'S BEEN A LOT OF WEIRD CULT SHIT GOING ON AND SOMEONE WITH YOUR--
JESUS CHRIST, NOT YOU TOO!
KAITO BEST
IT'S KIDS! IT'S FUCKING TEENAGERS HUFFING PAINT AND LISTENING TO SHITTY MUSIC, IT'S--
IT'S BEEN VIOLENT. IT'S BEEN WEIRD.
COINCIDENTALLY, SO HAS MY LIFE THE LAST FEW DAYS.
LOOK, MAN, I DON'T...
THERE ARE NO COINCIDENCES IN LIFE.
EVERYTHING CONNECTS IF YOU LOOK LONG AND HARD ENOUGH.
SOME HELP YOU ARE.
CATCH.
GONNA SEE A MAN ABOUT A HORSE BEFORE WE GET STUCK ON THE 405 FOR THE REST OF OUR LIVES.
LOS ANGELES POLICE

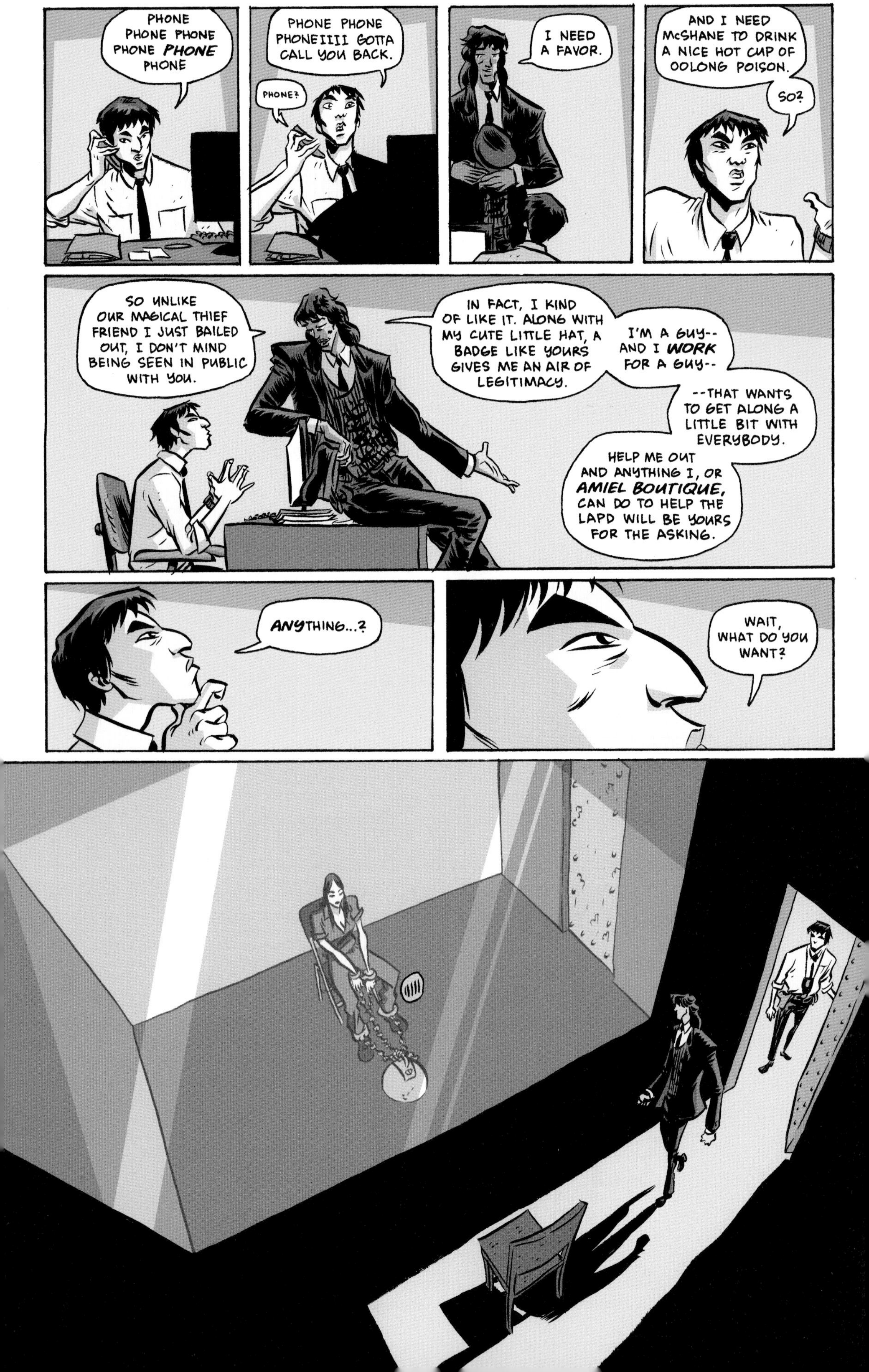
PHONE PHONE PHONE PHONE PHONE PHONE
PHONE PHONE PHONEIIII GOTTA CALL YOU BACK.
PHONE?
I NEED A FAVOR.
AND I NEED McSHANE TO DRINK A NICE HOT CUP OF OOLONG POISON.
SO?
SO UNLIKE OUR MAGICAL THIEF FRIEND I JUST BAILED OUT, I DON'T MIND BEING SEEN IN PUBLIC WITH YOU.
IN FACT, I KIND OF LIKE IT. ALONG WITH MY CUTE LITTLE HAT, A BADGE LIKE YOURS GIVES ME AN AIR OF LEGITIMACY.
I'M A GUY-- AND I WORK FOR A GUY--
--THAT WANTS TO GET ALONG A LITTLE BIT WITH EVERYBODY.
HELP ME OUT AND ANYTHING I, OR AMIEL BOUTIQUE, CAN DO TO HELP THE LAPD WILL BE YOURS FOR THE ASKING.
ANYTHING...?
WAIT, WHAT DO YOU WANT?

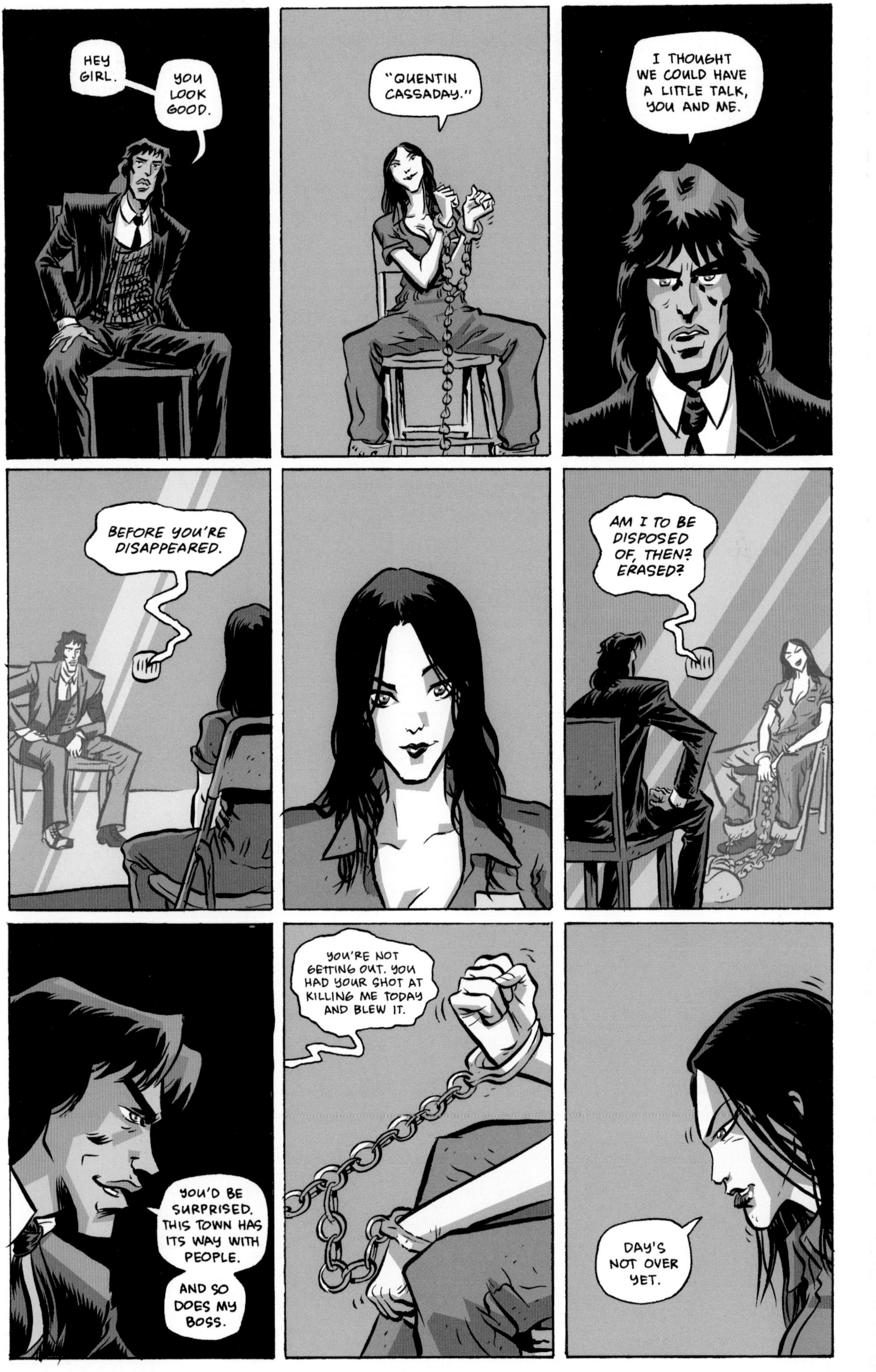
HEY GIRL.
YOU LOOK GOOD.
"QUENTIN CASSADAY."
I THOUGHT WE COULD HAVE A LITTLE TALK, YOU AND ME.
BEFORE YOU'RE DISAPPEARED.
AM I TO BE DISPOSED OF, THEN? ERASED?
YOU'D BE SURPRISED. THIS TOWN HAS ITS WAY WITH PEOPLE.
AND SO DOES MY BOSS.
YOU'RE NOT GETTING OUT. YOU HAD YOUR SHOT AT KILLING ME TODAY AND BLEW IT.
DAY'S NOT OVER YET.

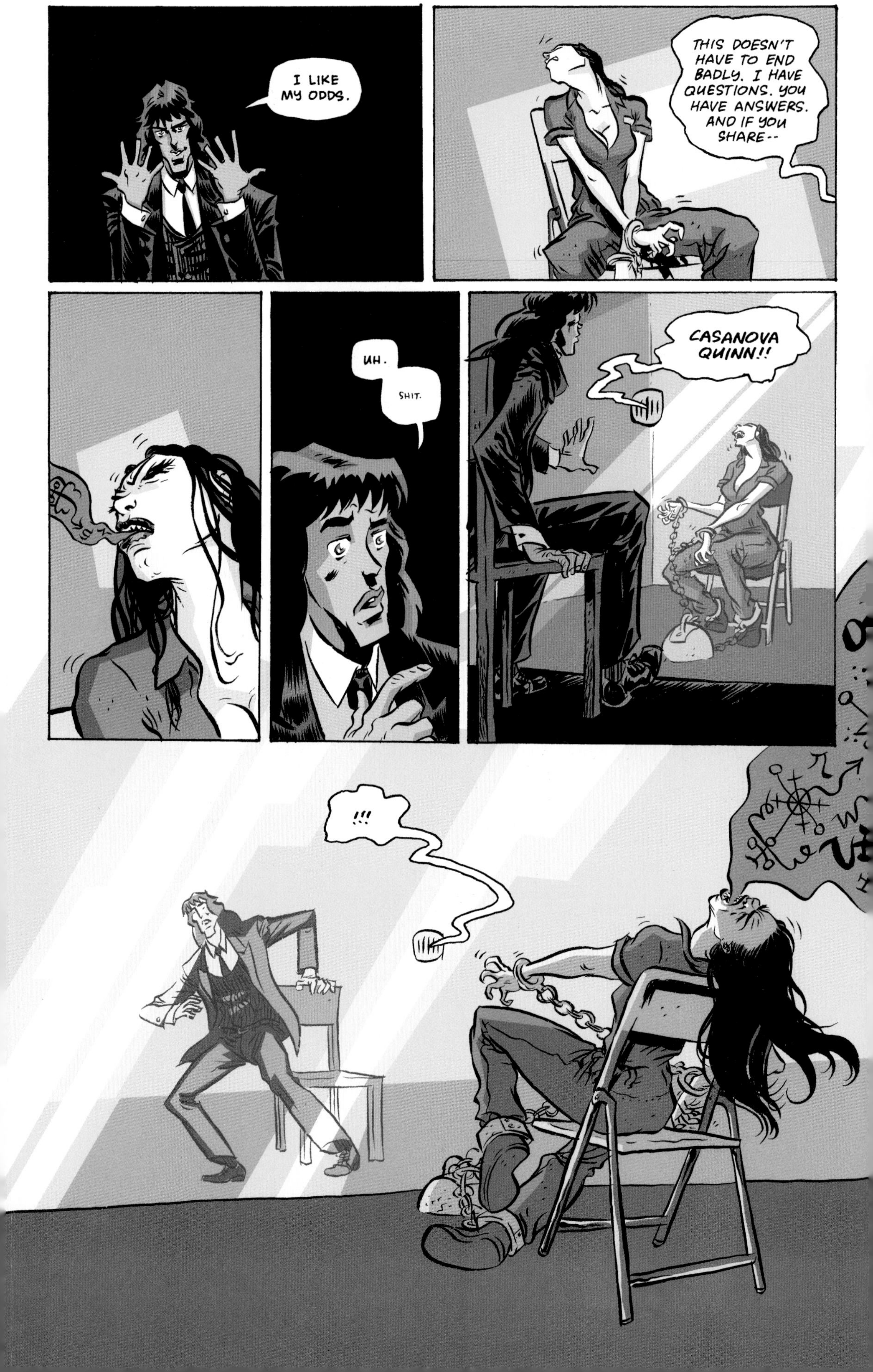
I LIKE MY ODDS.
THIS DOESN'T HAVE TO END BADLY. I HAVE QUESTIONS. YOU HAVE ANSWERS. AND IF YOU SHARE--
UH.
SHIT.
CASANOVA QUINN!!
!!!

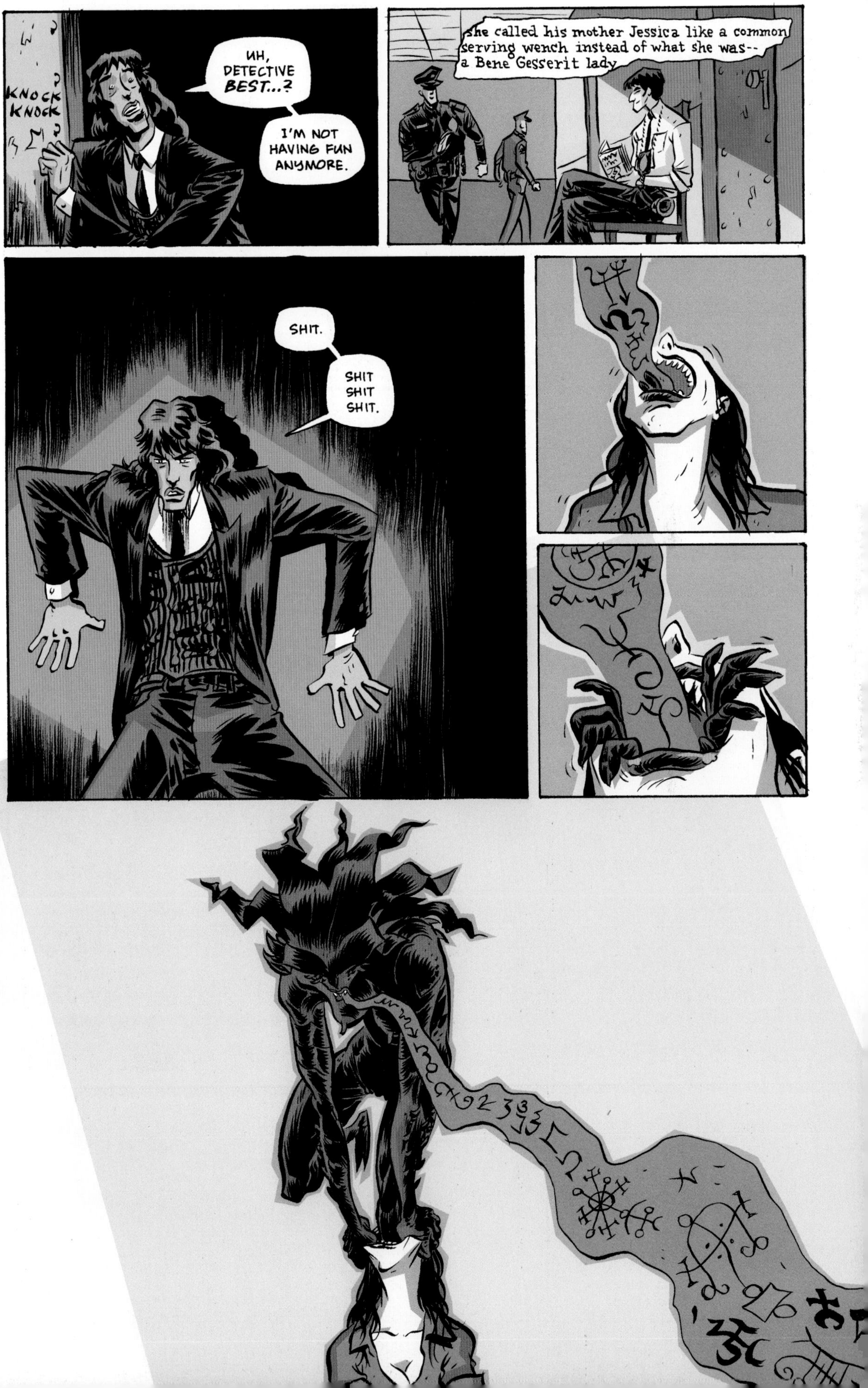
KNOCK KNOCK
UH, DETECTIVE BEST...?
I'M NOT HAVING FUN ANYMORE.
she called his mother Jessica like a common serving wench instead of what she was--a Bene Gesserit lady
SHIT.
SHIT SHIT SHIT.

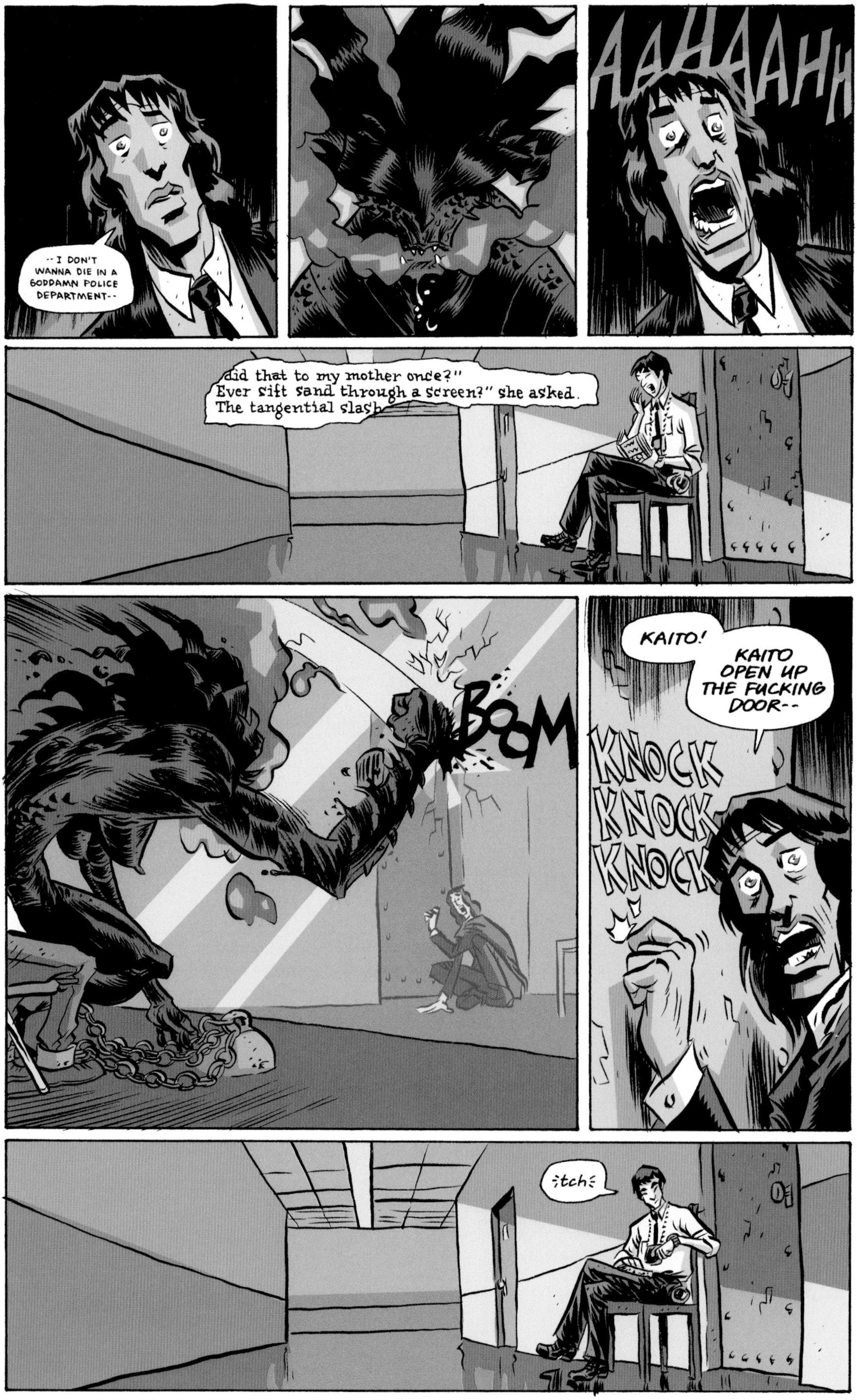
--I DON'T WANNA DIE IN A GODDAMN POLICE DEPARTMENT--
AAHAAAHH
did that to my mother once?"
Ever sift sand through a screen?" she asked.
The tangential slash
BOOM
KAITO!
KAITO OPEN UP THE FUCKING DOOR--
KNOCK
KNOCK
KNOCK
:tch:

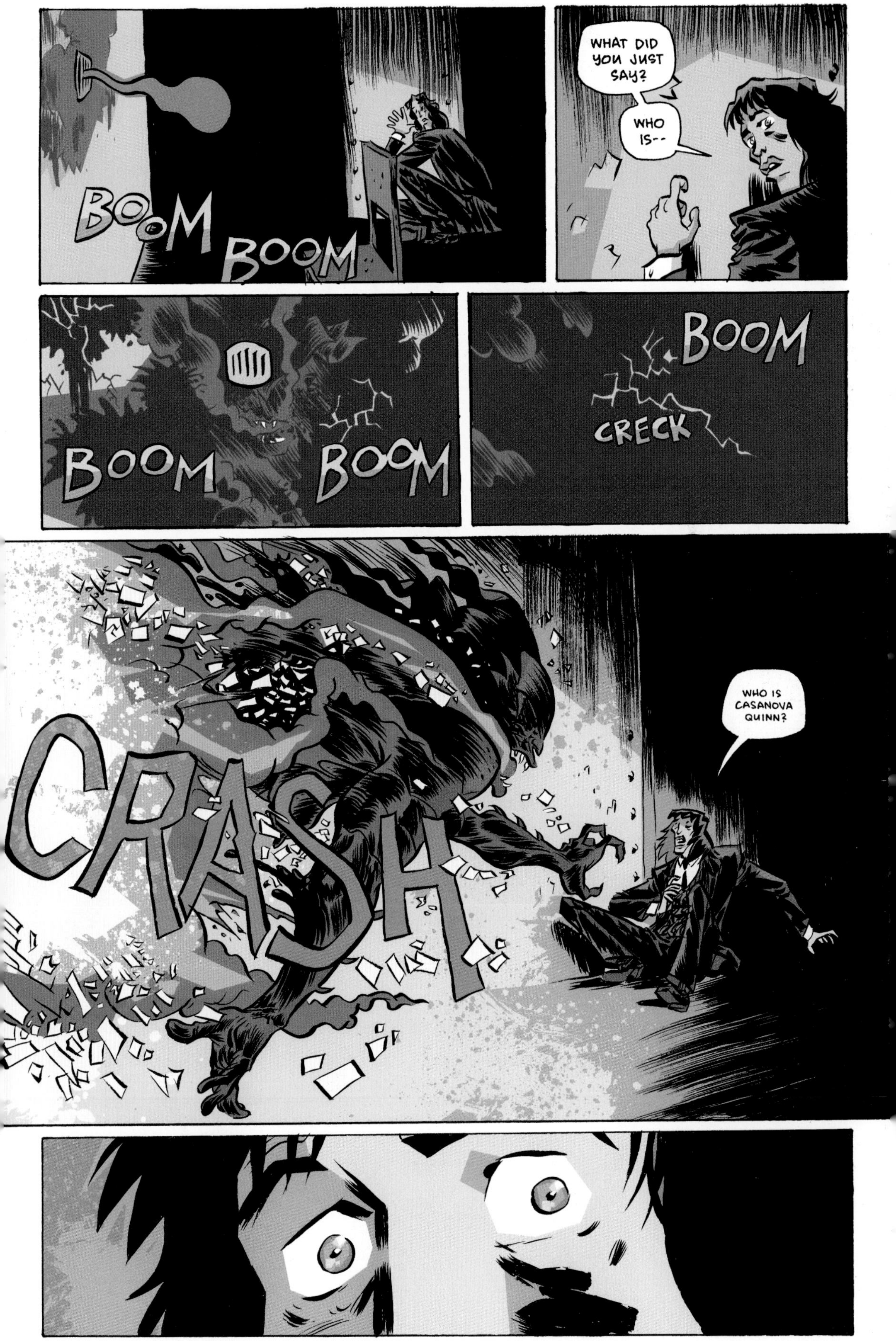
BOOM BOOM
WHAT DID YOU JUST SAY?
WHO IS--
BOOM
BOOM
BOOM
CRECK
CRASH
WHO IS CASANOVA QUINN?

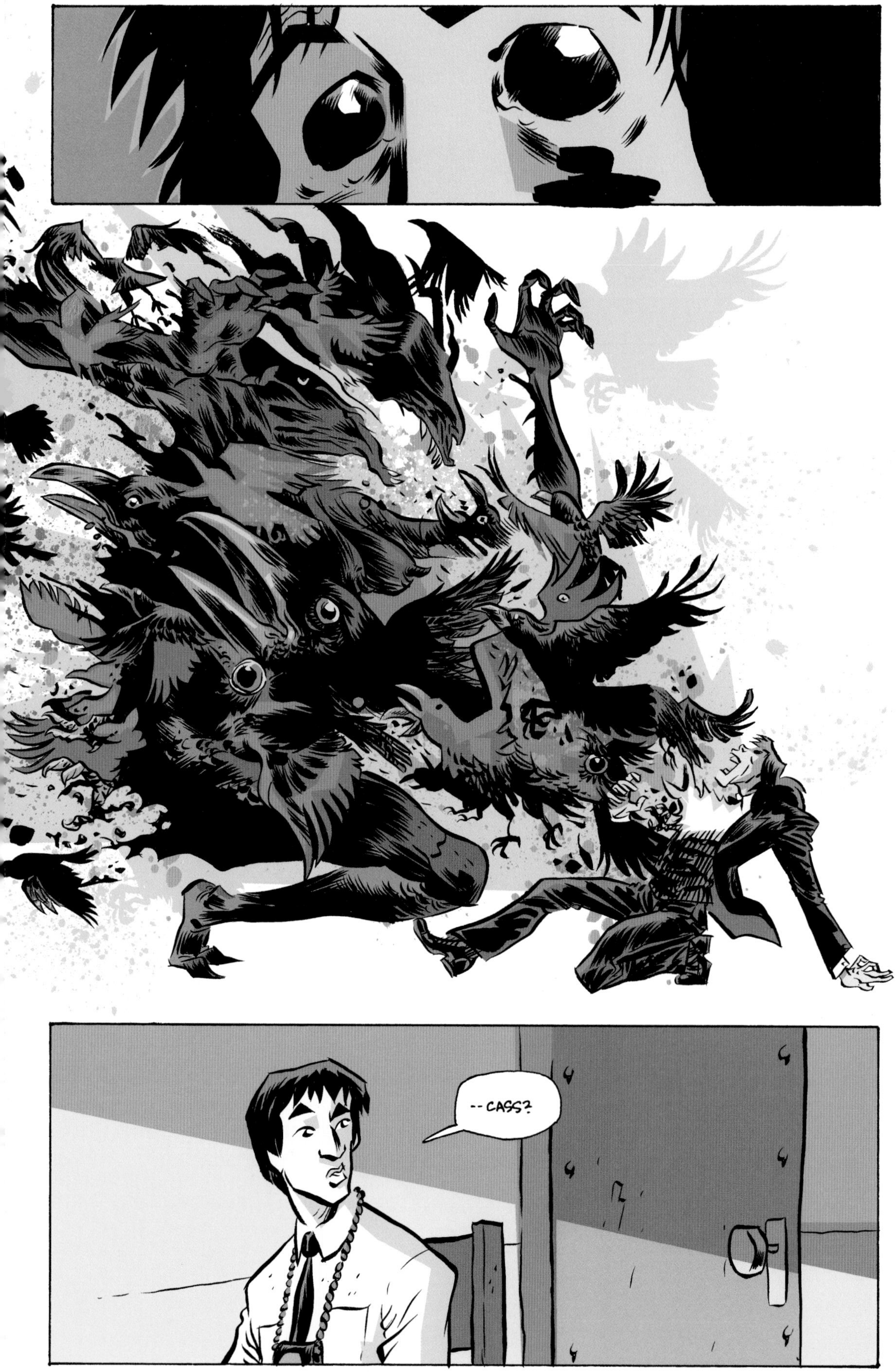
--CASS?

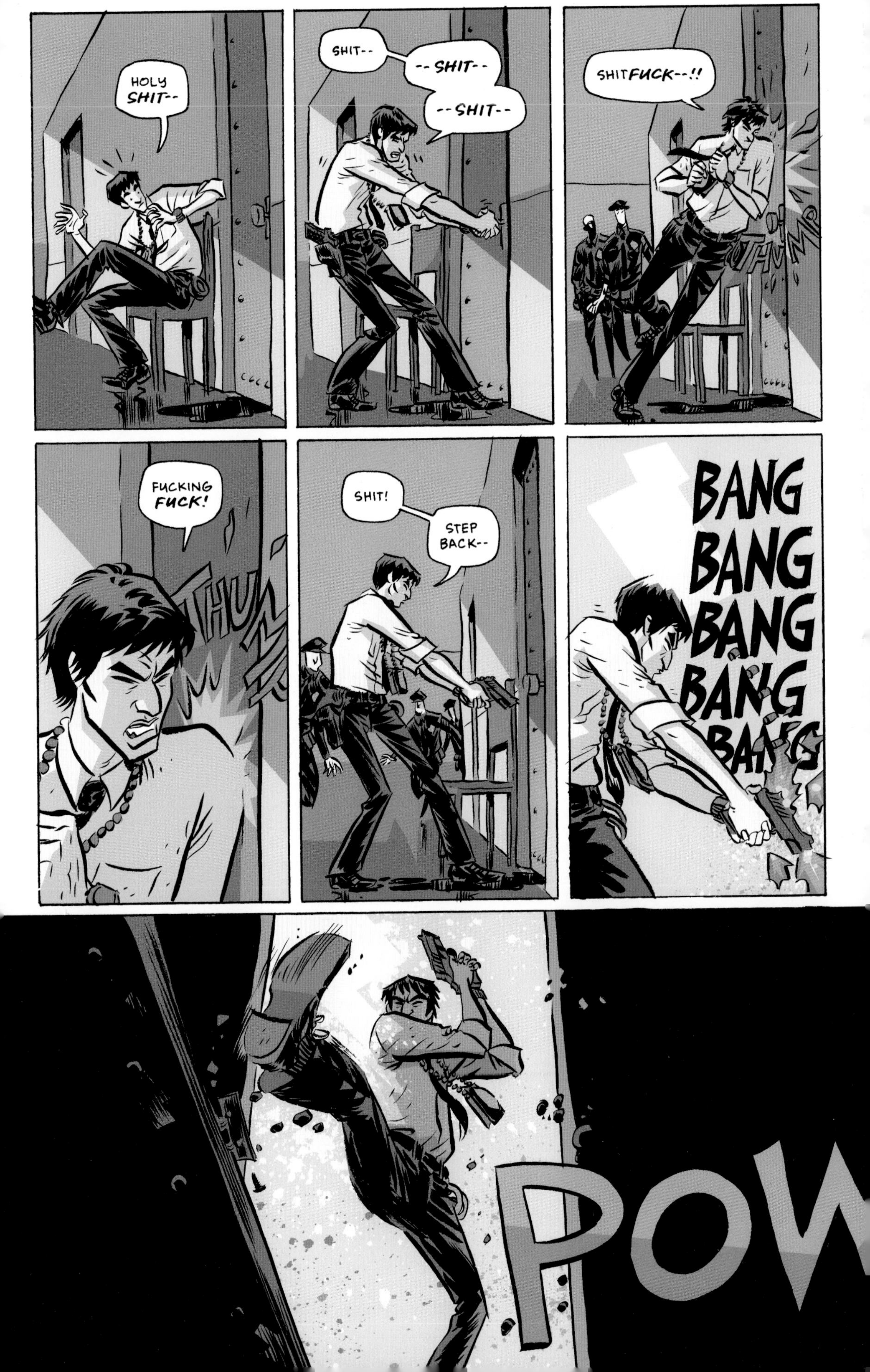
HOLY SHIT--
SHIT--
--SHIT--
--SHIT--
SHITFUCK--!!
THUMP
FUCKING FUCK!
THUMP
SHIT!
STEP BACK--
BANG
BANG
BANG
BANG
BANG
POW

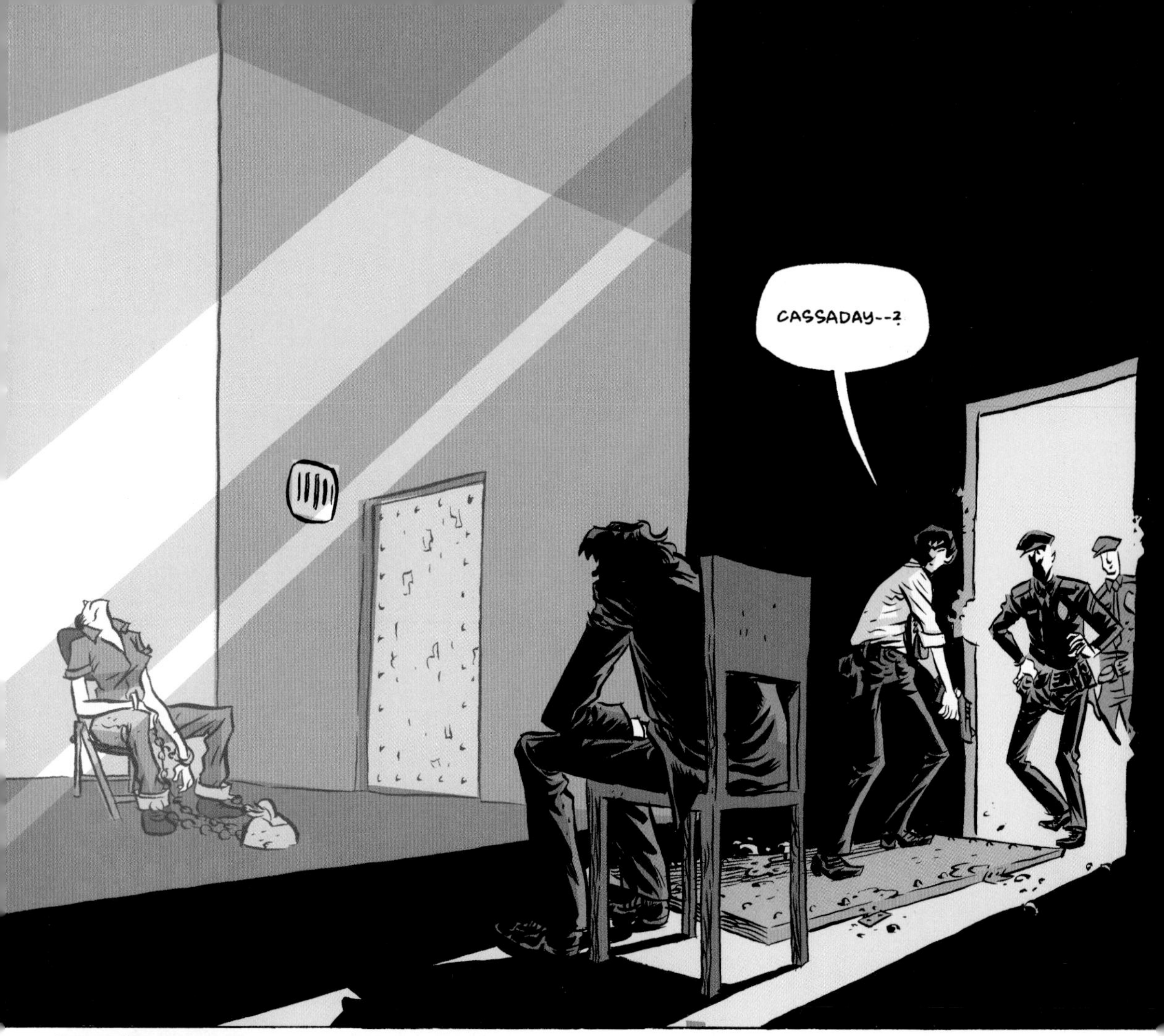
CASSADAY--?

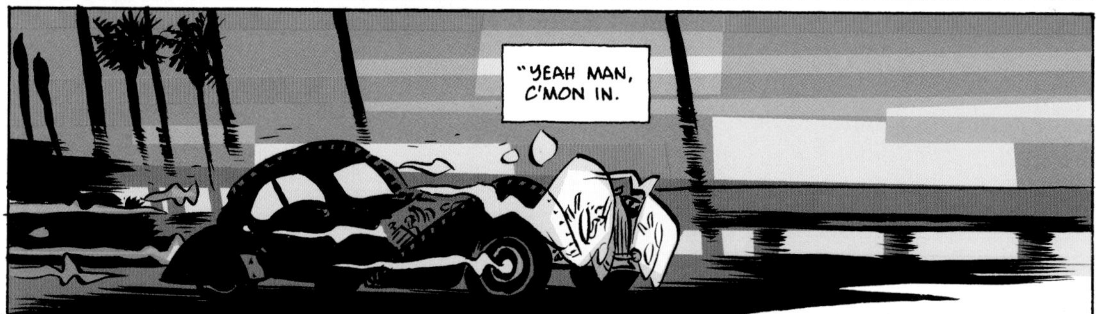
"YEAH MAN, C'MON IN.

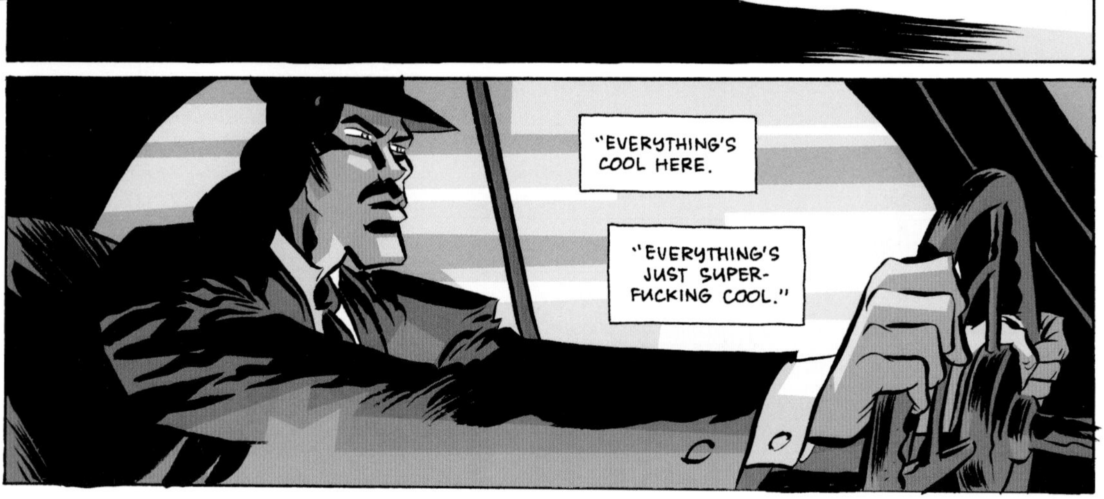
"EVERYTHING'S COOL HERE.
"EVERYTHING'S JUST SUPER-FUCKING COOL."

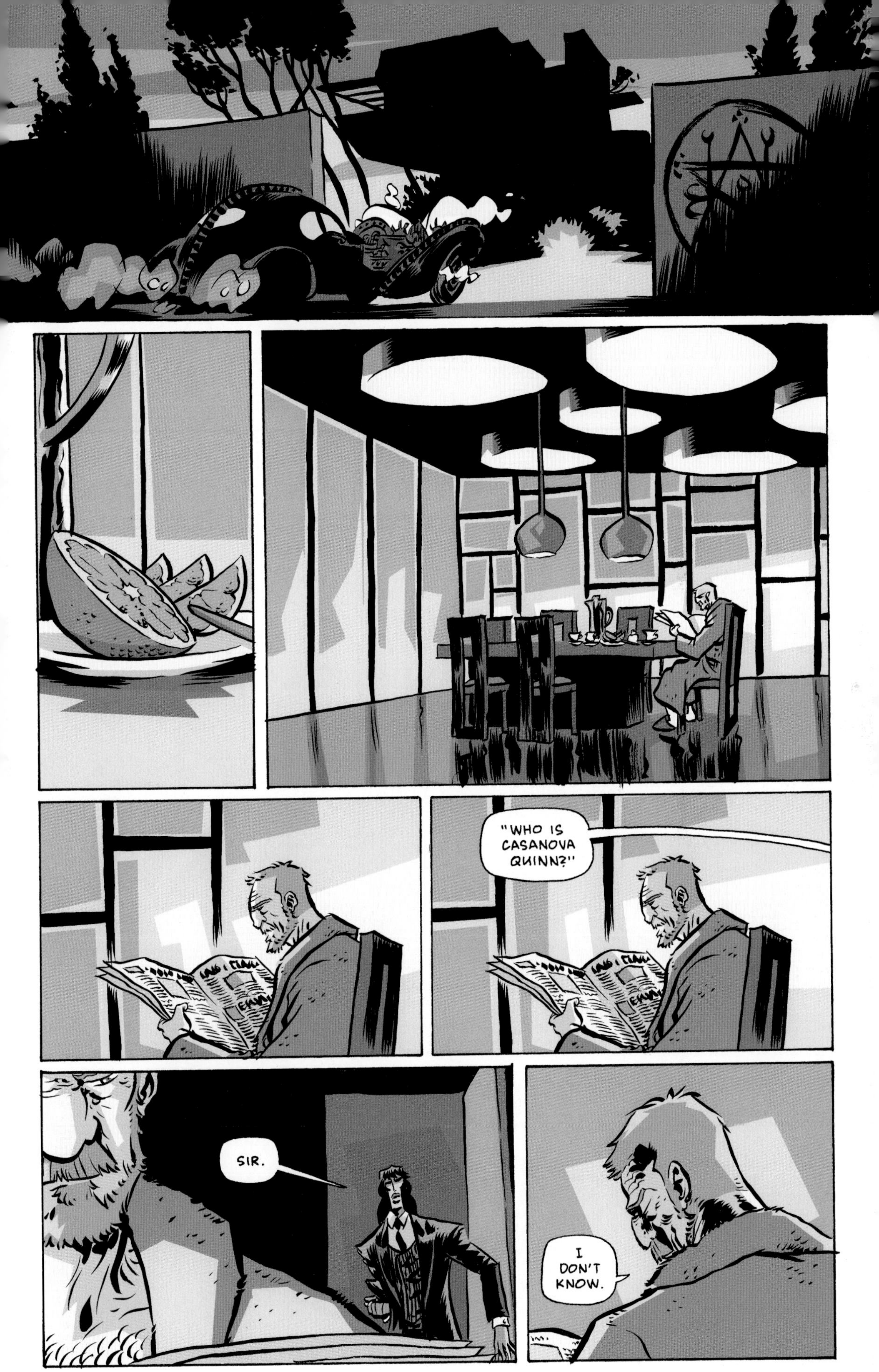
"WHO IS CASANOVA QUINN?"
SIR.
I DON'T KNOW.

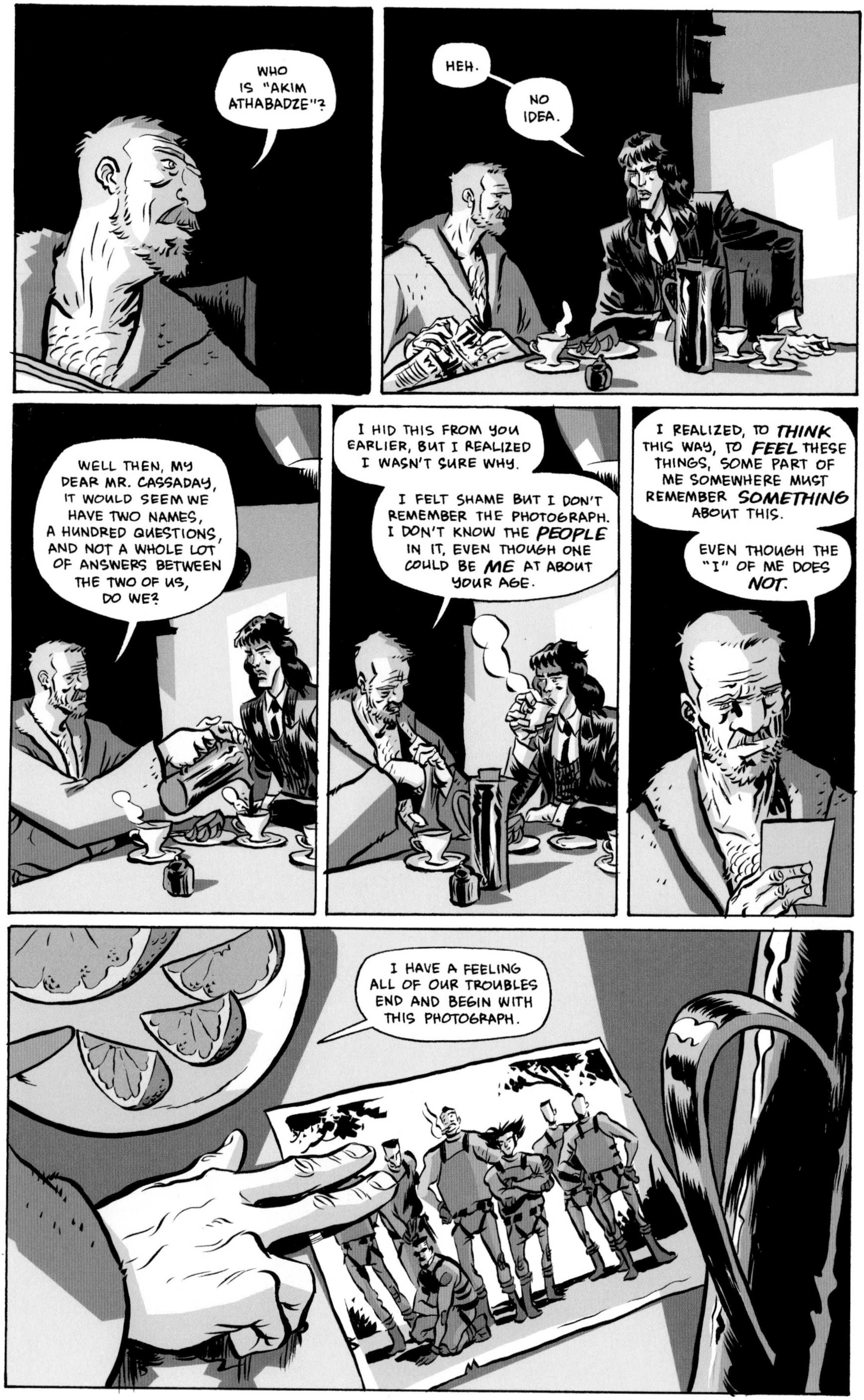
WHO IS "AKIM ATHABADZE"?
HEH.
NO IDEA.
WELL THEN, MY DEAR MR. CASSADAY, IT WOULD SEEM WE HAVE TWO NAMES, A HUNDRED QUESTIONS, AND NOT A WHOLE LOT OF ANSWERS BETWEEN THE TWO OF US, DO WE?
I HID THIS FROM YOU EARLIER, BUT I REALIZED I WASN'T SURE WHY.
I FELT SHAME BUT I DON'T REMEMBER THE PHOTOGRAPH. I DON'T KNOW THE PEOPLE IN IT, EVEN THOUGH ONE COULD BE ME AT ABOUT YOUR AGE.
I REALIZED, TO THINK THIS WAY, TO FEEL THESE THINGS, SOME PART OF ME SOMEWHERE MUST REMEMBER SOMETHING ABOUT THIS.
EVEN THOUGH THE "I" OF ME DOES NOT.
I HAVE A FEELING ALL OF OUR TROUBLES END AND BEGIN WITH THIS PHOTOGRAPH.

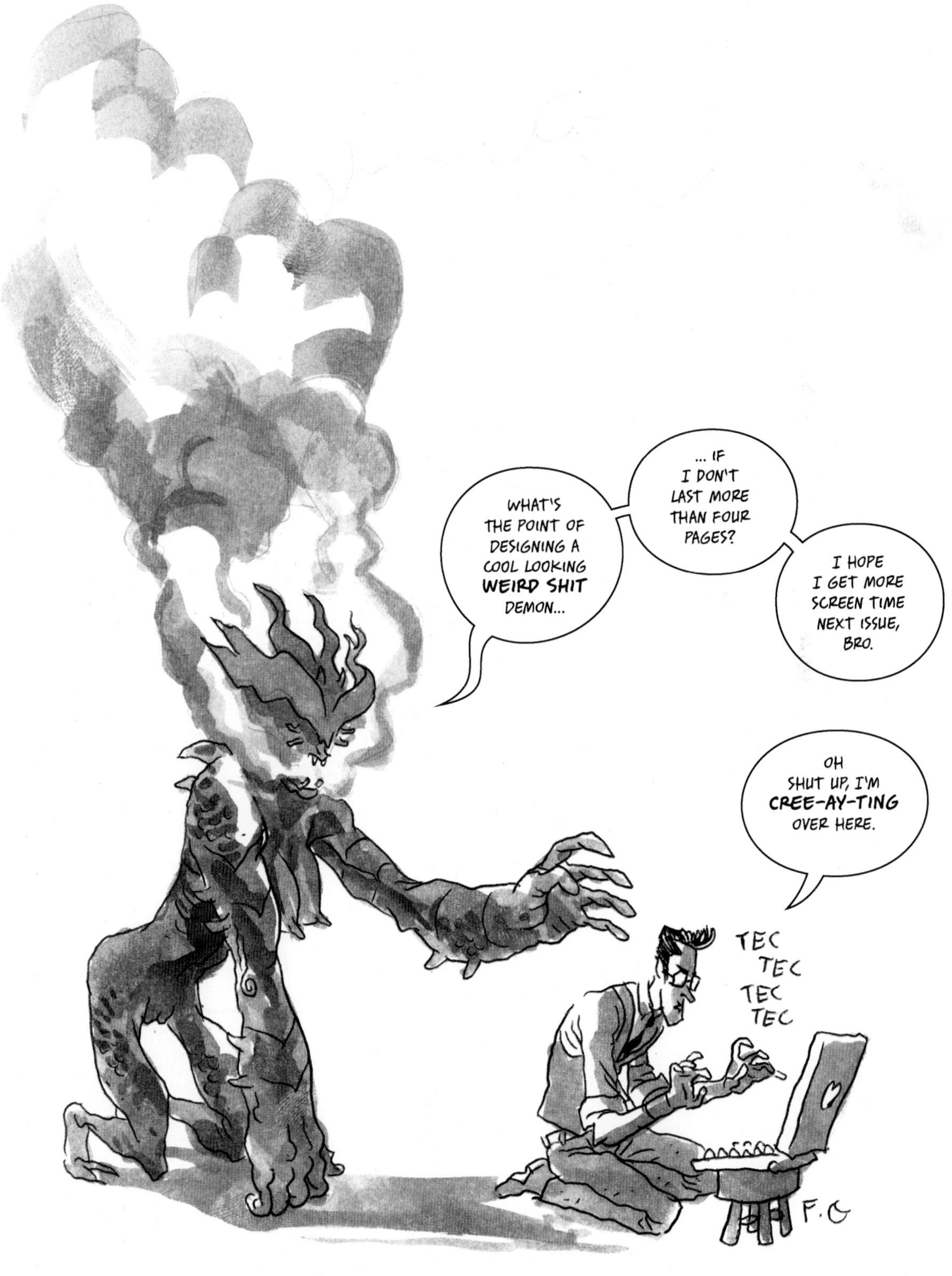
WHAT'S THE POINT OF DESIGNING A COOL LOOKING **WEIRD SHIT** DEMON...
... IF I DON'T LAST MORE THAN FOUR PAGES?
I HOPE I GET MORE SCREEN TIME NEXT ISSUE, BRO.
OH SHUT UP, I'M **CREE-AY-TING** OVER HERE.
TEC TEC TEC TEC
F.C

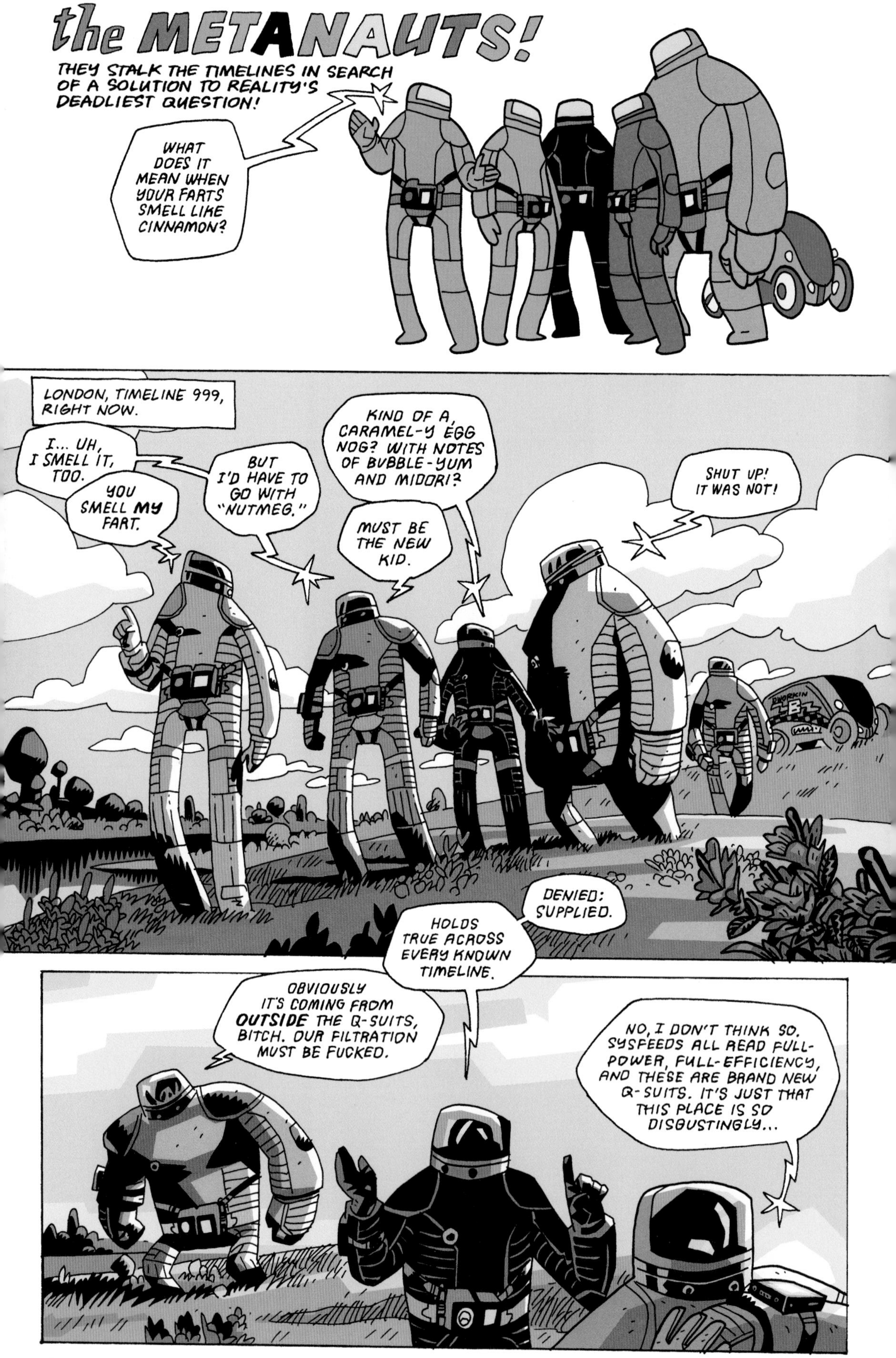
the METANAUTS!
THEY STALK THE TIMELINES IN SEARCH OF A SOLUTION TO REALITY'S DEADLIEST QUESTION!
WHAT DOES IT MEAN WHEN YOUR FARTS SMELL LIKE CINNAMON?
LONDON, TIMELINE 999, RIGHT NOW.
I... UH, I SMELL IT, TOO.
YOU SMELL MY FART.
BUT I'D HAVE TO GO WITH "NUTMEG."
KIND OF A, CARAMEL-Y EGG NOG? WITH NOTES OF BUBBLE-YUM AND MIDORI?
MUST BE THE NEW KID.
SHUT UP! IT WAS NOT!
DENIED: SUPPLIED.
HOLDS TRUE ACROSS EVERY KNOWN TIMELINE.
OBVIOUSLY IT'S COMING FROM OUTSIDE THE Q-SUITS, BITCH. OUR FILTRATION MUST BE FUCKED.
NO, I DON'T THINK SO. SYSFEEDS ALL READ FULL-POWER, FULL-EFFICIENCY, AND THESE ARE BRAND NEW Q-SUITS. IT'S JUST THAT THIS PLACE IS SO DISGUSTINGLY...

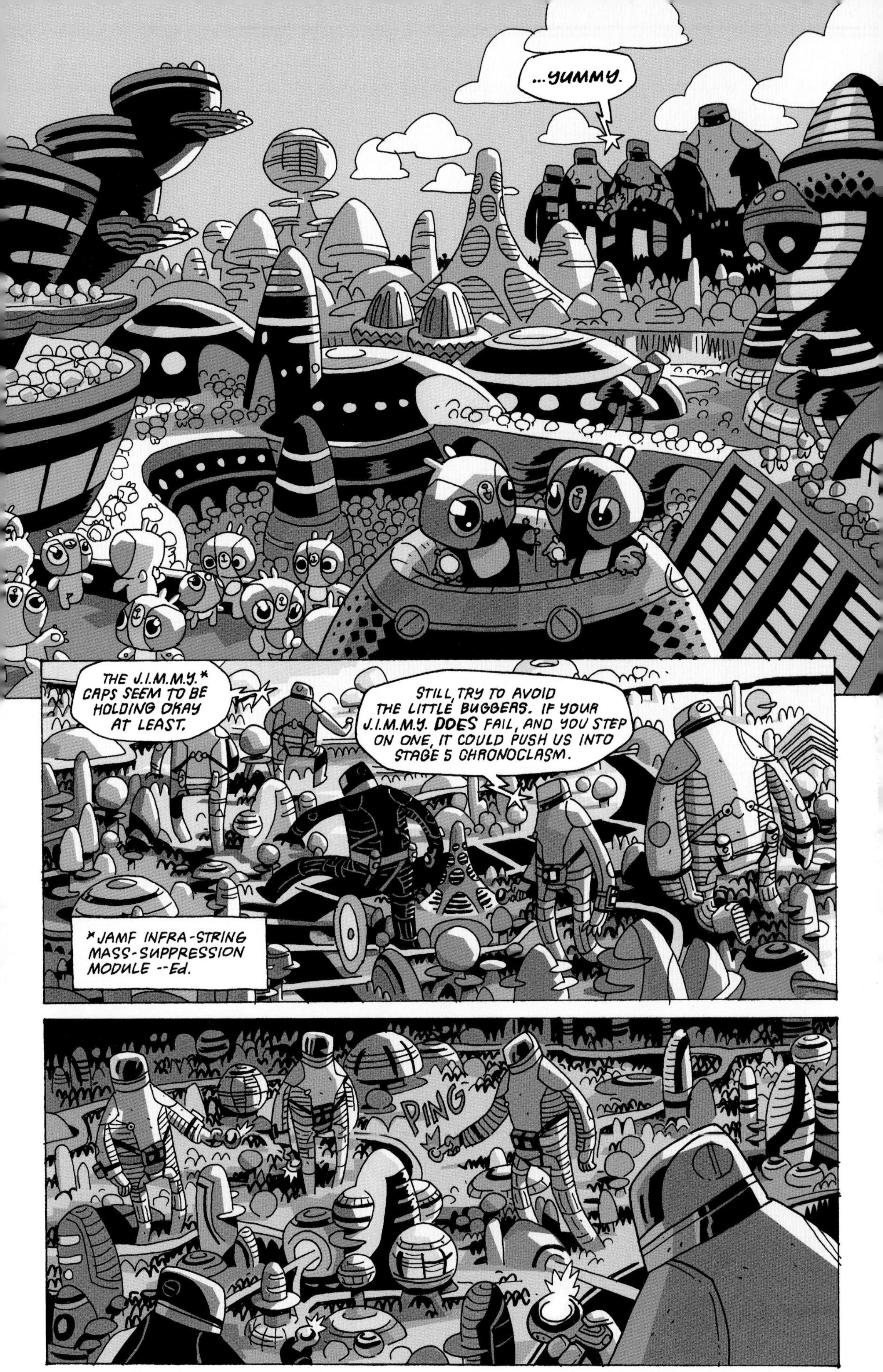
...YUMMY.
THE J.I.M.M.Y.* CAPS SEEM TO BE HOLDING OKAY AT LEAST.
STILL, TRY TO AVOID THE LITTLE BUGGERS. IF YOUR J.I.M.M.Y. DOES FAIL, AND YOU STEP ON ONE, IT COULD PUSH US INTO STAGE 5 CHRONOCLASM.
*JAMF INFRA-STRING MASS-SUPPRESSION MODULE --Ed.
PING

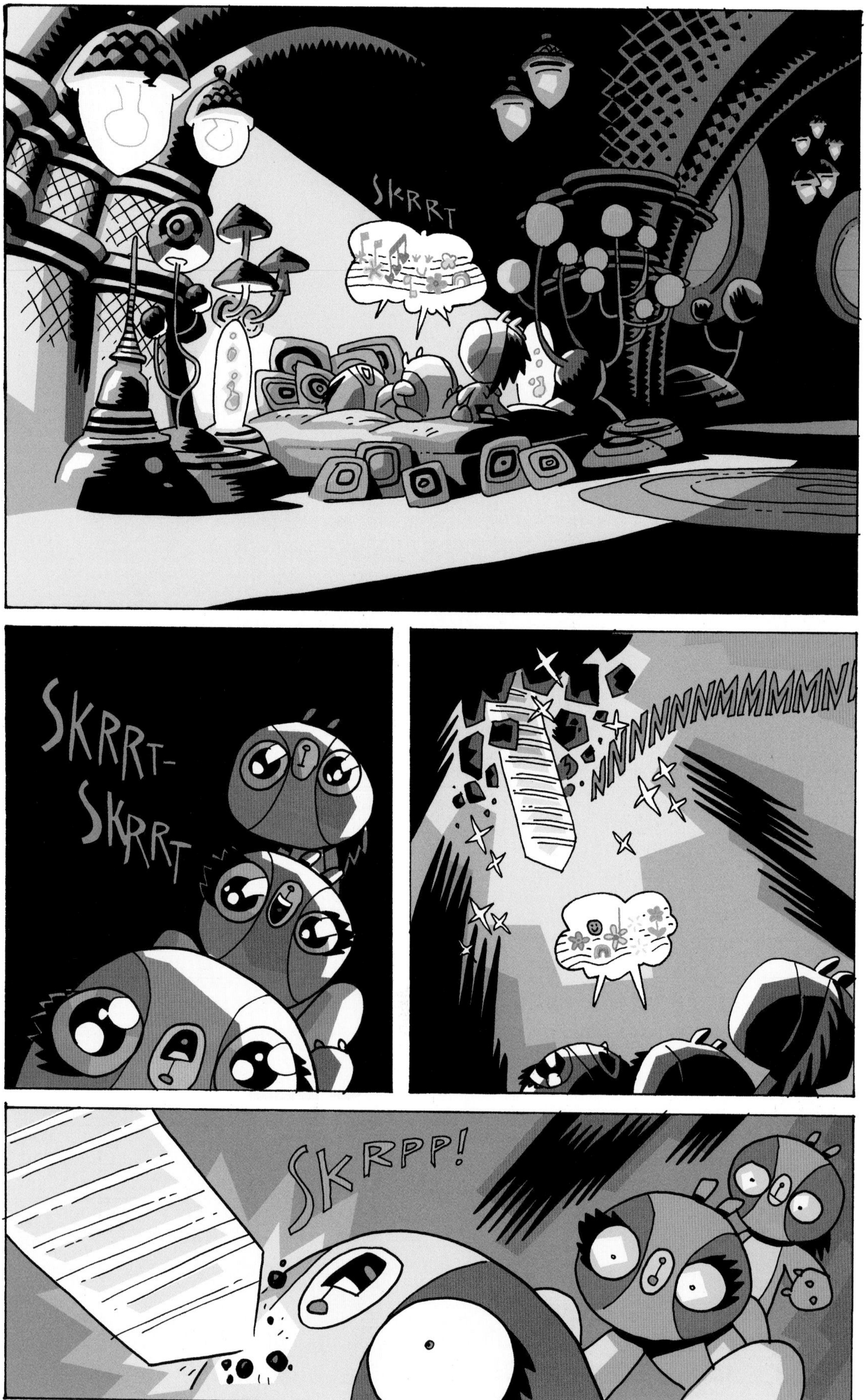
SKRRT
SKRRT-
SKRRT
NNNNNNNMMMMMN
SKRPP!

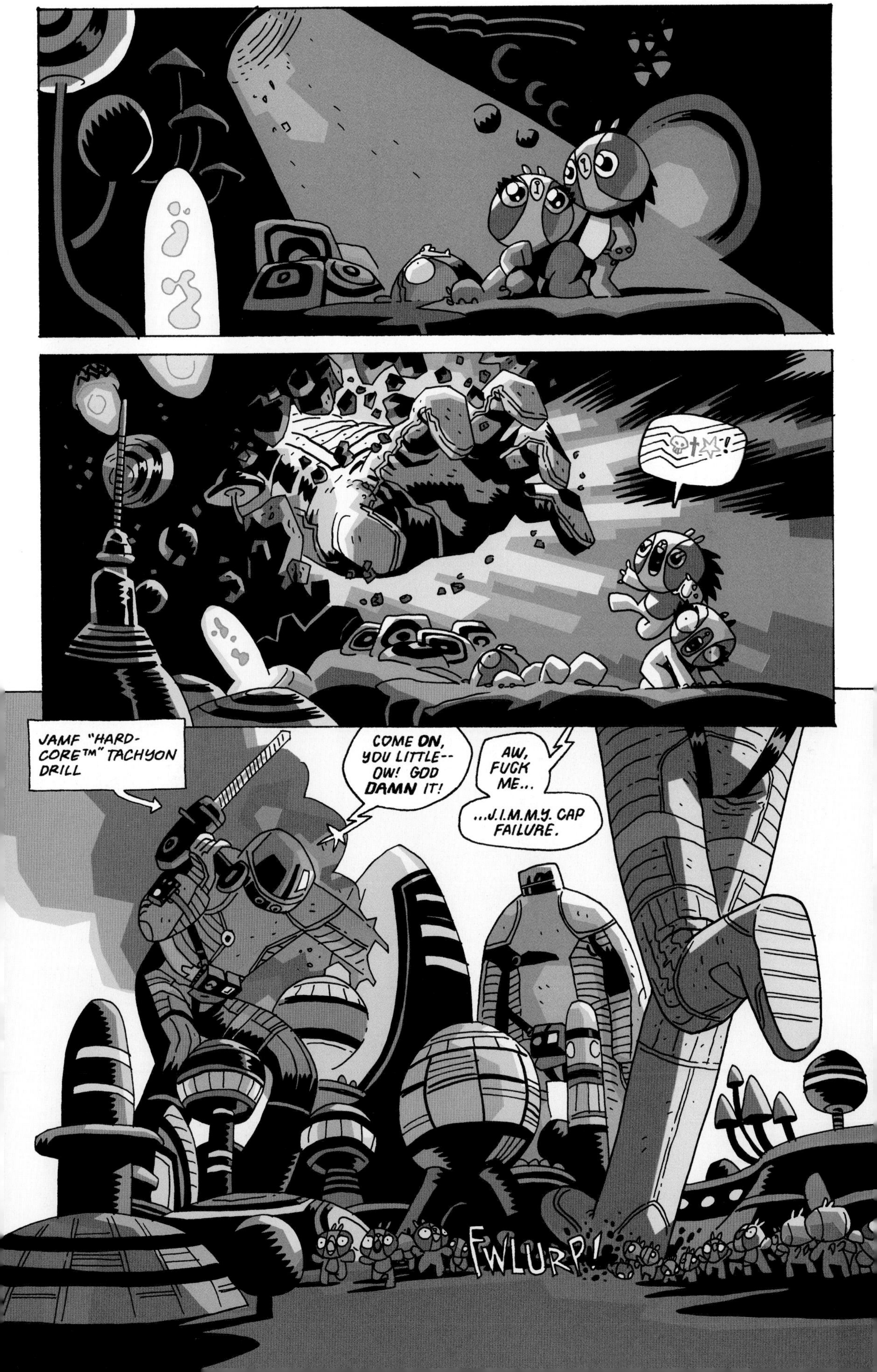
JAMF "HARD-CORE™" TACHYON DRILL
COME ON, YOU LITTLE-- OW! GOD DAMN IT!
AW, FUCK ME...
...J.I.M.M.Y. CAP FAILURE.
FWLURP!

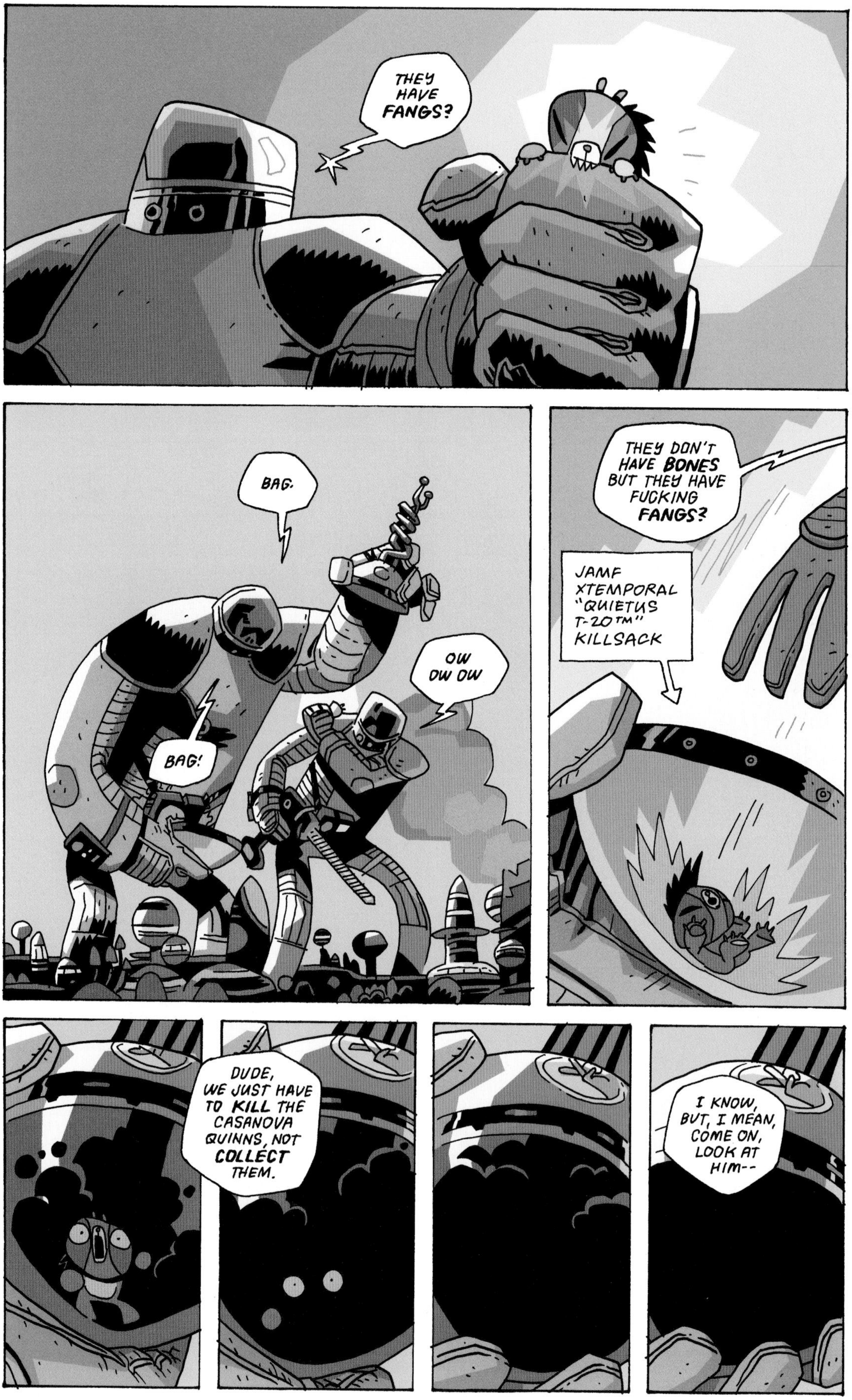
THEY HAVE FANGS?
BAG.
BAG!
OW OW OW
THEY DON'T HAVE BONES BUT THEY HAVE FUCKING FANGS?
JAMF XTEMPORAL "QUIETUS T-20™" KILLSACK
DUDE, WE JUST HAVE TO KILL THE CASANOVA QUINNS, NOT COLLECT THEM.
I KNOW, BUT, I MEAN, COME ON, LOOK AT HIM--

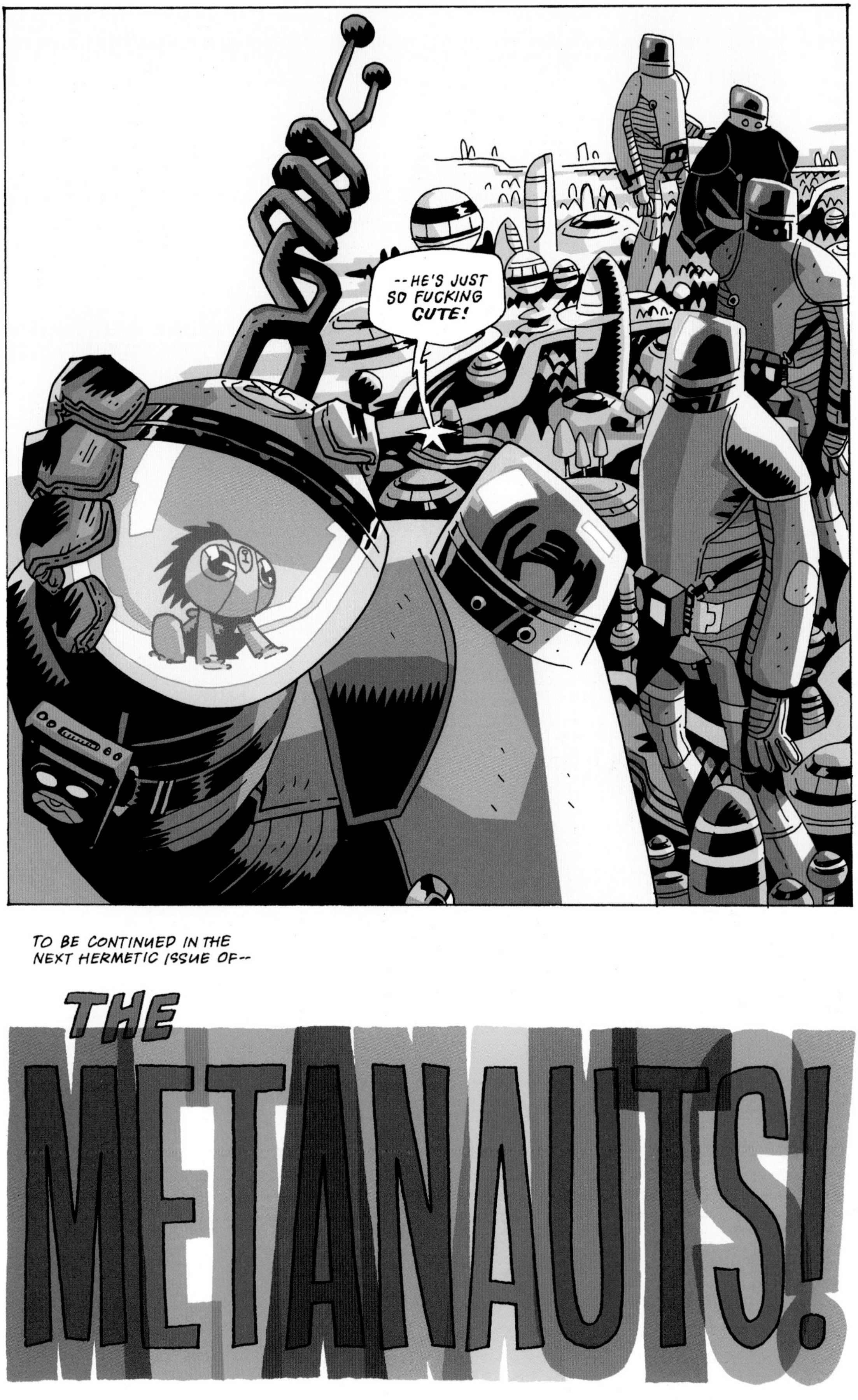
--HE'S JUST SO FUCKING CUTE!

TO BE CONTINUED IN THE NEXT HERMETIC ISSUE OF--

THE METANAUTS!

CHAPTER THREE
BLOOD BROTHERS

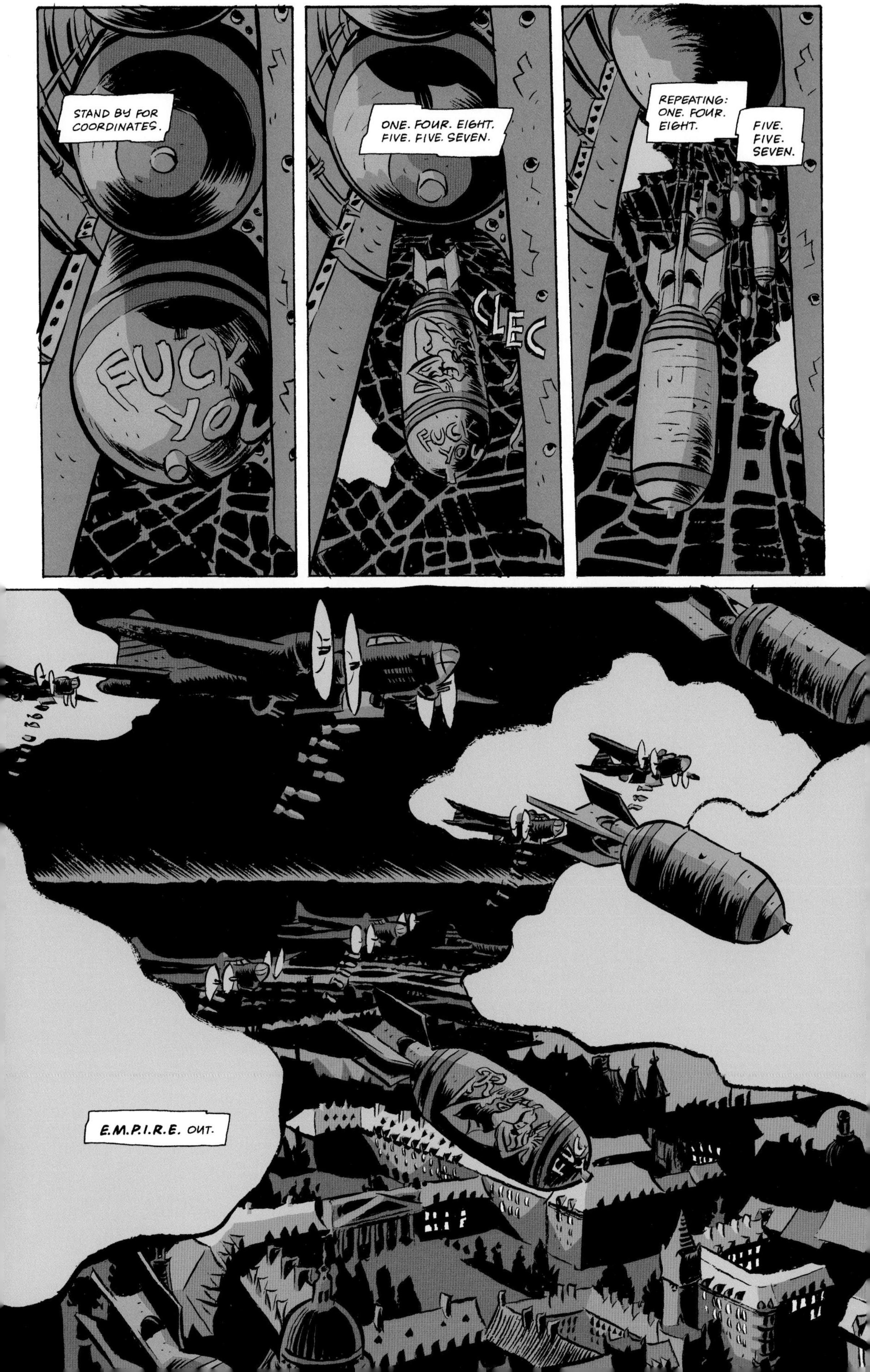
STAND BY FOR COORDINATES.
FUCK YOU
ONE. FOUR. EIGHT. FIVE. FIVE. SEVEN.
CLEC
FUCK YOU
REPEATING: ONE. FOUR. EIGHT.
FIVE. FIVE. SEVEN.
E.M.P.I.R.E. OUT.

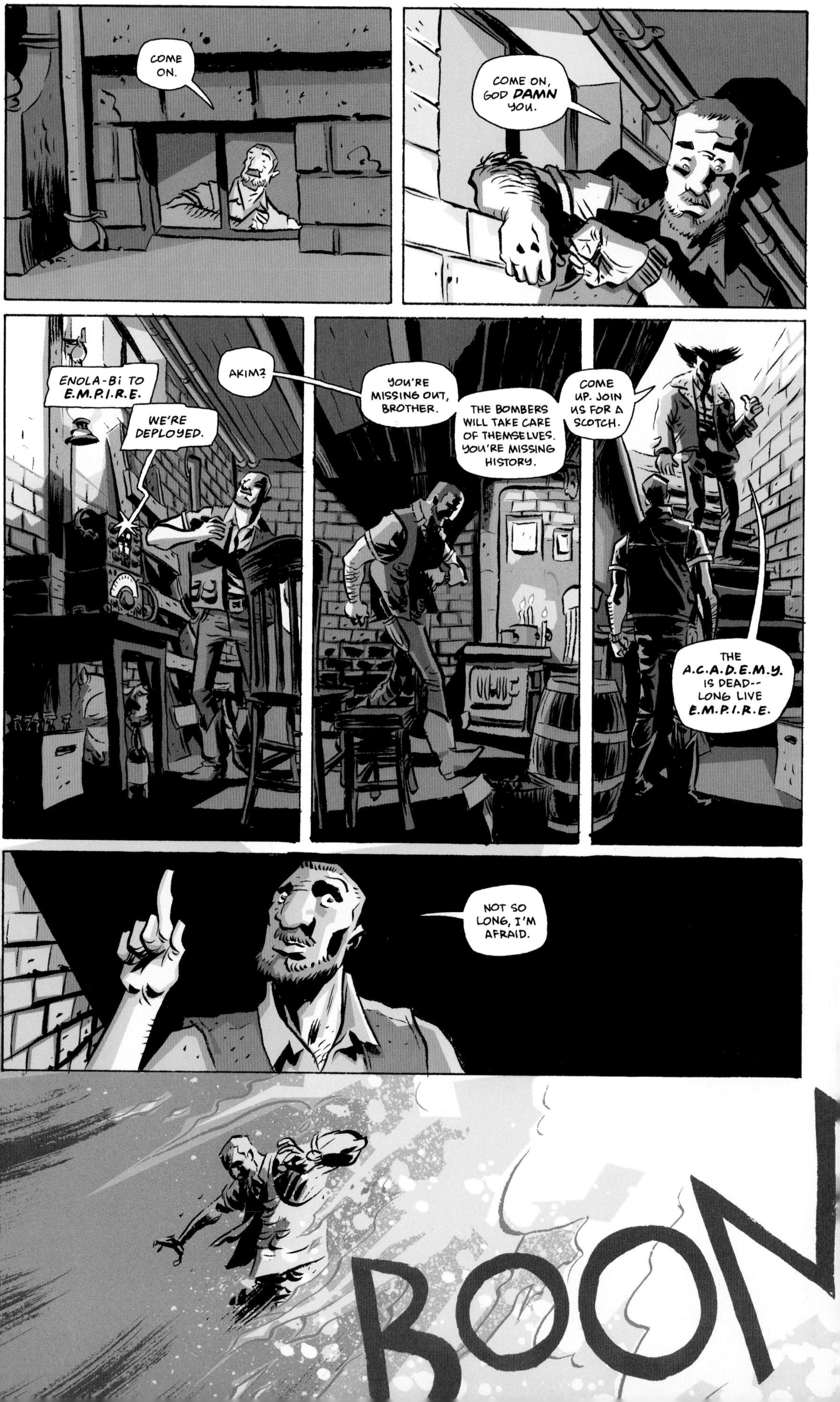
COME ON.
COME ON, GOD DAMN YOU.
ENOLA-Bi TO E.M.P.I.R.E.
WE'RE DEPLOYED.
AKIM?
YOU'RE MISSING OUT, BROTHER.
THE BOMBERS WILL TAKE CARE OF THEMSELVES. YOU'RE MISSING HISTORY.
COME UP. JOIN US FOR A SCOTCH.
THE A.C.A.D.E.M.Y. IS DEAD-- LONG LIVE E.M.P.I.R.E.
NOT SO LONG, I'M AFRAID.
BOON

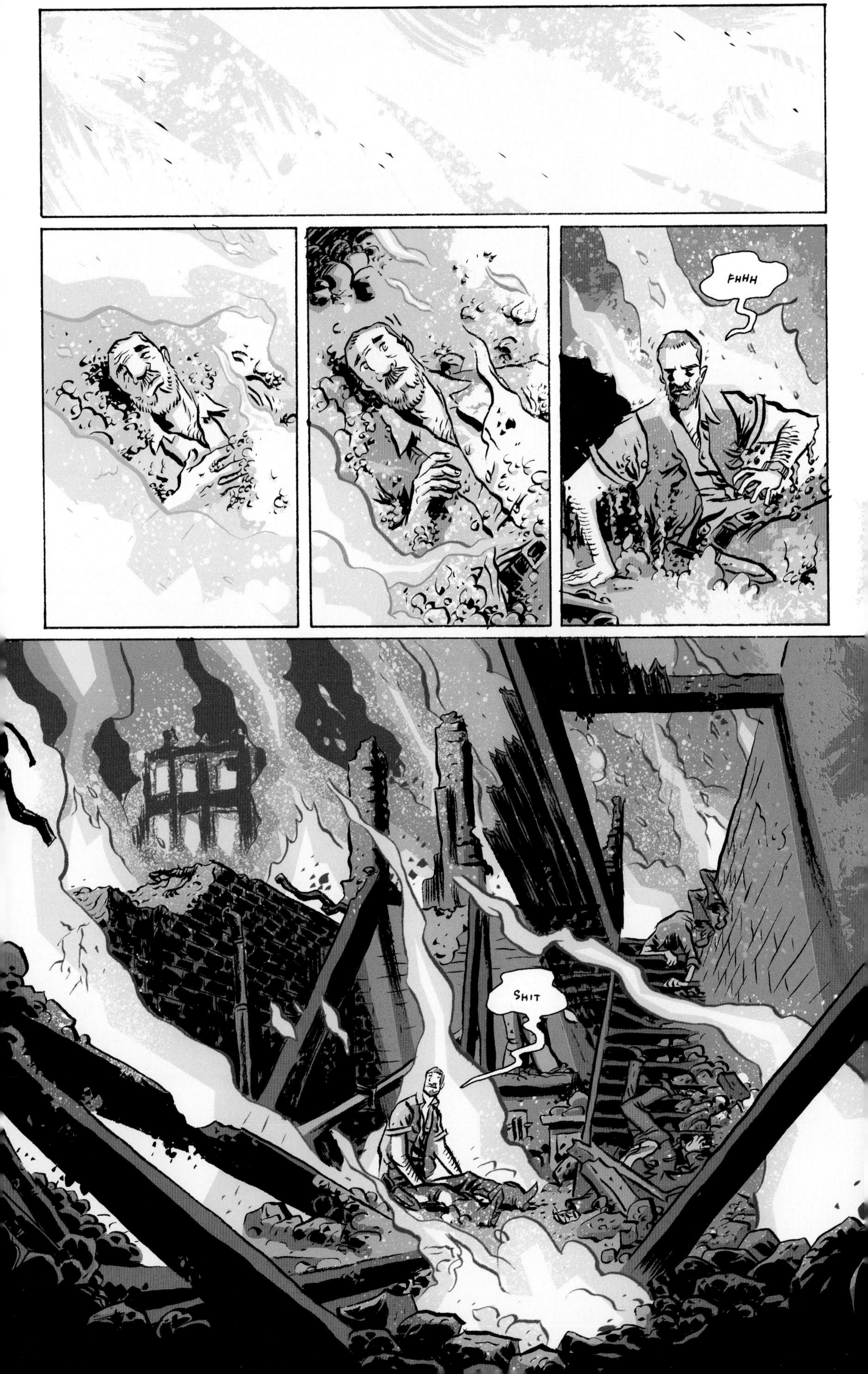
FHHH
SHIT

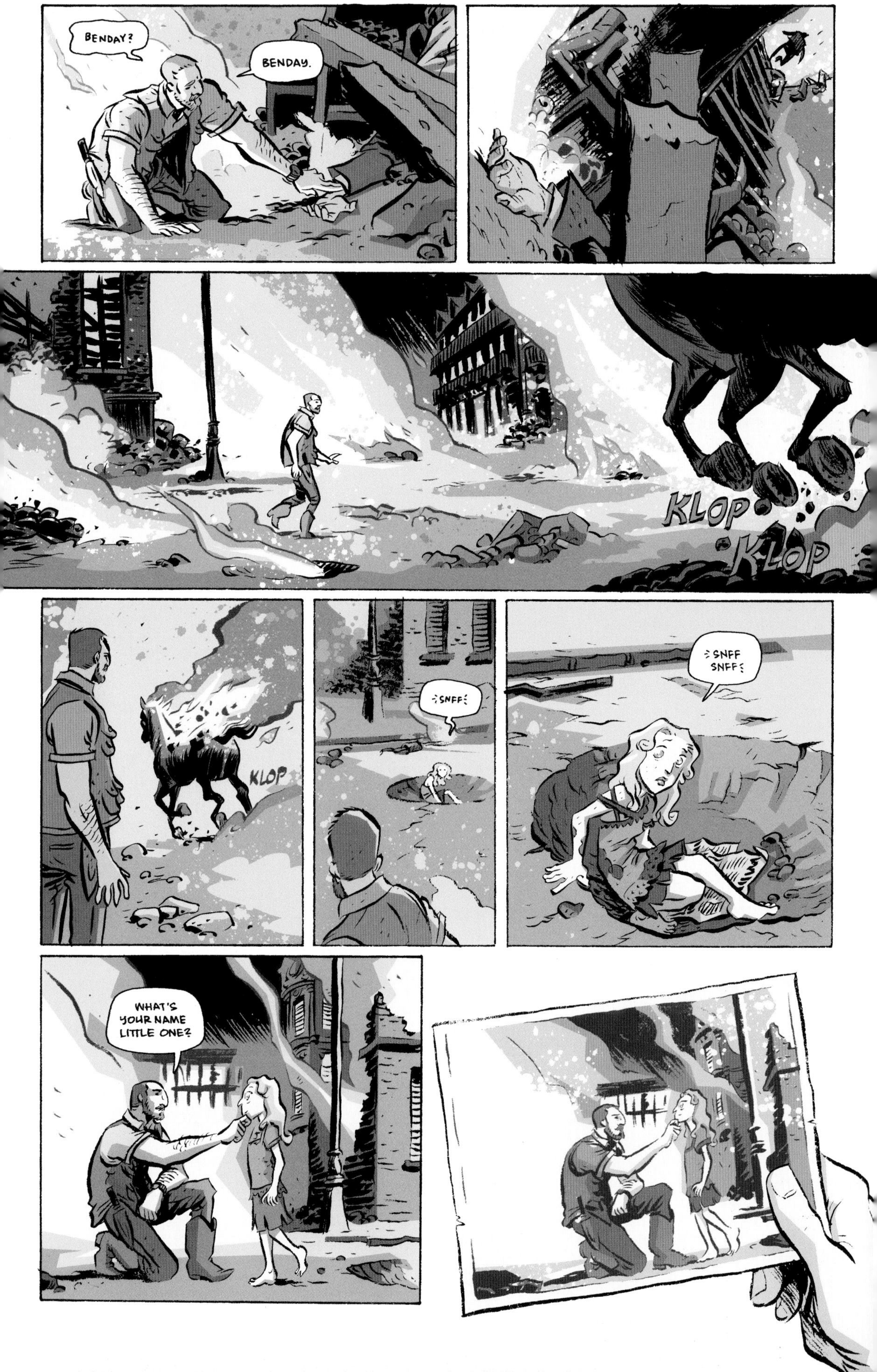
BENDAY?
BENDAY.
KLOP
KLOP
KLOP
SNFF
SNFF
SNFF
WHAT'S YOUR NAME LITTLE ONE?

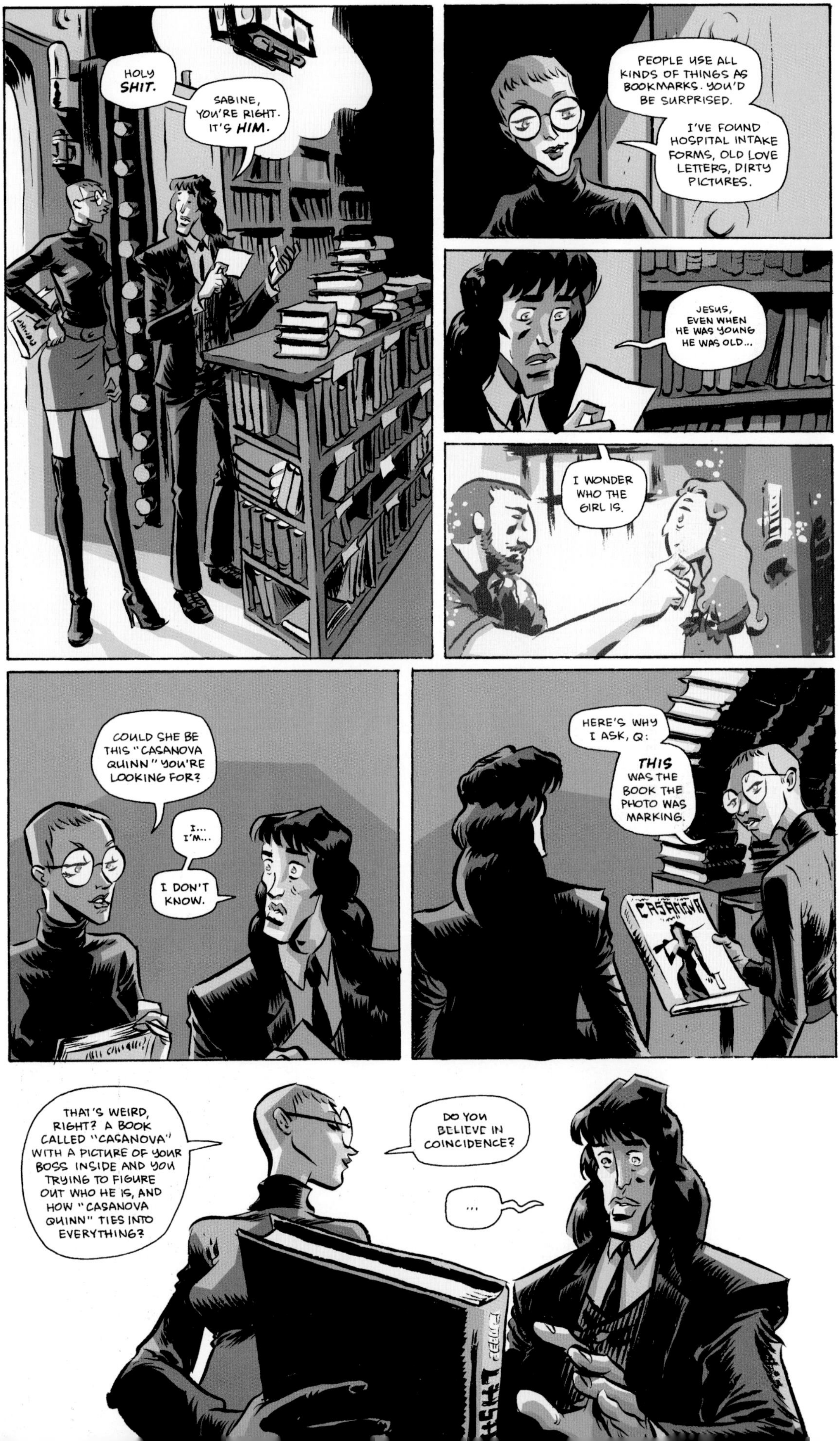
HOLY SHIT.
SABINE, YOU'RE RIGHT. IT'S HIM.
PEOPLE USE ALL KINDS OF THINGS AS BOOKMARKS. YOU'D BE SURPRISED.
I'VE FOUND HOSPITAL INTAKE FORMS, OLD LOVE LETTERS, DIRTY PICTURES.
JESUS, EVEN WHEN HE WAS YOUNG HE WAS OLD...
I WONDER WHO THE GIRL IS.
COULD SHE BE THIS "CASANOVA QUINN" YOU'RE LOOKING FOR?
I... I'M...
I DON'T KNOW.
HERE'S WHY I ASK, Q:
THIS WAS THE BOOK THE PHOTO WAS MARKING.
CASANOVA
THAT'S WEIRD, RIGHT? A BOOK CALLED "CASANOVA" WITH A PICTURE OF YOUR BOSS INSIDE AND YOU TRYING TO FIGURE OUT WHO HE IS, AND HOW "CASANOVA QUINN" TIES INTO EVERYTHING?
DO YOU BELIEVE IN COINCIDENCE?
...

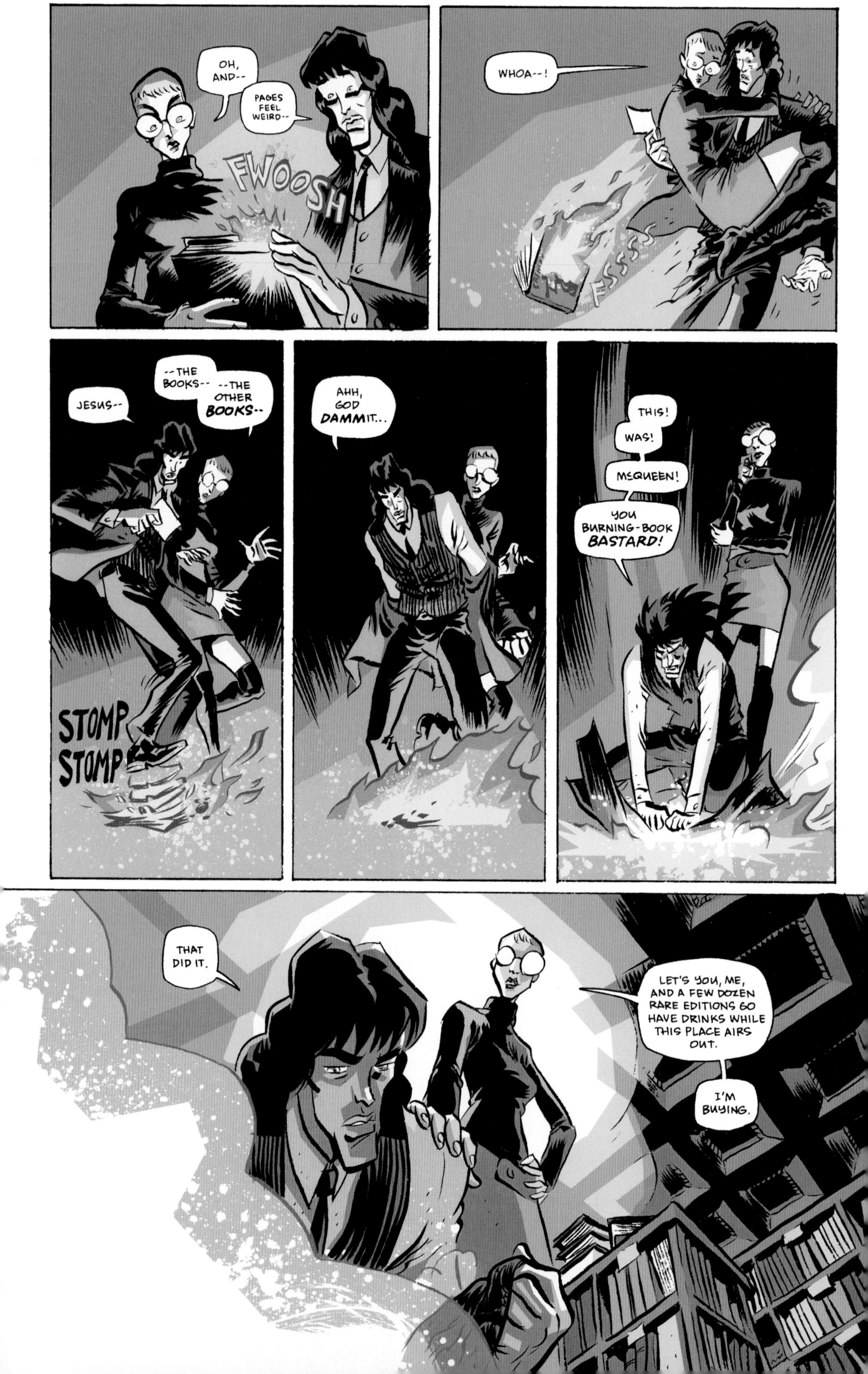
OH, AND--
PAGES FEEL WEIRD--
FWOOSH
WHOA--!
FSSSS
JESUS--
--THE BOOKS--
--THE OTHER BOOKS--
STOMP STOMP
AHH, GOD DAMMIT...
THIS!
WAS!
McQUEEN!
YOU BURNING-BOOK BASTARD!
THAT DID IT.
LET'S YOU, ME, AND A FEW DOZEN RARE EDITIONS GO HAVE DRINKS WHILE THIS PLACE AIRS OUT.
I'M BUYING.

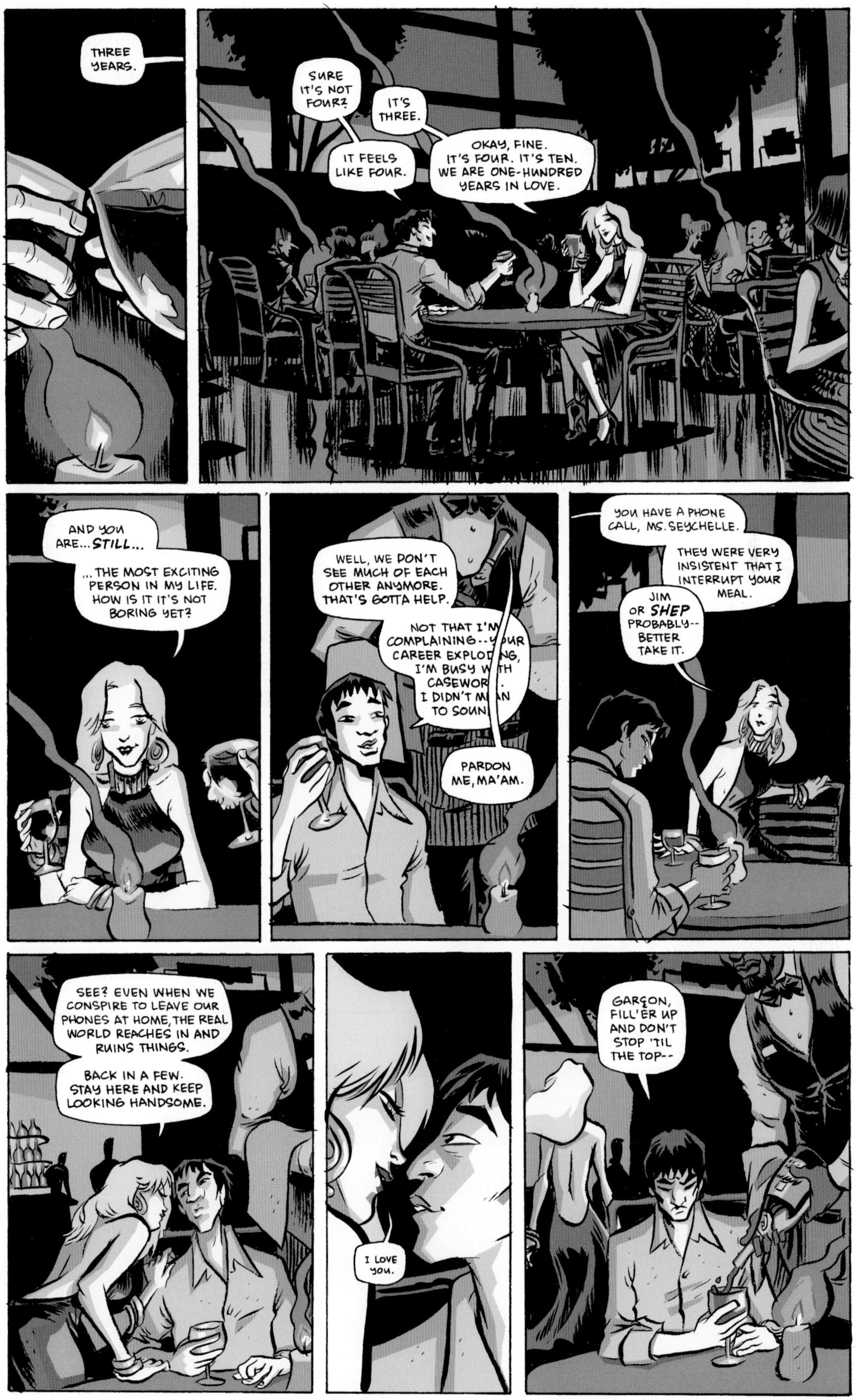
THREE YEARS.
SURE IT'S NOT FOUR?
IT FEELS LIKE FOUR.
IT'S THREE.
OKAY, FINE. IT'S FOUR. IT'S TEN. WE ARE ONE-HUNDRED YEARS IN LOVE.
AND YOU ARE... STILL...
...THE MOST EXCITING PERSON IN MY LIFE. HOW IS IT IT'S NOT BORING YET?
WELL, WE DON'T SEE MUCH OF EACH OTHER ANYMORE. THAT'S GOTTA HELP.
NOT THAT I'M COMPLAINING..YOUR CAREER EXPLODING, I'M BUSY WITH CASEWORK. I DIDN'T MEAN TO SOUND
PARDON ME, MA'AM.
YOU HAVE A PHONE CALL, MS. SEYCHELLE.
THEY WERE VERY INSISTENT THAT I INTERRUPT YOUR MEAL.
JIM OR SHEP PROBABLY-- BETTER TAKE IT.
SEE? EVEN WHEN WE CONSPIRE TO LEAVE OUR PHONES AT HOME, THE REAL WORLD REACHES IN AND RUINS THINGS.
BACK IN A FEW. STAY HERE AND KEEP LOOKING HANDSOME.
I LOVE YOU.
GARÇON, FILL'ER UP AND DON'T STOP 'TIL THE TOP--

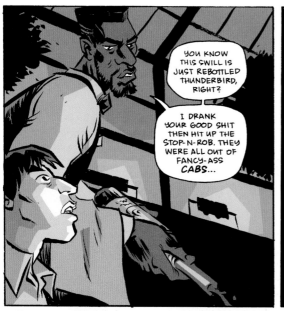

YOU KNOW THIS SWILL IS JUST REBOTTLED THUNDERBIRD, RIGHT?

I DRANK YOUR GOOD SHIT THEN HIT UP THE STOP-N-ROB. THEY WERE ALL OUT OF FANCY-ASS CABS...

THIS IS IT? THIS IS A BIT?

YOU'RE HERE TO FUCK UP MY NIGHT OFF?

WAS THERE REALLY EVEN A PHONE CALL?

THERE REALLY WAS A CALL. SO IT SEEMED A GOOD TIME TO BREAK COVER.

"COVER." BULL SHIT. YOU WORK HERE.

SUBWAY-MAGIC BUSKING ISN'T RECESSION-PROOF AND NOW YOU WORK HERE AND YOU'RE GONNA PUT YOUR DICK IN MY SOUP.

ACTUALLY I DID SOME DIGGING AROUND ON YOUR BEHALF AND I NEEDED TO GET WORD TO YOU--

CASSADAY HAS GOT US ALL IN A WORLD OF SHIT.

I NEED TO GET INTO THAT ROOM TONIGHT. SOON.

ROOM? THE FUCK'RE YOU--

SCRUB SCRUB

WHERE HE WAS ATTACKED.

SOONER THE BETTER. TICK TOCK. APOCALYPSE IS COMING.

GET OFF MY FUCKING DICK, MAN, IT'S MY ANNIVERSARY, FOR FUCK'S SAKE. I CAN'T GO BRO DOWN WITH YOU AND MICK JAG-OFF TO--

AAAAA AIIIEEEEE

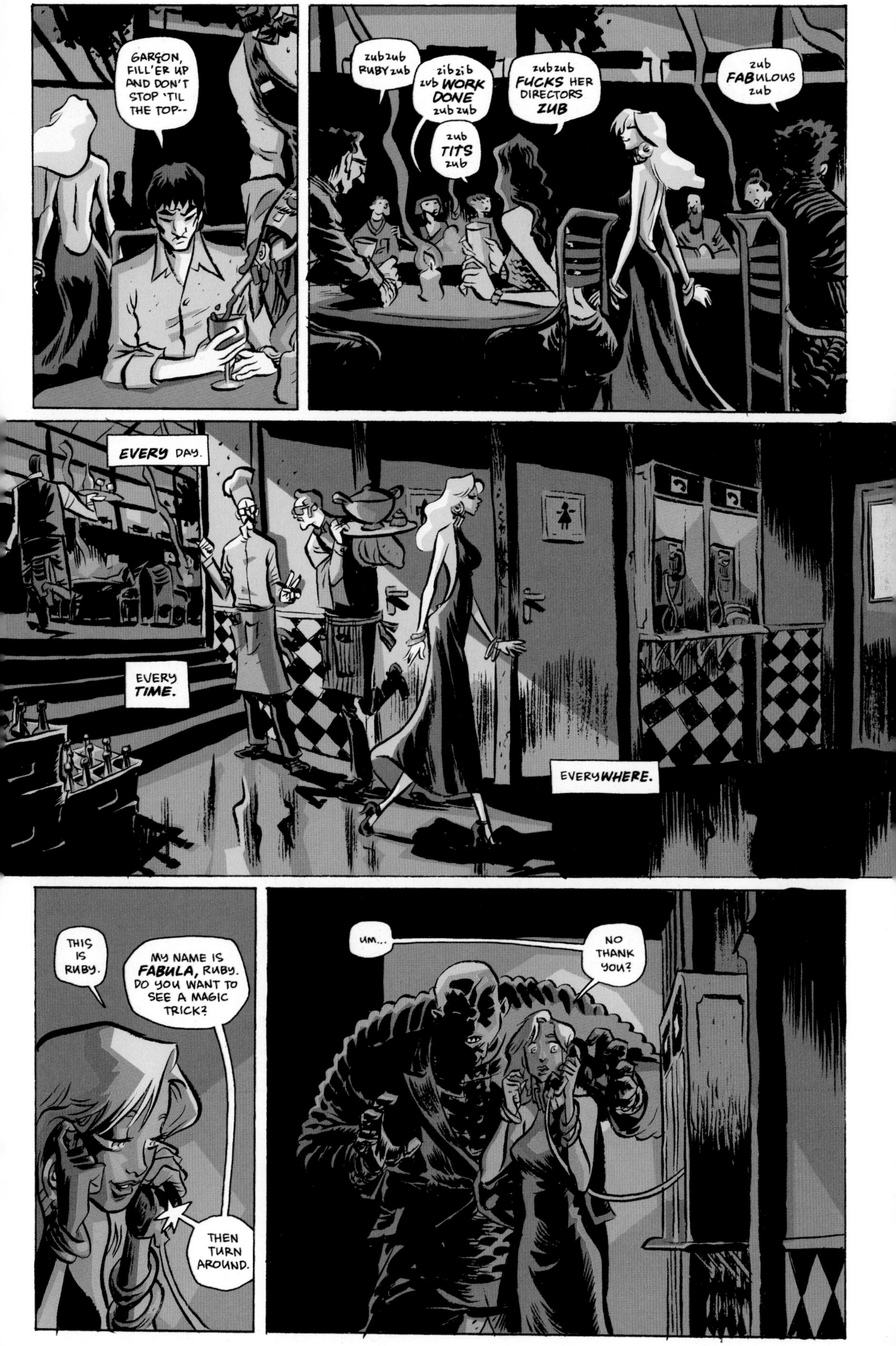
GARÇON, FILL'ER UP AND DON'T STOP 'TIL THE TOP--
zubzub RUBY zub
zibzib zub WORK DONE zubzub
zub TITS zub
zubzub FUCKS HER DIRECTORS ZUB
zub FABULOUS zub
EVERY DAY.
EVERY TIME.
EVERYWHERE.
THIS IS RUBY.
MY NAME IS FABULA, RUBY. DO YOU WANT TO SEE A MAGIC TRICK?
THEN TURN AROUND.
UM...
NO THANK YOU?

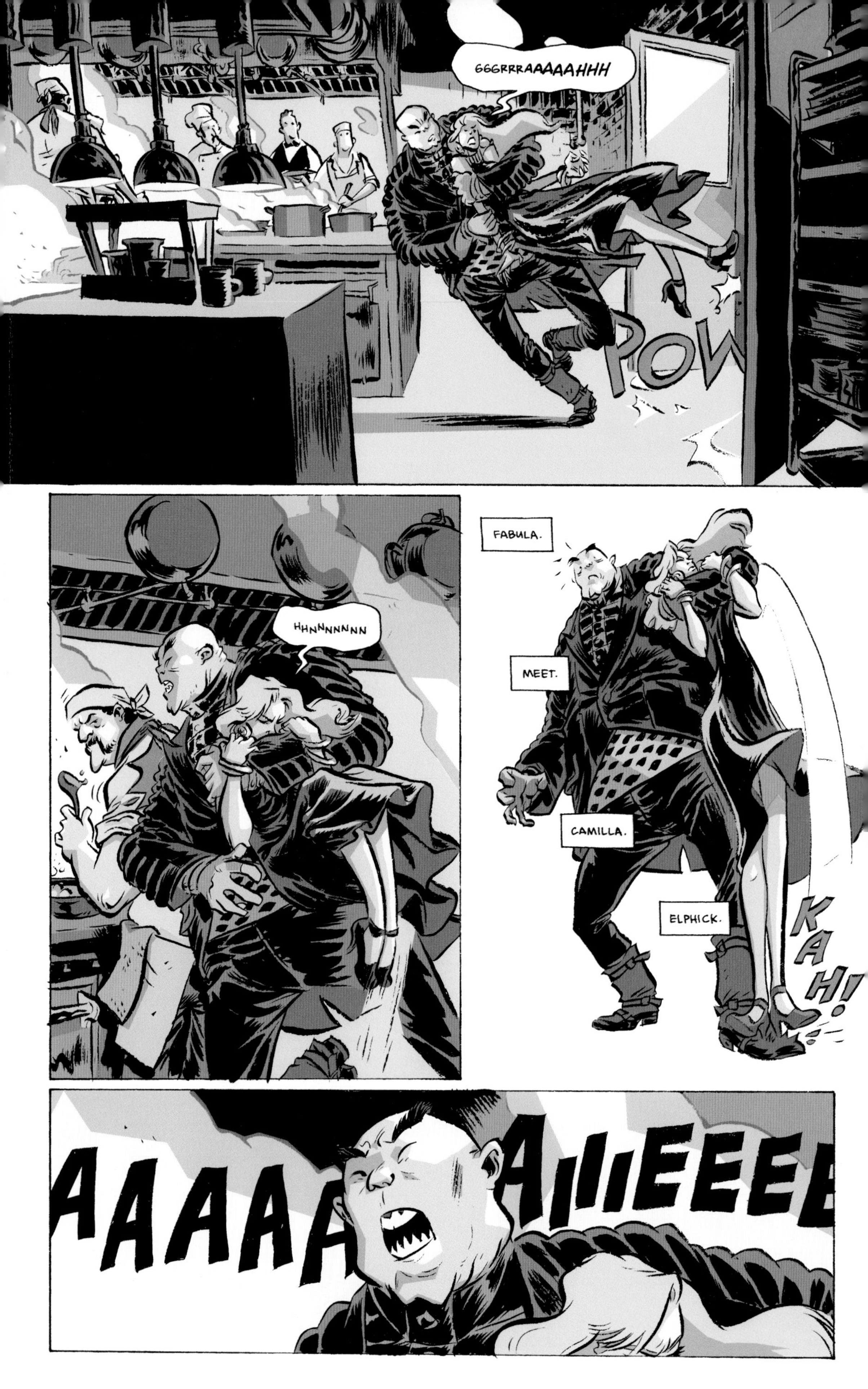
GGGRRRAAAAAHHH
POW
HHNNNNNNN
FABULA.
MEET.
CAMILLA.
ELPHICK.
KAH!
AAAAAAIIIEEEE

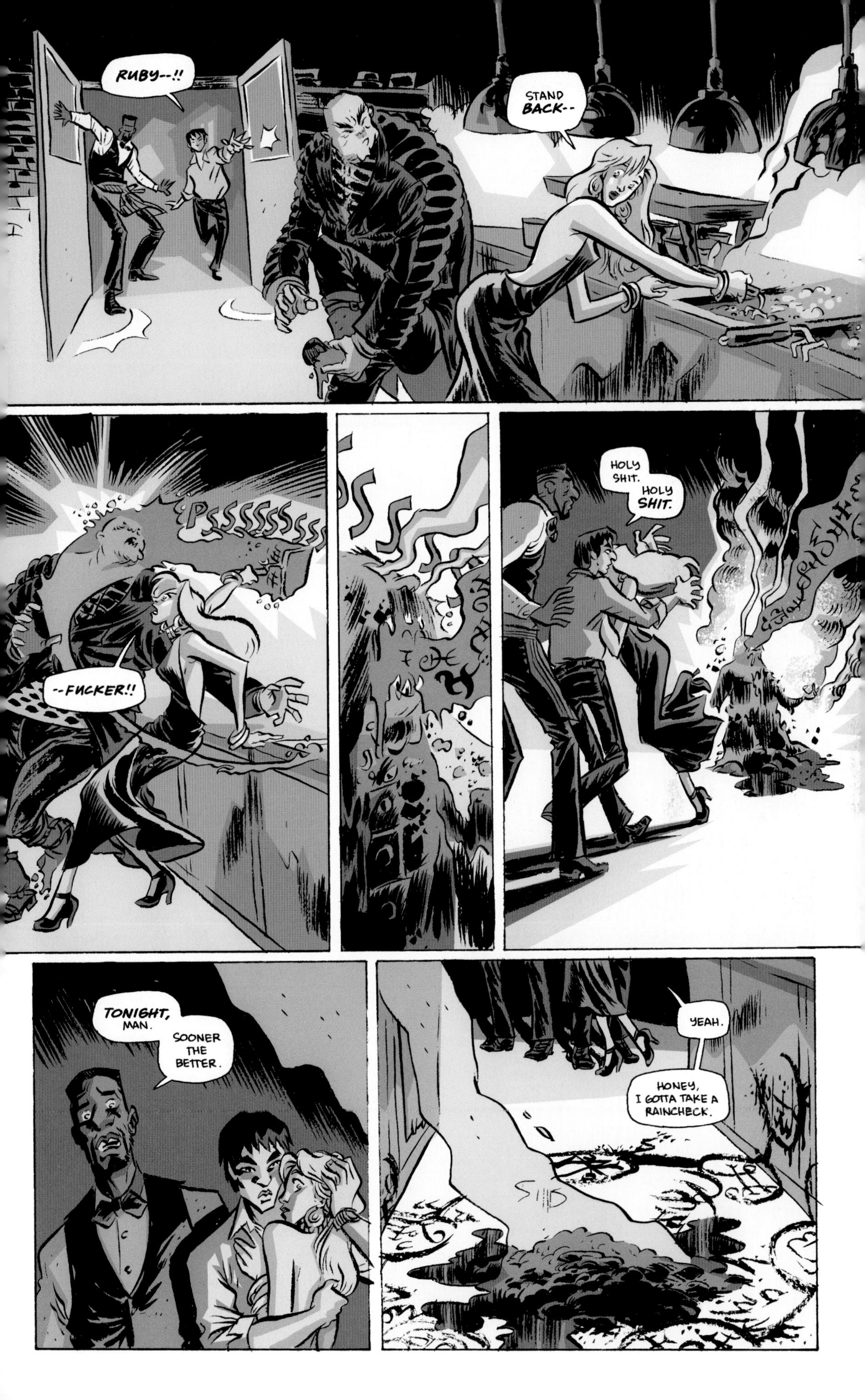
RUBY--!!
STAND BACK--
PSSSSSSSSS
--FUCKER!!
HOLY SHIT.
HOLY SHIT.
TONIGHT, MAN.
SOONER THE BETTER.
YEAH.
HONEY, I GOTTA TAKE A RAINCHECK.

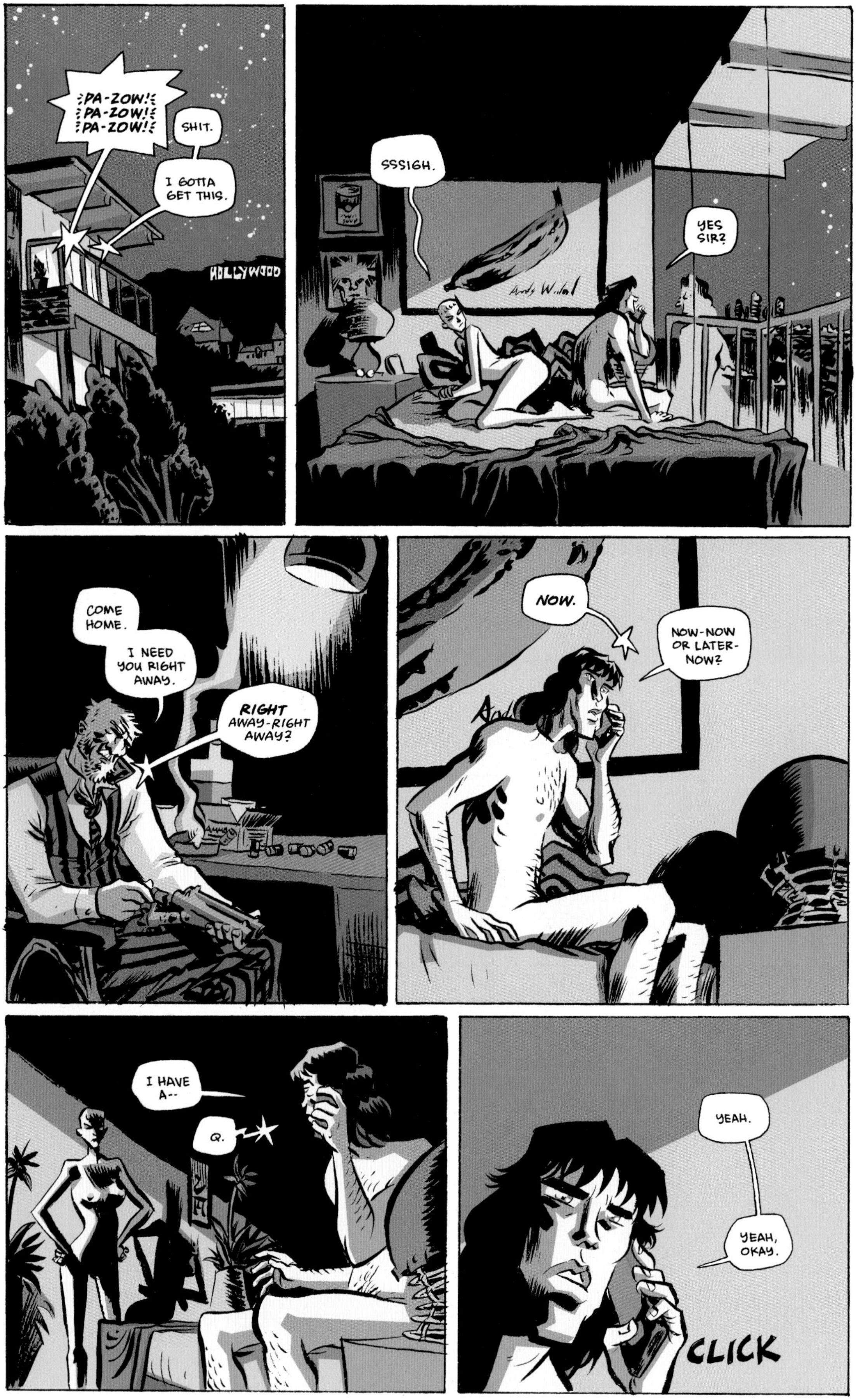
PA-ZOW! PA-ZOW! PA-ZOW!
SHIT.
I GOTTA GET THIS.
HOLLYWOOD
SSSIGH.
YES SIR?
COME HOME.
I NEED YOU RIGHT AWAY.
RIGHT AWAY-RIGHT AWAY?
NOW.
NOW-NOW OR LATER-NOW?
I HAVE A--
Q.
YEAH.
YEAH, OKAY.
CLICK

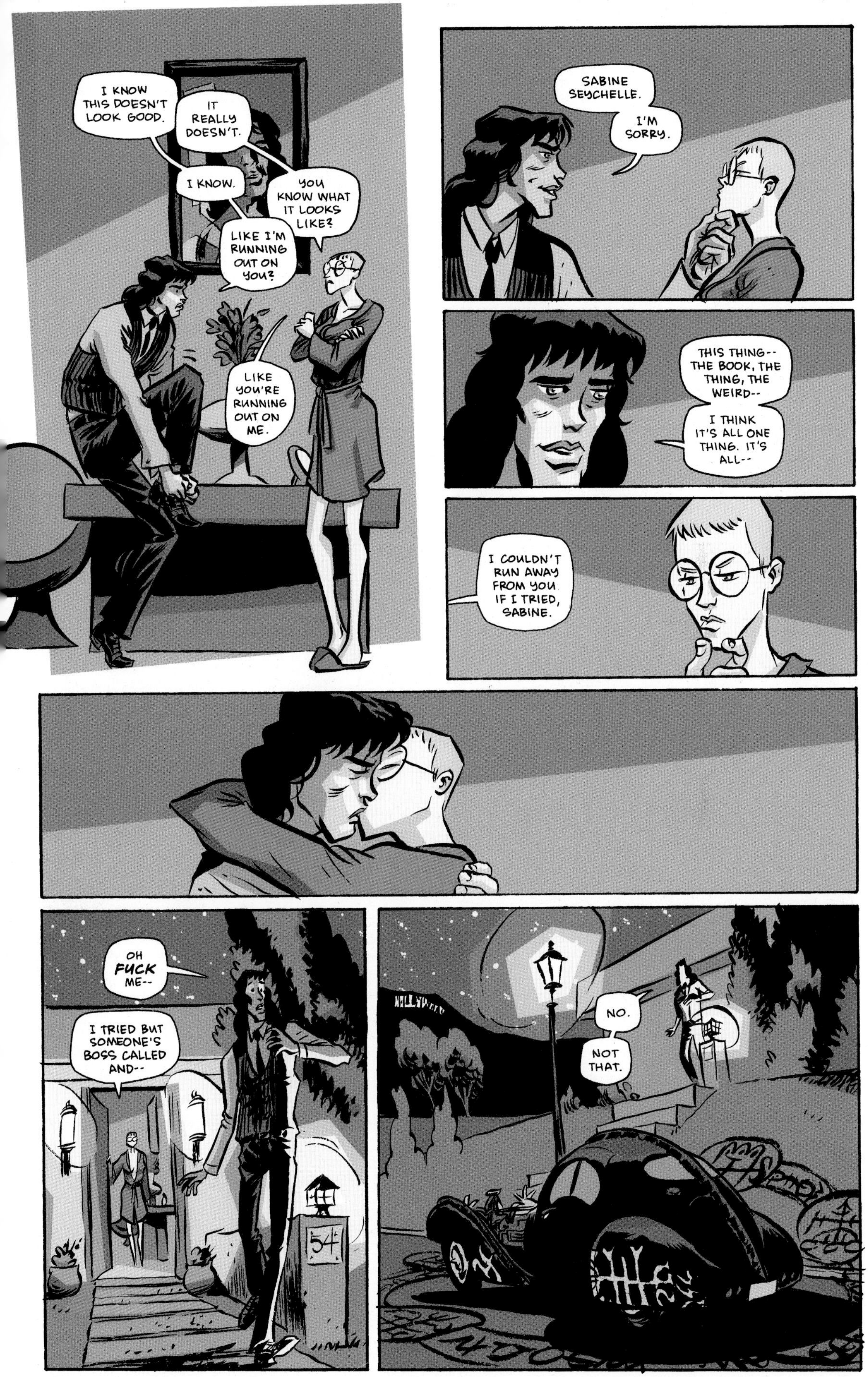

I KNOW THIS DOESN'T LOOK GOOD.
IT REALLY DOESN'T.
I KNOW.
YOU KNOW WHAT IT LOOKS LIKE?
LIKE I'M RUNNING OUT ON YOU?
LIKE YOU'RE RUNNING OUT ON ME.
SABINE SEYCHELLE.
I'M SORRY.
THIS THING-- THE BOOK, THE THING, THE WEIRD--
I THINK IT'S ALL ONE THING. IT'S ALL--
I COULDN'T RUN AWAY FROM YOU IF I TRIED, SABINE.
OH FUCK ME--
I TRIED BUT SOMEONE'S BOSS CALLED AND--
54
NO.
NOT THAT.

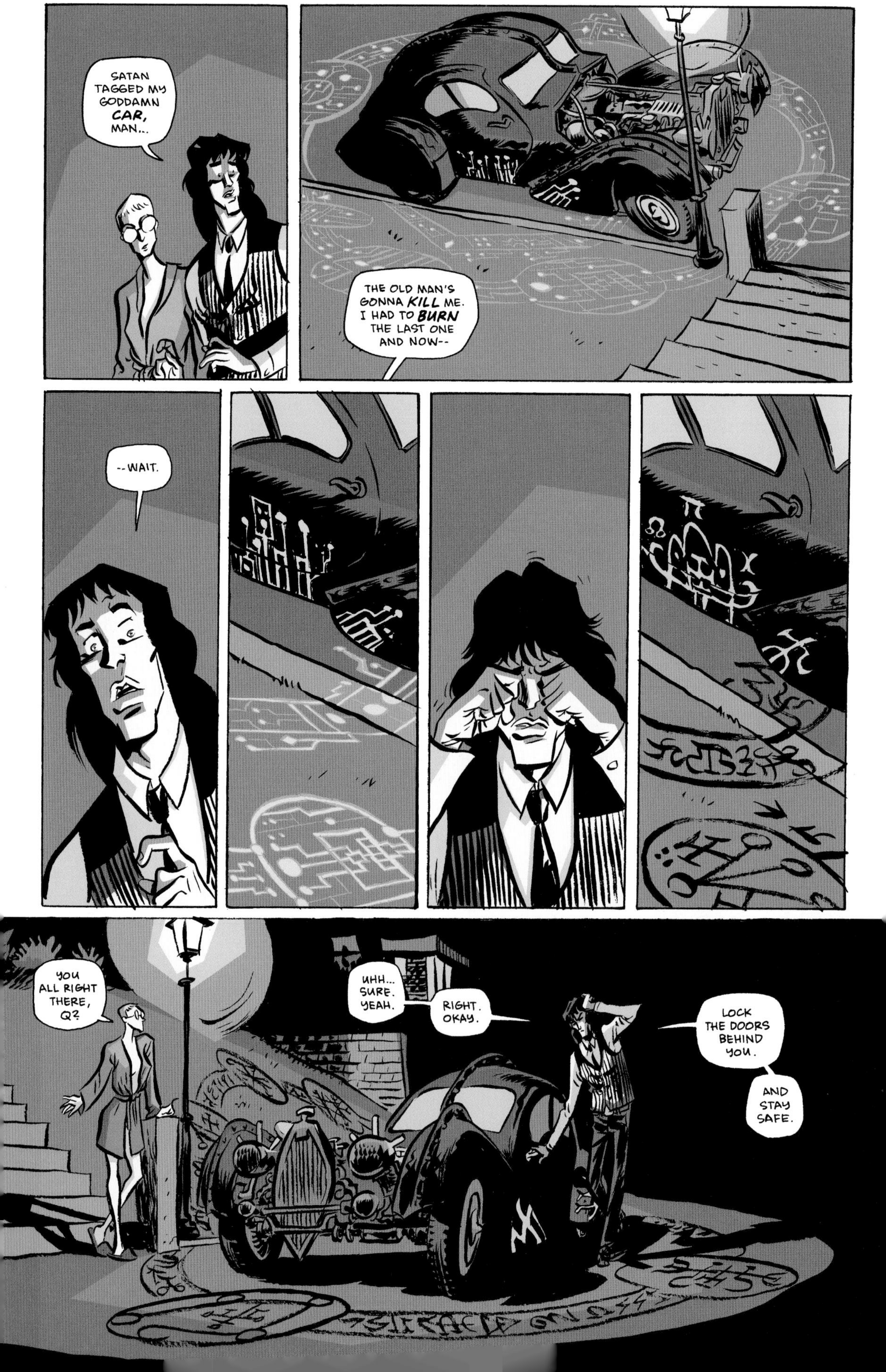
SATAN TAGGED MY GODDAMN **CAR,** MAN...
THE OLD MAN'S GONNA **KILL** ME. I HAD TO **BURN** THE LAST ONE AND NOW--
--WAIT.
YOU ALL RIGHT THERE, Q?
UHH... SURE. YEAH.
RIGHT. OKAY.
LOCK THE DOORS BEHIND YOU.
AND STAY SAFE.

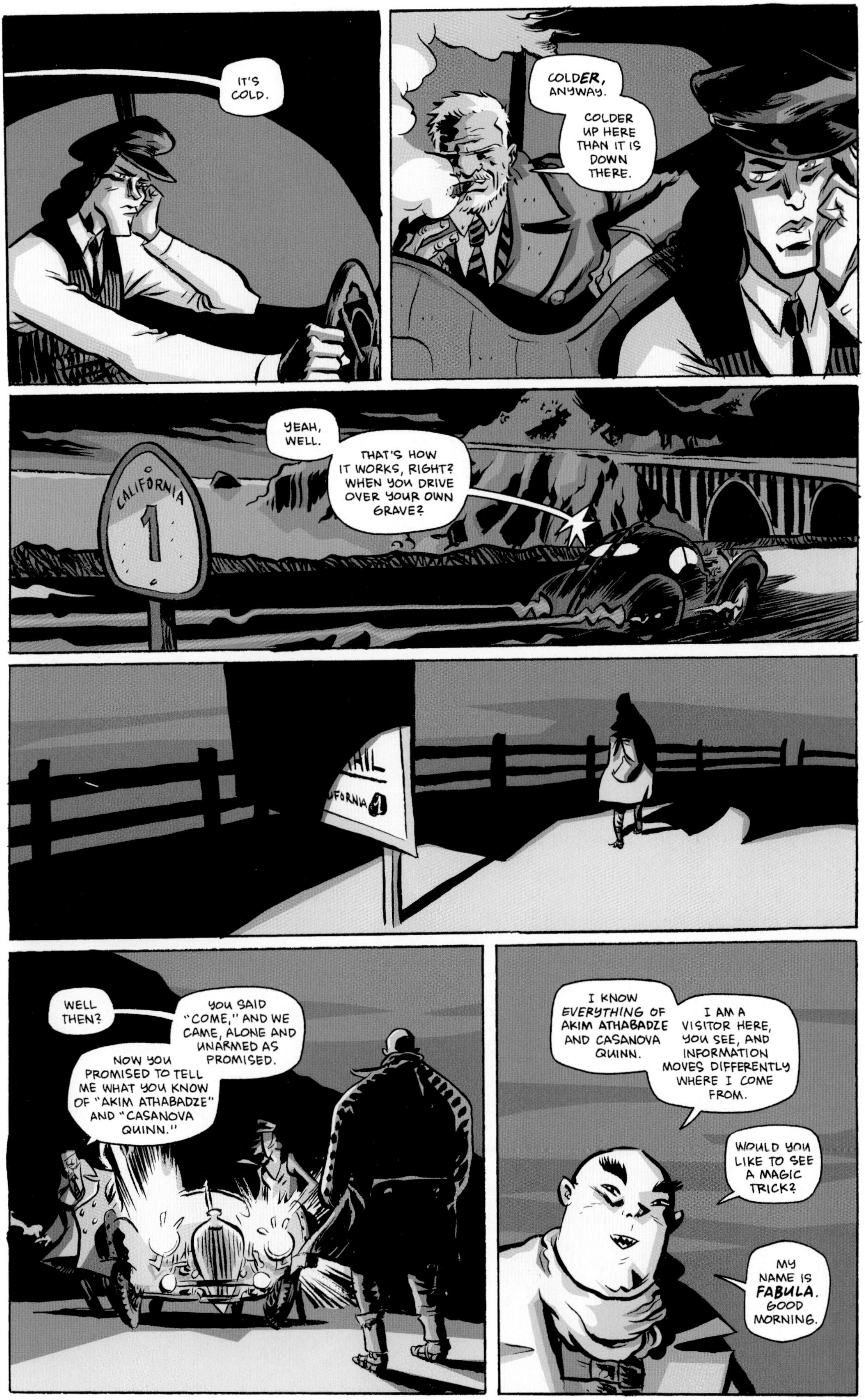
IT'S COLD.
COLDER, ANYWAY.
COLDER UP HERE THAN IT IS DOWN THERE.
YEAH, WELL.
THAT'S HOW IT WORKS, RIGHT? WHEN YOU DRIVE OVER YOUR OWN GRAVE?
CALIFORNIA
1
WELL THEN?
YOU SAID "COME," AND WE CAME, ALONE AND UNARMED AS PROMISED.
NOW YOU PROMISED TO TELL ME WHAT YOU KNOW OF "AKIM ATHABADZE" AND "CASANOVA QUINN."
I KNOW EVERYTHING OF AKIM ATHABADZE AND CASANOVA QUINN.
I AM A VISITOR HERE, YOU SEE, AND INFORMATION MOVES DIFFERENTLY WHERE I COME FROM.
WOULD YOU LIKE TO SEE A MAGIC TRICK?
MY NAME IS FABULA. GOOD MORNING.

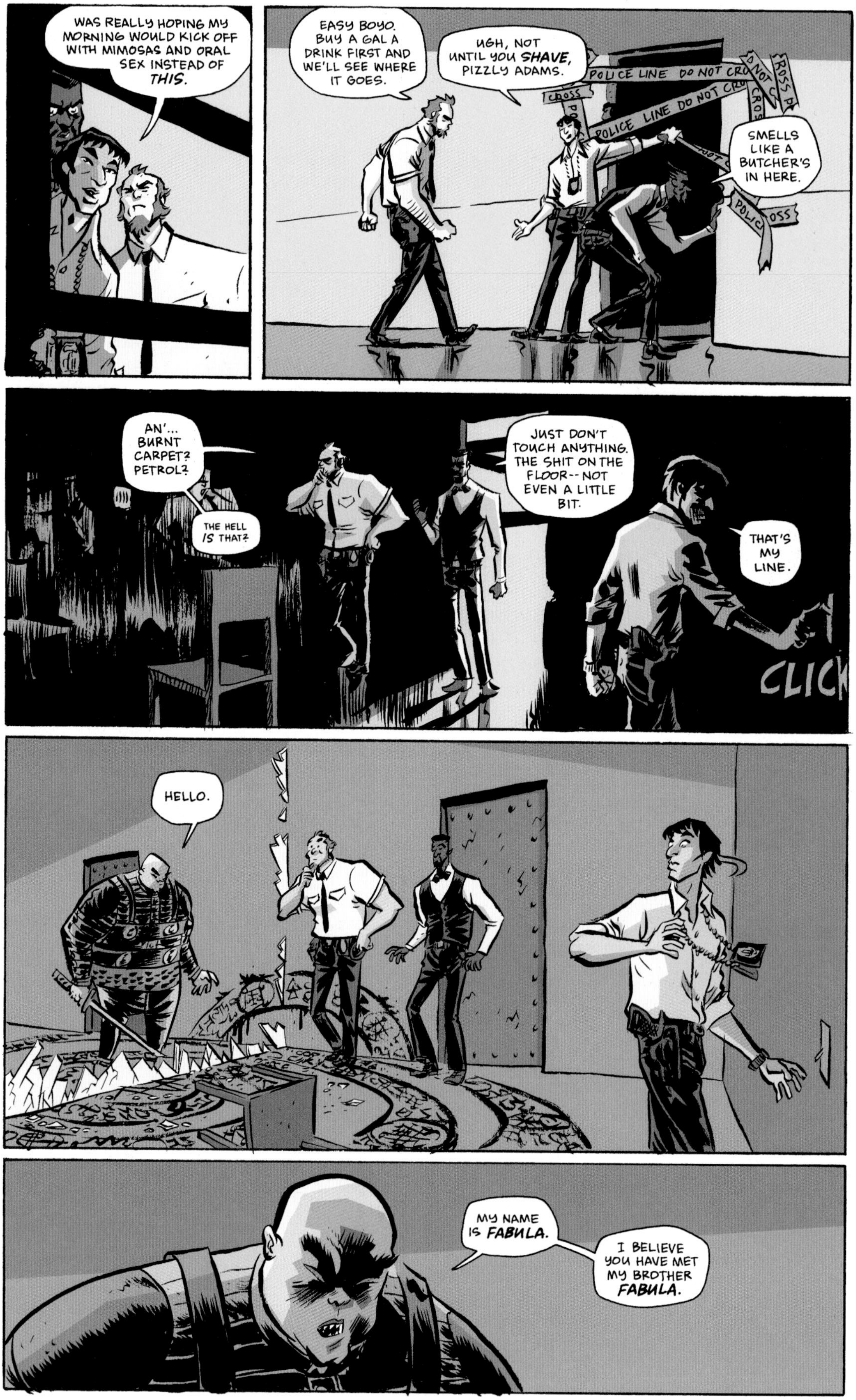
WAS REALLY HOPING MY MORNING WOULD KICK OFF WITH MIMOSAS AND ORAL SEX INSTEAD OF *THIS*.
EASY BOYO. BUY A GAL A DRINK FIRST AND WE'LL SEE WHERE IT GOES.
UGH, NOT UNTIL YOU *SHAVE*, PIZZLY ADAMS.
POLICE LINE DO NOT CROSS
SMELLS LIKE A BUTCHER'S IN HERE.
AN'... BURNT CARPET? PETROL?
THE HELL *IS* THAT?
JUST DON'T TOUCH ANYTHING. THE SHIT ON THE FLOOR--NOT EVEN A LITTLE BIT.
THAT'S MY LINE.
CLICK
HELLO.
MY NAME IS *FABULA*.
I BELIEVE YOU HAVE MET MY BROTHER *FABULA*.

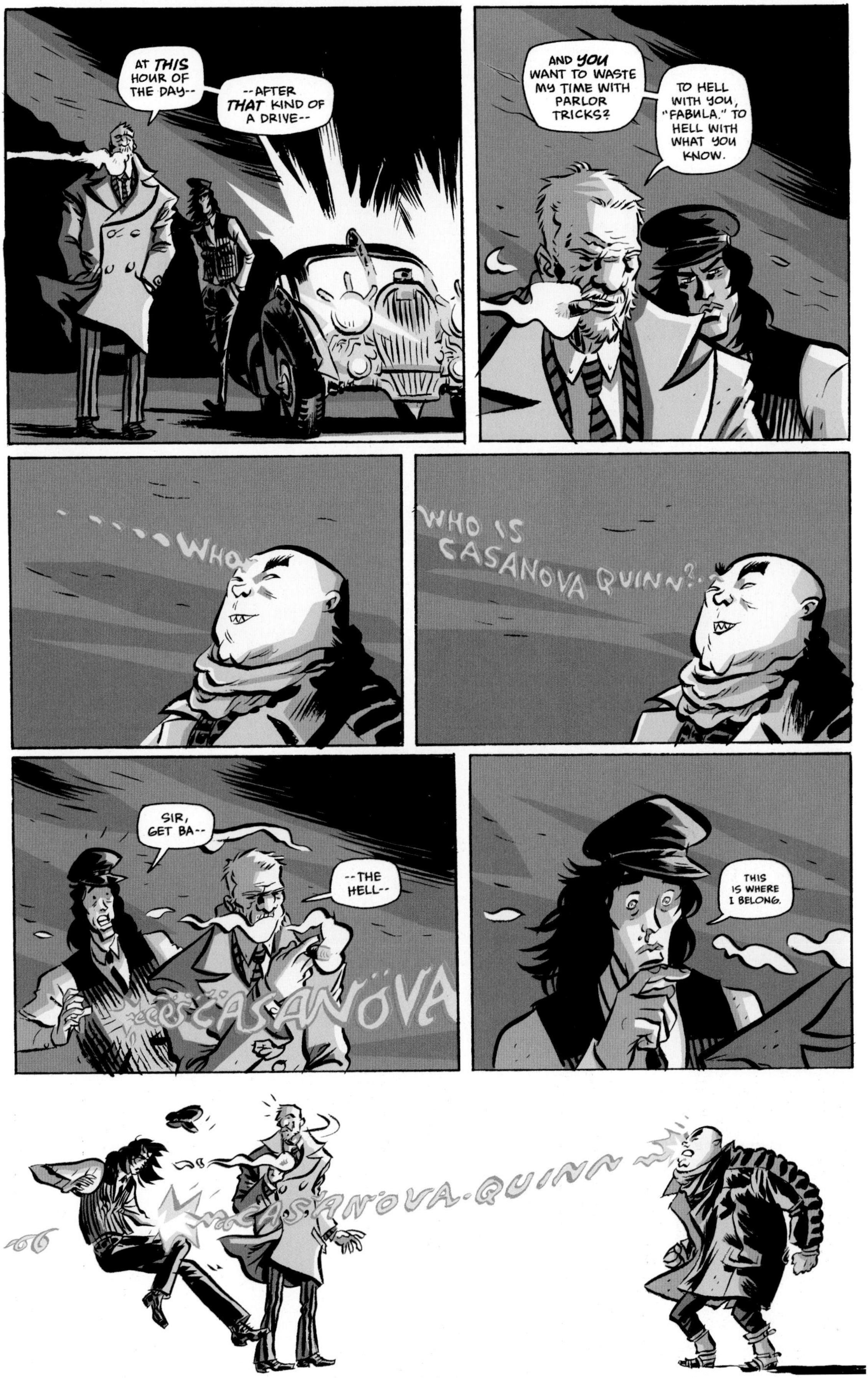
AT THIS HOUR OF THE DAY--
--AFTER THAT KIND OF A DRIVE--
AND YOU WANT TO WASTE MY TIME WITH PARLOR TRICKS?
TO HELL WITH YOU, "FABULA." TO HELL WITH WHAT YOU KNOW.
WHO
WHO IS CASANOVA QUINN?
SIR, GET BA--
--THE HELL--
CASANOVA
THIS IS WHERE I BELONG.
CASANOVA QUINN

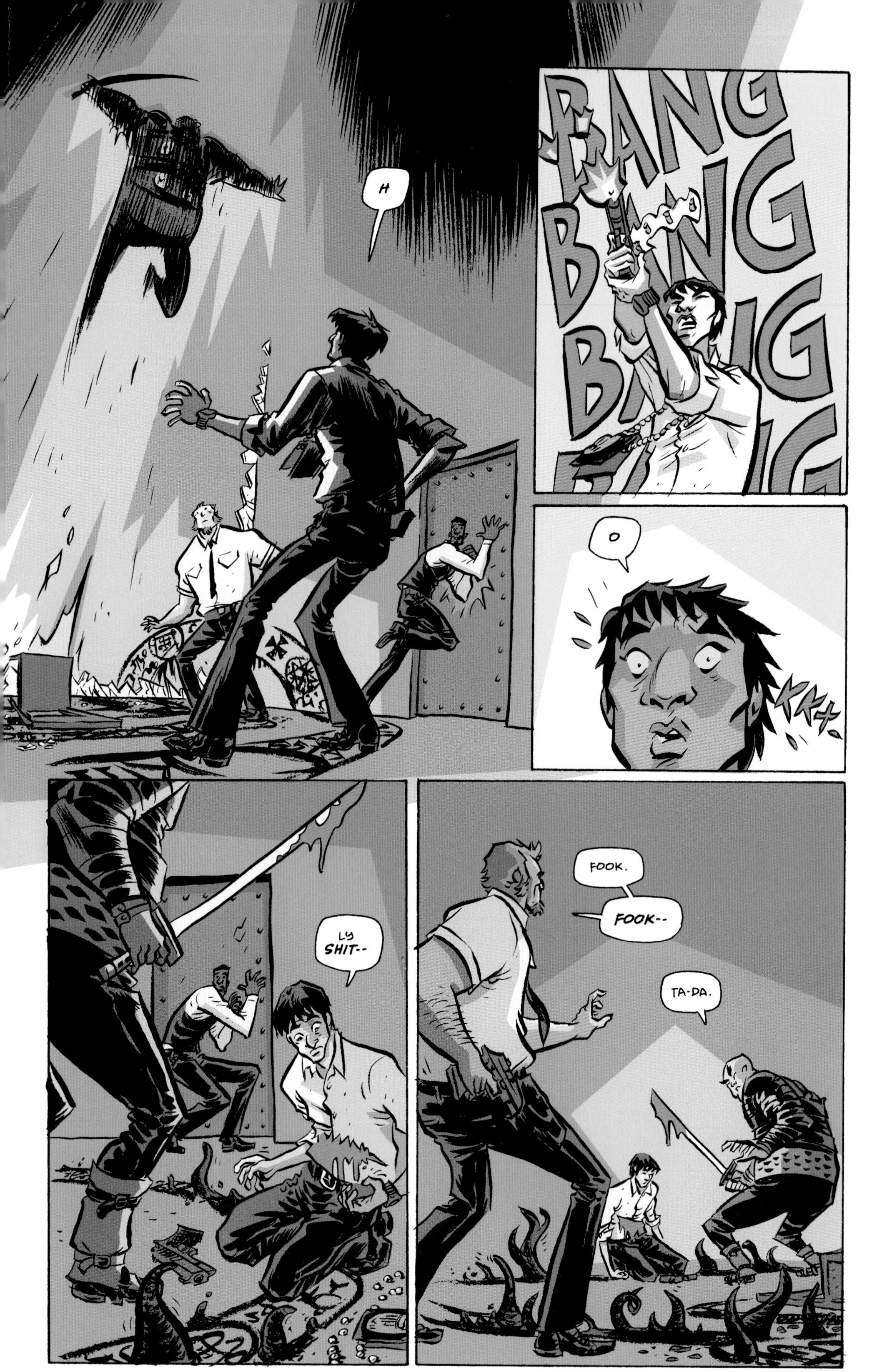
H
BANG
BANG
BANG
O
KKT
LY
SHIT--
FOOK.
FOOK--
TA-DA.

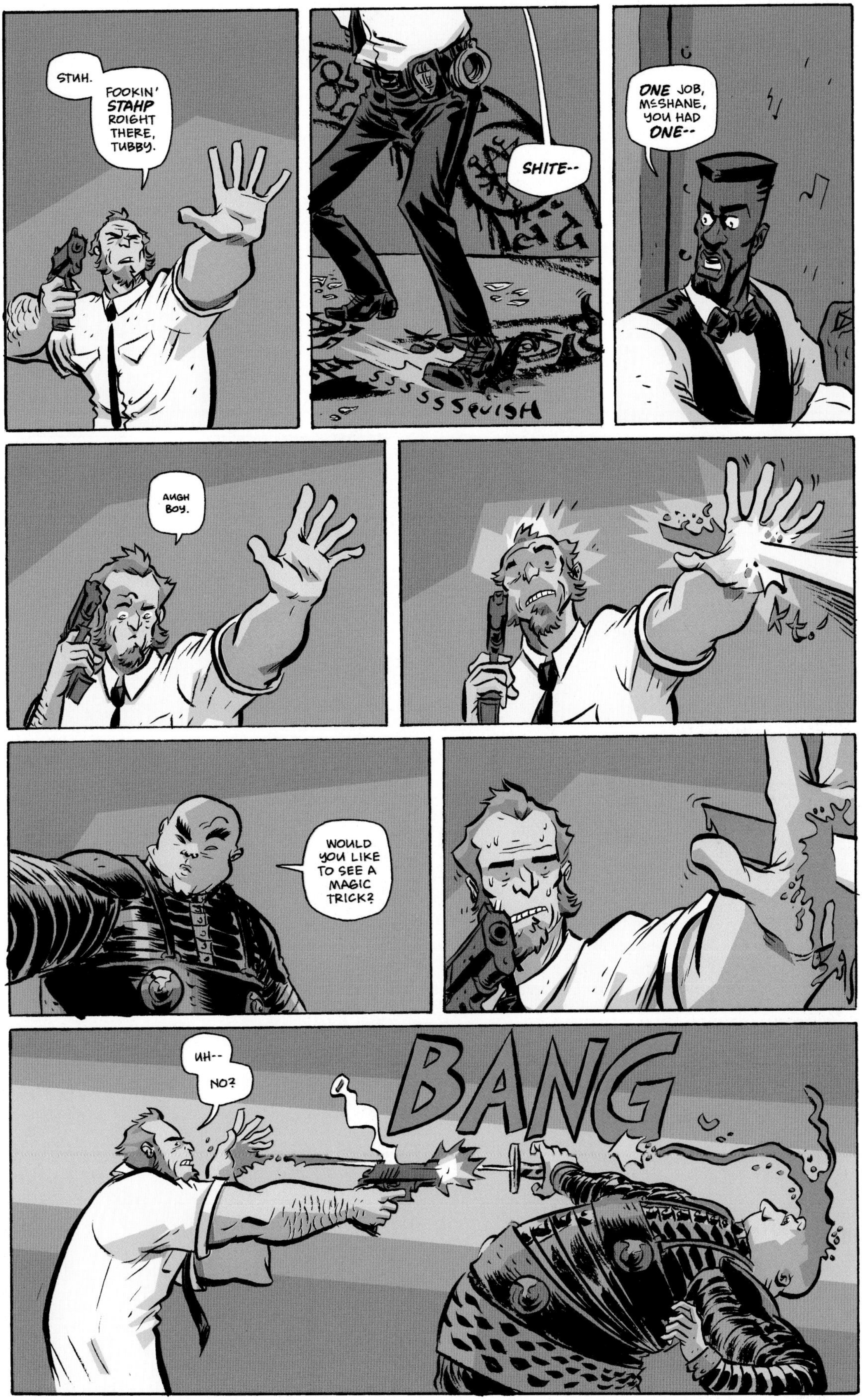
STUH.
FOOKIN' STAHP ROIGHT THERE, TUBBY.
SHITE--
SSSSSSSQUISH
ONE JOB, McSHANE, YOU HAD ONE--
AUGH BOY.
Kt.
WOULD YOU LIKE TO SEE A MAGIC TRICK?
UH--
NO?
BANG

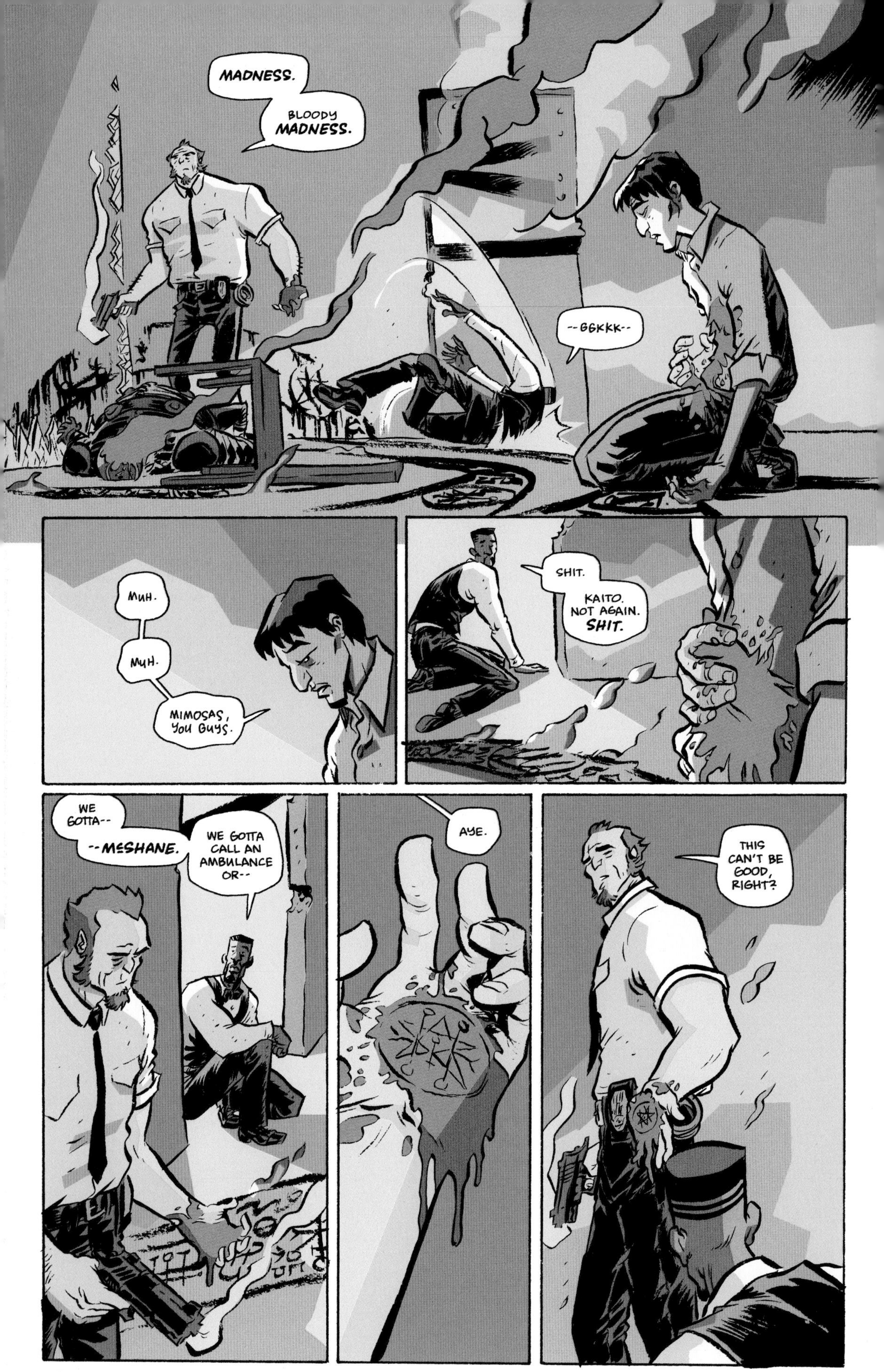
MADNESS.
BLOODY MADNESS.
--GGKKK--
MUH.
MUH.
MIMOSAS, YOU GUYS.
SHIT.
KAITO. NOT AGAIN. SHIT.
WE GOTTA--
--MCSHANE.
WE GOTTA CALL AN AMBULANCE OR--
AYE.
THIS CAN'T BE GOOD, RIGHT?

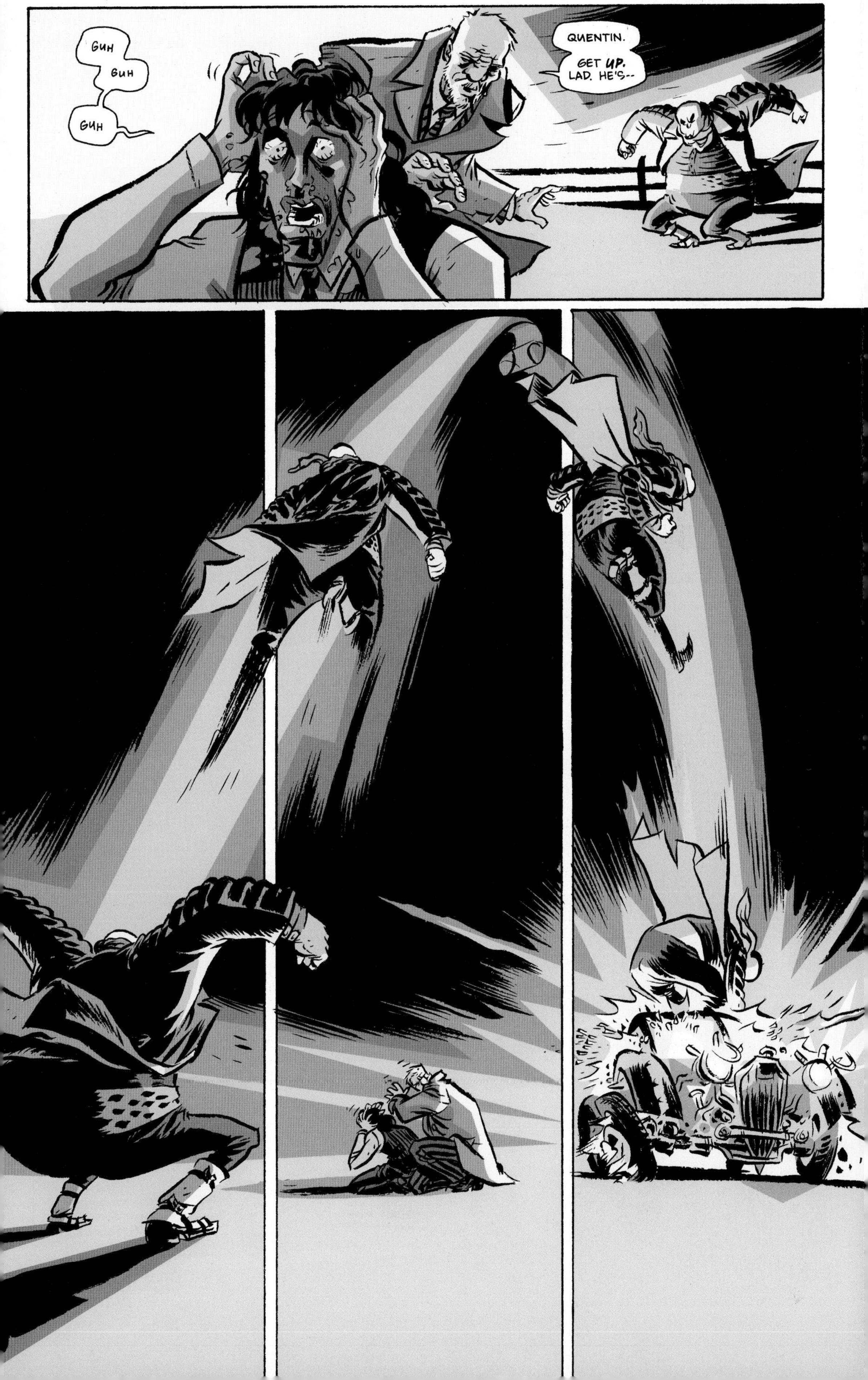
GUH
GUH
GUH
QUENTIN.
GET UP. LAD. HE'S--

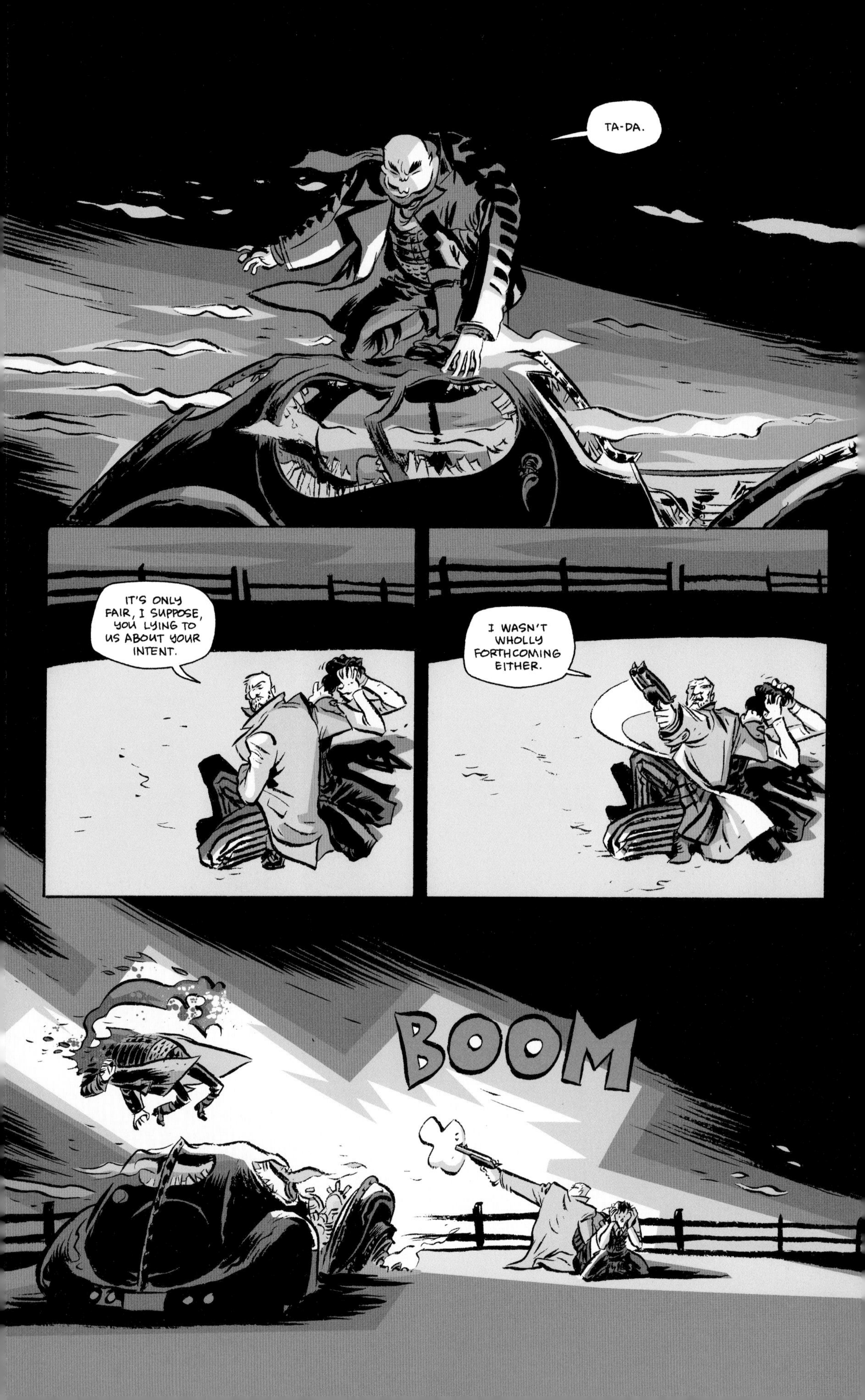
TA-DA.
IT'S ONLY FAIR, I SUPPOSE, YOU LYING TO US ABOUT YOUR INTENT.
I WASN'T WHOLLY FORTHCOMING EITHER.
BOOM

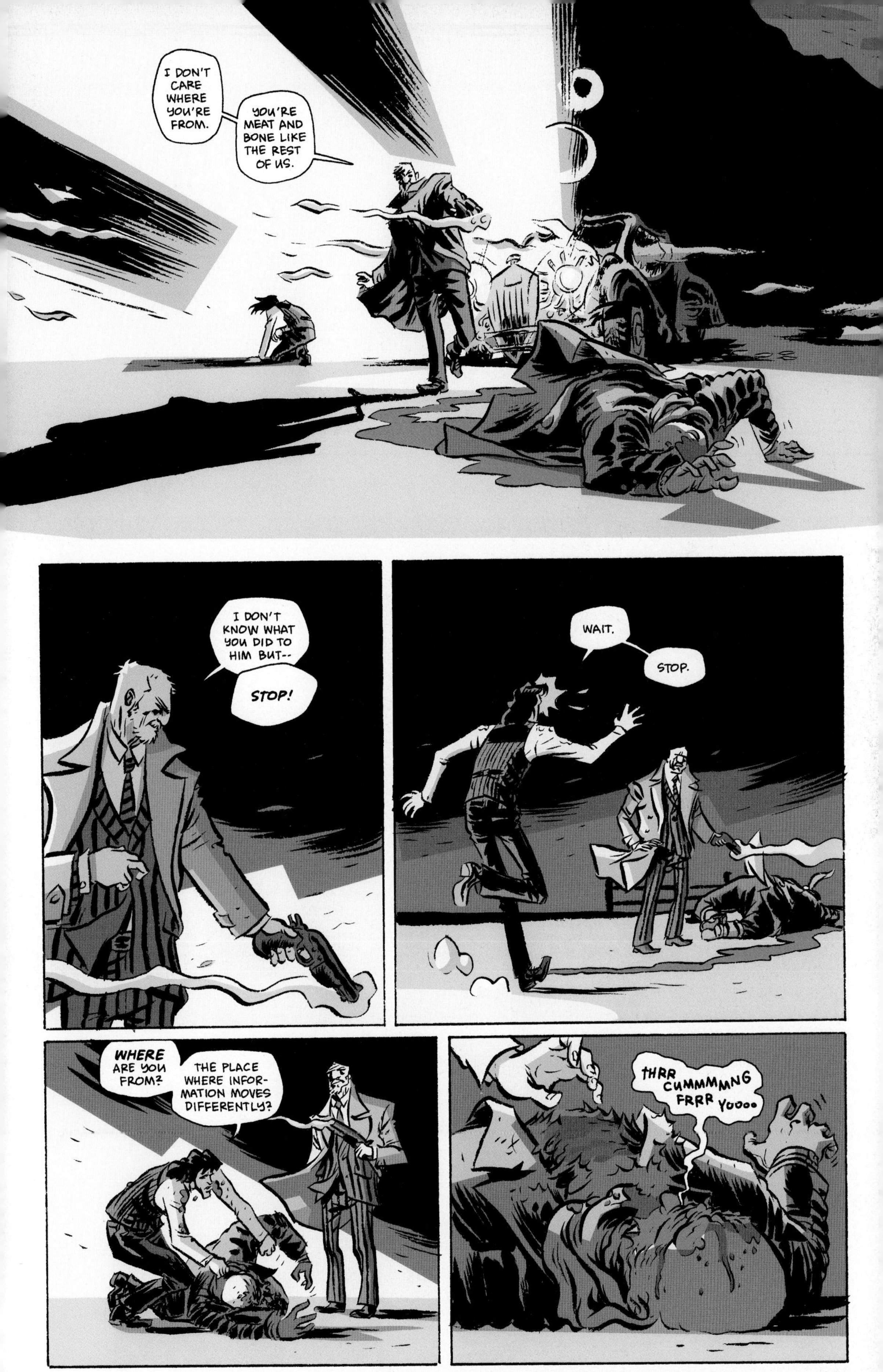
I DON'T CARE WHERE YOU'RE FROM.
YOU'RE MEAT AND BONE LIKE THE REST OF US.
I DON'T KNOW WHAT YOU DID TO HIM BUT--
STOP!
WAIT.
STOP.
WHERE ARE YOU FROM?
THE PLACE WHERE INFORMATION MOVES DIFFERENTLY?
THRR CUMMMMNG FRRR YOOOO

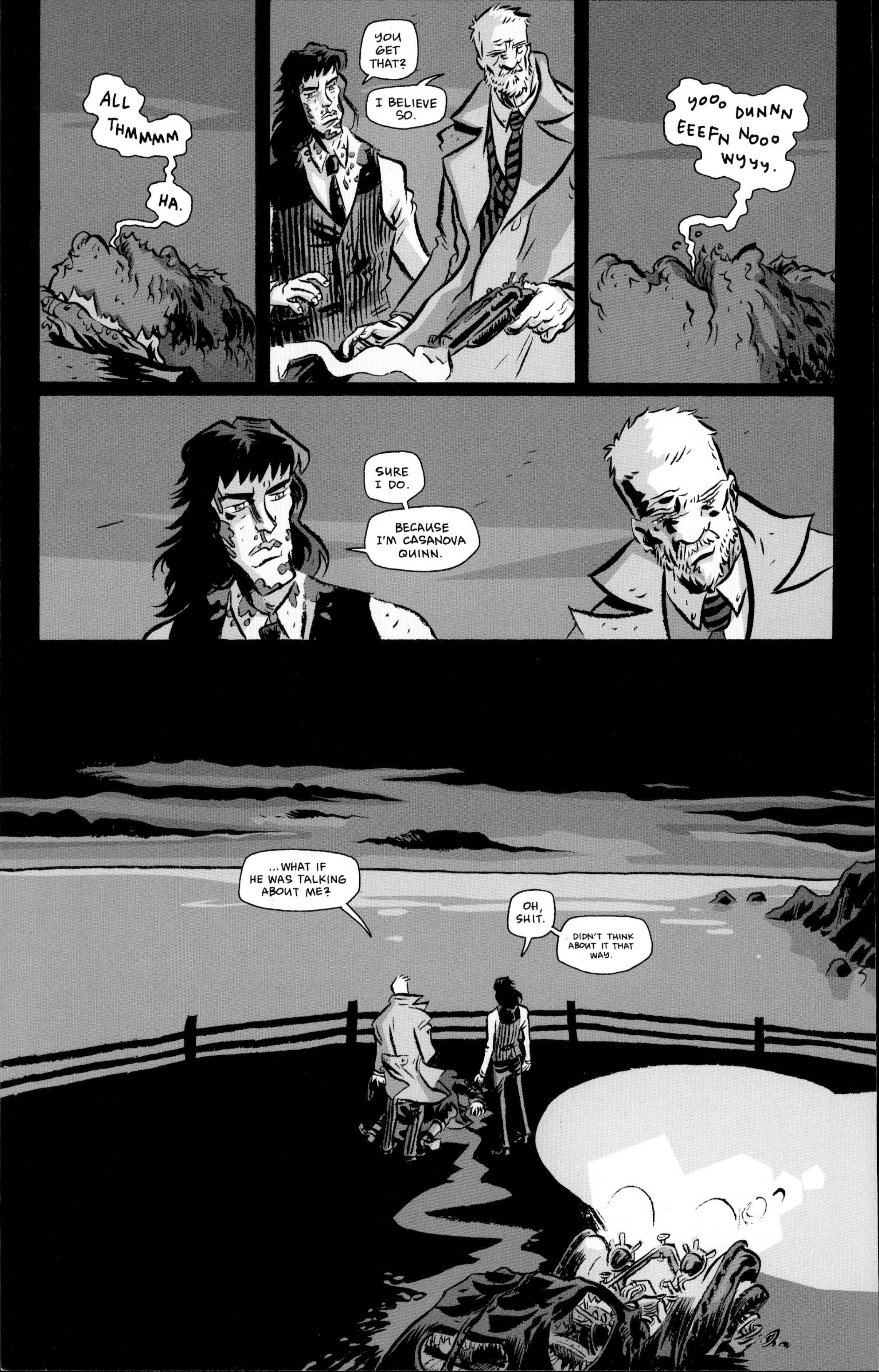
ALL THMMMM
HA.
YOU GET THAT?
I BELIEVE SO.
YOOO DUNNN EEEFN NOOO WYYY.
SURE I DO.
BECAUSE I'M CASANOVA QUINN.
...WHAT IF HE WAS TALKING ABOUT ME?
OH, SHIT.
DIDN'T THINK ABOUT IT THAT WAY.

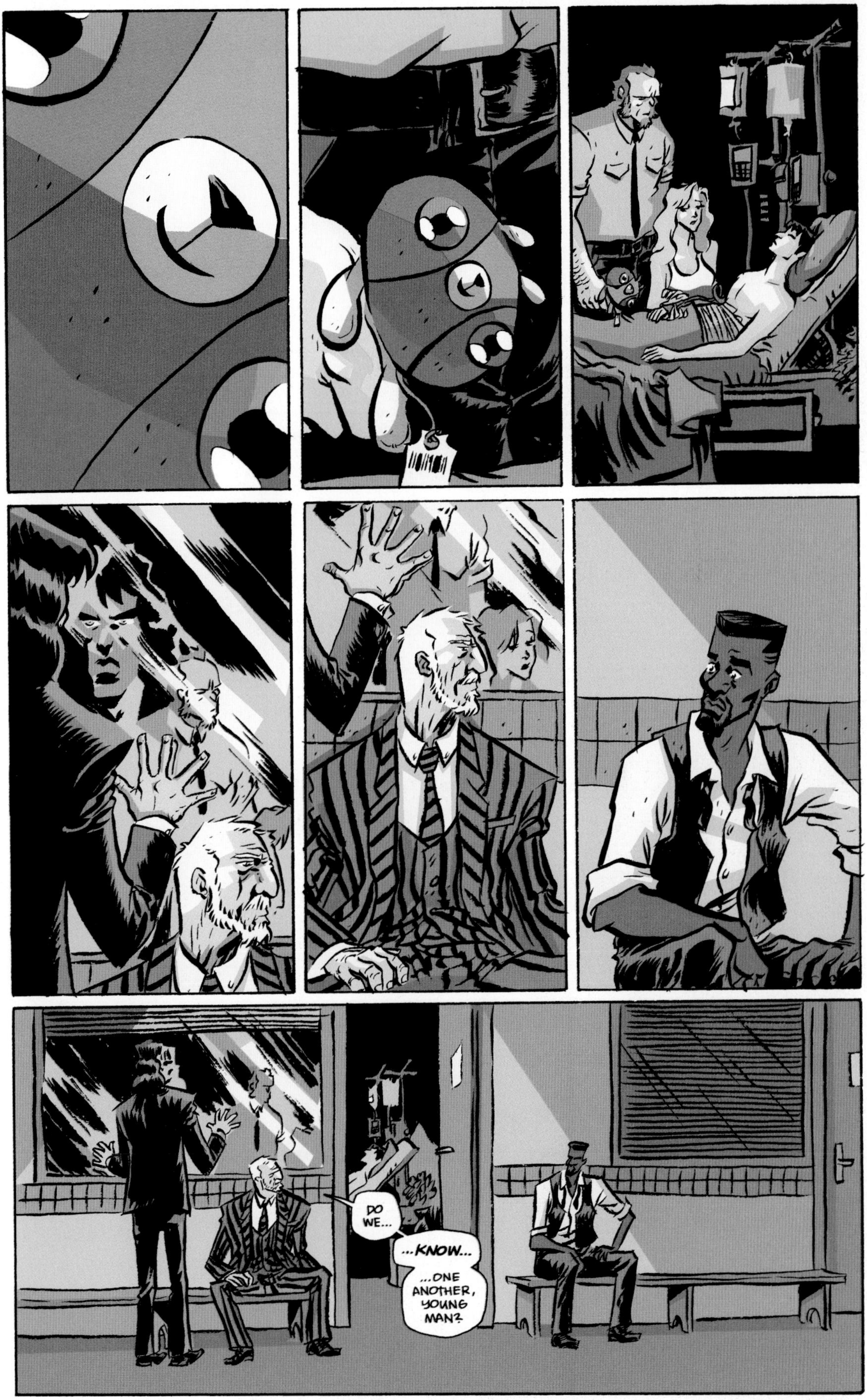
DO WE...
...KNOW...
...ONE ANOTHER, YOUNG MAN?

MOTHER OF GOD.

AKIM *REDIRECTED* THEM.

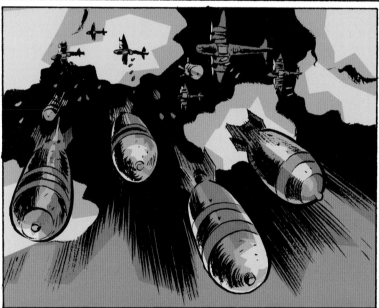

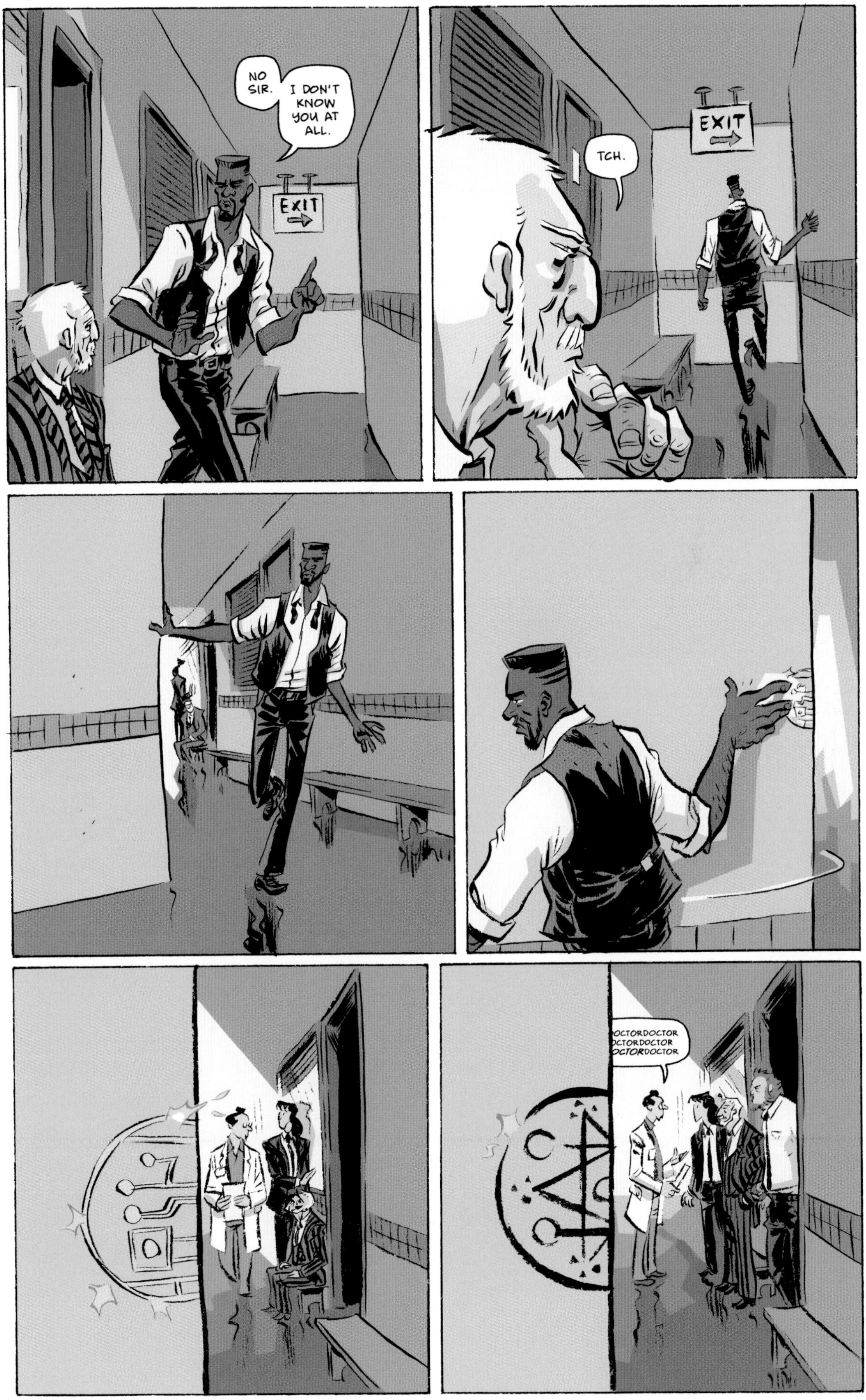
NO SIR.
I DON'T KNOW YOU AT ALL.
EXIT
EXIT
TCH.
OCTORDOCTOR
CTORDOCTOR
CTORDOCTOR

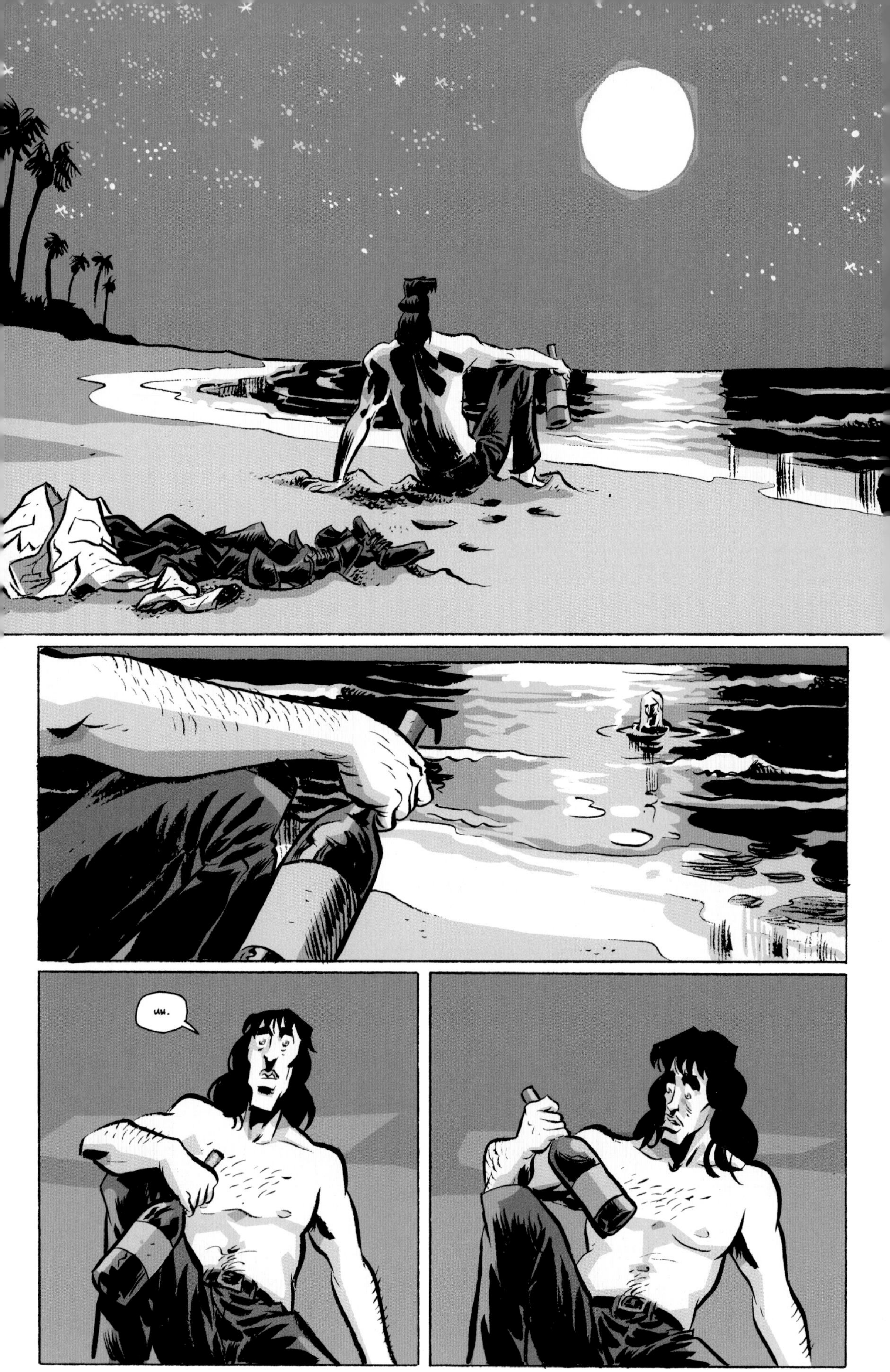
UH.

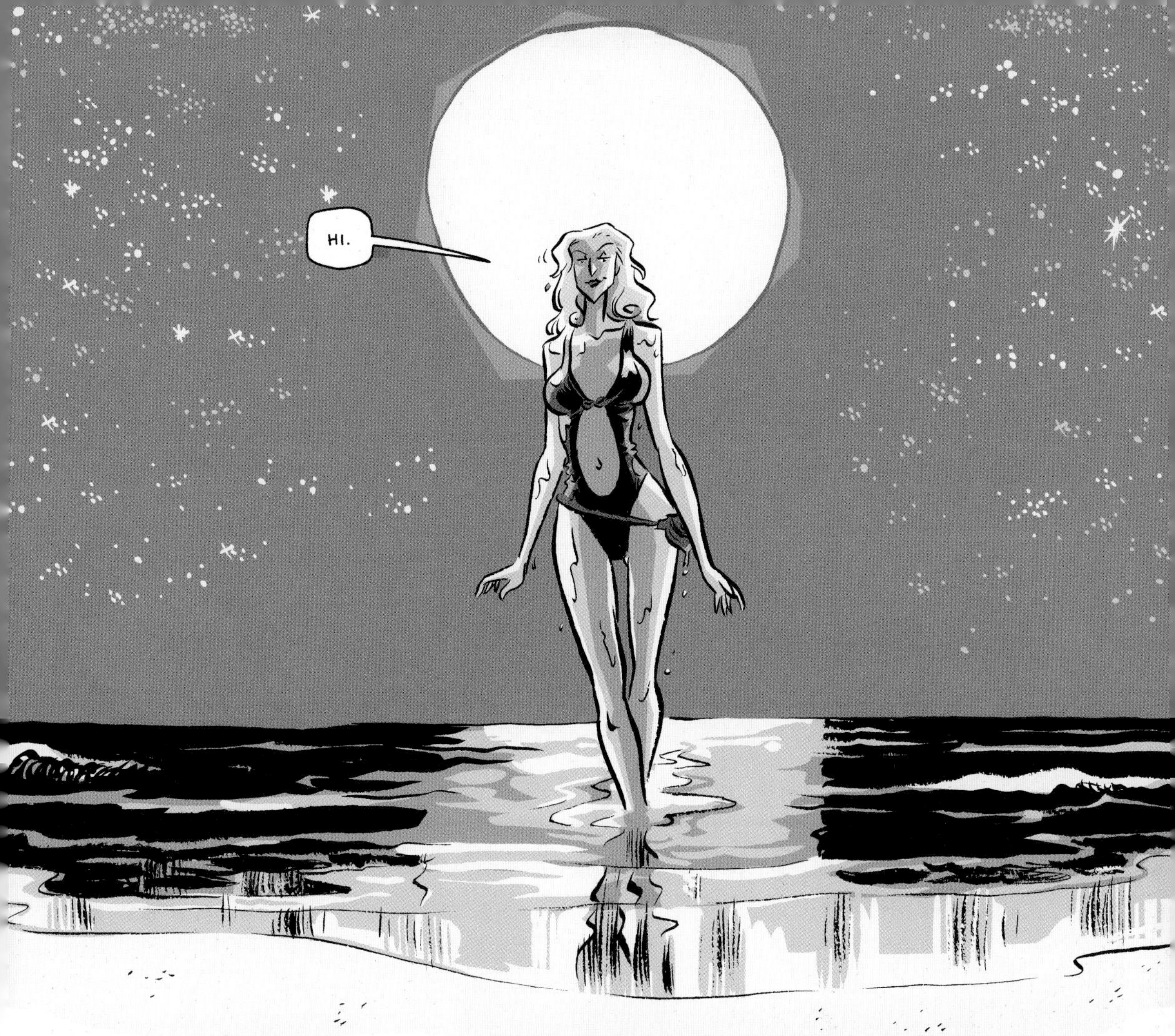
HI.

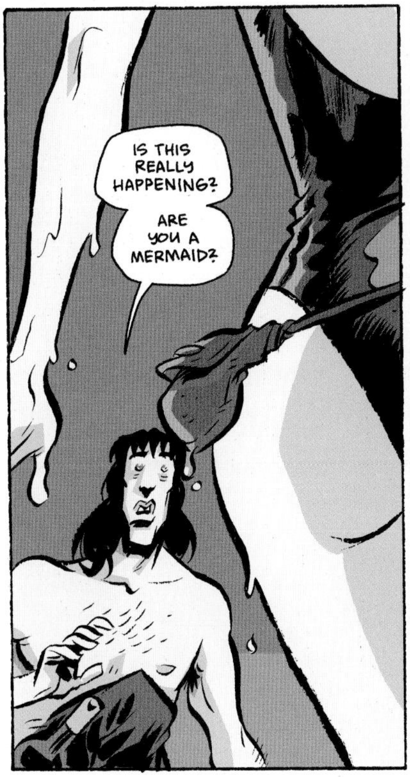
IS THIS REALLY HAPPENING?
ARE YOU A MERMAID?

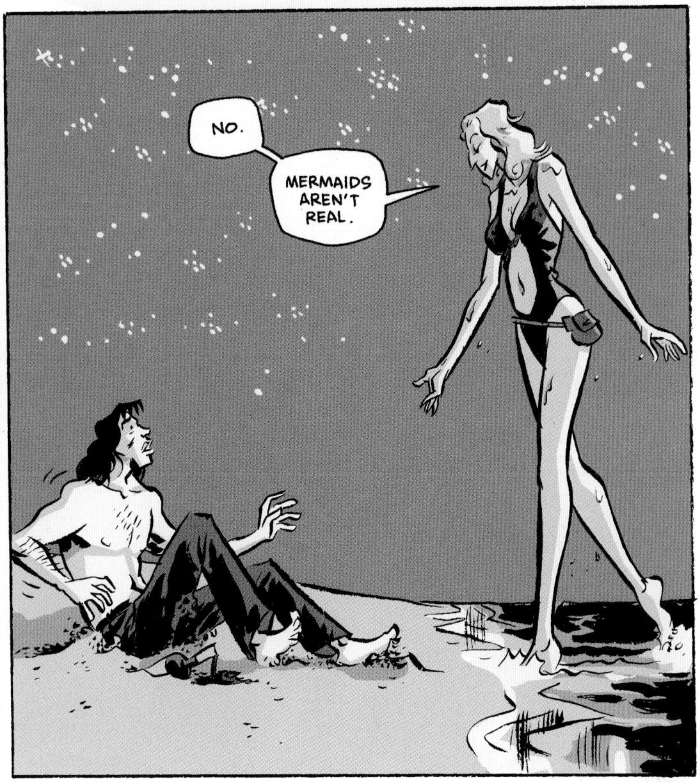
NO.
MERMAIDS AREN'T REAL.

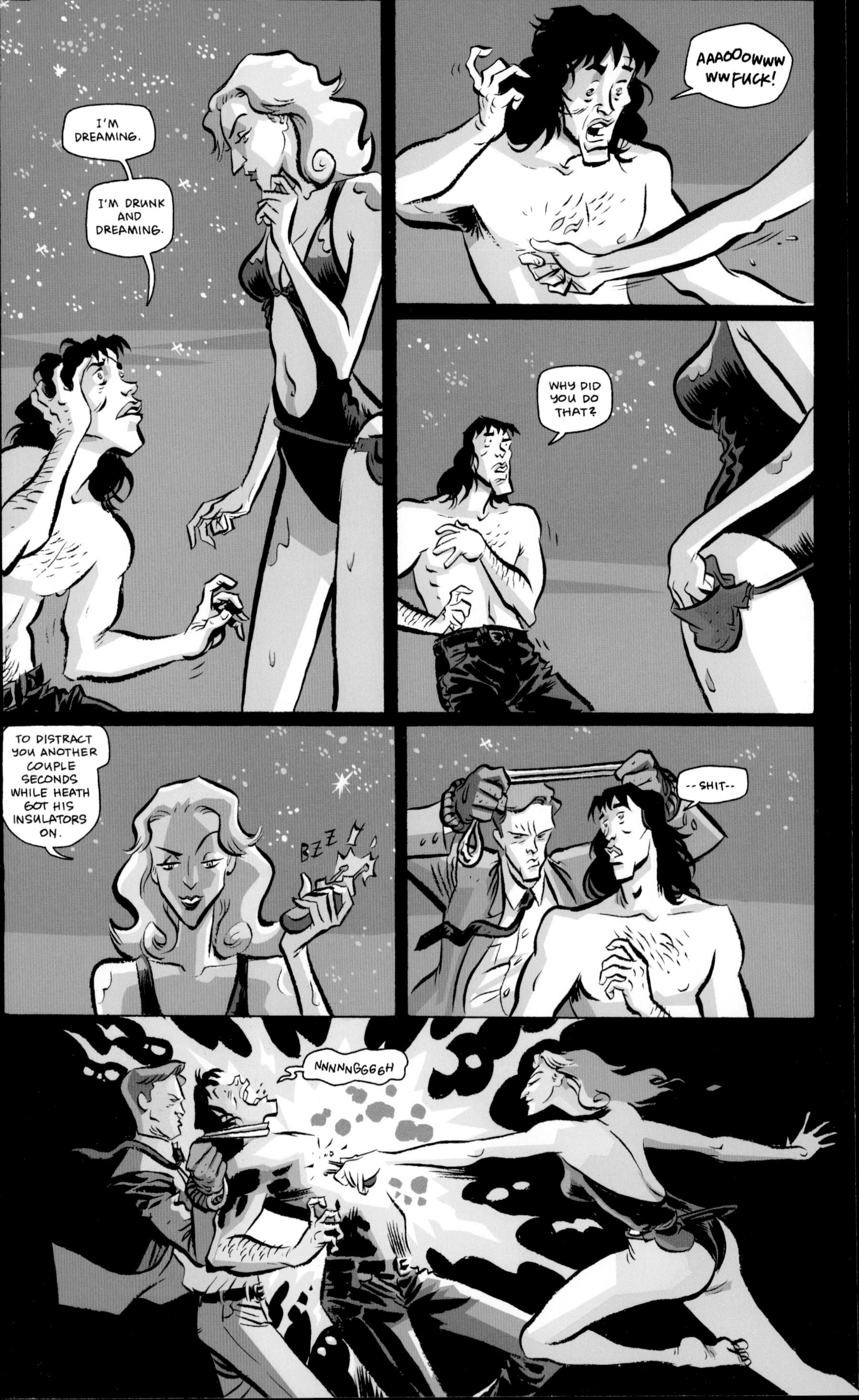
I'M DREAMING.
I'M DRUNK AND DREAMING.
AAAOOOWWW WWFUCK!
WHY DID YOU DO THAT?
TO DISTRACT YOU ANOTHER COUPLE SECONDS WHILE HEATH GOT HIS INSULATORS ON.
BZZ
--SHIT--
NNNNNGGGGH

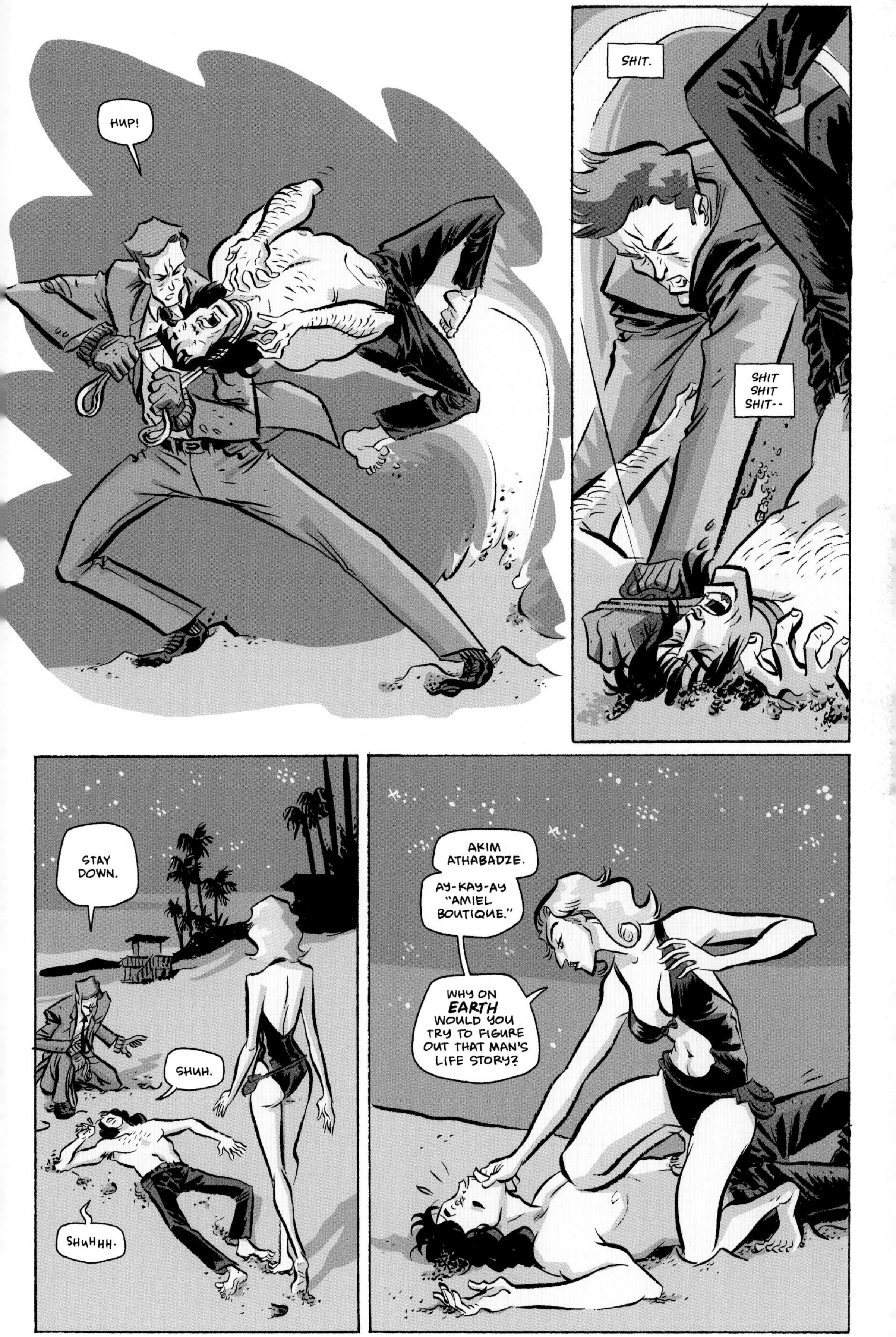
HUP!
SHIT.
SHIT
SHIT
SHIT--
STAY DOWN.
SHUH.
SHUHHH.
AKIM ATHABADZE.
AY-KAY-AY "AMIEL BOUTIQUE."
WHY ON EARTH WOULD YOU TRY TO FIGURE OUT THAT MAN'S LIFE STORY?

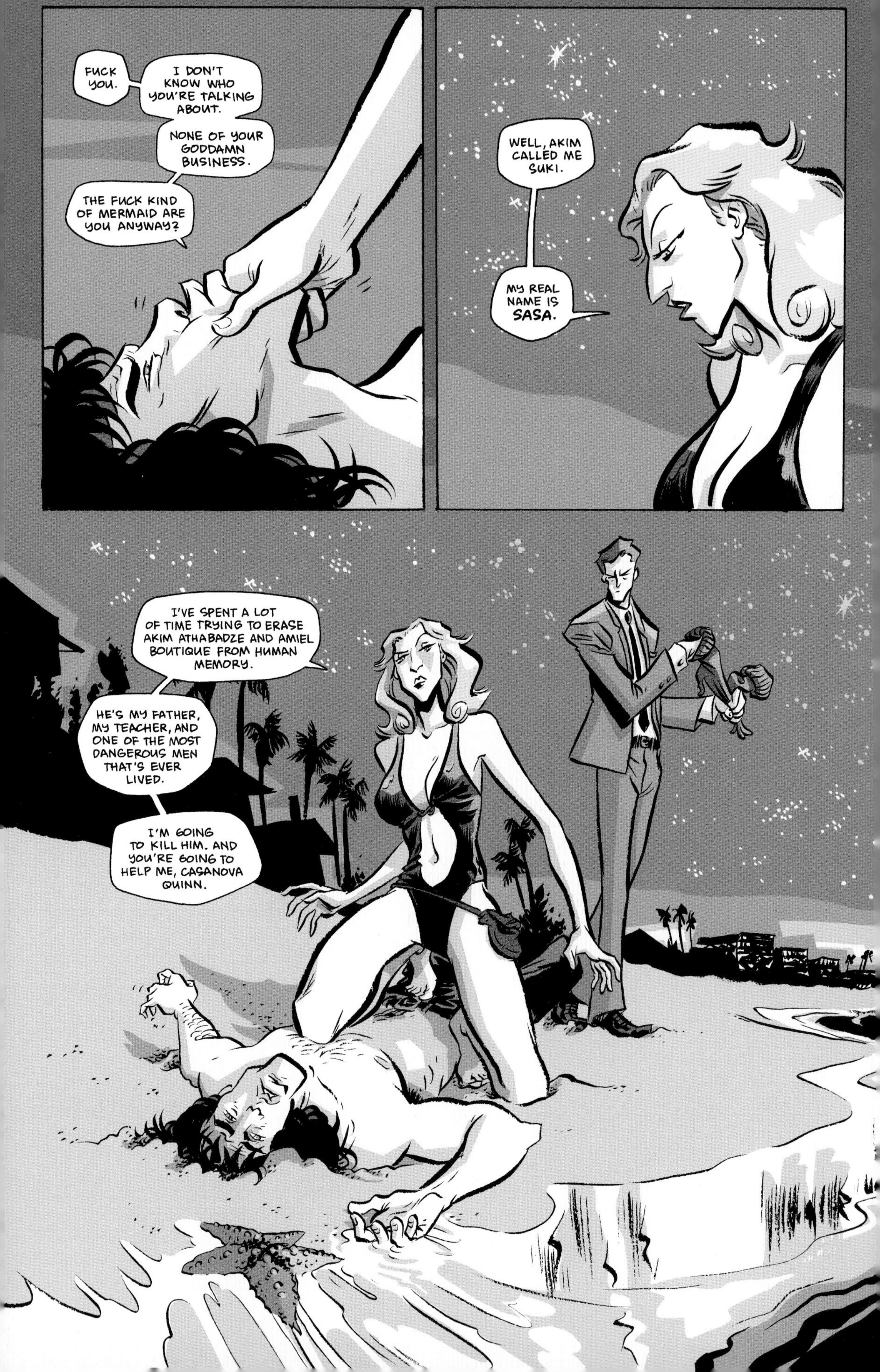

FUCK YOU.
I DON'T KNOW WHO YOU'RE TALKING ABOUT.
NONE OF YOUR GODDAMN BUSINESS.
THE FUCK KIND OF MERMAID ARE YOU ANYWAY?
WELL, AKIM CALLED ME SUKI.
MY REAL NAME IS SASA.
I'VE SPENT A LOT OF TIME TRYING TO ERASE AKIM ATHABADZE AND AMIEL BOUTIQUE FROM HUMAN MEMORY.
HE'S MY FATHER, MY TEACHER, AND ONE OF THE MOST DANGEROUS MEN THAT'S EVER LIVED.
I'M GOING TO KILL HIM. AND YOU'RE GOING TO HELP ME, CASANOVA QUINN.

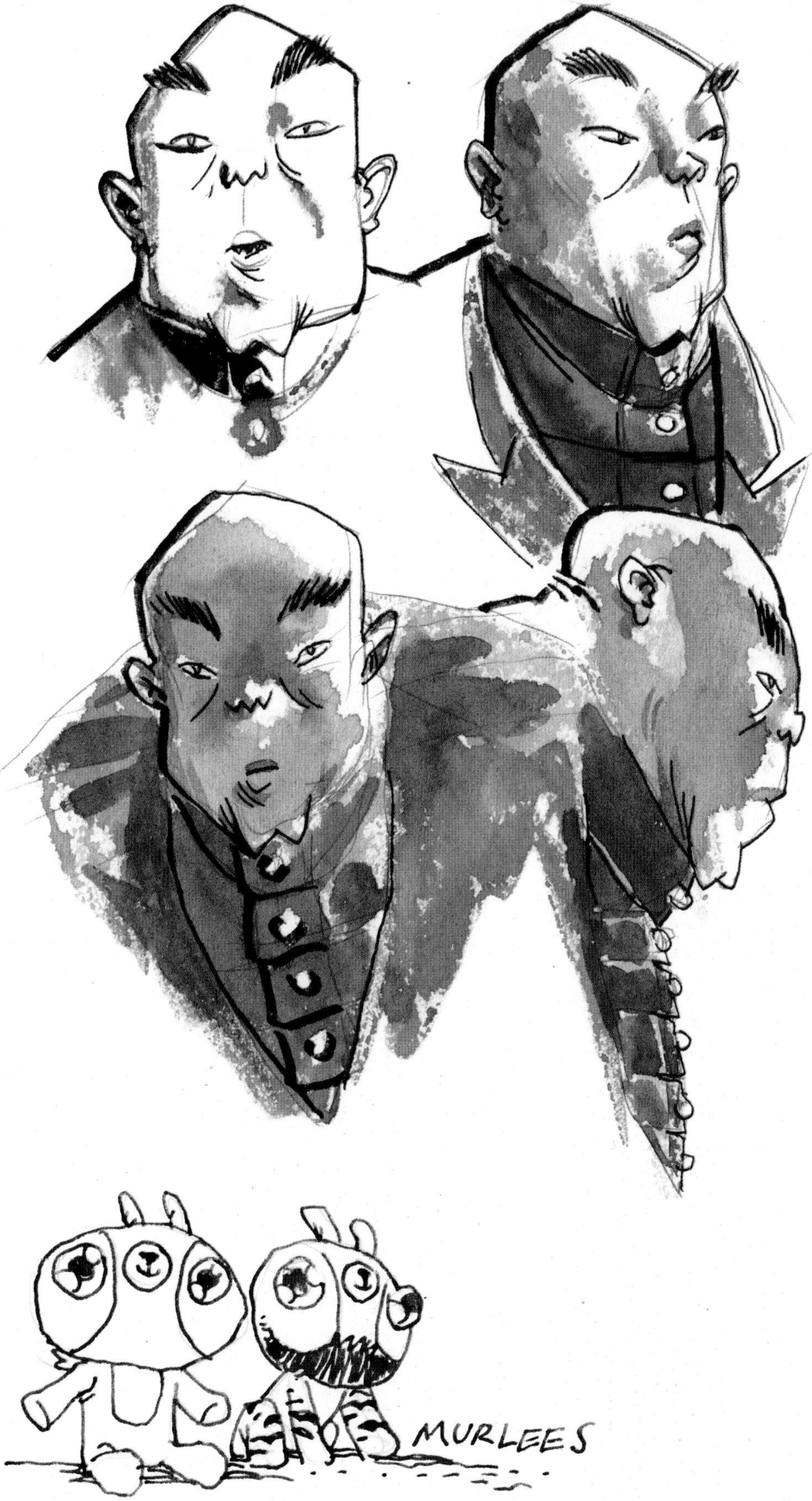
MURLEES

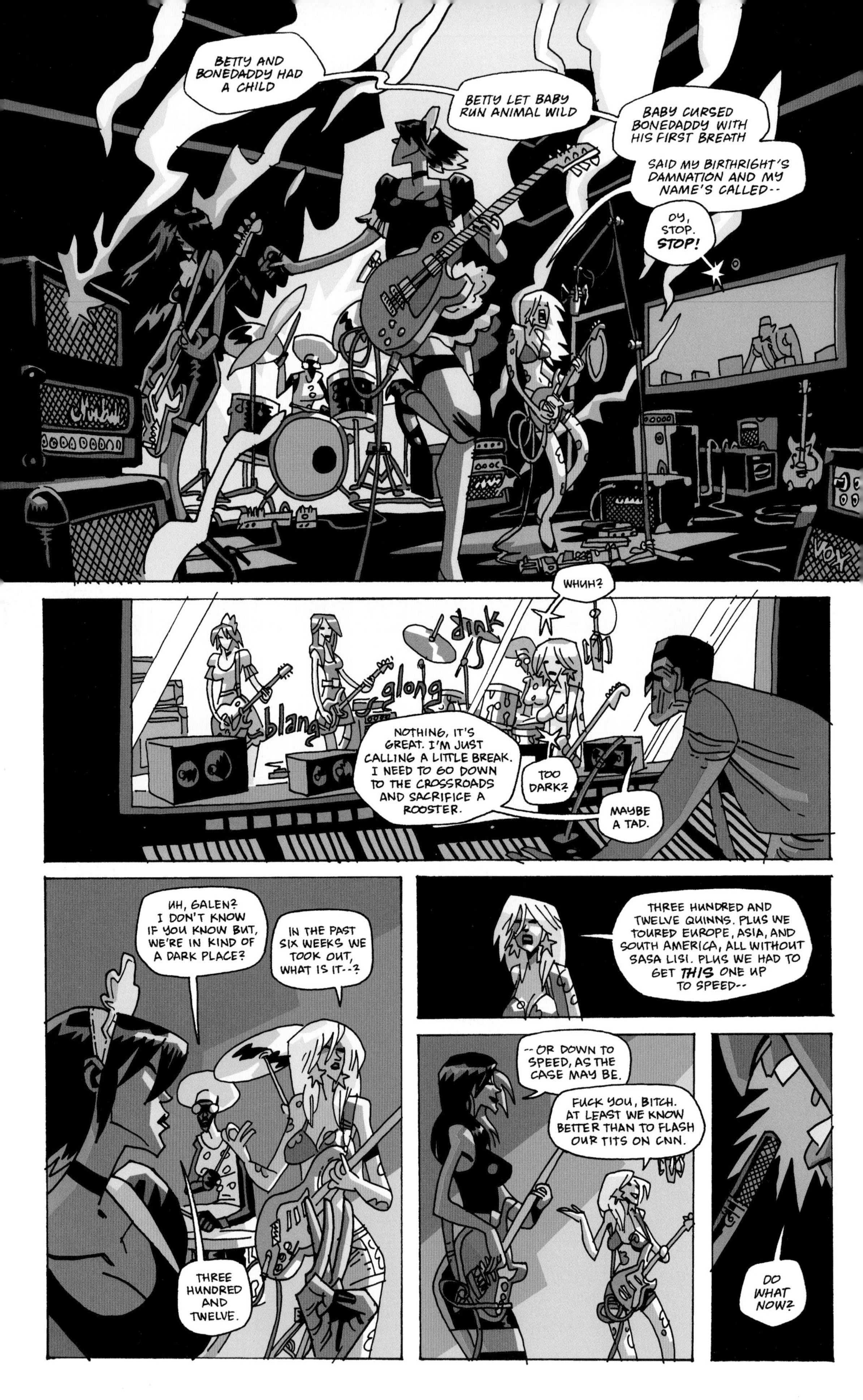
BETTY AND BONEDADDY HAD A CHILD
BETTY LET BABY RUN ANIMAL WILD
BABY CURSED BONEDADDY WITH HIS FIRST BREATH
SAID MY BIRTHRIGHT'S DAMNATION AND MY NAME'S CALLED--
OY, STOP. **STOP!**
WHUH?
dink
blang
glong
NOTHING, IT'S GREAT. I'M JUST CALLING A LITTLE BREAK. I NEED TO GO DOWN TO THE CROSSROADS AND SACRIFICE A ROOSTER.
TOO DARK?
MAYBE A TAD.
UH, GALEN? I DON'T KNOW IF YOU KNOW BUT, WE'RE IN KIND OF A DARK PLACE?
IN THE PAST SIX WEEKS WE TOOK OUT, WHAT IS IT--?
THREE HUNDRED AND TWELVE.
THREE HUNDRED AND TWELVE QUINNS. PLUS WE TOURED EUROPE, ASIA, AND SOUTH AMERICA, ALL WITHOUT SASA LISI. PLUS WE HAD TO GET *THIS* ONE UP TO SPEED--
--OR DOWN TO SPEED, AS THE CASE MAY BE.
FUCK YOU, BITCH. AT LEAST WE KNOW BETTER THAN TO FLASH OUR TITS ON CNN.
DO WHAT NOW?

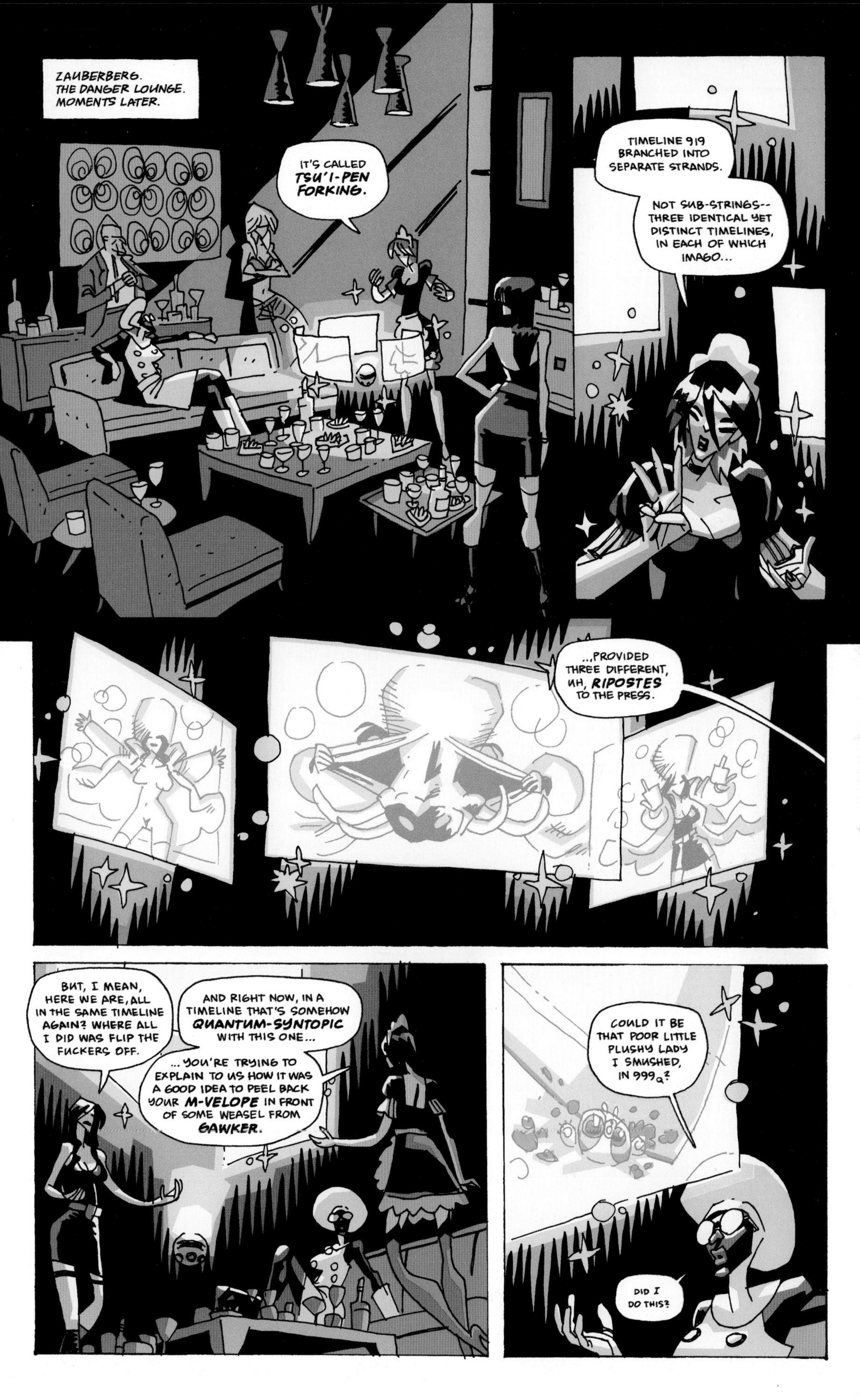
ZAUBERBERG.
THE DANGER LOUNGE.
MOMENTS LATER.
IT'S CALLED TSU'I-PEN FORKING.
TIMELINE 919 BRANCHED INTO SEPARATE STRANDS.
NOT SUB-STRINGS-- THREE IDENTICAL YET DISTINCT TIMELINES, IN EACH OF WHICH IMAGO...
...PROVIDED THREE DIFFERENT, UH, RIPOSTES TO THE PRESS.
BUT, I MEAN, HERE WE ARE, ALL IN THE SAME TIMELINE AGAIN? WHERE ALL I DID WAS FLIP THE FUCKERS OFF.
AND RIGHT NOW, IN A TIMELINE THAT'S SOMEHOW QUANTUM-SYNTOPIC WITH THIS ONE...
...YOU'RE TRYING TO EXPLAIN TO US HOW IT WAS A GOOD IDEA TO PEEL BACK YOUR M-VELOPE IN FRONT OF SOME WEASEL FROM GAWKER.
COULD IT BE THAT POOR LITTLE PLUSHY LADY I SMUSHED, IN 999a?
DID I DO THIS?

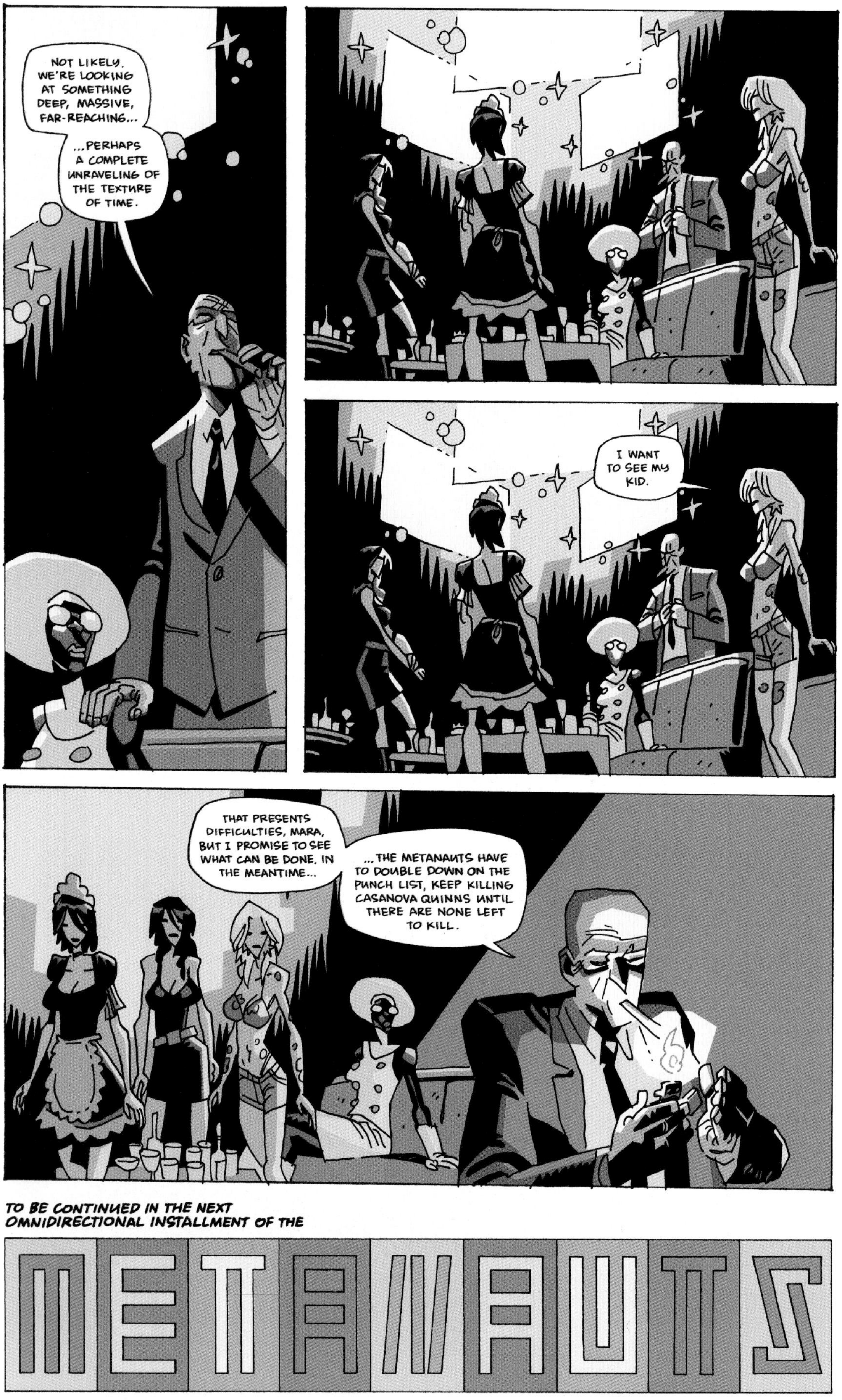
NOT LIKELY. WE'RE LOOKING AT SOMETHING DEEP, MASSIVE, FAR-REACHING...
...PERHAPS A COMPLETE UNRAVELING OF THE TEXTURE OF TIME.
I WANT TO SEE MY KID.
THAT PRESENTS DIFFICULTIES, MARA, BUT I PROMISE TO SEE WHAT CAN BE DONE. IN THE MEANTIME...
...THE METANAUTS HAVE TO DOUBLE DOWN ON THE PUNCH LIST, KEEP KILLING CASANOVA QUINNS UNTIL THERE ARE NONE LEFT TO KILL.

TO BE CONTINUED IN THE NEXT OMNIDIRECTIONAL INSTALLMENT OF THE

METANAUTS

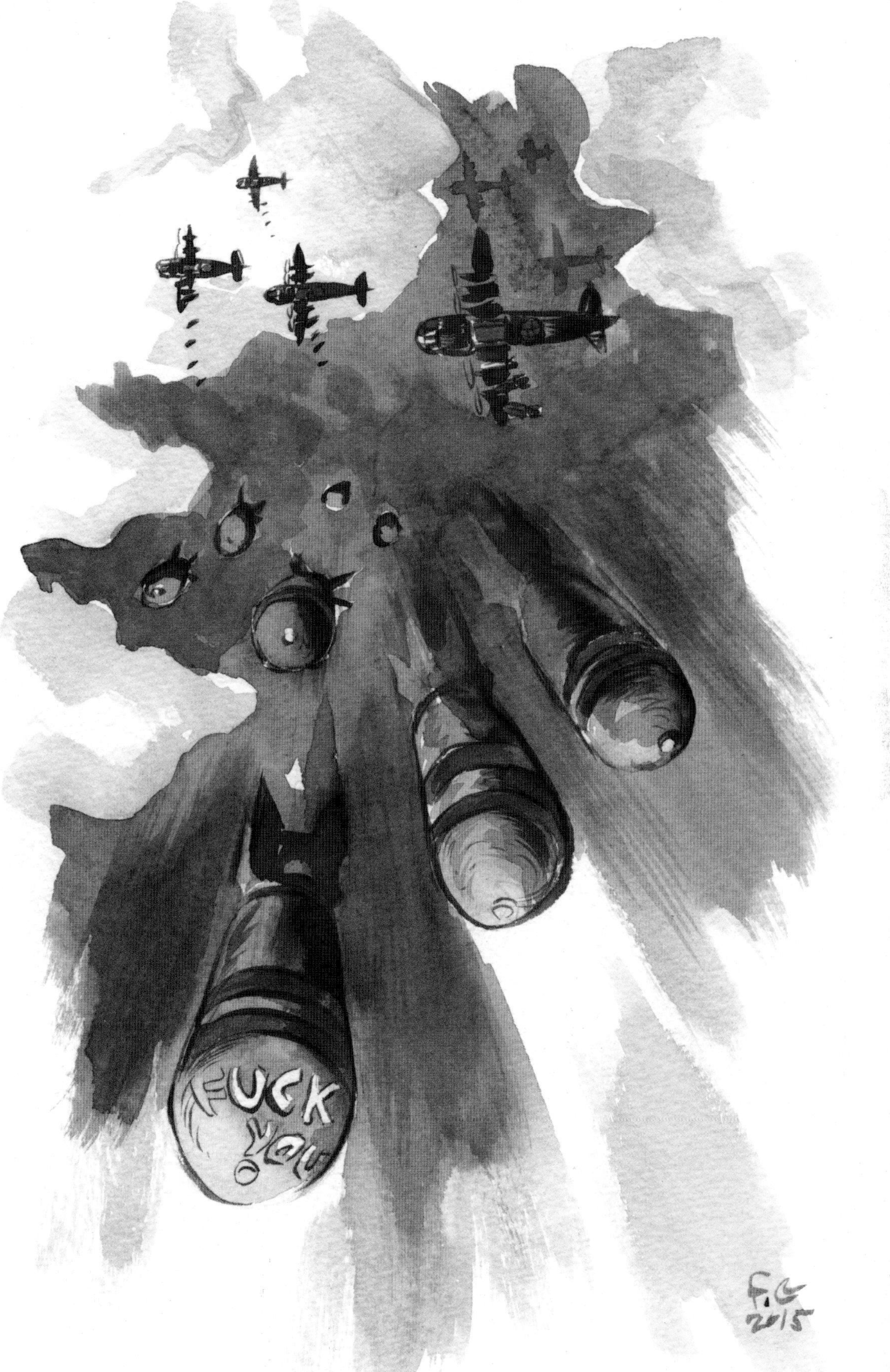
FUCK YOU

CHAPTER FOUR
AKIM ATHABADZE

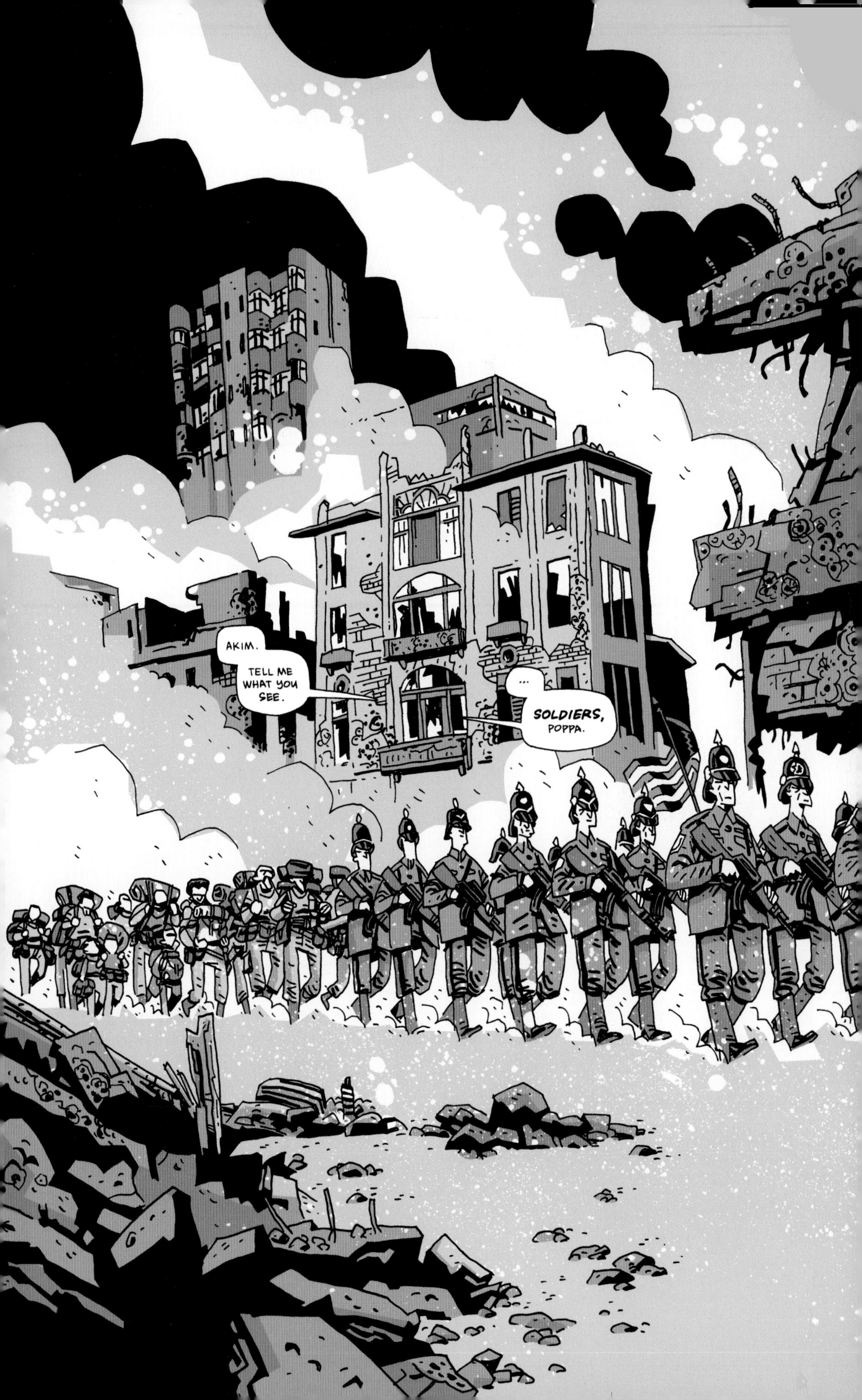
AKIM.
TELL ME WHAT YOU SEE.
...
SOLDIERS, POPPA.

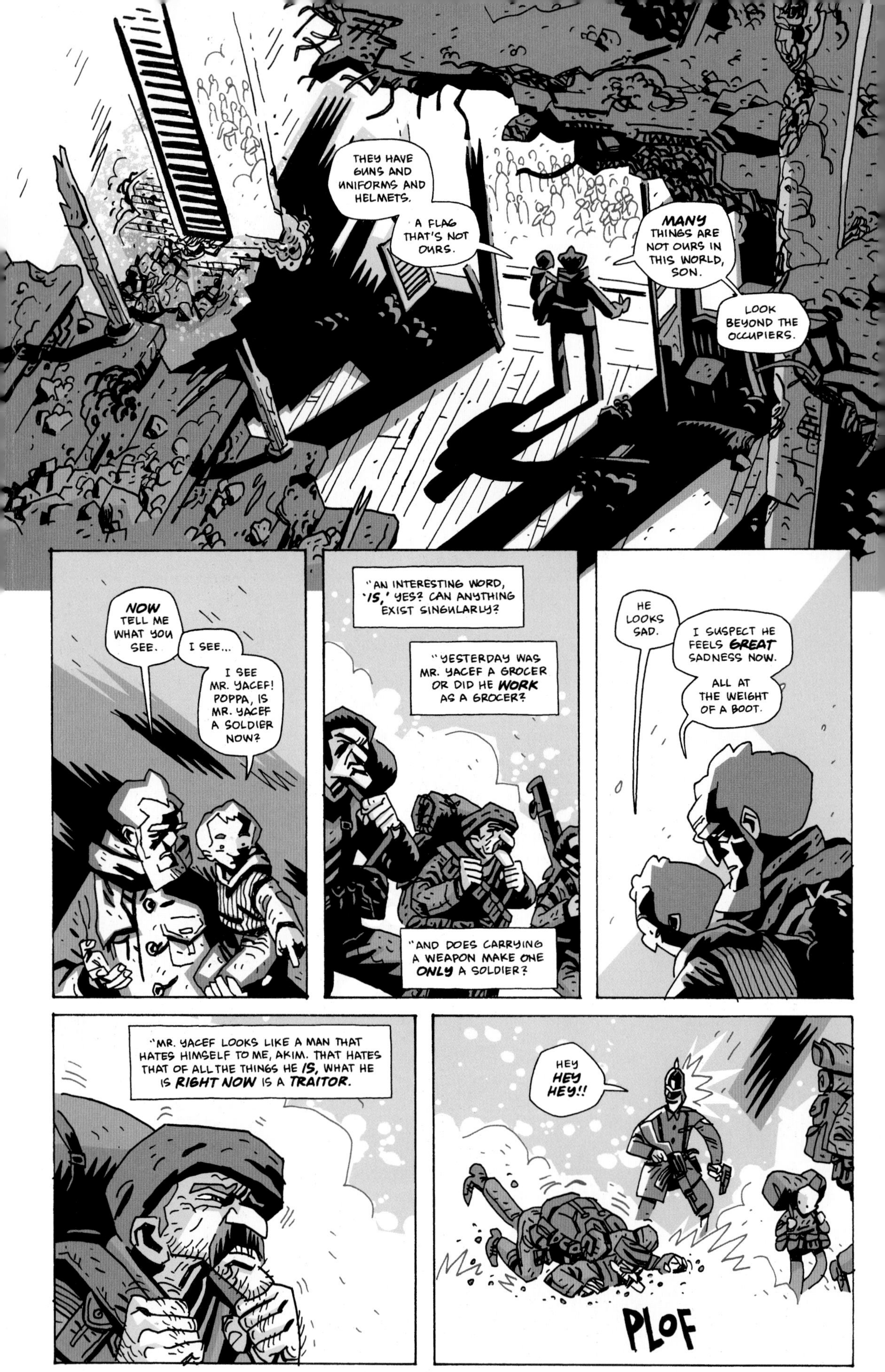
THEY HAVE GUNS AND UNIFORMS AND HELMETS.
A FLAG THAT'S NOT OURS.
MANY THINGS ARE NOT OURS IN THIS WORLD, SON.
LOOK BEYOND THE OCCUPIERS.
NOW TELL ME WHAT YOU SEE.
I SEE...
I SEE MR. YACEF! POPPA, IS MR. YACEF A SOLDIER NOW?
"AN INTERESTING WORD, 'IS,' YES? CAN ANYTHING EXIST SINGULARLY?
"YESTERDAY WAS MR. YACEF A GROCER OR DID HE WORK AS A GROCER?
"AND DOES CARRYING A WEAPON MAKE ONE ONLY A SOLDIER?
HE LOOKS SAD.
I SUSPECT HE FEELS GREAT SADNESS NOW.
ALL AT THE WEIGHT OF A BOOT.
"MR. YACEF LOOKS LIKE A MAN THAT HATES HIMSELF TO ME, AKIM. THAT HATES THAT OF ALL THE THINGS HE IS, WHAT HE IS RIGHT NOW IS A TRAITOR.
HEY HEY HEY!!
PLOF

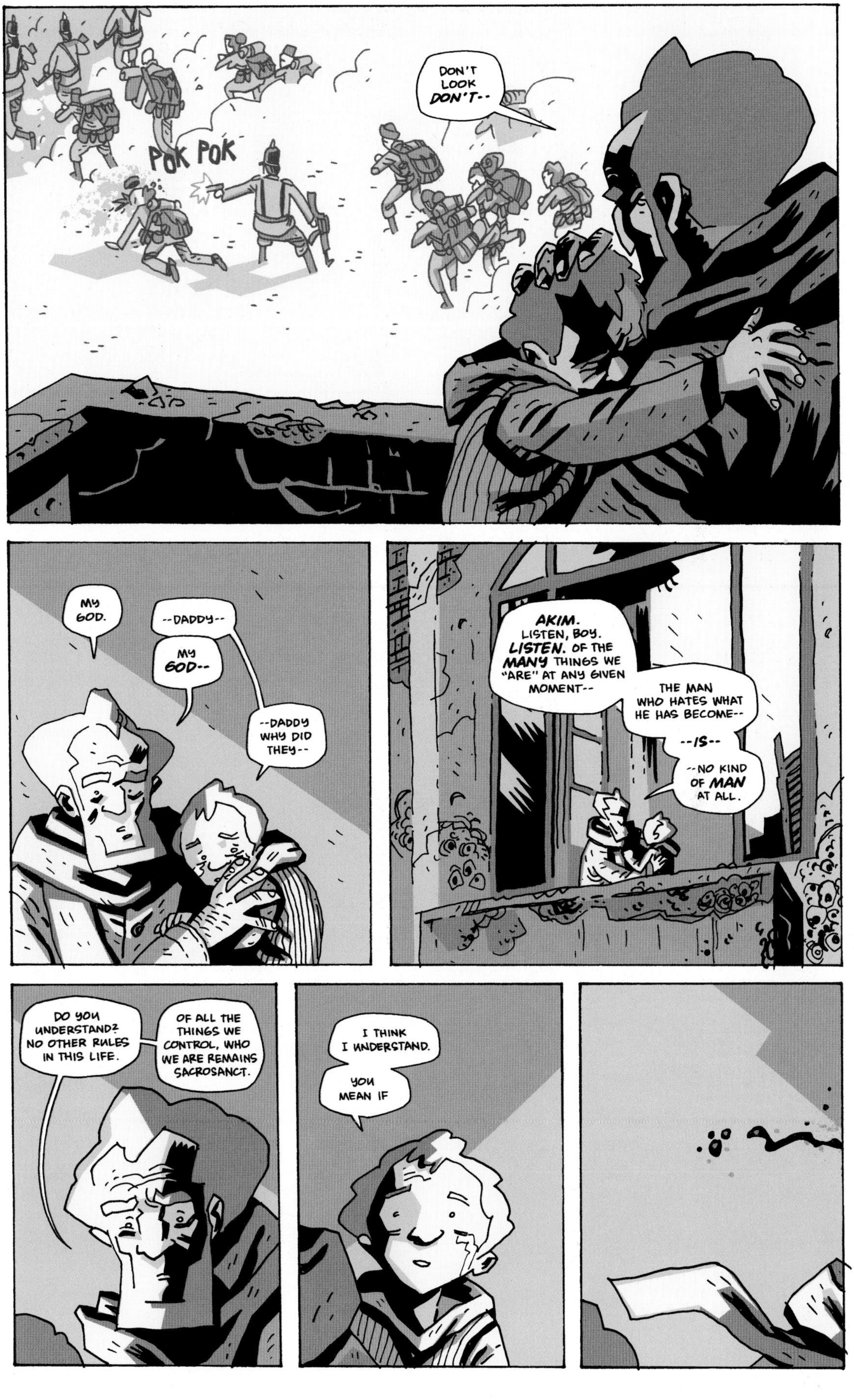
DON'T LOOK DON'T--
POK POK
MY GOD.
--DADDY--
MY GOD--
--DADDY WHY DID THEY--
AKIM. LISTEN, BOY. LISTEN. OF THE MANY THINGS WE "ARE" AT ANY GIVEN MOMENT--
THE MAN WHO HATES WHAT HE HAS BECOME--
--IS--
--NO KIND OF MAN AT ALL.
DO YOU UNDERSTAND? NO OTHER RULES IN THIS LIFE.
OF ALL THE THINGS WE CONTROL, WHO WE ARE REMAINS SACROSANCT.
I THINK I UNDERSTAND.
YOU MEAN IF

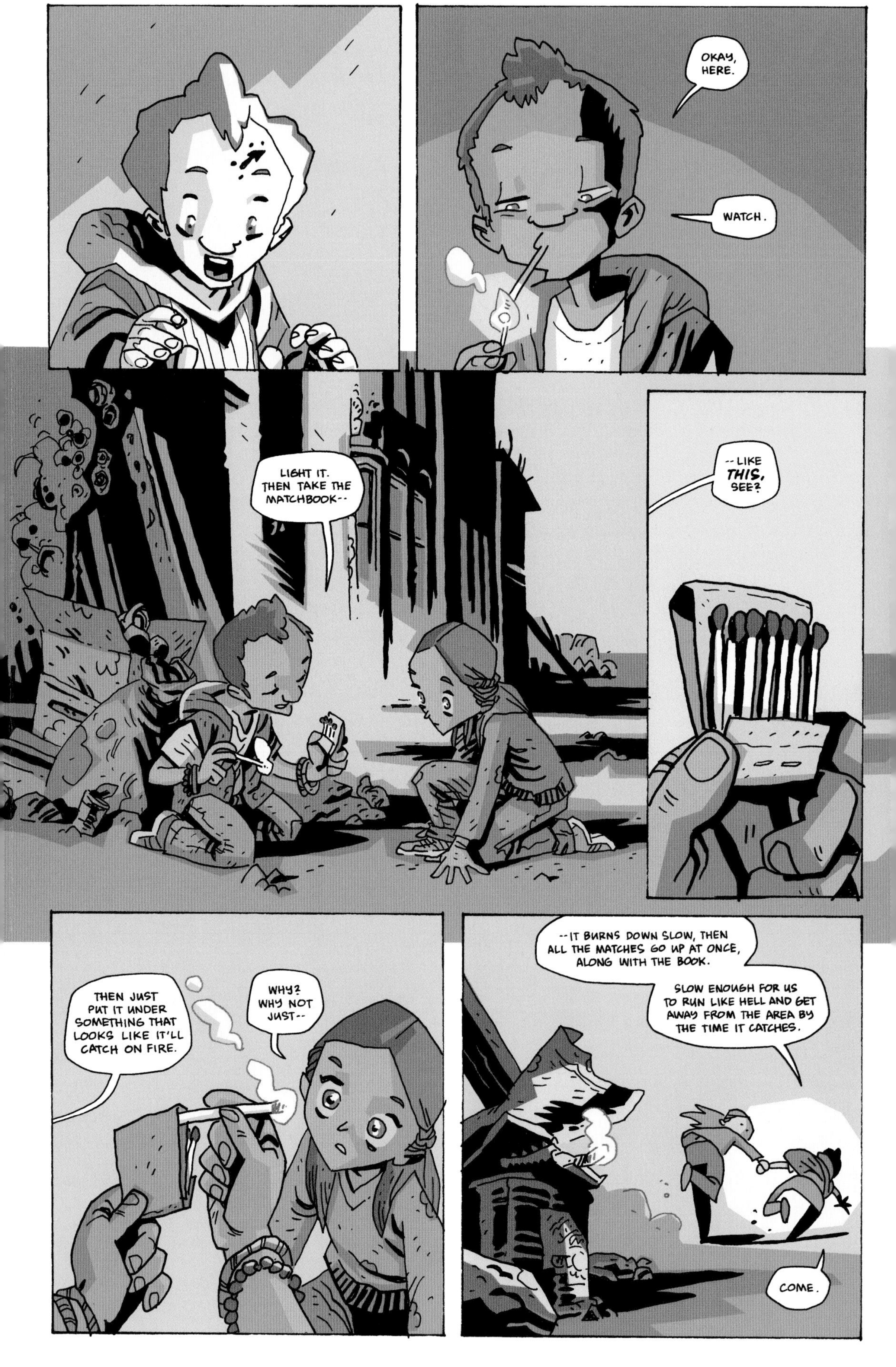
OKAY, HERE.
WATCH.
LIGHT IT. THEN TAKE THE MATCHBOOK--
--LIKE THIS, SEE?
THEN JUST PUT IT UNDER SOMETHING THAT LOOKS LIKE IT'LL CATCH ON FIRE.
WHY? WHY NOT JUST--
--IT BURNS DOWN SLOW, THEN ALL THE MATCHES GO UP AT ONCE, ALONG WITH THE BOOK.
SLOW ENOUGH FOR US TO RUN LIKE HELL AND GET AWAY FROM THE AREA BY THE TIME IT CATCHES.
COME.

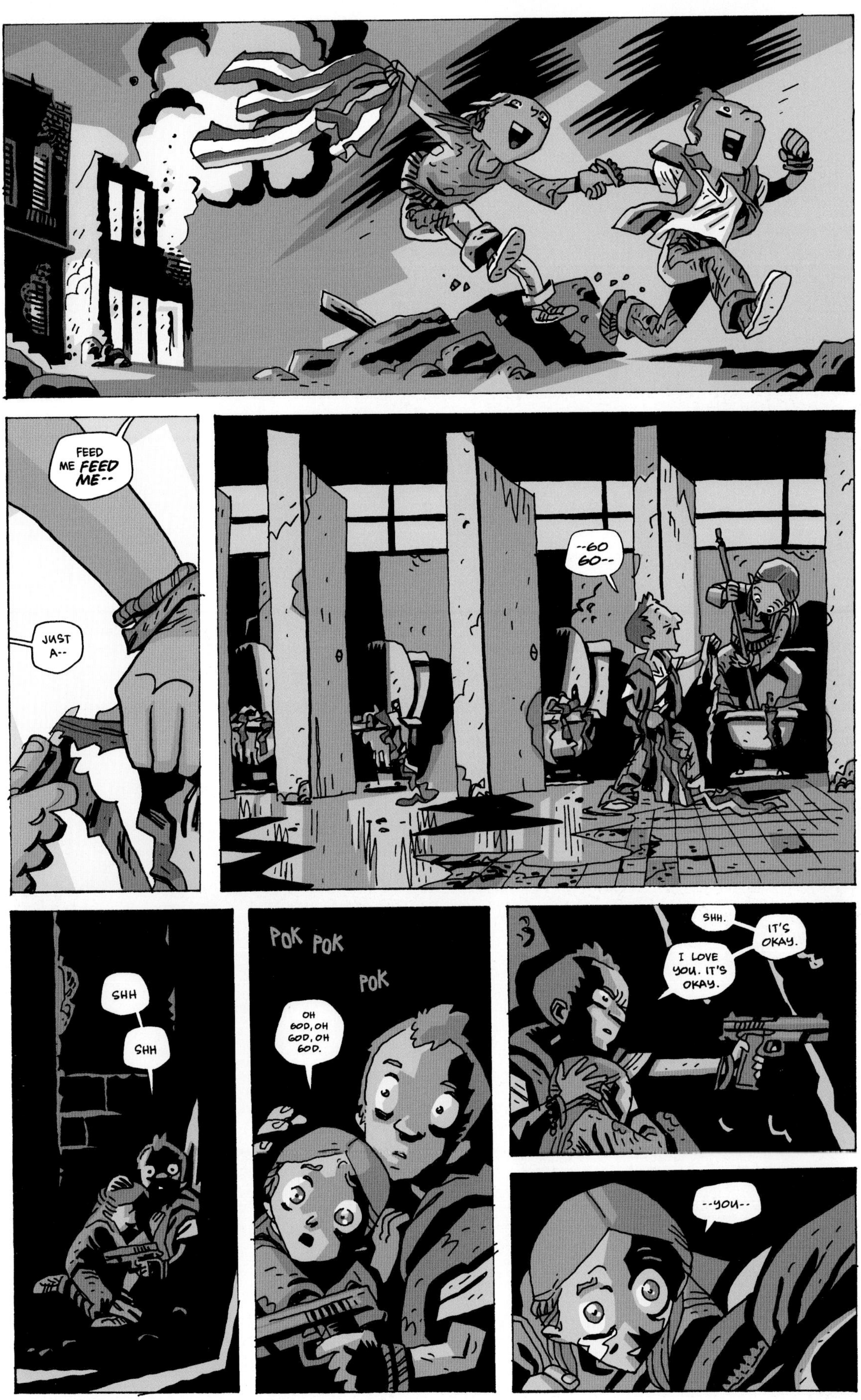
FEED ME FEED ME--
JUST A--
--GO GO--
SHH
SHH
POK POK
POK
OH GOD, OH GOD, OH GOD.
SHH.
IT'S OKAY.
I LOVE YOU. IT'S OKAY.
--YOU--

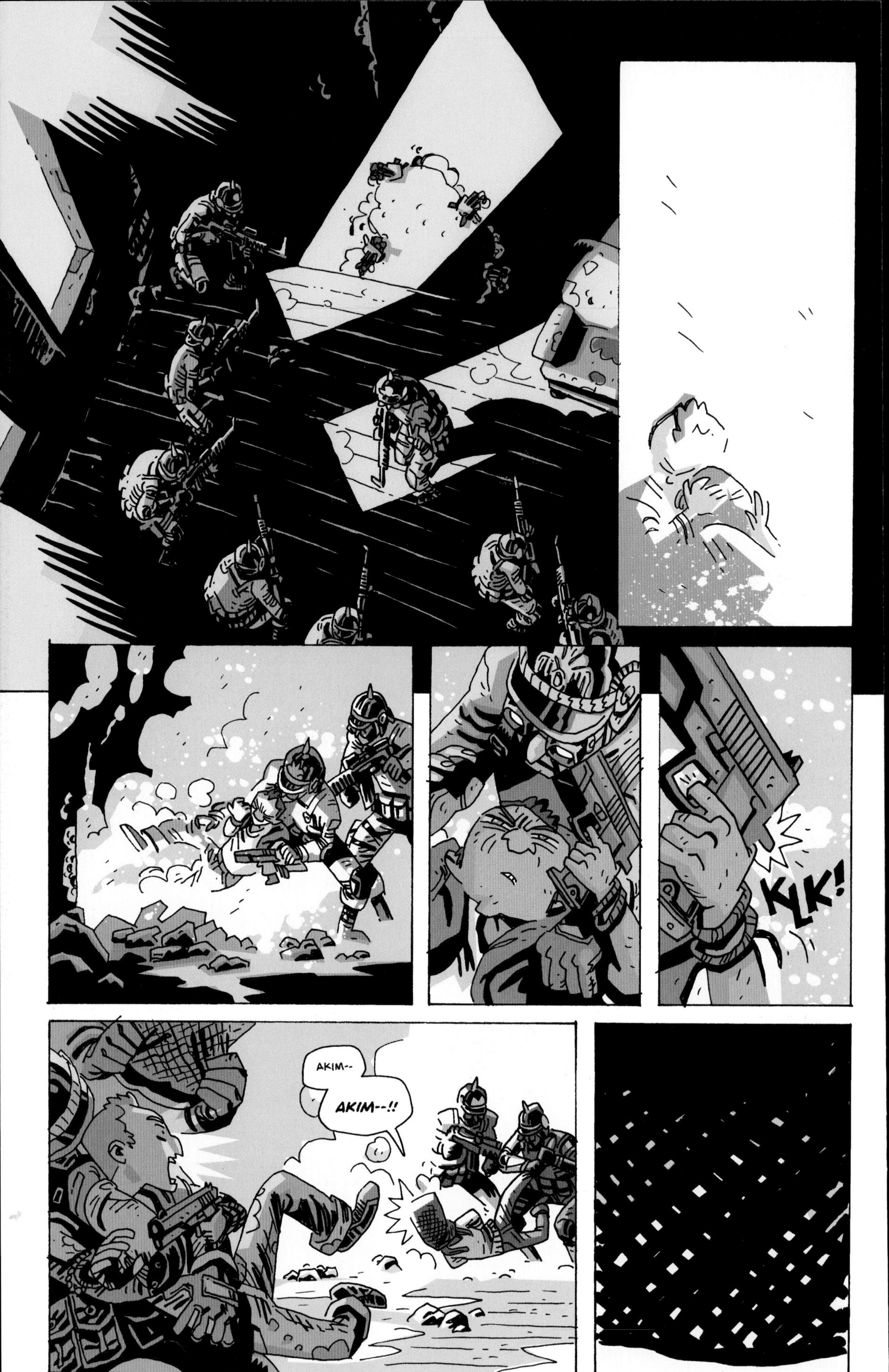
KLIK!
AKIM--
AKIM--!!

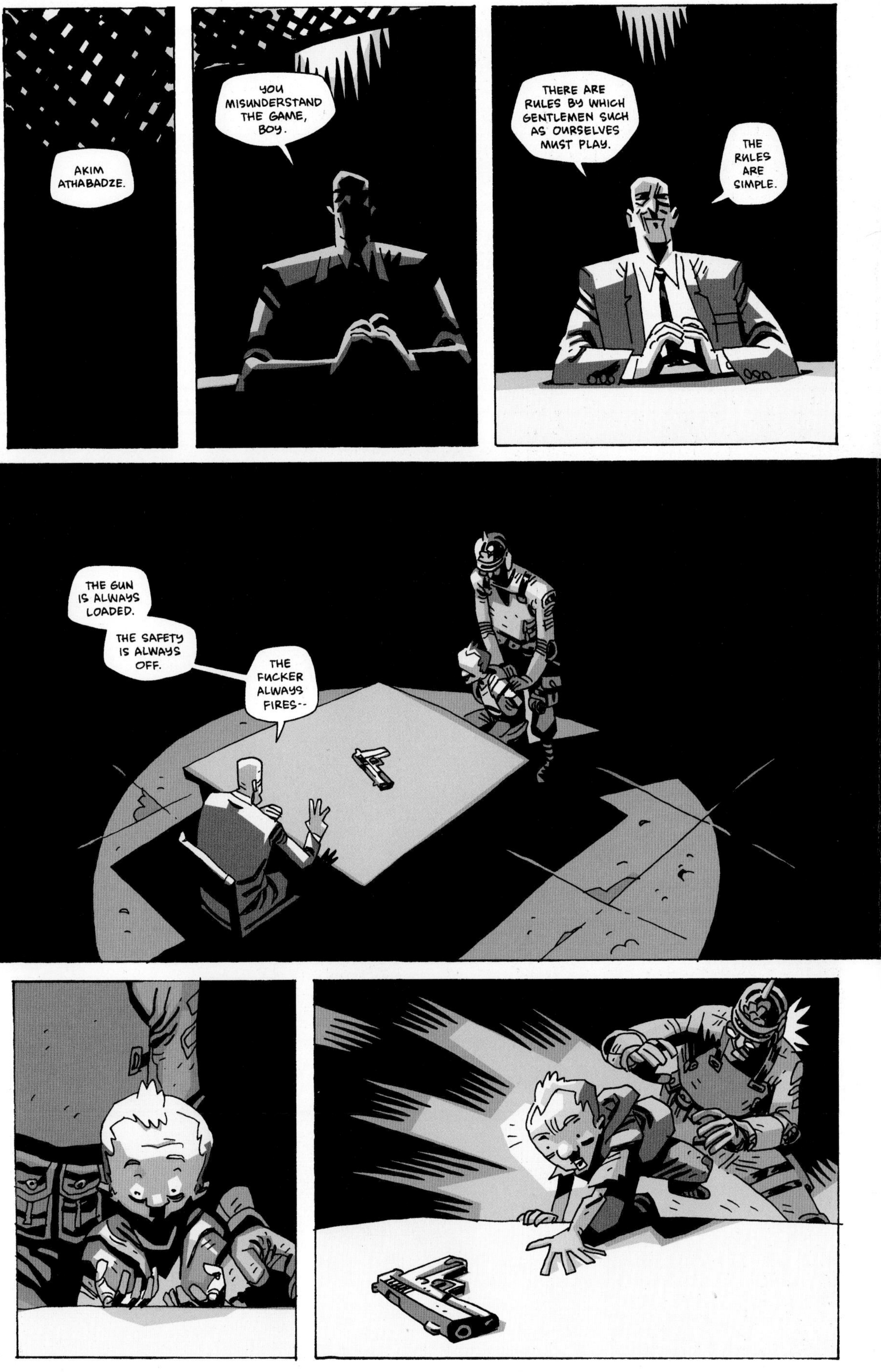
AKIM ATHABADZE.
YOU MISUNDERSTAND THE GAME, BOY.
THERE ARE RULES BY WHICH GENTLEMEN SUCH AS OURSELVES MUST PLAY.
THE RULES ARE SIMPLE.
THE GUN IS ALWAYS LOADED.
THE SAFETY IS ALWAYS OFF.
THE FUCKER ALWAYS FIRES--

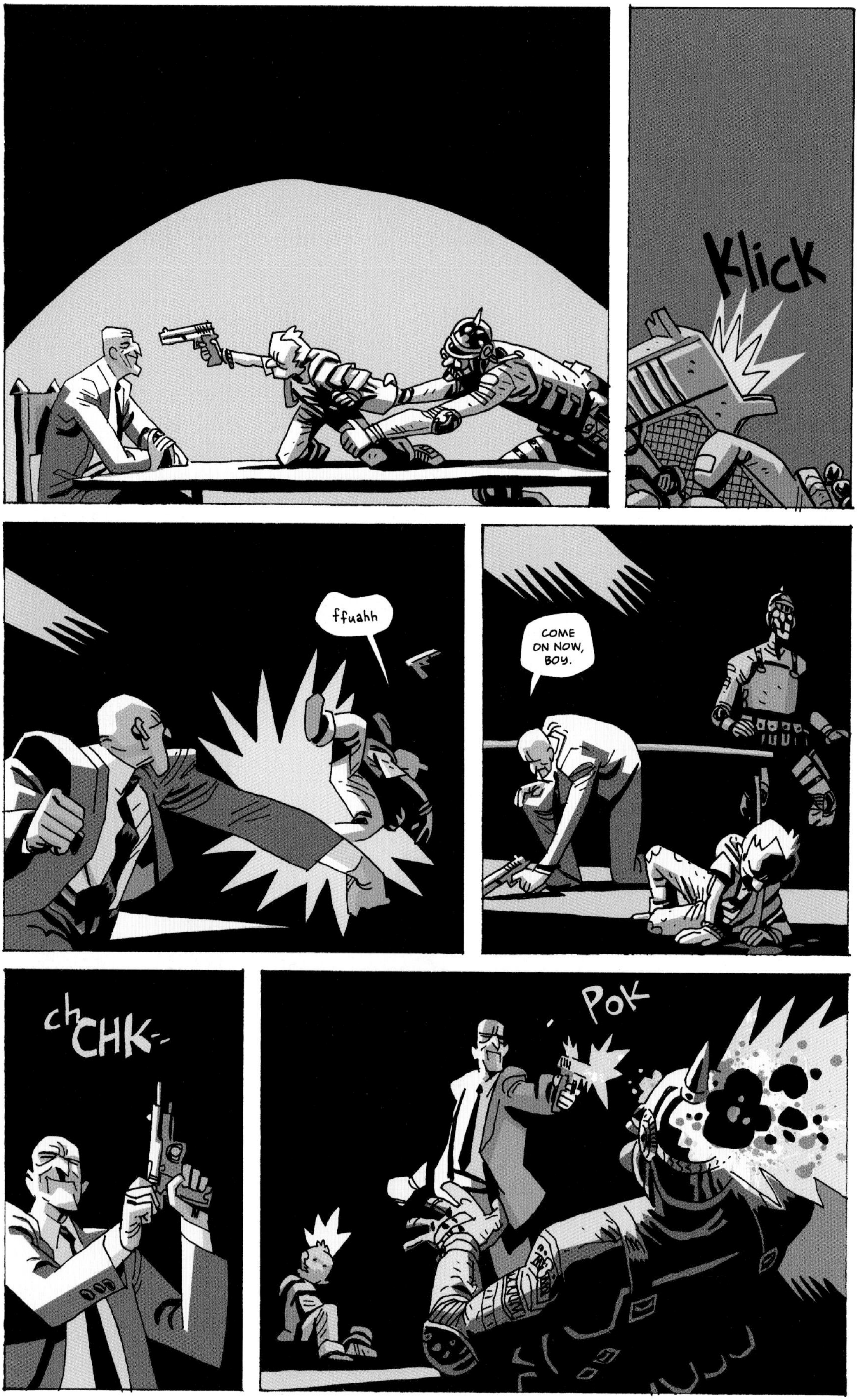
Klick
ffuahh
COME ON NOW, BOY.
chCHK
POK

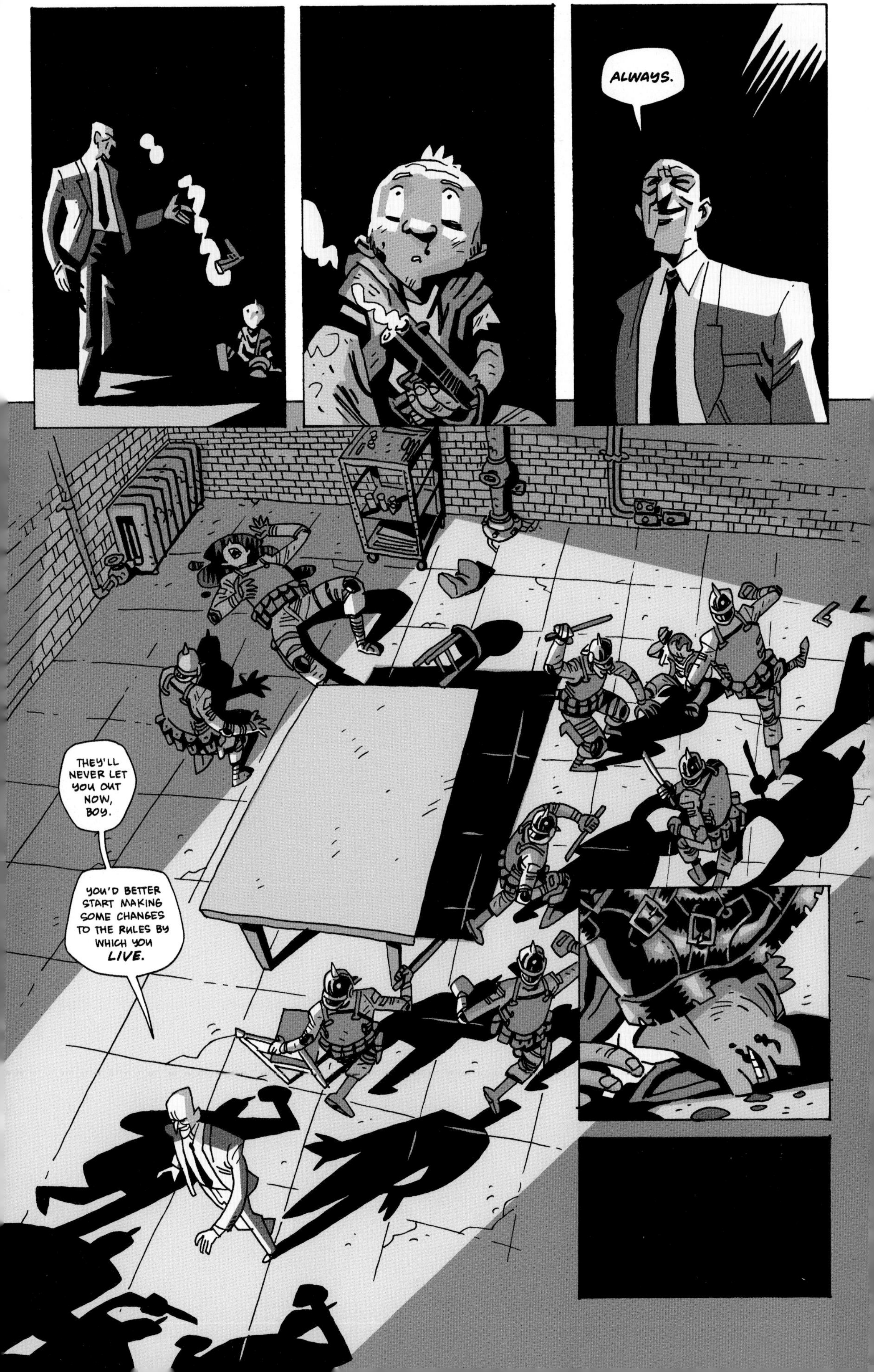
ALWAYS.
THEY'LL NEVER LET YOU OUT NOW, BOY.
YOU'D BETTER START MAKING SOME CHANGES TO THE RULES BY WHICH YOU LIVE.

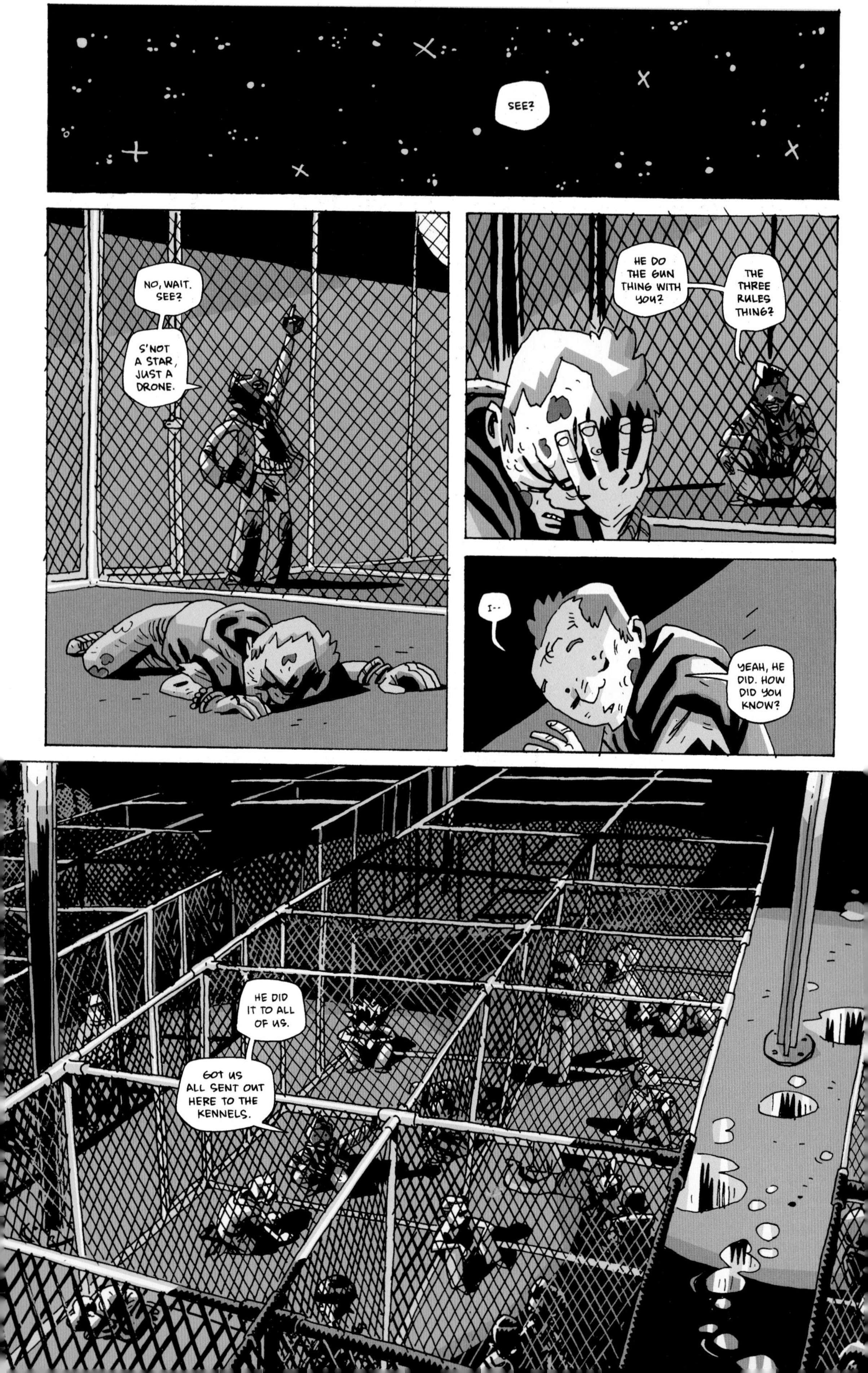
SEE?
NO, WAIT. SEE?
S'NOT A STAR, JUST A DRONE.
HE DO THE GUN THING WITH YOU?
THE THREE RULES THING?
I--
YEAH, HE DID. HOW DID YOU KNOW?
HE DID IT TO ALL OF US.
GOT US ALL SENT OUT HERE TO THE KENNELS.

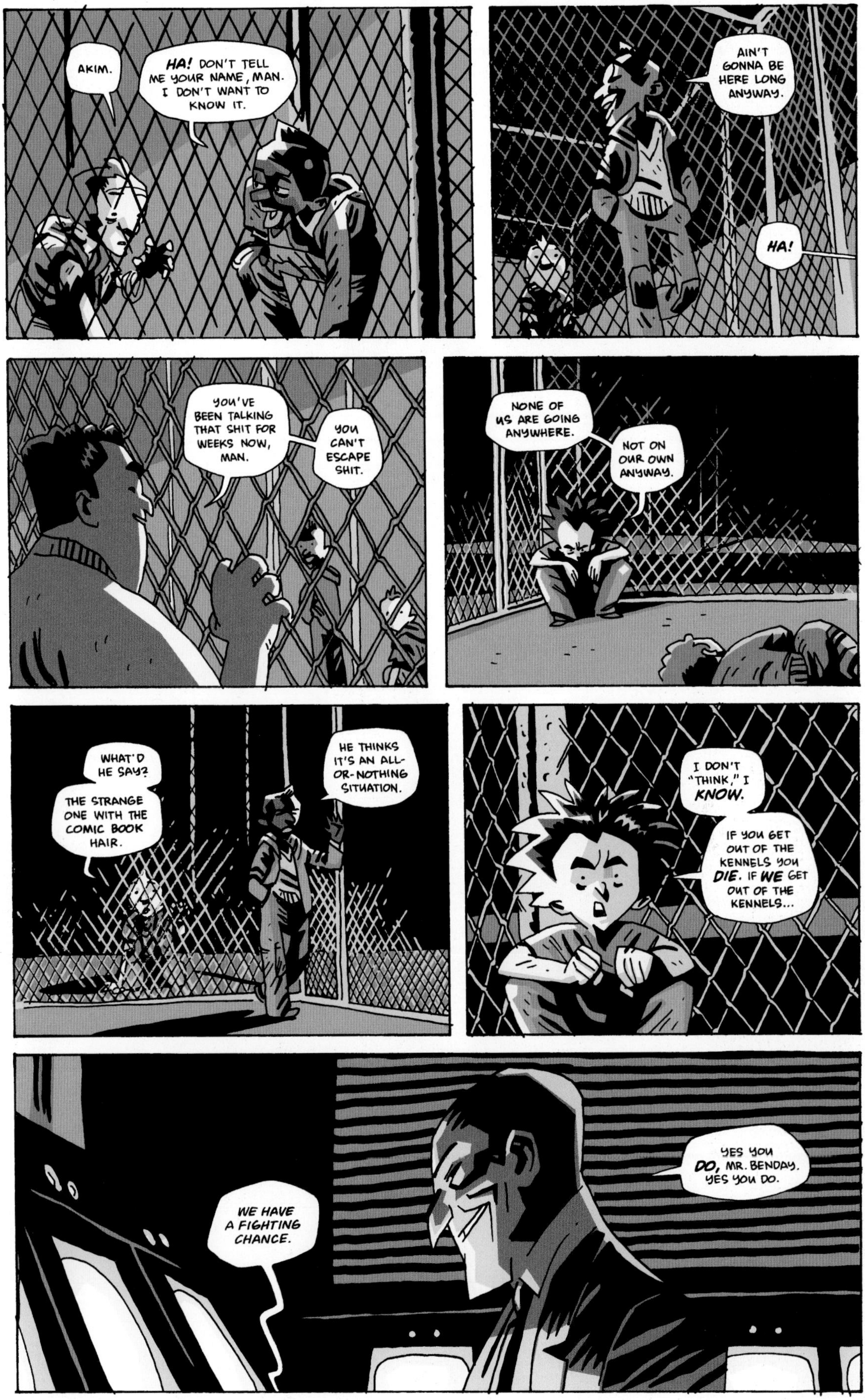
AKIM.
HA! DON'T TELL ME YOUR NAME, MAN. I DON'T WANT TO KNOW IT.
AIN'T GONNA BE HERE LONG ANYWAY.
HA!
YOU'VE BEEN TALKING THAT SHIT FOR WEEKS NOW, MAN.
YOU CAN'T ESCAPE SHIT.
NONE OF US ARE GOING ANYWHERE.
NOT ON OUR OWN ANYWAY.
WHAT'D HE SAY?
THE STRANGE ONE WITH THE COMIC BOOK HAIR.
HE THINKS IT'S AN ALL-OR-NOTHING SITUATION.
I DON'T "THINK," I KNOW.
IF YOU GET OUT OF THE KENNELS YOU DIE. IF WE GET OUT OF THE KENNELS...
WE HAVE A FIGHTING CHANCE.
YES YOU DO, MR. BENDAY. YES YOU DO.

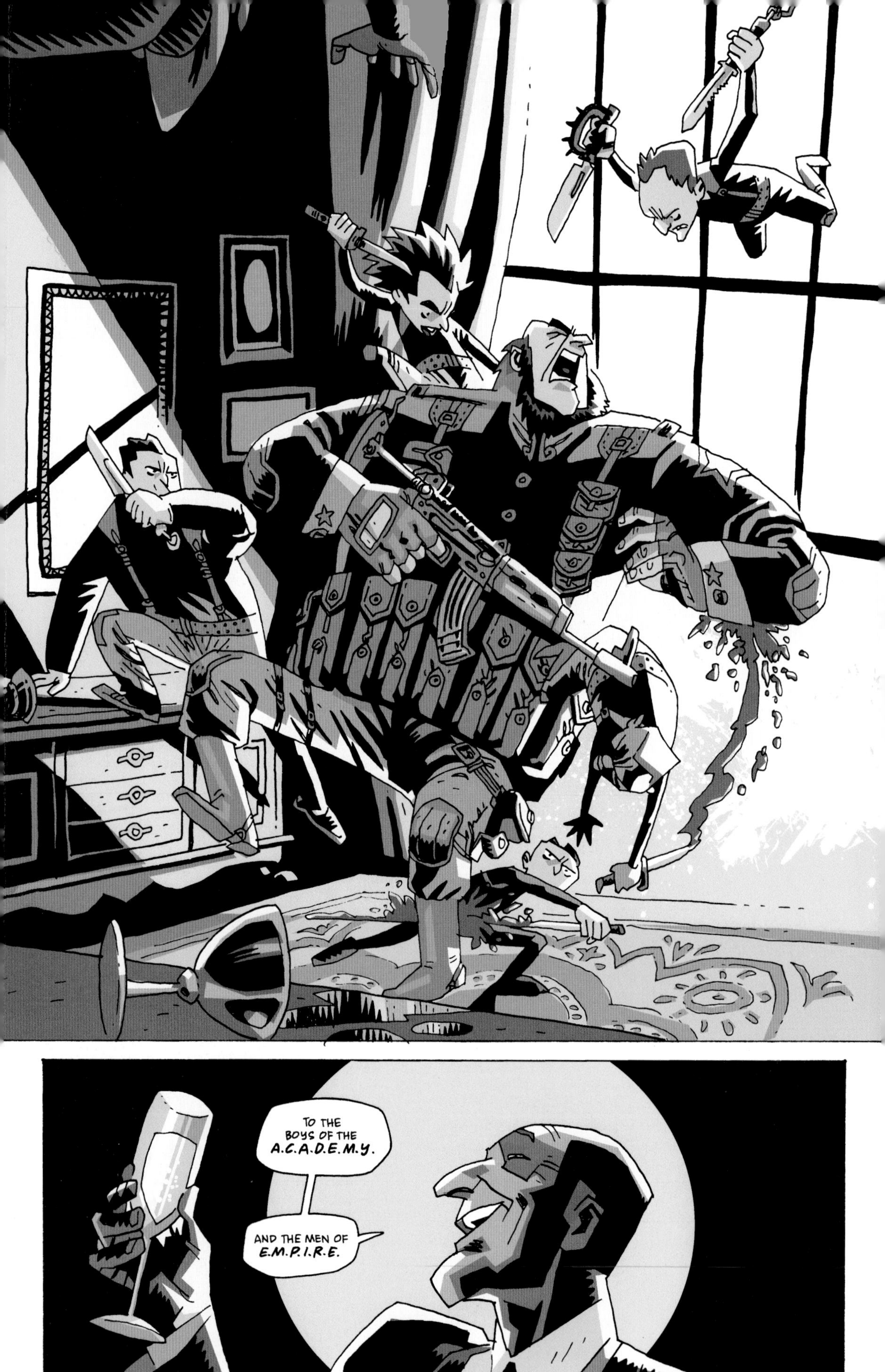
TO THE BOYS OF THE A.C.A.D.E.M.Y.
AND THE MEN OF E.M.P.I.R.E.

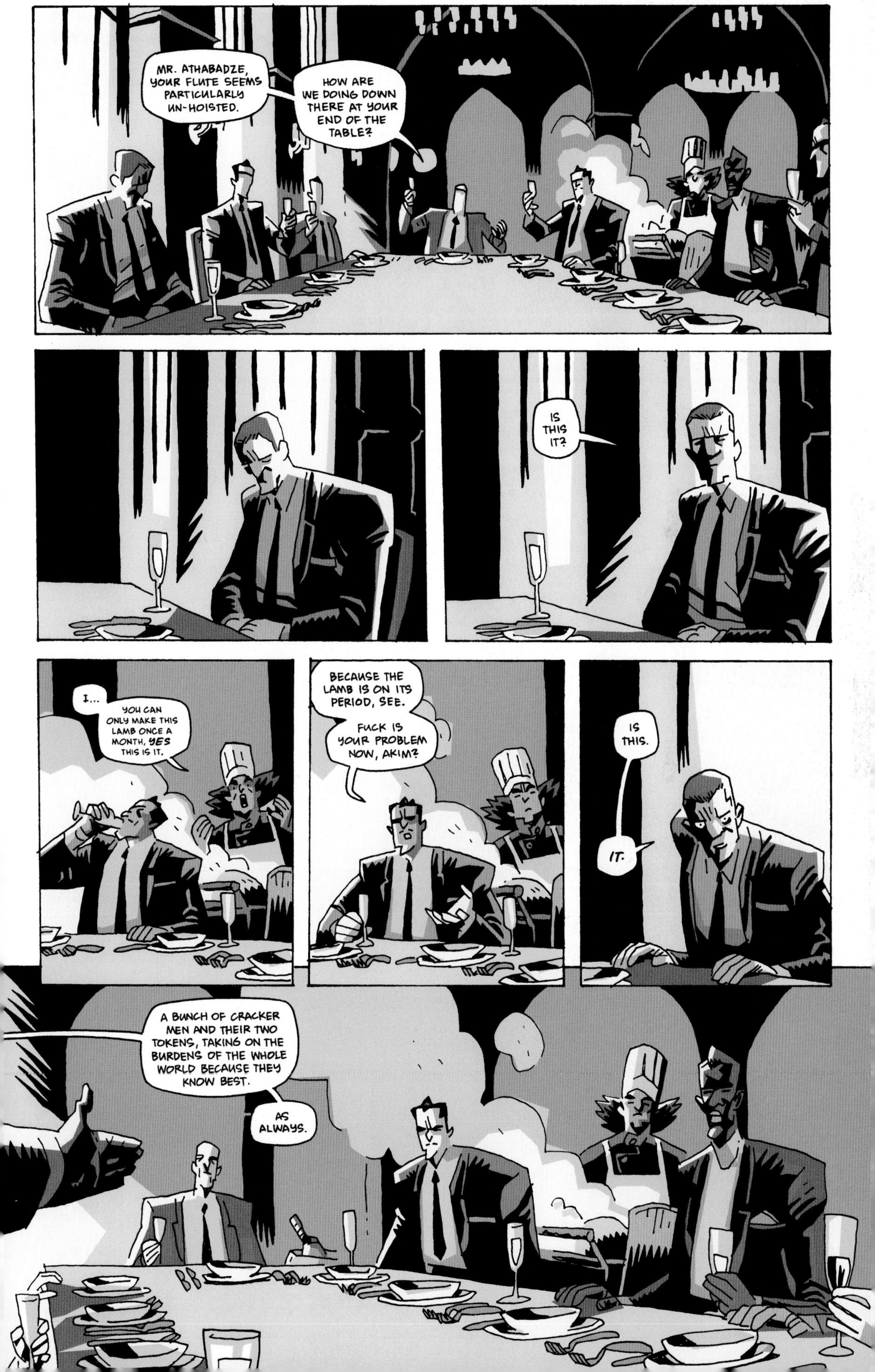
MR. ATHABADZE, YOUR FLUTE SEEMS PARTICULARLY UN-HOISTED.
HOW ARE WE DOING DOWN THERE AT YOUR END OF THE TABLE?
IS THIS IT?
I...
YOU CAN ONLY MAKE THIS LAMB ONCE A MONTH, YES THIS IS IT.
BECAUSE THE LAMB IS ON ITS PERIOD, SEE.
FUCK IS YOUR PROBLEM NOW, AKIM?
IS THIS.
IT.
A BUNCH OF CRACKER MEN AND THEIR TWO TOKENS, TAKING ON THE BURDENS OF THE WHOLE WORLD BECAUSE THEY KNOW BEST.
AS ALWAYS.

"HERE WE VIOLENTLY ASSERT OURSELVES AS *RIGHT* BECAUSE WE HAVE ALL BEEN SO WRONGED...

...TRYING TO REMAKE THE *WORLD* IN OUR IMAGE.

WE LOOK NOTHING LIKE IT BUT WE ACT THE SAME.

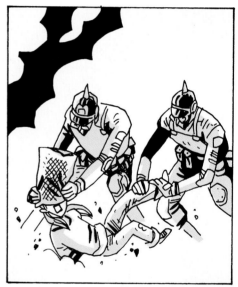

WHAT ARE WE BECOMING, CORNELIUS?

AKIM, COME *ON*, MAN.

YOU GONNA COME ALONG WITH ME ON THIS THING I GOTTA DO OR WHAT?

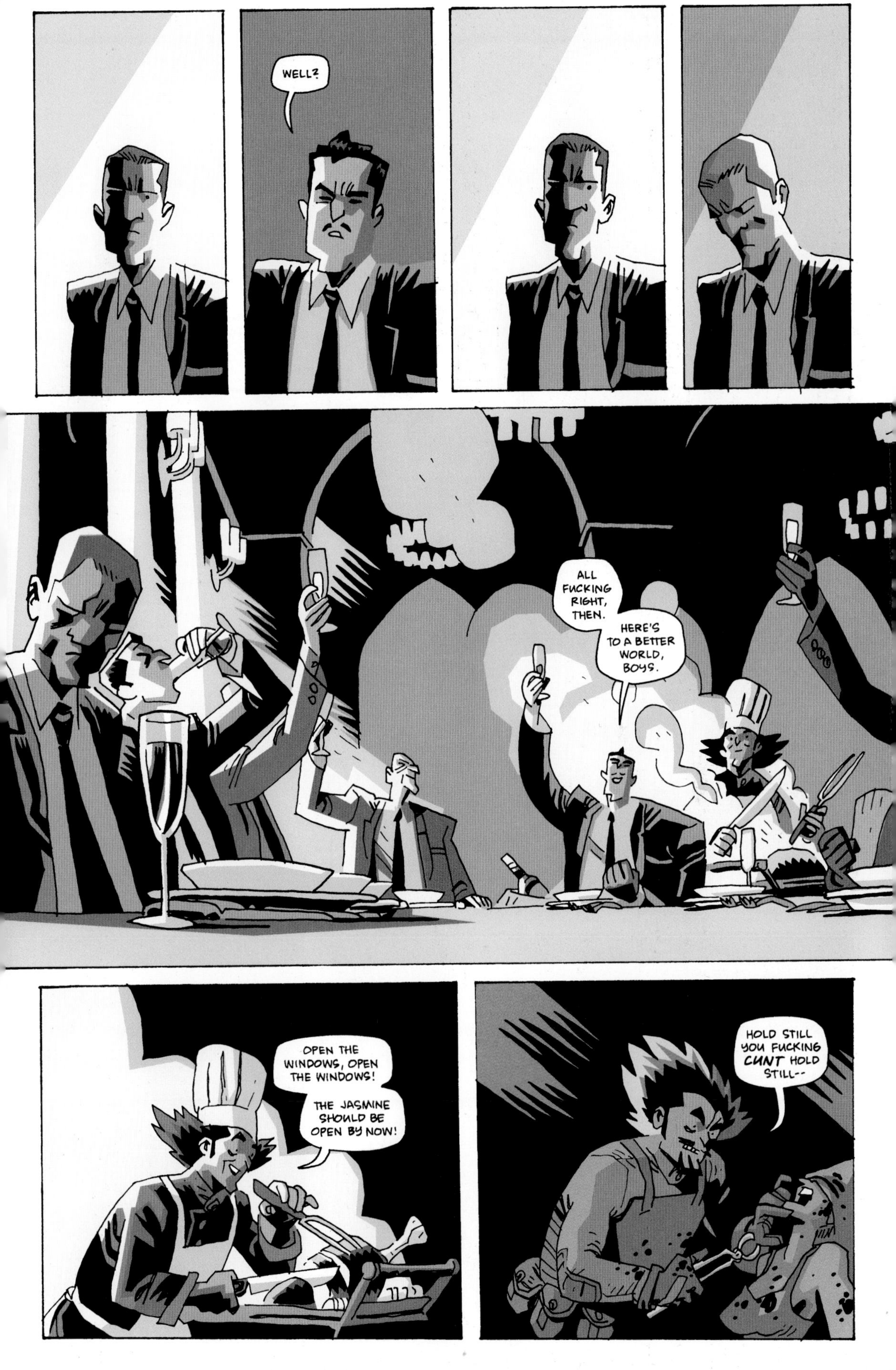
WELL?
ALL FUCKING RIGHT, THEN.
HERE'S TO A BETTER WORLD, BOYS.
OPEN THE WINDOWS, OPEN THE WINDOWS!
THE JASMINE SHOULD BE OPEN BY NOW!
HOLD STILL YOU FUCKING CUNT HOLD STILL--

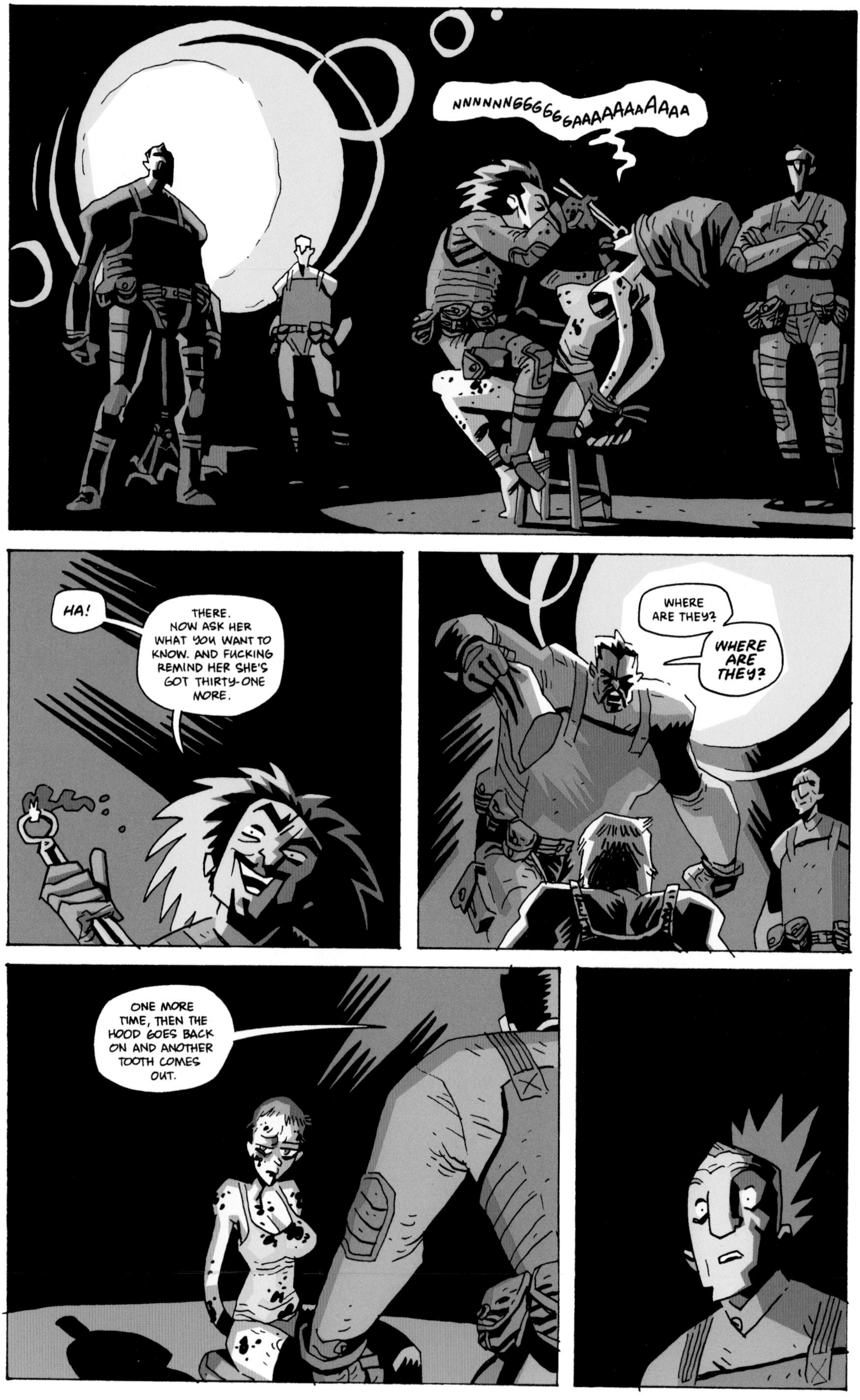
NNNNNNGGGGGGAAAAAAAAAAAA
HA!
THERE. NOW ASK HER WHAT YOU WANT TO KNOW. AND FUCKING REMIND HER SHE'S GOT THIRTY-ONE MORE.
WHERE ARE THEY?
WHERE ARE THEY?
ONE MORE TIME, THEN THE HOOD GOES BACK ON AND ANOTHER TOOTH COMES OUT.

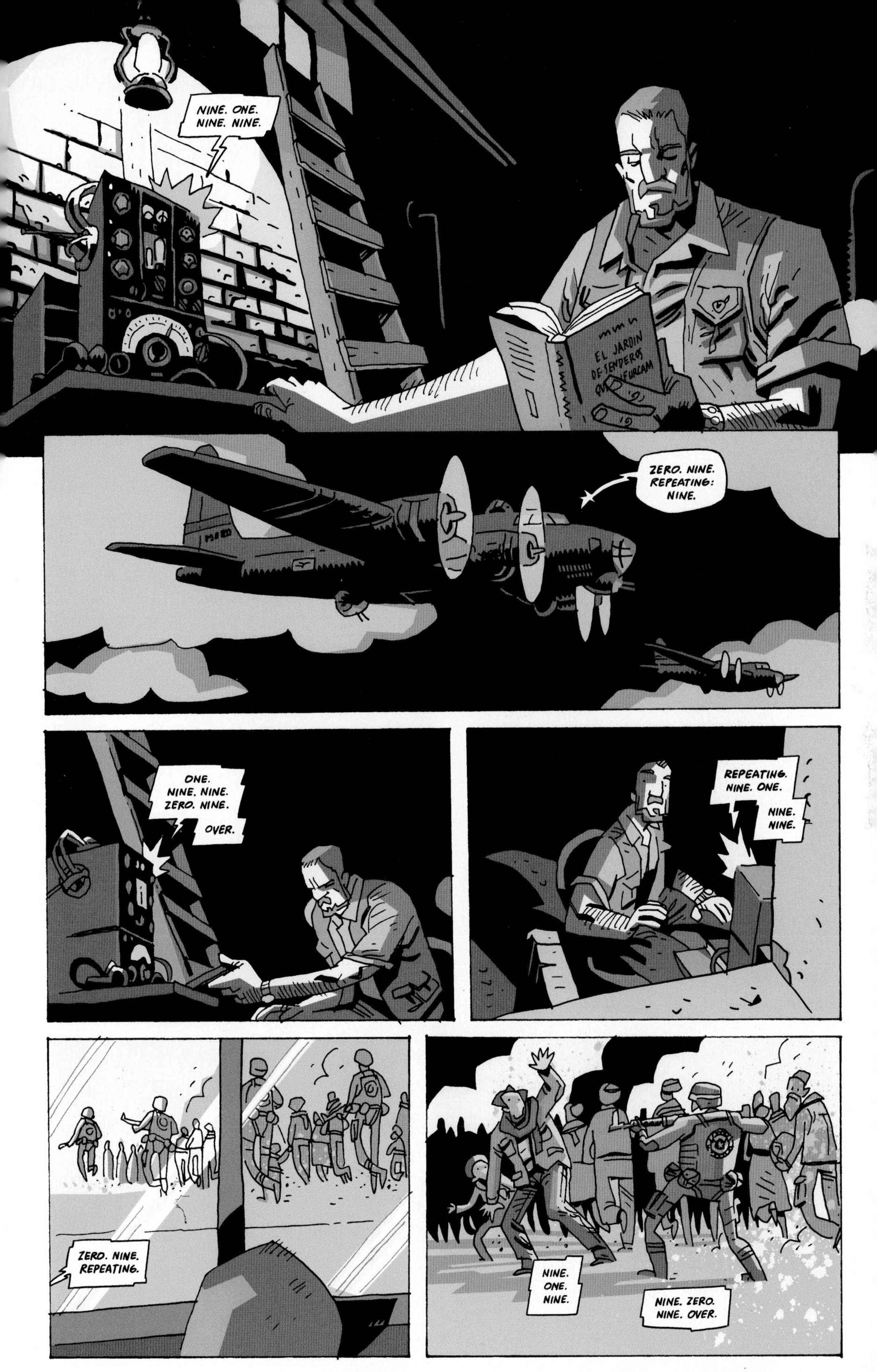
NINE. ONE. NINE. NINE.
EL JARDIN DE SENDEROS
ZERO. NINE. REPEATING: NINE.
ONE. NINE. NINE. ZERO. NINE.
OVER.
REPEATING. NINE. ONE.
NINE. NINE.
ZERO. NINE. REPEATING.
NINE. ONE. NINE.
NINE. ZERO. NINE. OVER.

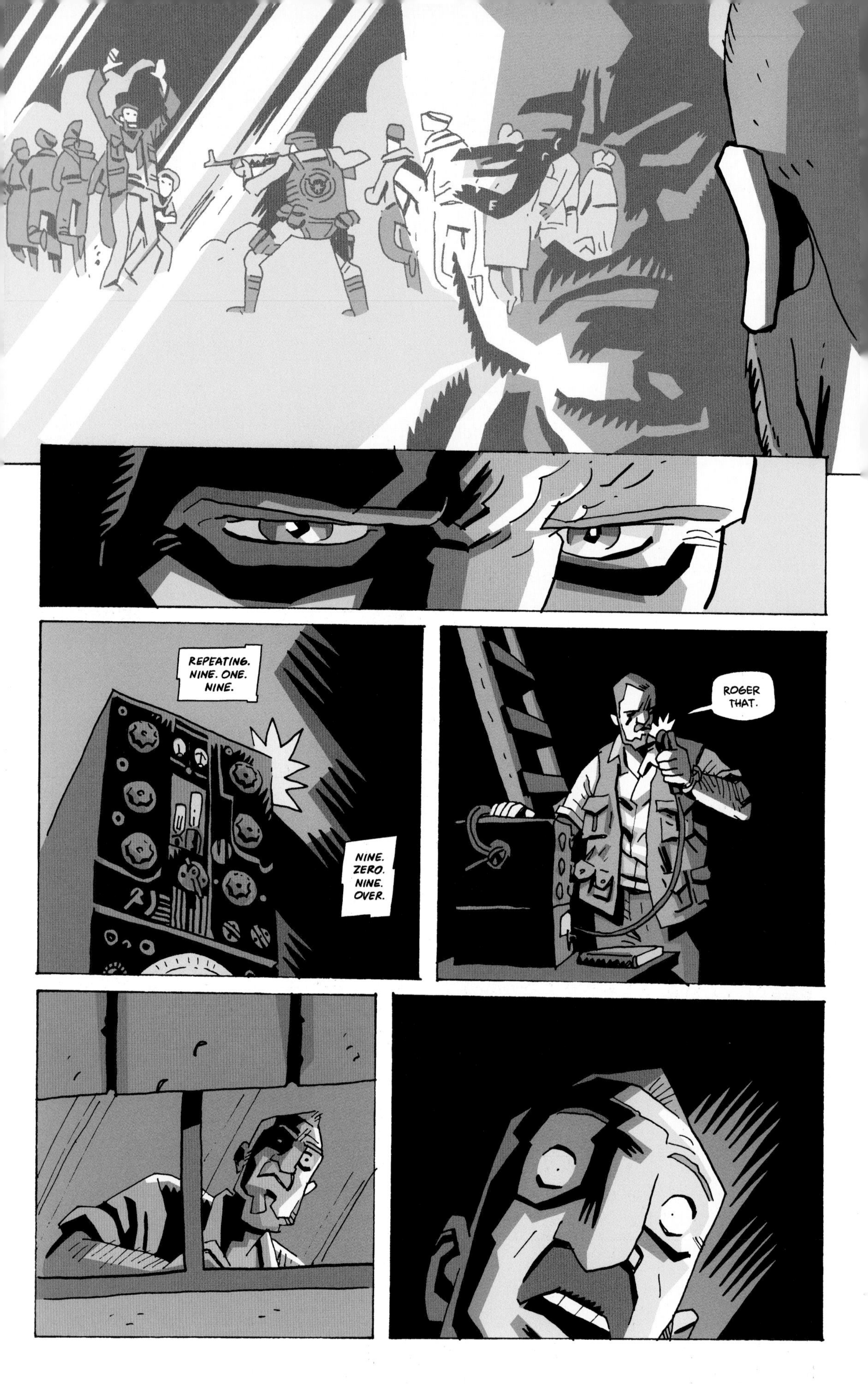
REPEATING. NINE. ONE. NINE.
NINE. ZERO. NINE. OVER.
ROGER THAT.

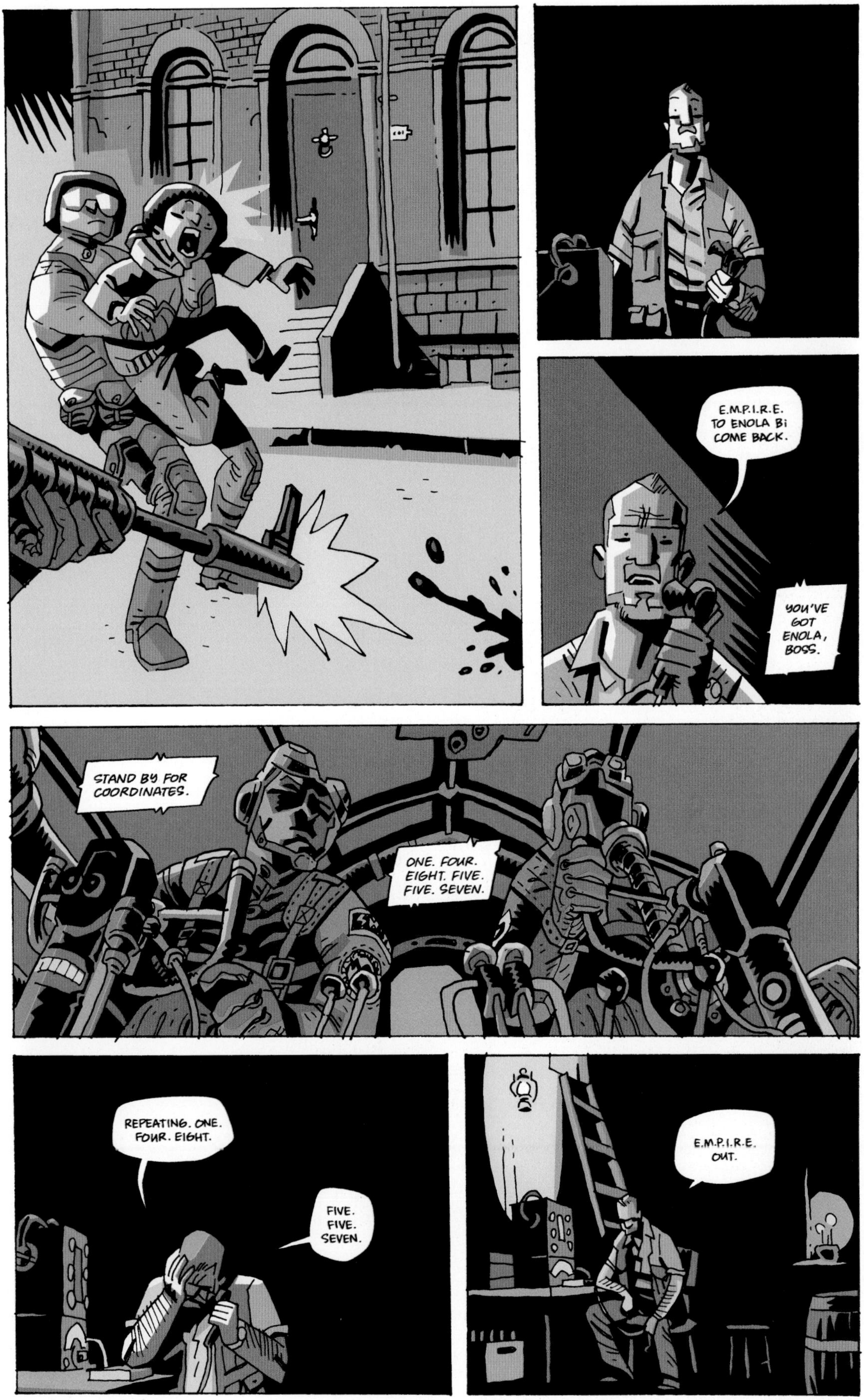
E.M.P.I.R.E. TO ENOLA Bi COME BACK.
YOU'VE GOT ENOLA, BOSS.
STAND BY FOR COORDINATES.
ONE. FOUR. EIGHT. FIVE. FIVE. SEVEN.
REPEATING. ONE. FOUR. EIGHT.
FIVE. FIVE. SEVEN.
E.M.P.I.R.E. OUT.

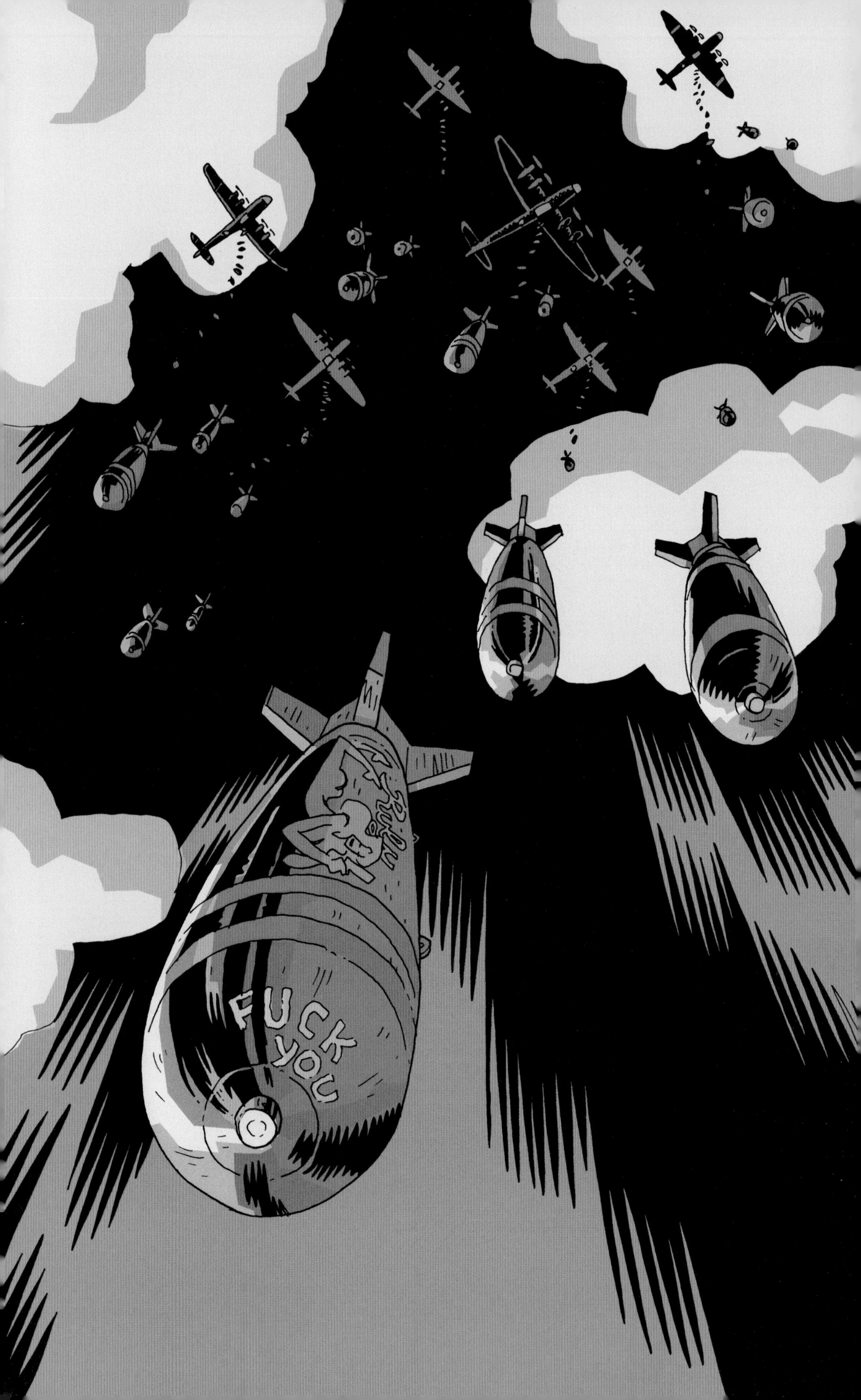
FUCK YOU

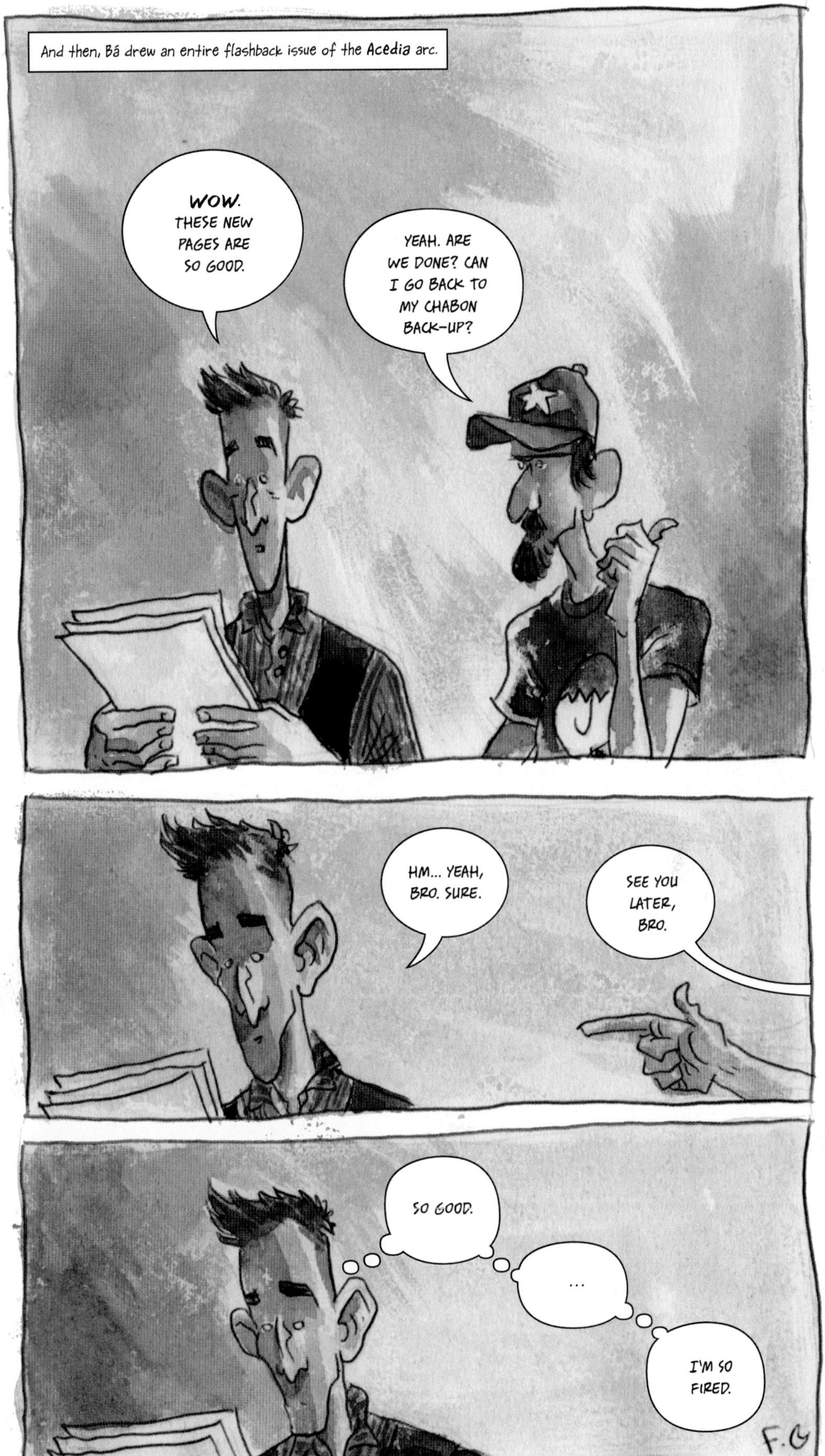
And then, Bá drew an entire flashback issue of the Acedia arc.
WOW. THESE NEW PAGES ARE SO GOOD.
YEAH. ARE WE DONE? CAN I GO BACK TO MY CHABON BACK-UP?
HM... YEAH, BRO. SURE.
SEE YOU LATER, BRO.
SO GOOD.
...
I'M SO FIRED.
F.G

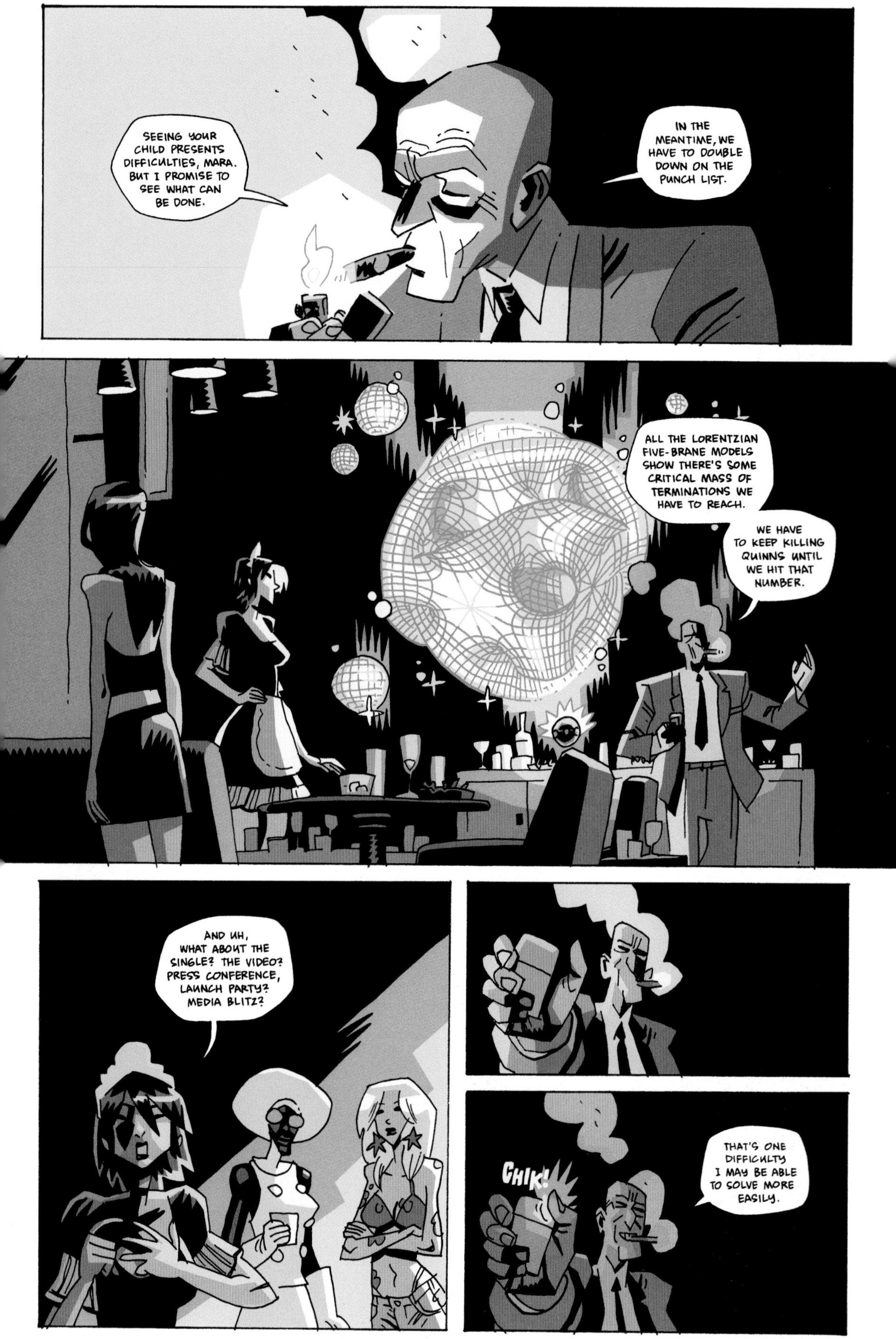
SEEING YOUR CHILD PRESENTS DIFFICULTIES, MARA. BUT I PROMISE TO SEE WHAT CAN BE DONE.
IN THE MEANTIME, WE HAVE TO DOUBLE DOWN ON THE PUNCH LIST.
ALL THE LORENTZIAN FIVE-BRANE MODELS SHOW THERE'S SOME CRITICAL MASS OF TERMINATIONS WE HAVE TO REACH.
WE HAVE TO KEEP KILLING QUINNS UNTIL WE HIT THAT NUMBER.
AND UH, WHAT ABOUT THE SINGLE? THE VIDEO? PRESS CONFERENCE, LAUNCH PARTY? MEDIA BLITZ?
CHIK!
THAT'S ONE DIFFICULTY I MAY BE ABLE TO SOLVE MORE EASILY.

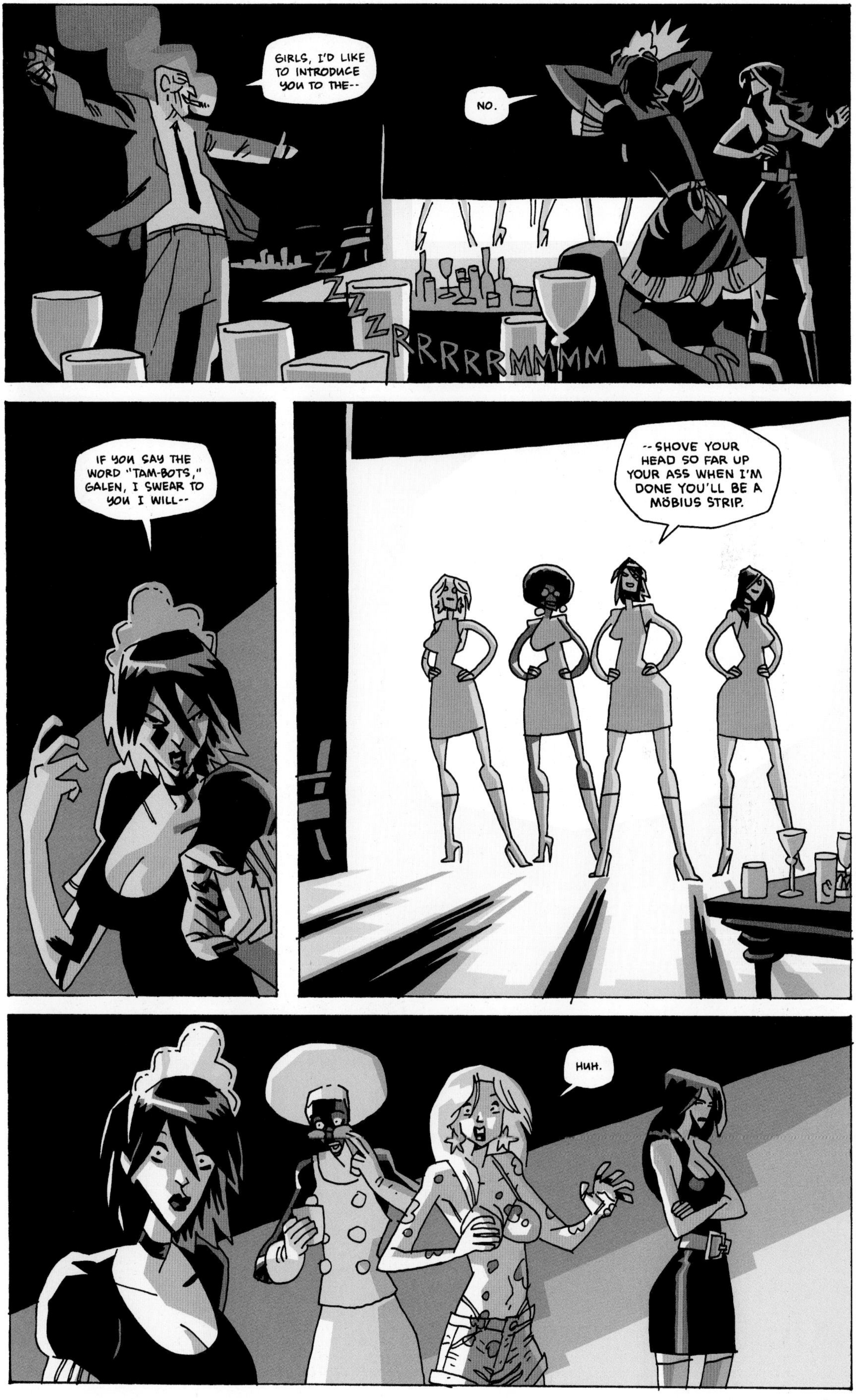
GIRLS, I'D LIKE TO INTRODUCE YOU TO THE--
NO.
ZZZZRRRRRMMMMM
IF YOU SAY THE WORD "TAM-BOTS," GALEN, I SWEAR TO YOU I WILL--
--SHOVE YOUR HEAD SO FAR UP YOUR ASS WHEN I'M DONE YOU'LL BE A MÖBIUS STRIP.
HUH.

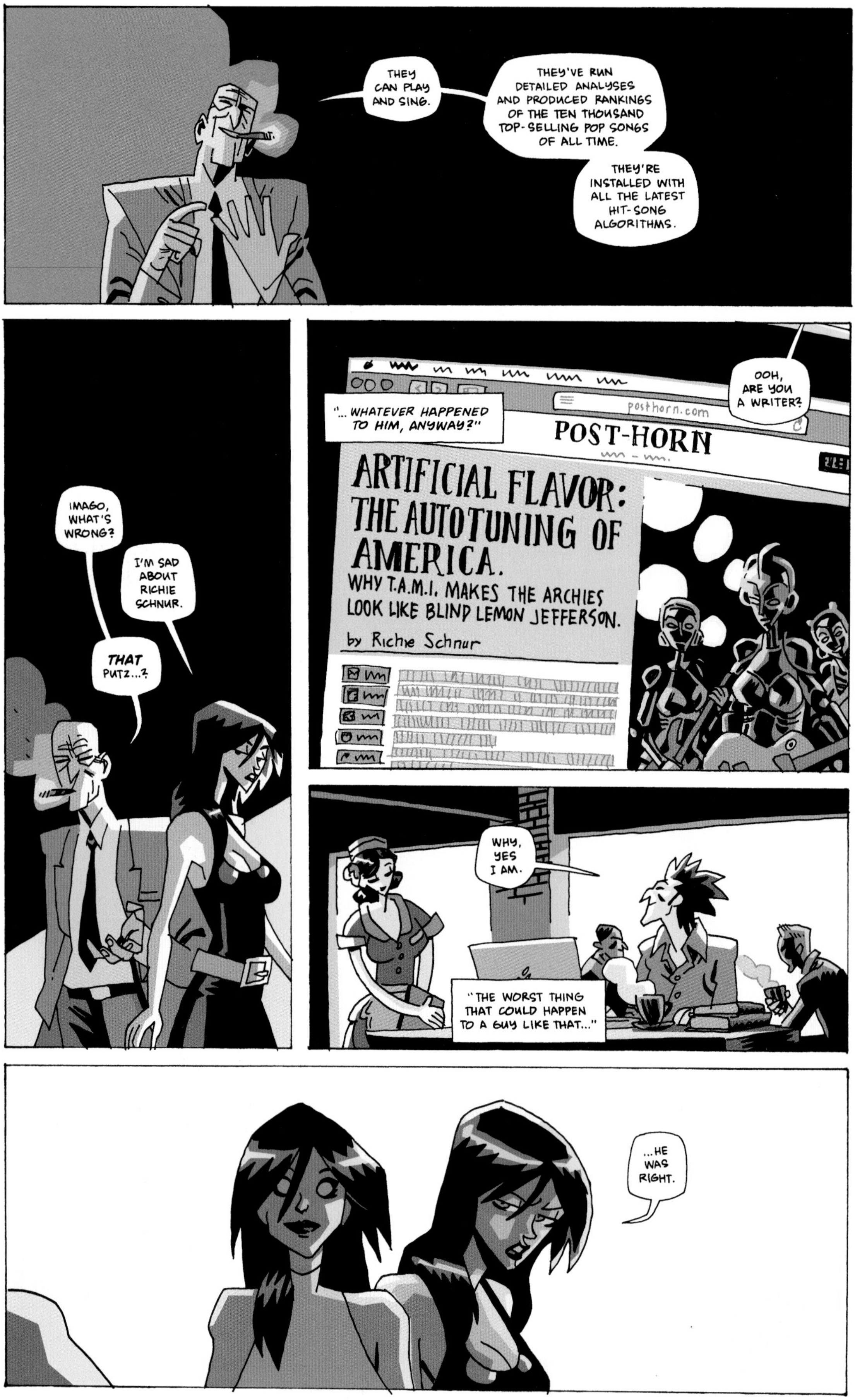
THEY CAN PLAY AND SING.
THEY'VE RUN DETAILED ANALYSES AND PRODUCED RANKINGS OF THE TEN THOUSAND TOP-SELLING POP SONGS OF ALL TIME.
THEY'RE INSTALLED WITH ALL THE LATEST HIT-SONG ALGORITHMS.
"... WHATEVER HAPPENED TO HIM, ANYWAY?"
posthorn.com
POST-HORN
ARTIFICIAL FLAVOR: THE AUTOTUNING OF AMERICA.
WHY T.A.M.I. MAKES THE ARCHIES LOOK LIKE BLIND LEMON JEFFERSON.
by Richie Schnur
OOH, ARE YOU A WRITER?
IMAGO, WHAT'S WRONG?
I'M SAD ABOUT RICHIE SCHNUR.
THAT PUTZ...?
WHY, YES I AM.
"THE WORST THING THAT COULD HAPPEN TO A GUY LIKE THAT..."
...HE WAS RIGHT.

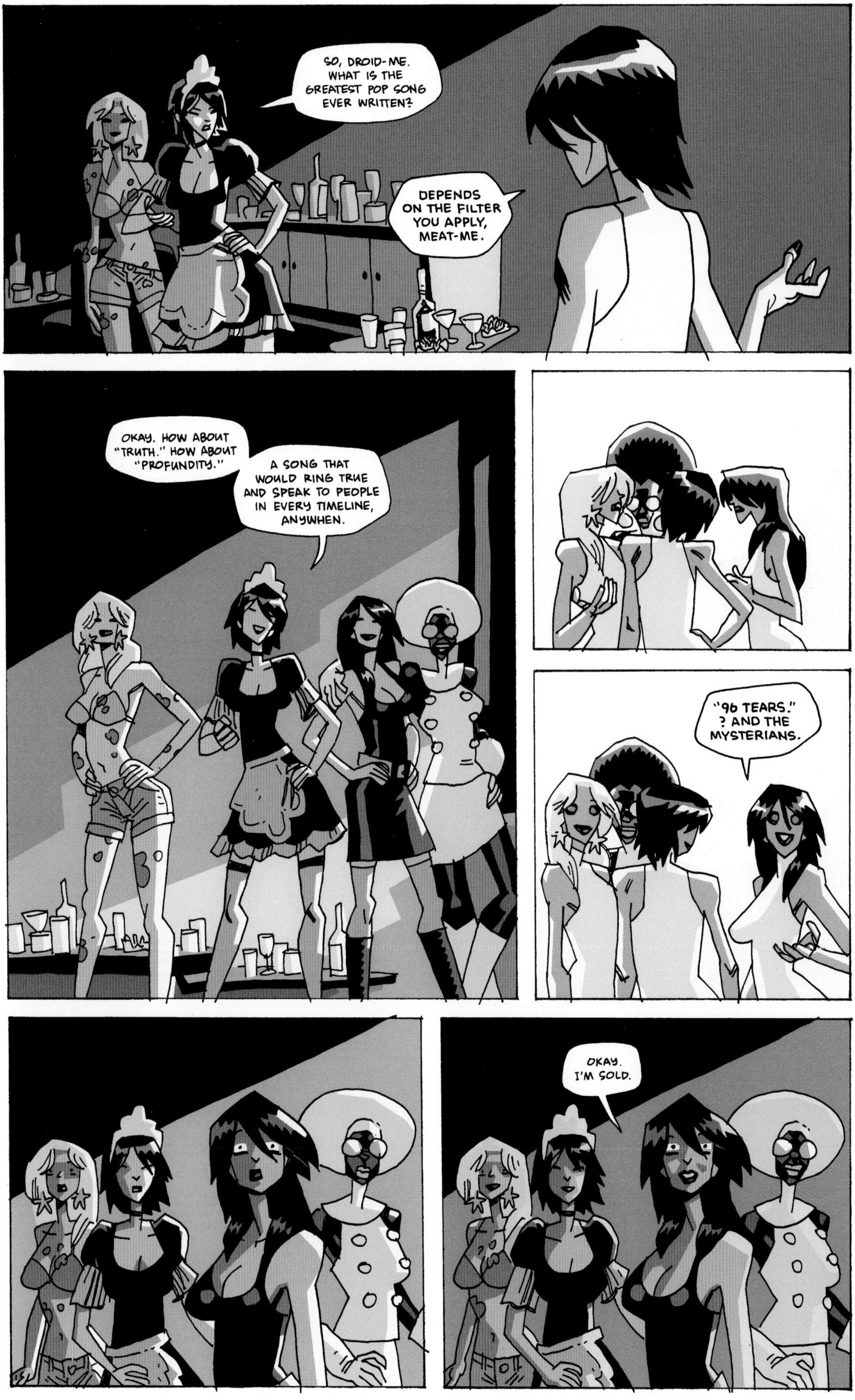
SO, DROID-ME. WHAT IS THE GREATEST POP SONG EVER WRITTEN?
DEPENDS ON THE FILTER YOU APPLY, MEAT-ME.
OKAY. HOW ABOUT "TRUTH." HOW ABOUT "PROFUNDITY."
A SONG THAT WOULD RING TRUE AND SPEAK TO PEOPLE IN EVERY TIMELINE, ANYWHEN.
"96 TEARS." ? AND THE MYSTERIANS.
OKAY. I'M SOLD.

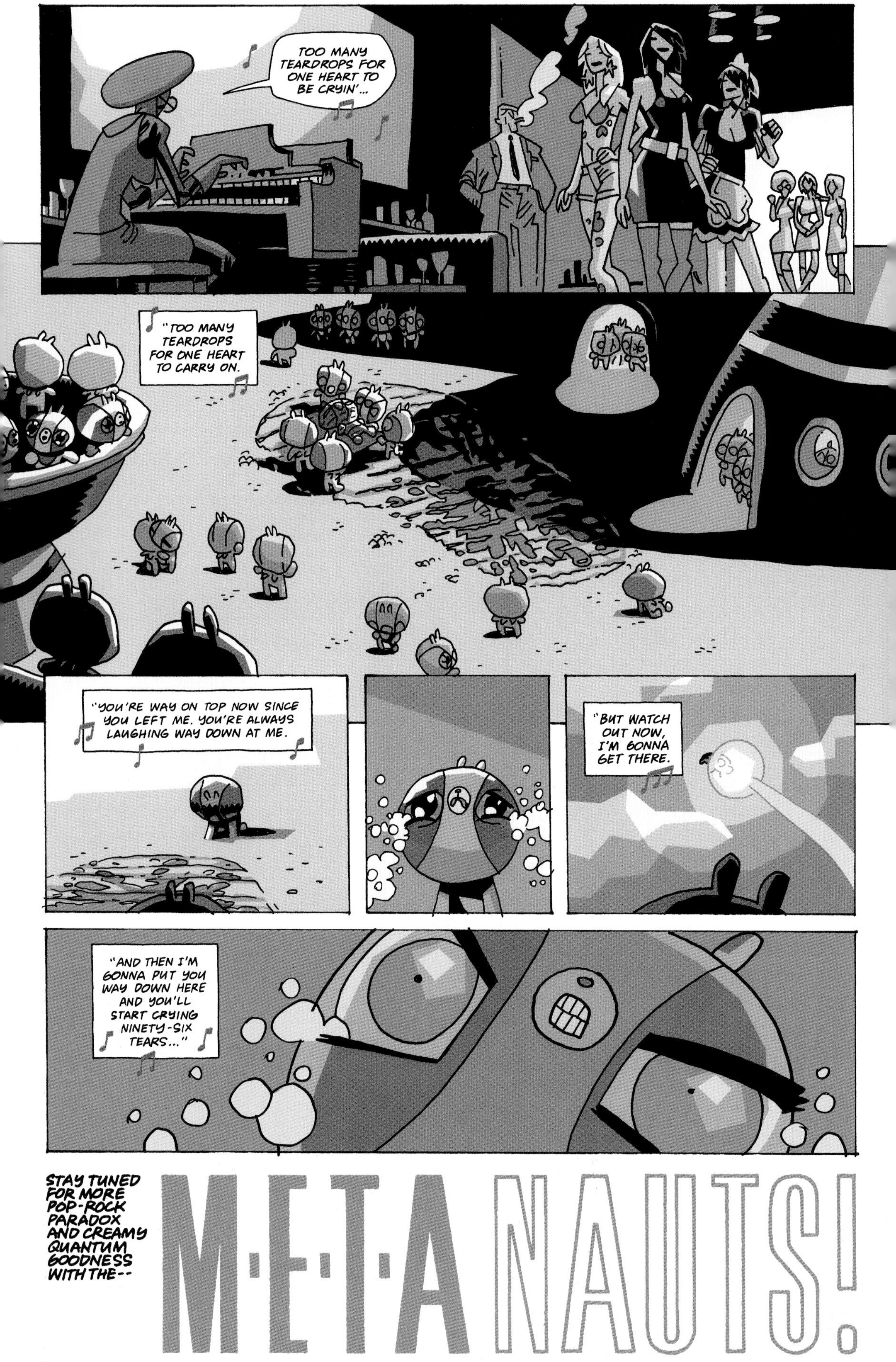

TOO MANY TEARDROPS FOR ONE HEART TO BE CRYIN'...
"TOO MANY TEARDROPS FOR ONE HEART TO CARRY ON.
"YOU'RE WAY ON TOP NOW SINCE YOU LEFT ME. YOU'RE ALWAYS LAUGHING WAY DOWN AT ME.
"BUT WATCH OUT NOW, I'M GONNA GET THERE.
"AND THEN I'M GONNA PUT YOU WAY DOWN HERE AND YOU'LL START CRYING NINETY-SIX TEARS..."
STAY TUNED FOR MORE POP-ROCK PARADOX AND CREAMY QUANTUM GOODNESS WITH THE--
M·E·T·A NAUTS!

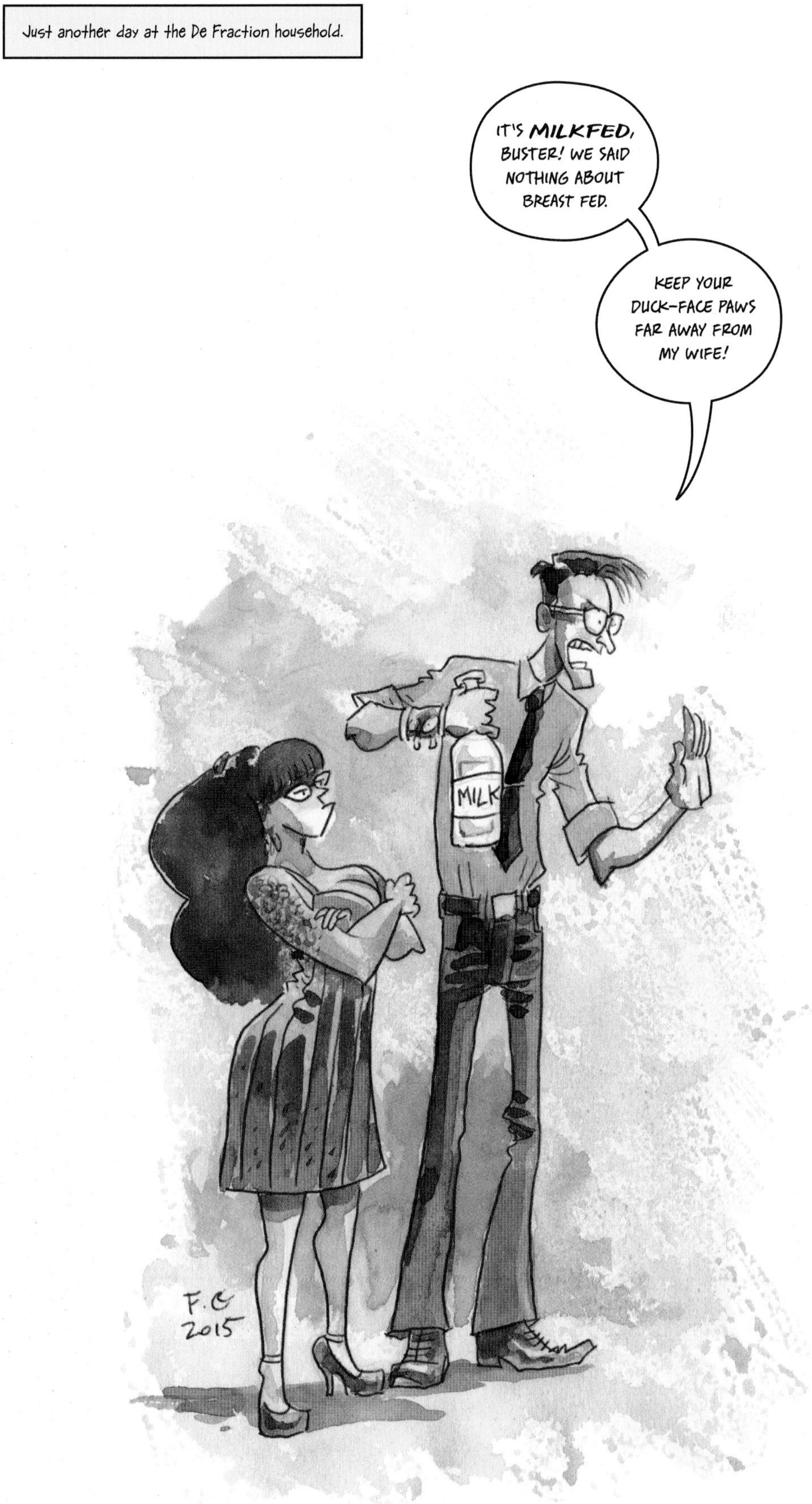
Just another day at the De Fraction household.
IT'S MILKFED, BUSTER! WE SAID NOTHING ABOUT BREAST FED.
KEEP YOUR DUCK-FACE PAWS FAR AWAY FROM MY WIFE!
MILK

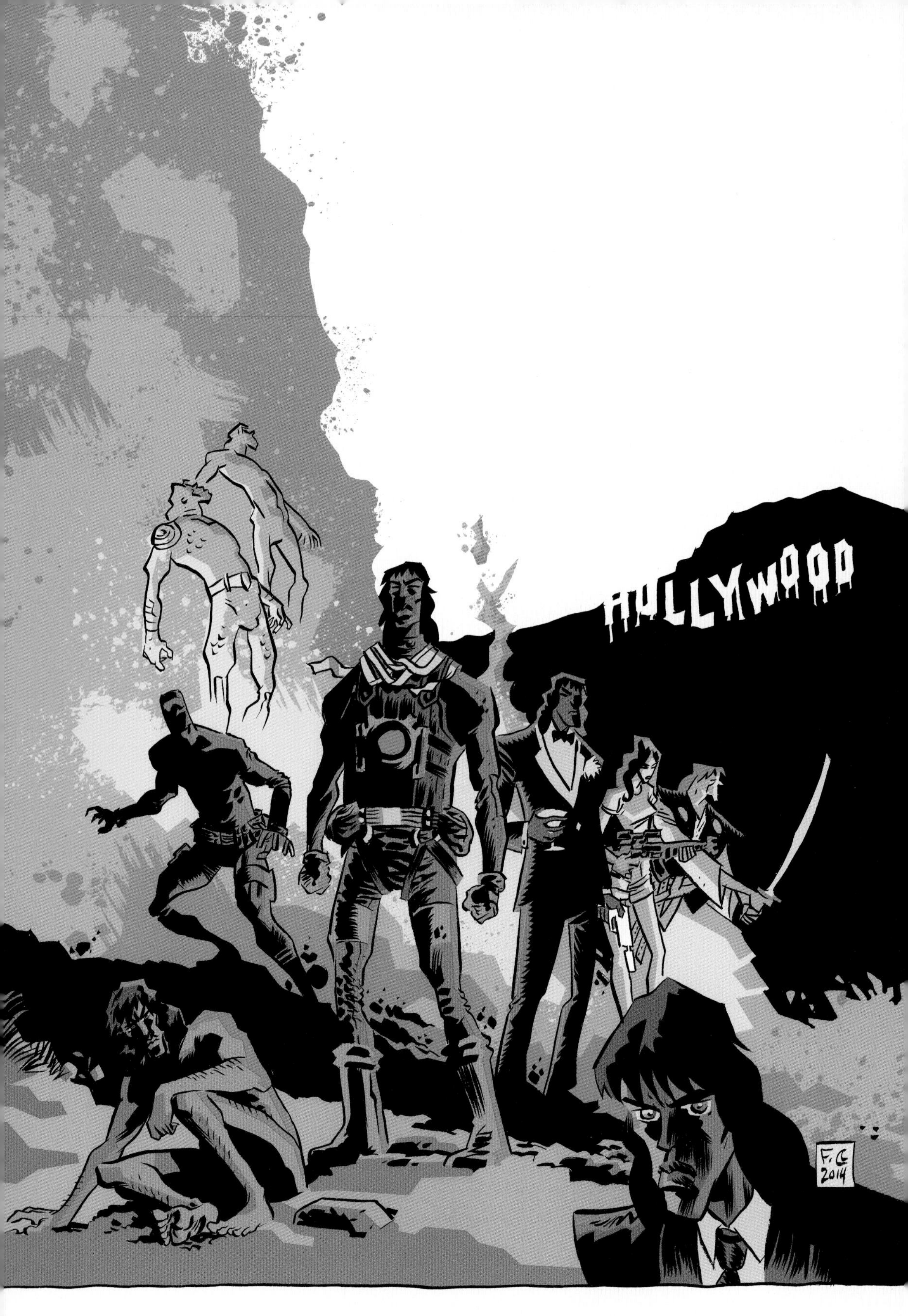
HOLLYWOOD
F.C 2014

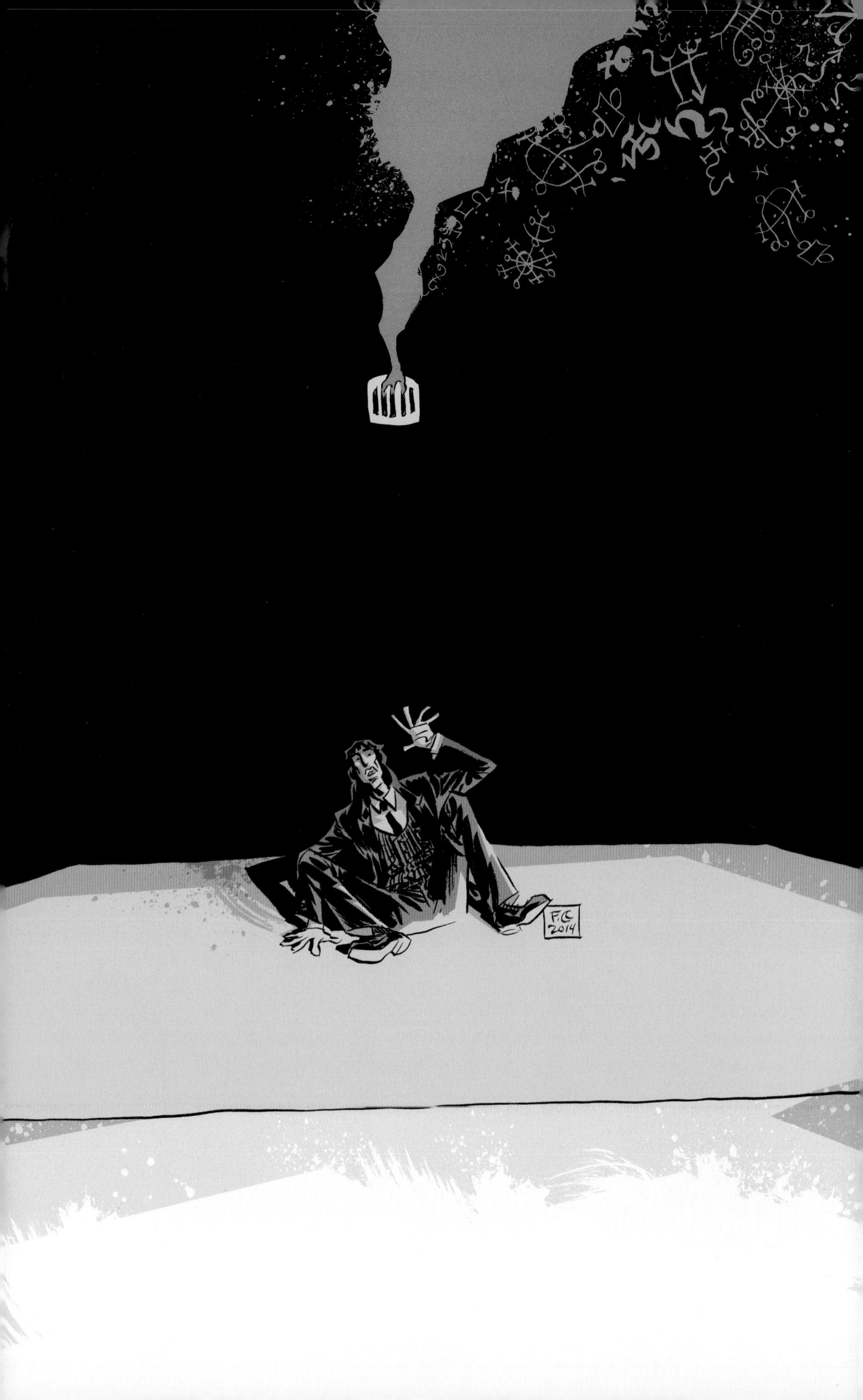
F.C
2014

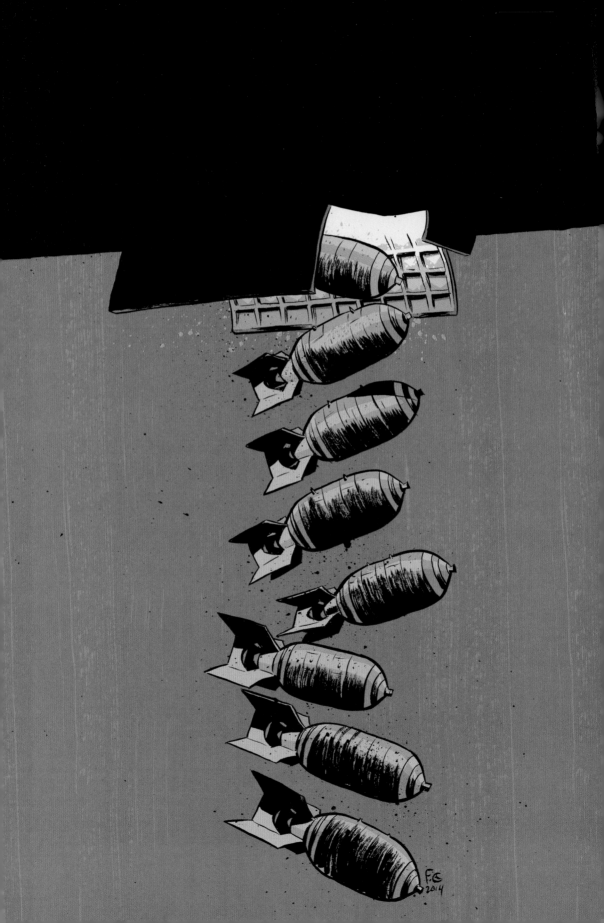